NO BONES ABOUT IT

COLD BED IN THE CLAY

RUTH SAWTELL WALLIS

INTRODUCTION BY CURTIS EVANS

Stark House Press • Eureka California

NO BONES ABOUT IT

The Peckhams and the Wests keep their loves and hates strictly in the family. Mattie Peckham is the keeper of the secrets, and takes great delight in tormenting everyone with them. Her brother Virgil West and his wife Charlotte live next door with their daughter Louise and her husband, Ralph Ogden. Ralph's secret involves the suicide of his first wife twelve years before. Then there is Duncan West, just returned from years spent living in Europe. His secret is hidden in a youthful letter he wrote Mattie years ago. Could it have anything to do with the mysterious blonde who moves in next door? When second cousin Janet comes to visit, she finds herself included in Mattie's cruel sport—but for Mattie Peckham, that sport is about to end.

COLD BED IN THE CLAY

Audrey Adriance and her husband Don move to the university town where he has been recently employed. They are welcomed into the neighborhood by next-door Professor Dexter and his wife Rachel, and are soon introduced to the rest of the group: Clifford Cox and his formidable wife, Beulah; the Grays, Thornton and Edna, and their daughter, Margaret; and the Dexters' guest, Detective Eric Lund. At a party that night, Audrey discovers an undercurrent of tension, heightened by her recognition of the unsavory Mr. Cox. Or could it just be that her immediate attraction to Thornton has set her on edge? Secrets are implied here. And perhaps the biggest secret is her own and Don's—a secret that soon leads to sudden death.

**Ruth Sawtell Wallis Bibliography
(1895-1978)**

Fiction/Mysteries:

Too Many Bones (1943; Dodd Mead; reprinted by Dell, 1946)
No Bones About It (1944; Dodd Mead; reprinted by Bantam, 1946;
    Eric Lund series)
Blood from a Stone (1945; Dodd Mead; reprinted by Bantam, 1947)
Cold Bed in the Clay (1947; Dodd Mead; Eric Lund series)
Forget My Fate (1950; Dodd Mead; Eric Lund series)

Non-Fiction:

Primitive Hearths in the Pyrenees (1927; with Ida Treat)
"Ossification and Growth of Children from One to Eight Years of
    Age" (1929, American Journal of Diseases of Children 37:61-87)
Azilian Skeletal Remains from Montardit (Ariege) France (1931)

ERIC LUND MYSTERIES— RUTH SAWTELL WALLIS

By Curtis Evans

Appealingly augmenting *Too Many Bones* (1943) and *Blood from a Stone* (1945)—the pair of fine nonseries mysteries by American anthropologist Ruth Sawtell Wallis which Stark House reprinted in one volume in 2020—in Wallis' small but distinguished crime fiction canon is a trio of series detective novels which came from the author's capable hands around the same time: *No Bones About It* (1944), *Cold Bed in the Clay* (1947) and *Forget My Fate* (1950). All three of these novels feature the criminal investigations of Wallis' appealing sleuth Eric Lund, a keen towheaded cop turned FBI lawman.

In his first appearance in *No Bones About It*, in a prologue dated from Christmas Eve, 1920, Eric Lund stands before the hovel deathbed of a once attractive female suicide, whom in life, it is imparted to us, was an emigre Polish princess. Then around twenty years of age, Lund is described as a blond policeman, "young enough to show distress" in the face of this beautiful woman's death. When Lund, now a police lieutenant in his early thirties, arises again in April 1932 in the main body of the novel, he is investigating the passing in suspicious circumstances of a malevolent old crone inside her hideous Victorian mansion; and he is given a lengthier description:

> The other man, tall, long-boned, and lean, carried himself easily and well in a light gray suit. His blue eyes, when he saw the bear and the armor [in the old woman's house], twinkled. To the girl in green leaning against the newel post, he took off his gray soft hat. His hair was the dull blond of a towhead turned thirty, his head narrow, long and high. Almost anyone would have guessed he was of Scandinavian origin but no one had ever called him a dumb Swede.

Lieutenant Lund also bears the stigmata of crisscrossed faded scars around his mouth—the legacy, as he explains, of one freezing cold winter's day in Minnesota, where he grew up as a boy. "I couldn't have got [the scars] in any less heroic fashion," he disarmingly confesses. "I was going to school one morning when I was about nine or ten and the wind on our beloved Minnesota prairie blew me into a barbed wire fence. It was twenty below, so I froze there, and when another kid pulled me loose, I left part of my face behind."

We additionally learn that Lieutenant Lund, after having industriously spent "five nights a week at law school for the last five years," has "just passed his bar examinations at the head of the list" and is soon "going into the F.B.I." By the time of the second Eric Lund mystery, *Cold Bed in the Clay*, which is set in June 1945, he has been in the Bureau for over a dozen years and is now a married man, having wed, presumably, not long after the completion of his murder investigation in the previous novel.

Certainly Eric Lund's first recorded case is one for the books. After the brief prologue in *No Bones About It* (which details to us the sad end, in a shack in the city of Watson, Massachusetts, of a wayward Polish princess), we are introduced to the protagonist of the story, twenty-three year old Janet Carter, a pretty, idealistic Minnesotan who has returned to Watson, her native town, to take a job with the "Committee for Cultural Relations with the Foreign-Born" and visit her surviving Watson relations: seventy-five year old Aunt Mattie Peckham, a cousin of her mother; Virgil and Charlotte Duncan West, Aunt Mattie's brother and sister-in-law; and Louis and Ralph Ogden, the Wests' daughter and son-in-law. Unexpectedly, Janet also encounters on her return trip her debonair second cousin Duncan West, Virgil and Charlotte's prodigal son of sorts, who has spent the last thirteen years of his life in Paris.

As portrayed by the author, Aunt Mattie—a wicked old witch of a woman who lives for prying out of the woodwork all the sordid details from her relations' lives that she can and using them to induce maximum embarrassment and distress within her not so cozy domestic circle—is a truly dreadful creature, one of mystery fiction's most deserving murderees. Only her Irish maid of four decades' standing, "Bridie" Callahan, seems able even to abide her. When, a third of the way into the novel, Aunt Mattie expires by means of a bottle of a stain remover brand felicitously named OUT, the phrase "she had it coming" should occur to readers' minds. Thus commences what in my estimation is one of the finest examples of genteel dysfunctional family murder cases on the fictional criminal record, following in the path of S. S. Van Dine's bestselling landmark Philo Vance detective novel *The Greene Murder Case* (1928)—though *No Bones About It* is far more compellingly characterized than the Master was ever willing, or able, himself to do in his detective novels.

In 1961 Ruth Sawtell Wallis—whose every book, whether criminal or anthropological, is graced with a powerful sense of setting, derived from her fascinating real life experiences—admitted, concerning the provenance of *No Bones About It*, that she had based Watson, Massachusetts on her own native city of Springfield in the same state and that she had "peopled it with fantastically blown-up and enriched mages of some of my kin." Concerning Mattie Peckham, Wallis divulged that Mattie's hardier real life model survived the fictive woman's imaginary slaughter at seventy-five to the highly venerable age of ninety-nine—to the end, doubtlessly, a cross to bear for her relatives. Tellingly the author dedicated *No Bones About It* to her widowed mother, Grace Quimby Mathewson Sawtell, who at the time of the novel's writing resided at 107 Dartmouth Street in Springfield, at the home of her late husband's spinster niece Florence Clark, a jigsaw cut Victorian mansion which had served as the Clark family domicile since the turn of the century. While far from the Gilded Age monstrosity which Mattie Peckham's house is lengthily described as being in *No Bones About It*, the Clark home most likely helped inspire it.

Similarly, the Duncan Rifle Works, the source of Charlotte West's family income, clearly was modeled after the Smith & Wesson Factory, founded in Springfield in 1856, and Janet Carter's place of summer employment, the Committee for Cultural Relations with the Foreign-Born, surely owed its derivation to Springfield's American International College, which, according to the College's website, "sought to educate newcomers to the United States and their children for citizenship and success." The College had been a pet project of the lineage-based patriotic organization the Daughters of the American Revolution, which at this time, at least, favored Americanization, rather than exclusion, of immigrants. Ruth Wallis' father, Joseph Otis Sawtell, had been a member of the DAR's lesser known masculine affiliate, the Sons of the American Revolution.

More surprisingly, given the author's staunchly New England Yankee background, in which her father obviously took great pride, Wallis had as well a family source for her portrayal of the Polish characters in *No Bones About It*, in that her father's younger brother, Edward Everett Sawtell (named after the famed nineteenth-century Massachusetts orator), in 1908 had married in Manhattan a native Polish woman by the name of Bertha Blusewicz (?). Seemingly this Sawtell brother, anyway, had put the American International College's policy into practice. Wallis' own sympathy with America's immigrant community is amply evident from the text of her novel.

In his notice of *No Bones About It* in the *New York Times Book Review*, Anthony Boucher roundly praised Wallis' second novel for its "[g]ood sketching of people and houses," "well-integrated and suspenseful narrative" and "fine period flavor of 1932," adding that not a single instance of what he dismissed as the foreboding, forced and feminine "Had-I-But-Known" style of writing favored by Mary Roberts Rinehart and her followers popped up to mar the intricately plotted criminal proceedings. Avis De Voto praised the novel's "Bay State atmosphere and characters," adding as well that the plot was "neat and clever"; while August Derleth deemed the whole affair "closely-knit, with ace-high characterization and plot."

On the other hand, a few other commentators have deemed Wallis' brief dénouement improbable, but to these unimaginative souls I would suggest that *Bones* is a novel deeply steeped in the legends and lore of New England Gothic, where one finds stranger things than are dreamt of in many a critic's book reviews. Murder can happen, as Rex Stout reminds us, even in the best of families, particularly among insular people who dogmatically venerate their ostensibly illustrious pasts. As Mattie Peckham's maid Bridie chattily confides to a native Irish policeman interviewing her in the kitchen:

> "I tell you, Mr. Murphy, they're funny, them Wests. Grown-up people all behavin' the way their fathers and mothers would have wanted them to. 'What would Father have said,'" she mimicked. "Mrs. Peckham, Mr. and Mrs. Virgil, still talking that way at their age, and Mrs. Ogden all set to carry on in the same way." *

No trace of New England Gothic is found in Wallis' *Cold Bed in the Clay*, which followed *No Bones About It* by three years and boasts a similarly strong, although altogether different, sense of place. An American academic mystery, like W. Bolingbroke Johnson's recently reprinted 1942 detective novel *The Widening Stain*, *Clay* owes its inception to the author's experiences during her time at the University of Iowa in Iowa City, a short tenure which ended when she married visiting professor Wilson Dallam Wallis in 1931 and returned with him to Minneapolis, where he held a teaching position at the University of Minnesota.

In this successor novel Eric Lund is described by the author as "a tall, lean man with the dull, slightly graying hair of a towhead turned

---

*For an actual murder case which likely influenced Wallis' novel, see the afterword.

forty" (though he should be closer to forty-five) and "a narrow, Nordic face with a fine network of scars around thin lips." To the novel's protagonist, pretty, twenty-three year old faculty wife Audrey Adriance, Lund explains, while making dinner in her kitchen, that he fell in love with his wife "because she was the only girl I'd ever met who didn't ask me if I got these scars in a romantic way," adding nonchalantly: "I blew into a barbed write fence when I was a kid. Twenty below on a Minnesota prairie. A helpful older sister [in the previous novel just "another kid"] pulled me off and some skin too. I'd frozen on the wire. Will this cream whip?"

Lund has come to the state university, another character explains, "just for a week to give some sort of memorial lecture on crime," but of course the pleasant towheaded lawman soon encounters real life crime at the campus when Audrey's husband Don, a decidedly unpleasant individual with an alcohol problem, is found dead on a local country road, seemingly the victim of a careless hit-and-run driver. Folksy Chief of Police Peterson suspects that Don, only lately hired by the university, may have been deliberately run down and that long-suffering Audrey may have been involved in his death—but Eric Lund has other ideas about the case, however unofficial his capacity. Yet if Audrey is not the one who did it, just who did deal out death to dipsomaniacal Don, and why?

Perhaps the culprit may be found among these faculty members and spouses who, not long before Don's demise, consorted with the Adriances at a small house party: interminably nosy Alfred Dexter and his scatterbrained wife Rachel; imposing Beulah Briggs Cox, a rare female professor, and her altogether objectionable new husband Clifford; and handsome anthropologist Thornton Gray and his kittenish young wife Edna. And what can the Dexters' black Labrador retriever, Cadwallader, and the Grays' precocious, crime magazine gazing young daughter, Margaret (whom Edna insists on calling "Sister," although she is an only child), contribute to the solution of the mystery? Altogether *Cold Bed in the Clay* is a gripping tale of murder and malfeasance, written with astringent humor and peopled with an all-too credible cast of characters. "Such things shouldn't happen to nice people," observed Nancy Barr Mavity of the deadly goings-on in *Clay* in her review of the novel in the *Oakland Tribune*, before adding: "Miss Wallis makes you believe that they can—and do."

In 1961 Ruth Wallis freely divulged that she set *Cold Bed in the Clay* in a "Midwest university town, a sort of University of Iowa." Although the text of the novel implies that the town is *not* located in Iowa but rather in a neighboring state (probably Minnesota), the neighborhood of The Bowery, where a pivotal event in the novel occurs, presumably is drawn, albeit in obscured fashion, from Bowery Street in Iowa City, described by *Little Village* as an area with a "largely working class" population, "employed by the factories and workshops that used to line Gilbert Street or by trades associated with the nearby railroad." The Bowery is distastefully described to Audrey by another character in *Clay* as "[t]he hangout of homeless men. Men who have always been homeless. The old casual laborers who can't work anymore. This was the hiring center for the wheat fields and the lumber camps and for the tile laying when they were in their prime. So now they drift back and stay....it's well to drive carefully here and watch out for the drunks." However, the inspiration for the mock-Tudor faculty houses which Wallis bemusedly describes at length in the novel came, according to the author, from dwellings on Minneapolis' River Road. (In Minneapolis the Wallises, wife and husband, themselves lived in a tasteful craftsman apartment which still exists today.)

Eric Lund made a most appealing mid-century series detective, yet he would appear in only one more Ruth Wallis novel before the author abandoned fiction writing in 1950. *Forget my Fate* "was my last murder mystery," Wallis wrote blithely in 1961. "Two more are planned in full detail, but they will not be written and I shall not care, for I have taken part in two quite different books, and two more are in process. They are part of my real life of wife, scientist, and another sort of writer." Asked "What do you plan to do within the next twenty years," Wallis with mordant bluntness replied: "I expect to die." She was right. Ruth Sawtell Wallis passed away seventeen years later in 1978 at the age of eighty-two, after a long and distinguished academic career and a shorter and insufficiently heralded stint as a crime writer. Renewed recognition of that accomplished aspect of her bountiful creative life has been long overdue.

—August 2021
Germantown, TN

....

Curtis Evans received a PhD in American history in 1998. He is the author of *Masters of the "Humdrum" Mystery: Cecil John Charles Street, Freeman Wills Crofts, Alfred Walter Stewart and British Detective Fiction, 1920-1961* (2012) and most recently the editor of the Edgar nominated *Murder in the Closet: Essays on Queer Clues in Crime Fiction Before Stonewall* (2017) and, with Douglas G. Greene, the Richard Webb and Hugh Wheeler short crime fiction collection, *The Cases of Lieutenant Timothy Trant* (2019). He blogs on vintage crime fiction at The Passing Tramp.

NO BONES ABOUT IT

·····················

RUTH SAWTELL WALLIS

To
Grace Quimby Sawtell

CHAPTER I

Prelude. December 24, 1920

There were four people in the room.

Raw light from the single gas jet fell direct upon the gloss of a dress shirt bosom, on brass buttons, on coarse linen covering what lay on the table.

In the shadows against the white-washed wall two figures sat motionless. The old man's bent profile had the strength of rock worn to human semblance. Beyond him a girl huddled, dark shawl masking bowed head and shoulders.

Across the poor room a candle flame, fluttering in the draft, made gaiety of the little wall shrine, the Virgin's blue robe, the pink and yellow paper flowers. Sleet scratching and bumping at the ill-fitted panes was the only sound until the policeman spoke. He was blond, and young enough to show distress when he said to the man on the other side of the shrouded table:

"Will you look at the body now, sir?"

The man in the wet raccoon coat, flung back from evening dress, nodded. "Yes," he said thickly.

He, too, was young, though older than the officer. Shock had driven most of the alcoholic flush from a face ordinarily handsome below a thick black pompadour.

The policeman drew back the sheet.

Two hours ago this had been a girl of twenty. Now it was mainly a heap of furs. A sable coat covered the body from neck to ankles, drawn close as if to warm death. A fur Cossack cap concealed all hair. The hands had been folded over a crucifix. Diamonds shone on the left hand, sapphires around the pale wrist. Someone had managed to close the eyes, but it had been impossible to do anything about the blue face and the rigid grin.

After a long look, the black-haired man covered his face with his hands. In one of them was a piece of stiff white paper. His words were almost inaudible. "It is my wife."

The policeman dropped the sheet over the body and came to his side.

The husband lowered his hands. "No one must see her."

"You are free to make any arrangements now, sir," the policeman told him. "The medical examiner would have waited, but it took quite a while to locate you. And it's Christmas Eve."

The other man's laugh was small and bitter. "And how!" He repeated low, intense, "No one must see her. Cremation. She ... she was the most beautiful thing I ever saw."

Behind him the old man raised his head. The girl leaned toward him, speaking soft gutturals.

"Do I keep this or give it to you?" Fingers unsteadily held out the stiff white paper to the policeman who shook his head.

"We know what she wrote to you," he said. "It wasn't sealed or addressed and they can't read much English, so they turned it over to us. It's a clear case."

The husband of the dead girl turned the paper over slowly. "Written," he said dully, "on the back of her shopping list. The name of what she took written on the same paper. Did she ... did it kill her right off?"

The policeman, his hand on the other's shoulder, was moving toward the door. "Yes. The medical examiner said it was mainly strychnine. And in her condition ..."

"Her what?"

"Because she was going to have a baby, sir."

The policeman's arm steadied the shuddering body. "God, I didn't know!"

Over the bowed black head the policeman saw the girl rise and come toward the light. The shawl fell from slim shoulders, and fair hair framed her face.

"I'll take him out to his car," the officer told her. "His mother's chauffeur is waiting. I'll be back." He closed the door.

When he opened it a few moments later, the old man was kneeling by the table. The girl stood at the old iron sink.

"This has been pretty hard for you," he said.

She looked up at him with wide, steady gray eyes. Her hair hung in fair braids over her shoulders, giving her a childish air, but there was strength in the face as well as beauty.

"Yes," she said. Even in the monosyllable her accent was marked.

The young policeman watched her quiet movements as she lifted dishes into a pan of water, picked up a rag; watched the lips of the kneeling old man.

"This has hit your grandfather harder than it has you, hasn't it?" He watched her closely again.

"Yes," she said again and went on with her work.

He stood silent.

She looked up at him. His eyes were blue and candid; his mouth thin and firm. The light brought out a fine network of scars around his lips.

The girl said, "It was my gran'father she come to see. In old country he was serving in big houses like she was born in. She was princess in our country. Talking together was … nice for them."

"So she came here to die."

The girl nodded.

"Why," he asked, "do you think she killed herself?"

She was silent a moment. "Sick," she said, "for old country. An' her husband … You saw …"

"Uh-huh. You naturally don't like him much, you and your grandfather. But you were sorry for him, too."

"Sorry?"

"I saw you when he heard about his wife's … you know."

She flushed and her straight gaze fell to the dishes in her hands. "A man," she said softly, "wants his son."

The policeman smiled down at her. "There's some of the old country left in you yet," he said. "An American girl wouldn't have been so quick to know how he felt."

She straightened. "I am going to be American. Old country. That is wrong. Here will be my country."

"O.K., sister," he patted the slender shoulder. "How you going to begin? Got a job?"

"Sometimes. With cateress."

He looked down at the hands in the dish pan, puffy from hot water, but with neat nails. The job explained them. "Like it?"

She shrugged. "I learn things."

"Going to night school?"

Again the wide gray eyes held his. "I will go," she stated.

"That's the spirit," he said. "I'm betting on you." He buttoned the blue ulster under his chin. "I'll be on my way. The undertaker'll be here soon and all your troubles will be over."

The girl's smile was shadowy. "All *her* troubles," she said.

After the door had closed behind him, she left her work and crossed the room to the old man kneeling by the body on the table. She laid her fingers on his shoulder. He raised his head and looked at her. Sunken eyes fixed on her hand.

"We are alone," she said, and the tones of their native speech were strong and clear. "We are alone, my grandfather."

Slowly he nodded. After a moment he again bowed his head in prayer. She slipped to her knees beside him.

CHAPTER II
April 1932, Wednesday, 4:30 P.M.

The Peckham house dominated Elm Street Hill. It was not the largest house, the finest, or the oldest. There was the Duncan-West French provincial chateau next door, an acre of gray stone. For two hundred years before Mattie Peckham's father got his architectural inspiration at the Philadelphia Centennial Exposition, houses in Watson, Massachusetts had been simple and lovely. But beside this embodiment of his dream, eclectic manor houses and Early Americana faded away. The Peckham house was the most horrible house in town.

It would perhaps not be too much to say that it was the most horrible house in the United States of America, at least in so perfect a state of preservation. In shabby sections of little towns you can sometimes find the tottering remains of the monstrosities of 1876, but on the Peckham house the paint was shiny new. A fine shade of mustard-and-water brought out its every feature: the central Gothic spire, flanked by four balconies, the overhanging peaks of the second-story windows like little Swiss chalets, and the miles of jig-saw carvings that enlaced porches, piazzas and porte-cochere. From the street a walk of bulging bricks led up between a weeping willow and a cedar of Lebanon. On the right the lawn showed a patch of pale green whence an iron stag had been tardily removed.

On closer view the house was worse. There was a mad quality about it. Under second-story gables, doors opened out onto space. The jig-saw patterns were insane. It smelled of owls in the attic and suicides in the cellar. It was not a house you would want to meet on a lonely road at midnight. It was hag-ridden.

On this sunny April afternoon the door opened and the hag stepped out.

Mrs. Mattie Peckham did not really look like a walking corpse. It was not that her face was so old, but that her teeth and her hair were so new. Too white, too black, and far too abundant. Under the inky puffs and pompadours her skin was shriveled and yellow, and the lips around the sparkling denture were purple and wide. But seventy years of peering into other people's business had not worn out the small, bright black eyes. She wore a red silk sweater, a spotted purple dress and beaded black slippers with French heels. She moved around the right-hand corner of the house, skirting a high hedge which she regarded with menace.

Past the house there was a narrow gap in the hedge. Mrs. Peckham, reaching it, looked through. A dumpy Irish woman came out the back door and joined her.

Through the gap they could see the lawn of the West chateau and a green-turreted entrance opening on the drive. A town car drove slowly up to this door from the direction of the garage. A chauffeur got out, a slim, dark little man in a well-cut uniform. He stepped up to the door smartly and went in.

"He's a Foreigner," said Mrs. Peckham. She had not turned, but she knew her retainer was at her side. "I wouldn't have hired a foreign chauffeur, Bridie."

"No, we wouldn't have a furriner, ma'am," agreed Bridie.

"My brother wouldn't either, if he had a choice. But it's her money." There was venom in her tone, but not much. She had said this every day for forty years.

Bridie just smiled.

"But you know, Bridie, what a wonderful man Mr. Virgil is. He made her cut the gap in the hedge. He wouldn't shut out his own sister."

"No, ma'am," said Bridie.

"She," said Mrs. Peckham with sharper spite, "wouldn't stand out in her yard and be friendly with the people who work for her, the way I am with you, Bridie. She makes poor Jerry get out of the car and come into the house and talk to her. I can't see them at the reception room window."

A door slammed behind them and Mrs. Peckham said, "You stand here, Bridie, and catch Jerry when he comes out. I've got something to do."

Bridie nodded, folded her hands on her stomach, and prepared to wait.

Mrs. Peckham crossed her backyard in the direction of the slammed door. No hedge protected the Georgian brick house next door. It was open, modest and commonplace, with a sun porch toward Mrs. Peckham's porte-cochere. You expected, when that door slammed, to see a small boy with a bike or a Scottie dog.

Instead there came down the step from the sunroom an old man in a clean white shirt without a collar, and black Sunday trousers with wide leather suspenders. He was short and strong.

"Good afternoon," called Mrs. Peckham. "Good afternoon, *Mr.* Baluta."

The old man bowed and murmured. Mrs. Peckham crossed her driveway. She smiled, not an encouraging expression.

"Are you enjoying your new home, Mr. Baluta?"

"I thank you, yes, ma'am," he said. The eyes sunk at either side of his craggy nose were patient, not interested. The accent was heavily foreign.

"I'm sure you are. It is such a very nice house. My cousin built that house, Mr. Baluta."

"So?" said Mr. Baluta,

"Yes. She moved away ten years ago. I'm expecting a visit from her daughter. She's coming on the *five o'clock train from New York*." Her tone underscored the last six words.

"So?"

"Yes. And my brother, Mr. Virgil West— You used to work for him, Mr. Baluta, until just last month, didn't you? ..."

"I work in Duncan shop," said Mr. Baluta.

"It's the same thing." There was an edge in Mrs. Peckham's voice. "My brother is also expecting his son on that train. Duncan has been away for twelve years. Do you remember Mr. Duncan West, Mr. Baluta?"

Mr. Baluta said, "I work at the shop for ten years only. Not know Mr. Duncan West."

Mrs. Peckham's smile deepened, purple lips pulled back to reveal more of the denture.

"We're all expecting someone today, aren't we? Mr. Duncan at my brother's house, my little cousin at my house. And—you're expecting your granddaughter, aren't you, Mr. Baluta?"

"You know that?" The tone was low, unstressed.

"Your housekeeper told my Bridie. And I was so interested. I've always been so interested in your granddaughter."

He spoke after a moment, looking at her carefully. "You know my granddaughter, ma'am?"

"You're surprised, aren't you?" Mrs. Peckham was pleased. "Oh, yes, I've followed her career from the very beginning."

"Her career?" His eyes said nothing.

"She's been a wonderful granddaughter to you, hasn't she? Such a smart girl, buying you this lovely house. But you have done a great deal for her, too, I'm sure. A great deal."

"I have done not'ing," he said. "She has done all." He bowed. "Good day, lady."

"Good-bye, Mr. Baluta. It's been so pleasant to have a little talk with you. I knew you'd be glad to hear how interested I am in your granddaughter's visit. And," she said slowly, "I know ALL about Helenka."

Mr. Baluta walked away to the front of his house. If, in spite of his low bow, this seemed a little abrupt, it appeared to delight Mattie Peckham. Something of her jack-o'-lantern smile of farewell was left over for the neat, dark chauffeur who followed Bridie through the gap in the family hedge.

"Oh, there you are, Jerry! Mrs. West let you go at last. Aren't you afraid you'll miss the train?"

"No, Madam," said Jerry.

"Isn't Mrs. West riding down with you? And Mrs. Ogden?"

"No, Madam. With Mr. Duncan's bags and with the young lady, your guest, and her luggage, Mrs. West felt there would not be room. She thought you might have planned to go to the station, Madam."

"Well, I'm not going," stated Mattie. "If Charlotte Duncan West doesn't think enough of her son to meet him at the train after he's been gone for twelve years, I don't see how she can expect me to be excited about a little second cousin. Do you, Bridie?"

"Maybe Mrs. West feels kind of upset about seein' her boy after all this time," suggested Bridie, "and would kind of like to be alone when it happens."

"You may be right. I wouldn't know how she'd feel about anything. I never have." She looked at the correct oblivion of the chauffeur. "Jerry, what are you waiting for?"

"For your orders, Madam."

"And it's no more than right that you should. I pay you part of your salary. It helps Mr. West during the Depression and its helps you, too, Jerry."

The ends of Jerry's black moustache twitched slightly. The scheme hadn't been an advantage to the chauffeur Mrs. Peckham had dismissed at the moment when jobs were hardest to get.

"And I send Bridie over every single day to clean your room."

Bridie looked superior virtue. Jerry looked ingratitude.

"I wouldn't stand around like that if I were you, Jerry," Mrs. Peckham told him, "not if I wanted to make the train."

"No, Madam. I may go?"

The great car swept down the curving Duncan drive. Through the gap in the hedge Mrs. Peckham watched. The blue lips pressed tight and curled; the little dark eyes glowed. "Bridie," she warned, "you'd better keep your eyes wide open from now on or you're going to miss something. Something I've been expecting for twelve long years."

"Yes, ma'am," promised Bridie.

CHAPTER III
Wednesday, 4:30 P.M., Continued

The blond young woman in gray moved exquisitely down the aisle of the chair car. Everything about her—her butterfly hat, the green orchid, her walk—was as perfectly finished as her make-up, as delicate as the contours of her face. Behind her trailed the faint perfume of lilies of the valley.

The dark-haired man in London tweeds glanced up casually from his book and, as casually, down again, but Janet Carter in the chair behind him gazed in open admiration. She's a movie heroine, Janet thought, just the opposite of a movie actress on a personal appearance tour. She's almost the most beautiful woman I've ever seen. Almost? Who was better looking? No one. Only that childish memory, a wraith in white. Mariska. I've remembered all this time only because she died that way. Going back to Watson makes me think of her now.

Janet turned back to the window.

The valley had widened out suddenly. The train was following the river. You could see ahead miles of winding water and small green hills.

"I beg your pardon," the man had turned his chair toward Janet. "I hate awfully to trouble you, but could you tell me what has happened to that mountain?"

He looked quite sane. He looked quite exciting.

Janet stared obligingly out of the window. "Mt. Hero? It isn't smoking, is it?"

"No, it still seems to be extinct, but isn't there something missing about it?"

Janet looked again, up the valley at the detached little old blue volcano. "There used to be a house on the top," she said, "but it burned down ten years ago."

"Thanks," he said, "it's good to know I haven't forgotten everything really important. I went away twelve years ago."

"I cried when I heard about the fire," Janet confessed. "I looked through my first telescope at the Mt. Hero House and that's where I saw my first movie."

"It couldn't have been an old maid smirking in front of a mirror?"

"That's just what it was."

"Surely," he said, "we're not contemporaries."

Janet grinned, and he added, "Impossible. I'm thirty."

"The film was a little worn when I saw it," said Janet, "but I thought it was wonderful."

"Me, too. It's marvelous to come back after all these years and find a younger generation who shares my ancient enthusiasms. Have you been growing up for me in Watson, Massachusetts?"

"No, my good old grandfather," said Janet smartly, "I have spent the last ten years in Minneapolis, Minnesota."

"Wonderful!" he said.

"Just why?"

"It's so completely American, I envy you. I was never out of New England until I went to France in 1920. I was eighteen."

"Do I say 'wonderful,' too?"

"You don't."

"Aren't you awfully glad to be at home?"

"I don't know," his slow smile, the mouth a little tired, was different from the boys she knew. "Is it home?"

"Your family ..." she stopped.

"There is a great deal of it. Frankly, I'm frightened."

"No," said Janet.

"Yes. Afraid of the strange politeness between me and my parents, afraid, I suppose, of its inevitable breakdown. 'Son,' the old man will say, 'you don't get fatted calf like this in Paris.' And I'll reply, '*Au contraire et malheureusement*, veal every day in the week.' You see?"

"I see. But I expect I'll get into just the same kind of trouble. I've got to stay with a horrible old cousin who thinks that in Minnesota we live on porcupines and tree bark."

"It could be. But I think your case, though sad, is a little less tragic. One can't escape well-meaning parents, but what compels you to stay with a 'horrible old cousin'?"

"It's called," said Janet, "strong family feeling. It's really cowardice. The H.O.C. has the family scared to death. Even after spending ten years a thousand miles away, Mother can't quite realize she's escaped. When the ogress wrote I was to come straight to her lair, Mother said 'how lovely.' But I shan't stay long."

"Oh, don't tell me you're going away from Watson?" There was challenge in the mocking eyes.

"No. I've got a job there for the summer."

"What sort?"

"I'm going to plan and put on an International Festival. All the local race and nationality groups." Janet smiled apologetically. She was proud of her first real job, but she didn't expect her pride to be shared.

"That's enormously interesting." Surprisingly, he seemed to mean it. "What's the background of most of the Watson foreign-born?"

"There are Italians, droves of them. French Canadians, of course. And Poles."

The look of interest left his face. "Poles. Yes," he said flatly.

Janet picked up her hat and purse. "I must go and repair the devastation of the voyage," she said awkwardly.

"No damage has been done." Intimacy came back to his tone. "You're a clever girl to do without rouge."

"It fades me. My hair is no-color."

"On the contrary. It's exactly right for your skin. Ivory and autumn leaf. I haven't seen that perfect combination for years."

"Or liverwurst and New York cheese," Janet said and went off to the dressing room. She hoped she had sounded nonchalant. She felt fluttered.

Parting the heavy green curtain, she drew in her breath against the first wave of dust and liquid soap, but this standard Pullman attribute was being conquered by lilies of the valley wafted on clouds of cigarette smoke. The blond woman was sitting before the mirror. In the glass her eyes met Janet's, gray under heavy black lashes. Seen at close range her beauty was authentic and only a little older. She moved to make room at the shelf and smiled.

Something faint but insistent stirred Janet's nerves, with This Has Happened Before. But, of course, it hadn't. She sat down at the glass, to brush her light brown hair from the widow's peak, to put on her hat.

"We are very nearly at Watson?" The voice was like Cousin Charlotte West's, the same delicate, precise intonation, but with a warmer undertone.

"Yes," Janet responded shyly. "I'm getting off there."

The lovely voice said, incredibly, "I, too."

Impossible to imagine where she would fit in the dead complacence of Watson, Massachusetts.

"I left there more than ten years ago. A long time. It makes one afraid."

Another one, thought Janet. "Really afraid?"

"Almost," the gray eyes were serious, while the exquisite lips smiled. "Afraid to meet the girl I left behind me, the self I used to be."

It was like a line in a play and it suited her. She picked up her silver foxes and Janet followed her into the car.

The man from Paris said, "Good old red gas tank. We're almost at Home Sweet Et Cetera. Miss Minneapolis, would you favor the idea of breaking me in gently ... let me ring you up and do a movie now and then in memory of the Mt. Hero House?"

She wanted to, awfully. "I could never," she said, "explain you to my relatives. They know exactly who my friends are in Watson."

"If that's the whole trouble, I'm sure we could think of something convincing. We both look enormously intelligent."

The train had stopped. "We haven't time," said Janet. And thought it was probably fortunate. He was fascinating, but not an entirely comfortable person. "We'll probably meet, anyway. Watson isn't a metropolis."

His answer was a good-humored shrug.

On the station platform of Watson, high above Main Street, the passengers from the New York Express were milling and shouting for porters. The blond lady, with nothing more apparently executive than delicate disdain, had successfully indicated eight gray suede bags to the only three Red Caps.

"Miss Carter?" The trim little chauffeur with the dark moustache was at Janet's side. "If you will tell me which bags are yours ..."

"Oh, good. Mrs. Peckham sent you. What a rescue." She turned to the ranged luggage. The train was pulling out. "These two and the typewriter are mine."

But the chauffeur was not at her side. She looked around, bewildered. The platform was now nearly empty. Two men came toward her, the chauffeur gesticulating, apologizing to a man in tweeds. "I looked all about for you at first, sir, and then I saw the young lady."

The man from Paris looked at Janet. He took off his hat. "I quite understand."

"But I don't," said Janet. "Is he your chauffeur or mine?"

"Well, I thought mine. But we might let him choose. Of course, I wouldn't win."

Jerry stepped forward. "Miss Carter," he smiled, "and Mr. West, the car is parked in front of the First Church. I'll have your bags down directly."

The bags—Janet's ingénue-new, beside the others sophisticatedly-worn and bright-labeled, "Firenze," "Helsinki," "Paris,"—were stowed away, and they had sunk into the deep limousine cushions behind a faintly smiling Jerry. Then, amused wrinkles about his eyes, Mr. West said, "Now, Mademoiselle Minneapolis, can you explain your charming but rather bewildering claim to my father's car?"

"Uh-huh. Because it seems to be your Aunt Mattie Peckham's car, too," and added, "Cousin Duncan."

"Cousin ... who the devil are you?"

"The name is Janet Carter."

A warm finger raised her chin. "Let me look at you." He did so. "Of course. Your coloring. I should have known. The little girl in the red brick house. You're ... you must be Janie-West."

"Right," she flushed a little at his touch, "only no one has called me that for ages."

"The hostess to whom you so feelingly referred on the train is my Aunt Mattie?"

"Yes," said Janet.

"I always thought she was a jolly old girl, you know."

"Did you?" said Janet.

"I did. Well, ogress or not, she can hardly object to our ... acquaintance."

"Wait and see," said Janet, "Cousin Duncan."

The car was climbing Elm Street Hill.

"You don't really feel that the prose of cousinship is going to spoil everything?" His eyes mocked her, "And you aren't going to be a lady and say 'what is everything?', are you, Janie?"

"I'm going to say again 'Wait and see'." It was not maidenly embarrassment that prompted Janet's reply. It was the presence of Jerry's apparently deaf back. Ogress was not exactly the word nor was dallying the pastime she wished reported to Cousin Mattie Peckham via the kitchen and a well-remembered institution known as Bridie. "Here is your house."

"I'll get out. I expect Mother is waiting. Jerry, take Miss Carter on, and come back with my things." Duncan West opened the car door. He stood for a moment, looking up the curving drive to gray stone towers above poplars faintly green. "Castles in Touraine and Spain and Watson," he turned and took Janet's hand. "*À tout à l'heure, ma cousine* and something more."

Hat in hand he strode across the lawn and the car moved on to Mrs. Peckham's gravel drive.

As the saffron conglomerate of Mattie's house loomed before her, Janet shuddered. She turned her head away toward the familiar red brick normality of the house on the left.

On the step where Janet had often bumped down her bicycle and her doll buggy, the glamorous lady of the train, silver foxes slipping from her shoulders, stood directing the disposal of her multiple luggage by a taxi driver and an old man in black Sunday clothes.

Nor was Janet her total audience. Bridie, under the murky yellow porte-cochere, unclasped her hands from her stomach as the car stopped, but her round blue eyes did not falter from the house next door. Jerry, opening the car door for Janet and holding out a stiff gauntlet for her descent, stared like a sleep-walker at the farther scene.

"Jerry—Jerry and Bridie,"—it struck down at them, a gloating command from above. Jerry's neat head turned ridiculously in all directions, seeking the sound. Bridie took a step toward the car. There followed a rasping laugh. Mattie Peckham's black hair and white teeth gleamed down from one of her doghouse balconies. "Jerry," she repeated, "will you *please* bring in Miss Carter's valises as soon as you have finished *what you are doing now?*"

CHAPTER IV
Wednesday, 6:30 P.M.

In her cool chintz-hung sitting room Charlotte Duncan West sat straight and tall and still on her great grandmother's sofa. Her white hair rose like a crown. The hands that held her knitting looked older than her face. Her dress was ice blue. So were her eyes.

There was a small sound, and she glanced at the armchair where Virgil, her husband, was doing what he called "just looking at the paper." The sound came evenly from behind it.

Louise Ogden, her daughter, standing by the window where long curtains floated gently in the spring breeze, asked, "Mother, shall I call the boys?"

"No, dear," said Charlotte definitely. Louise looked disappointed. She was thirty-five, with red cheeks and dark, curious eyes, suggestive of her Aunt Mattie Peckham's. Her wrists and ankles were slender, but her arms issued heavily from a sleeveless rose-flowered gown.

"I suppose they'll know it's dinnertime as soon as Aunt Mattie sounds off," she said. "Mother, did we have to dine at her house on Duncan's first night at home?"

"We always dine at your aunt's on Wednesdays."

Louise's flush deepened. "Mother, what do you think about Duncan?"

Charlotte's cool face relaxed. "It's wonderful to have him here."

"I think he looks a little, well, foreign."

"That's just his clothes, Louise. He's getting to look so much like his grandfather Duncan. My father was a very fine-looking man."

"Duncan isn't bad looking," Louise agreed. "He may be snooty."

"We shall all find it a little strange at first," said Charlotte smoothly. "Twelve years is a long time to be separated."

Louise eyed her mother steadily as the needles slipped across two rows of snowy wool. She took a deep breath. "Mother," she asked, "why did Duncan leave home?"

Her mother counted stitches before she said, "Why do you ask me something you know as well as I do? The Kent boys were going to Europe for a year with their tutor. Duncan had finished at St. Philip's in June. He wasn't at all sure he wanted to go to Yale. It was a good opportunity for him to join them. Your father and I both urged him to go."

"I know," Louise was impatient, "but Duncan didn't want to go. He hated the whole idea. I remember perfectly well the night of my dance he was swearing he wouldn't go near old Europe for anything on earth, anyway not till the football season was over. Then the next morning he was tearing around like mad after passports and letters of credit and mumbling about a fellow needing to know the world. Mother, what happened? Why did Duncan leave home?"

Mrs. West's cold eyes held her daughter. "Nothing happened," she said quietly. "You know as much as I do, Louise. Pick up your father's paper."

The floorward descent of the *Watson World-Democrat* (it was one hundred per cent local and Republican) revealed the gentle heave of pouter-pigeon torso which supported the plump old chin and hands of Mr. Virgil West.

Louise stooped for the paper. "Aunt Mattie ought to be too busy prying into Duncan's past to bother with Ralph tonight. Mother," her face was flushed and solemn, "if Aunt Mattie doesn't let Ralph alone, someday I shall kill her."

Charlotte said, "She is your father's sister. Remember how lovely she was to you when you were a little girl."

"I remember exactly how lovely!" Louise watched the tense line of her mother's jaw. "And so do you. Aunt Mattie spoils everything."

"She tries," said Charlotte calmly.

Duncan West, standing at a casement window in his boyhood tower room, looked down far below him and thought as he had thought long ago: below this house like a castle, below that great stone parapet and the cliff, there should be an ocean rolling in, fog and cold salt spray. But there had never been anything like that. Only black smoke from the Duncan Rifle Works on the river flats. Grandfather Duncan had liked to overlook the source of his security.

The smoke was not so thick as Duncan had remembered it. For 1932 was a year more conspicuous for peace than for prosperity.

There was a tap on the door and his brother-in-law, Ralph Ogden, came in, carrying bottles, ice and tall glasses on a tray. There was something about Ogden's carefully brushed black hair, florid face, solid, slightly stooped figure that suggested he was more commonplace than he had started out to be. In this Depression year, Ralph and his wife, Louise, had, as he said at the Club, moved in their income with the old people to bring social security to the West butler.

Duncan put out his hand for a glass. "Should this be viewed with alarm?"

Ogden shook his head. "Pre-war bourbon from Grandfather Duncan's well-known cellars, and there's plenty more where this came from. Your father hasn't touched a drop since Prohibition."

"Not a drop of liquor?" Duncan's brows rose. "How un-American!"

"I wouldn't quite say that." Ralph poured himself a small drink. "At first he didn't. Ethics, patriotism, something like that. Then the boys at the Club got talking about their home brew and that awakened the old competitive spirit in your Dad. So now he sticks to his own brand. He says there's always novelty in it."

"And what else?"

"Carrots," said Ralph.

"God," said Duncan.

They sat silent. The early spring evening lay about them, cool and quiet. From the road far below there rose a faint toot of an automobile horn. Bridie, beyond the hedge, was calling, "Kitty ... Kitty ... Kitty."

Duncan said, "You know my family better than I do."

"Well," said Ralph slowly, "I married one of them."

Duncan held expression from his usually mobile face. What did he know about that marriage which had taken place nearly two years after he left home? Nothing. And hadn't there been an earlier marriage for Ralph?

"Your Dad," said Ralph, "is a fine old boy."

As for the rest, his tone implied, find out for yourself.

Duncan turned back to the window. "The river road has changed. There used to be a daisy field below Aunt Mattie's barn. And all those little shacks."

"Polack town? They tore those down when they made the boulevard. Three or four years ago."

There was no parapet behind the yellow-spired carriage house of Mrs. Peckham where the cliff had begun to fall sharply. Behind the modest two-car garage of Mr. Baluta, land sloped almost gently to the river. On this slope, outlined against the sky, were two figures, an old man and a blond woman, a sharp silhouette in black.

"Who," asked Duncan, "is that old man?"

Ralph shrugged. "Old Steve, your Dad calls him. He retired from the shop a few months ago. Used to live down there in Polack town."

He leaned toward the window, looking idly down. The woman raised an arm to her head. Seen against the sky, it was a gesture of peculiar grace.

Duncan saw Ogden's back stiffen. He chose his words with amused deliberation. "Odd companion for that particular girl."

Ralph whirled around. His breath came a little quick. "You know the girl?"

"Want to meet her?"

Ralph did not smile. "For a moment I thought she was someone I used to know. Where did you meet her?"

"I didn't. She was on the train."

Ralph's color was healthier, his tone matter-of-fact. "The old man bought your cousin's house for cash. It's not a cheap house."

"The girl could have supplied it. She's expensive."

"Meaning?"

"One way or another she could have earned it. I wouldn't know."

"It's a dull trip from New York." Ralph's tone leered. "Don't tell me you missed your chances."

"There was," said Duncan, "another girl."

The woman's golden head had vanished over the brow of the hill, the old man following.

"Not," said Ralph, "the little Carter cousin?"

"Yes. Type not common in international circles."

"Janie was a funny kid," Ralph set down his glass. "She was some sort of flower girl at Louise's wedding. And I distinctly remember that she was the only female there who didn't kiss me. Refused to, and meant it. It was a relief."

"Though not altogether flattering." Duncan's tone was pleased.

A sudden hoarse sound broke in.

"*Nom de Dieu,*" said Duncan, "what was that?"

It was repeated, a teeth-setting range from squeal to squawk.

Ralph was unmoved. "You'll get used to it," he said, "if you stick around here very long. That is Aunt Mattie Peckham, calling us for dinner."

"Why, for God's sake, does she do it?"

"It's supposed to be some secret signal that she and your father had when they were kids. He says he doesn't remember it. She stands where you can't see her, just behind the gap in the hedge."

There was a shriller screech.

"Sounds like the 'view halloo' for the hounds of hell."

"They'll break loose all right," said Ralph, "if we don't get going."

They started down the turret stair. "I've always had a warm spot in my heart for Aunt Mattie," insisted Duncan. "I used to go to her with my troubles when I was a kid. I wonder if she remembers it."

Ralph regarded the back of his brother-in-law's head. "She never forgets anything," he gave grim assurance.

The squall rose to a final height.

"She really does that," Ralph added, "to get your mother's goat."

"And does it?"

"That," said Ralph, "I've never been able to make out."

On the hill behind his Georgian Colonial house, Mr. Baluta and his granddaughter stood silent in the pale spring evening.

An inhuman cry cut into the quiet.

Mr. Baluta crossed himself. The girl shuddered. "The owl," she said, "I hate it. The bird of death."

"It is not an owl," said Mr. Baluta. "It is worse. An old witch woman calls to her own."

CHAPTER V
Wednesday, 7 P.M.

They dined together in the lurid gloom of art-glass windows. Four women, three men. Not in a decade had so many members of the West family sat down together. These seven would never dine together again.

Mattie Peckham in purple and diamonds which gleamed in contrast to their dirty old settings, darted her little chipmunk eyes around the table. At Charlotte West, her sister-in-law, consciously serene; at Louise Ogden, her niece, obviously bellicose; at Ralph Ogden, bored and bland; at the exotic nephew from Paris. Only when they rested on her old brother, Virgil West, were they kind. She did not bother to look at Janet West Carter.

But no one else neglected Janet. Across the table from her, Duncan, detached, faintly amused by everyone else, glanced at her now and then with a secret warmth, more disconcerting than his family's questions. There were a lot of questions. Tonight the famous West curiosity was reenforced by a special need. They wanted so much to question Duncan, but what could they ask about a life utterly unknown? About a son and brother now almost as alien as the lands in which he had chosen to live? And so, they collected information about Janet.

Cousin Charlotte, cool and gracious, said, "It is nice for you to find work, dear," and waited for Janet to say her father was doing badly in business.

Janet said, "Thank you, Cousin Charlotte."

"Janet," Louise was earnest, "you've got to be terribly careful about your volunteer committees. If you get the wrong people at the start, nothing will go. I *know*."

"Oh, I hope everyone will be interested," Janet told her. "We want every nationality group to be fully represented."

"Oh, those," Louise flushed with impatience. "I didn't mean those foreigners. I mean the people who count."

"So did I," said Janet, and met Duncan's eyes.

Louise hadn't heard. "I can give you a lot of advice. I've been doing Day Nursery and Red Cross and clinics for years, and only a few people are worth bothering about."

"Thank you," said Janet.

No one else asked her about the pageant. Only Louise was interested in community activities. The Junior League post-dated Mattie Peckham and Charlotte West; they had never known a good reason for doing good works.

Cousin Virgil, from the foot of the table opposite his sister, napkin tucked under chin, and tucked under that, great forkfuls of roast pork and apple sauce, asked gently, "How much are they giving you, Janie?"

Mattie Peckham's beady eyes were on Janet now. So were Louise's, and the ice-blue aristocracy of Cousin Charlotte was not without interest. An old feeling rose in Janet Carter, a wave of heat, a wave of cold. She hadn't felt that since she was thirteen years old, since she had moved away from Watson and the family. What it meant was complete frustration, the frozen certainty that she couldn't say: none of your damned business.

"A hundred and fifty a month," said Janet.

"How much is that a week?" Mattie Peckham's question was a demand.

"The Community Fund pays your salary, doesn't it, dear?" asked Cousin Charlotte. She made it sound like charity.

"It's thirty-five dollars a week," said Louise, caressing the pearl in one cushiony ear lobe.

"Thirty-four dollars and sixty-two cents," her father corrected her gently. "That's quite a lot of money for a little girl like you, Janie."

Duncan kept his eyes on his plate.

"It's a damned poor salary when you consider that the job lasts only three months," said Ralph Ogden.

Janet, seated at his right hand, turned toward him in gratitude. She had hated Ralph Ogden since she was eleven years old, and not from a childish whim. However, she was not above recognizing a little understanding in the present bleakness.

"Aren't you a little strong in your expression, Ralph?" said Mrs. Peckham, and smiled.

"Ralph," said Duncan with condescending tact, "I suppose you play a lot of golf?"

"No," said Ralph. "Too lazy or something. Fishing's my sport. Land-locked salmon in a few weeks now."

"We all know what these fishing trips are like," Mrs. Peckham implied.

An angry flush rose in Ralph's face, an angrier one in his wife's. "Uncle Eli was a great fisherman," Louise blurted out.

There was a silence. The late Mr. Eli Peckham had expressed his complete commonplaceness with a silence so rare in their ranks that he was known to all the Wests as a wonderful man. No one had ever suggested that his lonely and assiduous fishing had an alcoholic angle.

Mrs. Peckham turned her lush wig toward her niece. Louise poked violently at her fruit salad.

Charlotte West said, "Your mother must miss her home here very much."

Janet said, "We have a modern house."

"Of course, dear," said Cousin Charlotte. "We know that they now have plumbing all through the West."

"Yes," said Janet unadvisedly, "and the Indians seldom ride into town on buffaloes any more. There's hardly any reason to go to Minnesota now."

"There never was," said Mattie Peckham.

Duncan said, "Who did your house?"

"A protégé of Frank Lloyd Wright."

"Oh, I say, marvelous. I must see it."

"It's in the *Architectural Forum*, two pages of pictures."

"It wasn't," said Louise, "in *House and Garden*."

Cousin Virgil chewed to a slow finish and asked in quiet fear, "Is it one of those steel-and-window things, Janie?"

"It is," said Janet.

Louise said rather timidly to her brother, "Duncan, do they have scavenger hunts in Paris?"

His eyebrows rose. "I imagine so. Through the sewers. The rats do, anyway. You can see them when you go through in boats."

"How disgusting," said Louise. "No, I mean parties where everyone is given a list of the craziest things they have to find and bring in at midnight. You know, things like a hoop-skirt or a hair from a policeman's head."

"I didn't know," said Duncan. "You like them?"

"They're great fun," said Louise. "Of course, I always win the prize for the most complete list. That's because Aunt Mattie has everything you could imagine in this house."

"Except," said Ralph, "the hair from a detective's left temple."

"What if he didn't like it?" returned Louise. "That was nothing in comparison with turning in an iron stag."

Duncan's eyes lighted with recognition. "The stag," he said. "Eve. I knew I missed something when I came up to the house. Aunt Mattie, you never let her steal Eve?"

"I don't know why you called the stag that," said Mattie crossly. "Virgil and I always called it 'Monarch of the Glen' when we were children."

"Mattie," Virgil corrected her softly, "I think that when Father bought the deer I was twenty and you were twenty-five."

"Well," said Duncan, "when Louise and I were in the 'Lady of the Lake' phase of our education, it was the 'Stag at Eve' to us. Eve for short."

"I have a sweet picture of you riding it," said his mother. "I'm sure," Duncan smiled at her. "And now Eve is salvage. Why did you let them do it, Aunt Mattie?"

"I was in bed," snapped Mrs. Peckham.

"It wasn't so hard to do," said Louise proudly. "Eve was just bolted to the pedestal."

"The pedestal wasn't on your list?"

"Oh no, and Aunt Mattie called in a junk man next morning and sold it for a lot of money. Anyway, for cash. It was solid metal."

"And Eve?"

"Monarch of the Glen," said Mrs. Peckham, "is in the carriage house. She was hollow."

"But still a friend," said Duncan. "I shall pay her my respects. Go on. Tell me more about the social life of Watson. Does one still dance at the Hilltop Club?"

"We have a new club, dear," said Charlotte. "No one we know belongs to the Hilltop Club now."

"The Longvale Club," said Ralph, "is in a hollow, bordering a swamp. It is very exclusive."

"It was the Kingstons' home," said old Virgil. "They were having a little difficulty keeping it up."

"There's a dance at Longvale a week from Saturday night," said Louise.

"Good," said Duncan. "May I have the honor, Cousin Janet?"

"We never go," said Louise. "Ralph doesn't like to dance."

"No," said Mattie, pleasantly. "Ralph just likes to stay home and—er—fish."

Louise took up the charge. "He likes to read quite deep books."

"Book-of-the-Month stuff," muttered Ralph. "Sheer hatred of waste. Family subscribes. Somebody might as well read 'em."

"You *like* reading, darling," Louise told him and the table. "You like it better than movies."

"Never go near those," said Ralph.

Mrs. Peckham's eyes were fixed upon him with a peculiar gleam. Her breath sucked in eagerly between the shining dentures.

"You miss," she said dramatically, "a great deal."

She looked around the table. At her right Duncan, Louise at his side, his father at the foot of the table. At Virgil's right sat Charlotte, placed by Mattie as far as possible from the son she had just retrieved after twelve years. Next to her was Ralph, then Janet. They were all settling down to frozen pudding and fruit cake. Mattie Peckham, whenever she felt like saving on food, remembered that her even more saving father had been proud to be a good provider.

In the light of the ugly old chandelier, she drew her blue lips into a tight smile for the pleasure of herself alone. No one knew what was coming. No one was afraid. In just a moment now ... "Bridie," she said to her minion, "put the coffee on the table and don't come back." There was a glitter in her eye which could be read: Don't stay at the door of the butler's pantry.

"Yes, ma'am. No, ma'am," said Bridie.

And now they were alone. The moment had come. After twelve years. How much should be told now? A little. Save it. Bring out a morsel from time to time. Mrs. Peckham did not touch her pudding. This was her great moment.

She started mildly, repeating almost without emphasis her last remark to Ralph Ogden. "Yes," she said, "you miss a great deal if you don't go to the movies. And Ralph never goes near them. Did you see a lot of American movies in Paris, Duncan?"

"Not many, Aunt Mattie. Charlot of course, every chance I got. Perfect artist."

"Char-low? Who is she?"

Janet said, "I think he means Charlie Chaplin, Cousin Mattie."

"He should say it, then," said Mattie. "We aren't French."

"I beg your pardon, Aunt Mattie."

She looked at him hard. "What *did* you do in Paris, Duncan? We don't know very much about you. Of course, we are just your family."

"I know," said Duncan with his most charming smile. "I've always been a rotten correspondent."

And now there was joy and triumph in her blue smile. "I have," she said distinctly, "a letter from you."

Duncan looked at her with suddenly blank eyes. "Yes?"

"A very," she said, "very interesting letter. I shall keep it as long as I live."

Everyone had heard her. Everyone looked up. Janet, seeing Duncan's face, thought with a certain satisfaction: He hasn't quite such a warm spot for her in his heart right now. He looked briefly as if he had murder there.

Then he was saying, "Tell me about the stars of Hollywood. Are they really as enchanting as one hears?"

"There are some kind of pretty girls," admitted his father slowly.

"Norma Shearer," Louise breathed, "and Kay Francis are simply stunning. Didn't you love Jean Harlow in 'City Sentinels'?"

Charlotte West spoke with decision. "There is only one actress in the movies who is really a lady."

Mattie Peckham's eyes gleamed. "Of course, Charlotte," she said, "you would be the best judge of that."

Charlotte regarded her with virulence, controlled and cold.

"Who is that, Cousin Charlotte?" asked Janet.

"Mary Alden," said Charlotte West. "Have you seen her, dear?"

Mattie Peckham leaned toward her sister-in-law. For once there was gratitude in the look. Charlotte had said exactly what she had hoped she would. "Why do you like her so much?" she encouraged.

"Because," said Charlotte, "you can tell at once that she is well bred and well brought up. I feel sure she must have been born in New England."

"Do you, indeed?" breathed Mattie Peckham.

"What's she like?" asked Ralph idly. "That sounds pretty pale to me."

"I saw her once," said Janet, "in *So Long as Life*. She's lovely, blond and graceful."

"Did any of you," asked Mattie avidly, "see her in *Candle in the Night?*"

They had not. Louise thought it was the early picture in which she made a hit in a small part, overshadowing the star. It was.

"They're reviving it now at the small theatres, since she's become the rage. It's at the Bijou Theatre now. Out Morgan Park way."

Mrs. Peckham said, with a solemnity that surprised them, "I want you all to promise me that you will go to see *Candle in the Night*. I am sure that most of you would find it of the greatest interest."

"Morgan Park?" said Janet. "Isn't that on the other side of the river? I remember going there once—with you, Cousin Mattie. Didn't you stop the car and take me into a drugstore and give me a chocolate nut sundae?"

Mattie Peckham gave Janet her entire attention. "You have quite a memory," she said. "Do you remember anything more about it?"

She really, thought Janet, wants to know. It was easy to oblige. "The sundae had cherries and whipped cream and marshmallow. The girl who brought it to us had yellow bangs and she slopped the cream and you laughed. That's all. Except when I got home."

"Your memory," said Mattie Peckham, "is remarkable. Almost as good as mine. It was in 1921."

Virgil beamed at her. "Mattie never forgot a thing in her life."

"Well," she said, "I get a lot out of life that other people miss because they have poor memories. Or because," she paused, "they don't go to the movies."

"We can't," said Duncan, "all have the same pleasures."

"You," she said to him, "missed a great deal today."

"Oh, no I didn't!" He bowed across the table to Janet.

"You," said Mrs. Peckham, "and Janet missed a great deal, a very great deal. You traveled on the train with Mary Alden."

"No!" said Janet. But yes, she thought. The lovely lady. That is why I had the queer moment of recognition in the dressing room. But she was made up to look very differently in *So Long as Life*.

"What? The glamorous blonde?" asked Duncan.

"How do you know this, Mattie?" Charlotte inquired. "How do you know that Mary Alden was on the train with Duncan? I thought you didn't go to meet the train."

"I did not," said Mattie, "no more than you. Bridie," she went on, "thought it was very strange, Charlotte, that you didn't go down to the station when you hadn't seen Duncan for twelve years. But I said to her, 'Bridie, you know Mrs. West feels upset about seeing her son after so long, and she would not want to display feeling in a public place.'"

"That was understanding of you, Mattie," said Charlotte with formidable sweetness. "I'm glad that you explained it correctly to Bridie."

"Aunt Mattie," said Louise, "how did you know about Mary Alden?"

"I know everything." Mattie said it as she had to Mr. Baluta. "I know where she was born. I know where she used to live. I know what her real name is. I know where she is at this moment."

"Well, Mattie," said old Virgil, "since Bridie isn't here just now, you might explain it to all of us."

"I intend to," said Mattie. "I'd be delighted to do it." Her eyes mocked the cool certainty of her sister-in-law. "Mary Alden," she said, "was not born in New England. She was born in Poland. She used to live on the river flats, in a shack down behind the Carters' garage. Behind the house she bought for old Steve Baluta. She's in that house now."

The beautiful blonde on the doorstep of my old home, thought Janet. Of course. Cousin Mattie is right.

"Good heavens!" gasped Louise. "Mary Alden here. I ... I can't believe it."

"I haven't yet told you her name," said Mattie Peckham. "It was Helenka Baluta."

Charlotte said, "I have never heard that name before."

"Nor I," said Louise.

"Some of you have," said Mattie. She waited a moment. No one spoke.

"Wasn't it you, Duncan," she asked, "who knew Helenka Baluta? No, of course not." She laughed and then she pounced, cat on mouse. "It was *you*, Ralph, who had so much to do with Helenka."

He seemed astounded. "Never heard the name in my life."

"Oh, yes, you have," said Mattie.

"Not me," said Ralph.

Louise leaned forward, her face red, lips parted. Virgil cleared his throat.

Mattie said softly, "It was in her house that your wife met with her little accident."

Ralph's shoulders quivered. The knuckles of his hand on the table looked tight and white. He said slowly in the silence, "I had forgotten the old man's name was Baluta. I don't remember a girl."

"Don't you? She was very much there."

Ralph looked at his hand.

"Ralph," said old Mr. West, "I'm sorry I didn't tell you that the old Steve who bought the Carters' house was named Baluta. I didn't think you need ever know or that if you did, it would be," he looked at his sister, not tenderly, "in any painful way. All that was a long time ago."

"I know, sir," said Ralph.

"And I don't believe it," flamed Louise, "not a word of it. How could a common Polack girl like that be such a lady?"

"Perhaps by observing your manners, darling," said her aunt. "She used to serve at your parties now and then."

"It's a lie," Louise screamed suddenly, "the kind of rotten lie you would make up, just as you always do to pick on Ralph. I wish," her voice rose shrill, "that I had something to kill you with. We'll all be better off when you are dead."

Charlotte's hand fell sharp on her cheek. "Stop, Louise."

Ralph was on his feet, at his wife's side, raising her now sobbing figure, leading her from the room. Charlotte followed them into the hall.

In a silence more melodramatic than any Mattie Peckham had been able to create, the four remaining members of the family sat in the hideous old room. Duncan and Janet stared at the yellowed mess of their melting pudding and crumbled cake. Across the long, littered table where pools of brown and red from the stained glass chandelier lay like spots of blood, old Virgil West stared at his sister Mattie Peckham whose black eyes, now opaque and tired, neither faltered nor answered him.

The door to the butler's pantry swung silently open. Bridie stood with her hands folded on her stomach. She spoke.

"Please, ma'am, it's a long distance call on the phone. From Hollywood, Californy. It's for Mr. Duncan."

CHAPTER VI
Thursday, 5 P.M.

Throat tight, cheeks flushed, Janet Carter approached the house where she was born. The house, comfortable, solid, commonplace, showed no effects of foreign invasion. Its pleasant red brick, broken in regular spaces by green-shuttered windows, its sloping roof with three dormers and two chimneys, its white door with fanlight and brass knocker, were the standard English Colonial scattered all over the United States of America.

Outwardly Janet also looked standard, a pretty American college girl in a dusty-rose suit and saddle shoes, but inwardly there was tumult. Everything about Janet that was professional and ambitious urged her up the walk; everything that was a New England lady retarded her footsteps. And there was the added brake of Cousin Mattie's murky suggestions about Helenka Baluta and Louise's hysterical response. However, though in dilute form, she had the West curiosity. Janet West Carter mounted the circular brick steps and clanged the knocker.

Waiting, her lips formed dryly over and over, "Is Miss Alden in?" Behind that door she visualized a maid approaching with a card tray.

The door opened. Janet gasped. She had to speak. She said, "How-do-you-do, Miss Baluta."

Gold hair wound high on her head, very slim in black linen, the granddaughter of Steve Baluta looked down at Janet. She was Mary Alden all right. Something more had to be said. Janet said it hastily and not well. "We met on the train."

"Yes," said Miss Baluta, not unpleasantly, not warmly. Janet stuttered, "I'm Jan-Janet Carter. I ... I was born in this house."

It seemed a particularly silly thing to have said, when she saw the hall behind that dramatic figure. A whitewashed wall, a heavy carved chest, a glaring lithograph of Christ crowned with thorns.

"And you would like to see the house again? Naturally. Come in, of course." It was graciousness from a distance.

Janet went in, ashamed, following Miss Baluta's gesture toward the room on the right. There were more religious pictures, gaudy against white walls, heavy, handsome peasant bureaus and chests, a radio, an advertising calendar from Preszmylski's grocery. Hand-woven draperies framed the windows.

Janet sat awkwardly on a stiff leather chair. Through the curtained windows of the adjoining sunroom she could see the mustard of the Peckham mansion. She felt she couldn't be even vaguely like Cousin Mattie for a minute longer. She looked at the beautiful, faintly inquiring face of her hostess and blurted out of her distress, "I've got to tell you why I'm really here and you can throw me out if you want to."

The gray eyes were guarded, the tone cool. "Why are you here?"

Janet looked steadily at her, pleading for understanding. "I'm directing ... I'm hired to direct a pageant for the foreign-born groups. It's to be given on the Fourth of July. And I thought ... by myself ... I haven't talked to anyone else ... that it would be wonderful if you would help us. For the Polish group, you know. It would be really something for them to ... and for all of us ... to work with ... a person like you."

"What do you mean by a person like me?" There was no help in that cold voice.

Janet said, "Miss Alden ..." and stopped.

The woman had stiffened in every line of face and body. She rose. Janet expected to be ordered from the house.

"Your pageant people sent you here? They know about this?"

"No. No one but me. I wasn't sure you would want to do it. It was just my idea." She got to her feet.

"You thought this out yesterday on the train?"

"No, no. Although I've seen *So Long as Life*. And thought you were wonderful. I ... I thought so on the train, too. But I didn't dream you were Miss Alden."

"Why," she was admitting nothing, "do you call me that now?"

"Because, last night at dinner, Cousin Mattie—Mrs. Peckham who lives next door—told all the family about you."

"She told ...?"

"That," this was hard to say, "you were Helenka Baluta and that you used to live on ... on River Street. And that you were visiting your grandfather here. In the house he bought from my parents. And that you were Mary Alden."

For a moment Mary Alden loomed before her, too white with hands pressed too tightly together. Suddenly she relaxed, color came softly along the planes of her cheeks. She smiled.

"Sit down, Miss Carter," she said. "No, not there. Here on the settee in the sunroom. At least there are cushions. You smoke? We will talk this over like two businesswomen."

They were together on the wooden settee, Mary Alden leaning back easily against a red pillow. Lilies of the valley and cigarette smoke again enchanted Janet.

"Now if," the tone was clear cut, with now and then a faintly foreign tone, "you could bring to your committees the cooperation or even the name of a Hollywood star, it would help you a good deal in your standing with them, wouldn't it, Miss Carter?"

Janet blushed, but answered frankly, "It would."

"Your career is just beginning, isn't it? My own, the important part of it, is also new. One great success, the first big contract signed. The future not yet assured. You could ruin all that for me."

"But I thought publicity ..."

"Was the life of a Hollywood star? And also her death. The wrong kind. Miss Carter, I want you to understand. I am proud of being Polish, proud of the country where I was born, and I am prouder than you can ever dream of the little house on River Street and the long way I have come from there." She paused, watching Janet's eager eyes.

"Through certain circumstances I have been built up as an actress with a one hundred per cent American background. Part was publicity. Part, a large part, from fan mail. People saying over and over that I am to them ... just that."

"I know. My Cousin Charlotte West is terribly sure you're the only well-brought-up girl who ever went into the movies. She knew you were born in New England, and she didn't like it when Cousin Mattie Peckham said you weren't."

"You see? The public must always be right. If it can be right for ten more years—and with luck it can—I ask for no more. For luck and your help."

"Of course," vowed Janet.

"Good," the gray, faintly shadowed eyes were appraising, not quite accepting. "And in return, I can offer you some help. For several years, I have been buying old furniture, hangings, court costumes, peasant dresses from Poland, Russia, Hungary. Many of these would be useful in your pageant. My grandfather, Mr. Haluta, would be glad to lend these to you for the use of you and your committee. Is it a bargain?"

"Oh, yes," agreed Janet, "but Miss ... Baluta?"—the actress nodded— "Miss Baluta, you don't need to make one with me."

Miss Baluta looked at her steadily. "I don't believe I did," she admitted. "Let us have tea."

She crossed the room, called something in Polish at the kitchen door.

"I was about to have my tea when you came. It will be very hearty and served on the dining table, Old Country style."

On a black oak table with a red-checked cloth an old woman with a broad, pale face was laying out cheese, sausage, dark shiny bread, strong tea. Helenka Baluta again spoke to her in Polish. She nodded and left the room.

"She is from my grandfather's church," said Miss Baluta. "She works here by the day. She is strong and clean and not very bright and her English is little. However, one never knows. I have sent her to work in the garden."

She poured the tea into brown pottery cups. "Now, tell me, how did this Mrs. Peckham know that Helenka Baluta and Mary Alden were the same person?"

"I don't know," said Janet, "unless from your grandfather or the woman who works for him."

"That is not possible. They do not know it. She not at all. He, only that I work in Hollywood. He is trustworthy beyond the grave. I have told him I am a model. He would tell everyone that or nothing."

"She must have recognized you when she saw you in the movies."

"Perhaps. It was a chance I thought I could take after one successful picture. After another I knew I could not come here incognito. I shall not come here again. But my grandfather is old. I wanted to see him in this house which meant so much to him. We lived, you know, just below here in a little old shack. He stayed there until they tore it down.... He can see the spot from here."

She smiled sadly, softly. Janet was entranced.

Miss Baluta leaned toward her. "You did not recognize me on the train. But this old lady, who had not seen me, told you who I was last night."

"She was up on her balcony when you got out of the taxi."

Helenka said slowly, "She must have known me well ... long ago. But that is impossible. I do not remember her."

"Not necessarily. Cousin Mattie never forgets anyone she's ever seen. Didn't you ever ... work for her? They said something about it last night. You couldn't forget that house."

Miss Baluta laughed. "It is a blown-up nightmare. I worked a little while for a cateress. Serving at parties. She is now dead. Cigarette?"

"Thank you."

"You have been away from Watson for a long time, too?"

"Ten years. I was just an infant when we left. Thirteen."

"We return as prodigals together." The smile was comradely, the tone in which she continued casual. "And until this winter I understand the house was rented to some old friends of your parents. Your relatives must have been sorry to lose congenial neighbors. It would be natural for them to resent the purchase of the house by a workman."

"But they didn't," Janet protested. "Father, particularly, wrote to ask Cousin Mattie Peckham if she objected. Cousin Mattie is a little difficult. But she didn't mind in the least. In fact, Father said she seemed delighted."

Miss Baluta lighted a cigarette. "And Mrs. Mattie Peckham, delighted but difficult, announced last night that Helenka Baluta is Mary Alden. To whom did she tell her tale?"

"Just to the family. The Wests. They live in the chateau effect on the other side of Cousin Mattie's."

"Were they much interested? Enough to talk?"

The answer to this took a bit of thinking out. Louise's outburst would, Janet was sure, make Mary Alden a taboo topic to the family for some time to come. Until Louise herself recovered and carried it to the Junior League.

Janet said, "Some of the family weren't interested at all. One of them didn't believe it. I suppose any one of them may circulate the news sometime, but I'm rather certain they won't for a while. Except possibly Cousin Mattie."

"Let us hope not. They sound like hundreds of people. If they are to be my neighbors, perhaps I should know who exactly is who."

Janet laughed. "There are really only six. In that yellow Hag's Nook lives Mrs. Peckham. She is my mother's cousin. I am staying with her until tomorrow morning. Next door lives Mr. Virgil West in the chateau which was built by old Mr. Duncan who founded the Rifle Works. Cousin Virgil married Miss Duncan, the Cousin Charlotte, who admires you so much. Duncan West is the son of the chateau. He's the third prodigal. He's been in Paris since 1920. He was on the train yesterday. We didn't know we were cousins."

"Black haired and tweedy?"

"Yes. And different. To me. I expect you know a lot of men like him."

"Several. And the rest of the family?"

"Louise, Duncan's sister. She and Ralph came to live with the Wests this spring."

"Ralph is ...?"

Janet did not want to say this to Helenka Baluta. "He is Louise's husband. Ralph Ogden."

Janet did not look at Miss Baluta's face. It must have been a terrible experience for her, that tragedy in the house on River Street. Christmas Eve, 1920. Janet, a little girl, hearing the family talk, afterwards stealing away to read it all in the paper, had never ceased to shrink from

Ralph Ogden. But Helenka, who had known Mariska's loveliness, who had perhaps seen her die, what must his name mean to her?

She heard a tea cup rattle against the saucer, then, quiet and even, the question, "And how did he receive the story, this Mr. Ogden?"

Janet looked at her. Was she whiter? Otherwise she seemed completely unmoved.

"At first he wasn't interested. Then Cousin Mattie reminded him ... of his wife's death. He hadn't been told about your grandfather's buying the house. Not his name. He said he didn't remember you."

There was a silent moment. "He did not remember me," said Miss Baluta, "but this Mrs. Peckham did?"

"Yes, and she's a lot more dangerous than Ralph."

"Yes," said Helenka. "Much. He will ask nothing but never again to hear my name."

Janet said, "I don't see how he could have wanted to live after Mariska was dead."

"You knew her?" The tone was sharp, the eyes intent.

"Oh, yes," said Janet. "That is ..."

The knocker clanged. She rose to go.

"Wait," said Miss Baluta. It was a command. She crossed the hall swiftly and flung open the door. She spoke distantly. "Good afternoon."

A voice Janet knew came out to her. "Miss Baluta, may I come in?"

Miss Baluta said, "You are ...?"

"You don't know?"

"No," politely.

"The name," he said, "is Duncan West."

"The cousin of Miss Janet Carter? Come in."

There was a silence.

"We play it this way?"

"Your cousin," she said, "is here for tea."

They came into the dining room, Helenka leading, glamorous, assured. Behind her, a pale, nervous Duncan West. "Janie, darling," he was too glad to see her.

"Not Janie, darling or otherwise," she tried to help his embarrassment. "I'm Miss Carter on business. Miss Baluta is going to ask her grandfather to lend me all sorts of priceless costumes for the pageant. Duncan, she's here incognito. You won't tell anyone, I know. And do you think can throttle a few members of your family?"

"I can try," he looked from one girl to the other. "My parents have essentially the right instincts, my sister, too. There's actually no one who needs to be murdered except Aunt Mattie. I am beginning to think it might be a pleasure."

"And you, yourself?" Miss Baluta asked him, in her face, in the inclination of her body, the beauty of the girl who had won America in *So Long as Life*, "Are you discreet?"

"I," said Duncan, looking at her hard and blank, "have as much of a stake in this as you. I also am here on business. I had a phone call last night from Hollywood. From World-Wide Studios. Subject to your approval, they may do a story of mine for your next picture."

"Who called you?"

"Sam Wells. And very hush-hush. No names mentioned. I was to go to 90 Elm Street and ask for Miss Baluta, and tell about his call. The Mary Alden angle, as Janie has evidently told you, was supplied by my dear aunt."

"I see," said Miss Baluta. "It is to your advantage to be still. World-Wide does not want their New England lady denounced as a Polack girl. Leave your story with me. When I have read it, I will send for you."

"Thank you," said Duncan West. "Coming, Janie?"

CHAPTER VII
Thursday, 6 P.M.-11 P.M.

The meticulously elegant young man strolling past the Peckham house stopped in his tracks and swore. The words were not English, but the meaning would have been clear to any passer-by.

"Jerry," the scream had come down from the Swiss-Gothic peaks. "Jerry, come here."

When he stepped into the Gothic hall she was waiting, standing at the foot of the staircase between a suit of Japanese armor and a stuffed grizzly bear. Her eyes ran all over Jerry, seeing the coat, a little shabby at the seams, but better tailored than Duncan's, much better than Ralph's.

She pushed her "transformation" straight, "I want you to pick up Bridie tonight at her cousin's. At exactly half-past nine."

"Madam," said Jerry positively, "Mr. West has given me the night off."

"I know," said Mrs. Peckham, "but you haven't had a stroke of work to do all day. No one has been out in the car."

"No, Madam."

"Then you get Bridie at nine-thirty sharp."

"Madam," said Jerry, "I have plans for evening." There was white anger in his face.

"You have plans," mocked Mrs. Peckham. "Have you, indeed. And so have I. You will have Bridie here before ten o'clock."

Jerry took a step toward her, a trim, fashionable figure, not without menace.

"What's all this?"

He wheeled, facing Ralph Ogden.

"What's all this about anyone going for Bridie? I never knew she was too feeble to come home on the bus."

He looked hard at Mrs. Peckham.

"I especially want Bridie called for today."

"Why?"

She looked as if she would refuse to answer. Then she said, "Bridie and I had a few words this noon."

To the West family the threat that Bridie, she who took so much devilment that would otherwise have fallen upon them, might some day leave Mrs. Peckham was real.

"O.K.," said Ralph. "I'll pick up Bridie. I'm going out anyway. Beat it, Jerry. Boss's orders. And kiss your girl for me."

Jerry left, whistling, but in a minor key.

"Where are you going tonight, Ralph?" asked Mrs. Peckham.

"Annual dinner of the Fly-Casting Club. And before you say anything about its being the Incorporated Boozers of America, let me point out that it was founded by your late husband."

"What's in that bottle?"

"Cleaning fluid. Yours. Louise told me to return it."

"Why'd she do that? Isn't she coming over tonight for our bridge?"

"No. She isn't feeling so good. Duncan's taking her place."

"Sulking," said Louise's aunt happily.

"Lay off Louise," said Ralph with force.

She spoke slowly, sweetly. "You've always been a fine husband, Ralph. And I'm sure you would have been a wise father."

Ralph Ogden, at the door, turned and looked at the gleaming porcelain beneath the wig that resembled a witch's black hat. "Have you ever thought," he asked, "that you might go a little too far?"

"No," said Mrs. Peckham.

When she was alone, she closed her eyes and stood still, clutching the neck of the grizzly bear. With wrinkled lids closed over those bright beads, she looked already dead. After a minute she roused herself and crept toward the reception room. There, under a ceiling of grimy cupids rendered ambiguous by garlands of roses, she sat down and began to feel like herself again. After all, at seventy-five one must expect to feel a little tired once in a while, particularly if one's favorite pastime is of an emotional nature. Such as last evening. She hadn't had a real headache for ages. She was glad she had found one of those capsules Dr.

Taylor had given Eli. She felt a little dizzy now.

Mrs. Peckham, in her fringed red velvet chair, began to feel very happy indeed. It was Thursday, the night for bridge with her brother and his family. Cards were the whole intellectual life of Mattie Peckham, and she had not lost her grip. Never questioning the value of a pursuit is a help to maintaining form, and with one exception bridge was to her the only worth-while occupation in life. The other was raising hell with her family.

There had been a time when her horizons had been broad enough to include the inner circle of Watson society. Mattie's father, in the days when tuna was called horse mackerel, had been a wholesale dealer in fish. Unlike Charlotte, daughter of a rifle king and caring unforgivably little for the privilege, Mattie had not been born into the state she wished to be accustomed to, but her snapping black eyes, her skill at cards, and the correct and quiet Eli had finally scaled the pinnacle for "that lively little Mrs. Peckham." A thick skin had also helped.

With the coming of old age, all that was past. The struggles, the triumphs, the despairs. Mattie Peckham was satisfied now with her two simple pleasures.

Today she had a prospect of both, with the added attraction of a sound cash profit. She was fully herself again when she heard Janet in the hall.

"I'm in here," she called. "What are you fishing out of the clothes closet?"

"Just something I bought downtown. I put it in here while I went on an errand." The tones were muffled. "Bring it here."

Janet came in, flushed. She had had quite an afternoon. She was carrying a dress box.

"'Marguerite's'," read Mrs. Peckham. "Going to wear it to the Longvale Club dance? You're pretty particular about what you wear when you go out with just a cousin."

Janet bit her lip. Mattie chuckled.

"Did you pay for the dress?" she asked.

"Of course."

"You must have lots of money."

"I haven't now." Janet tried to be pleasant.

Mrs. Peckham looked alert and strong. "How," she asked, "do you expect to live until you get paid?"

"That's all settled," explained Janet. "I've arranged to room and board at the Y.W. They pay part of my salary and they're glad to give it to me that way. I'm going to pack now and leave right after dinner."

"Oh, no, darling," Mrs. Peckham's lips met tight and stretched out in the blue line that she considered a very meaning smile. "No, no! Cousin

Mattie couldn't think of letting you live anywhere else but here. The Young Women's Christian Association is no place for a girl like you. What would your mother say?"

"She'd think it was highly respectable. And she wouldn't want me to impose on you, Cousin Mattie."

Mattie's smile stretched wider. "You won't be," she said. "How much would it cost you to live at that place?"

"About fifteen dollars a week."

"Darling. I couldn't let you do it. You must stay here with me. I've written to your mother today, telling her how happy it makes me to have you here. I told her you had agreed to stay. Bridie mailed the letter when she went out."

Janet looked at the gloating old face. Jerry's recent remarks covered her feelings perfectly.

"I couldn't impose on you for three months, Cousin Mattie."

"No, darling. Cousin Mattie wouldn't let you. Every Thursday morning you will give Cousin Mattie twenty dollars."

"Wh-at?"

"Because, of course, my home is not to be compared with a boarding-place for working girls. Twenty dollars seems to me a very small sum for a little girl who earns thirty-four dollars and sixty-two cents a week."

Janet looked at her shoe.

"Of course, dear, if you feel it is too much, I can write again to your mother and perhaps she could lend you a little. Or do you have to send money home?"

There is really only one thing to do, thought Janet. Kill her. She has insulted my father for not being a West and for not being, as she hoped, a failure. She has me by the throat. For if I don't do as she says, Mother will never forgive me. She has known Mattie Peckham always and yet I could never make her believe that this lovely little scene occurred. How could anyone not know what Cousin Mattie is like, really? My word against the Family. Strong Family Feeling. Sacrificing the young to the old, the decent and honest to the lying and mean.

Beside Mrs. Peckham there stood a bulging cabinet of gilt and glass. It held the card party prizes of half a century, little cloisonné vases, a Leaning Tower of Pisa, a bridge of elephants from the boardwalk at Atlantic City. A tabouret supported the overflow; in an ivory case with a golden tassel lay a snick-a-snee. When she was a child, Eli Peckham had showed the blade to Janet. He had told her it was deadly.

Mattie spoke again. "Cousin Virgil and Cousin Charlotte would never understand it if you lived anywhere except with the family." She paused.

"Isn't Louise very intimate with the members of the committee who pay your salary?"

Janet stood up. She felt weak and sick and beaten. "All right, Cousin Mattie. I'll stay here."

"That's very nice," said Cousin Mattie. "This is Thursday. Suppose you give me twenty dollars now."

"I can't," said Janet. "I've only got seven dollars to last until the first of the month. I won't be paid until the first of May."

Mrs. Peckham sat silent. Her lips moved.

Perhaps, thought Janet, that will free me.

"Then," said Mrs. Peckham, "I'll just add six per cent each week. That will make it $21.20. That'll do nicely. I'll write out a statement of our agreement for you to sign. Now go to the kitchen and put our supper on the table. Bridie's out."

The tonic engendered in Mattie Peckham's tough old system by her encounter with Janet continued throughout the evening bridge game. She won. And Duncan turned out to be as good a player as Louise and much quieter. Mattie followed only one of her passions at a time. While a game was in progress she played it. Gossip and malice would keep.

Every week in the fifteen years since Eli Peckham had died, Mattie and three other members of the family had sat at a card table in the library from seven until half-past nine. The library was small and dark and crowded, though not by books. At nine-thirty they had a light lunch left by Bridie on a tray, and at ten Bridie returned and the Wests went home. Bridie had her own little ways, and it had long ago seemed easier to have a train of changing laundresses and cleaning women under her sway, and no other resident servants.

Tonight at nine-thirty, Virgil West neatly added the score and said, "Mattie, aren't we going to ask Janet down to have a little lunch with us?"

"Of course we are." Duncan sprang up and made for the hall.

"You take the words right out of my mouth," said his aunt.

Charlotte, looking regal, returned from the butler's pantry carrying a tray of cheese crackers, jam tarts and carrot wine. Mattie smiled. Charlotte, she knew, liked to do things that emphasized the fifteen years between their ages. Let her do it.

Behind her, Janet, in pale green, entered with Duncan. She looked just a little too perky, Mattie thought, and quite aware of his hand just touching her shoulder. That will soon be over. The tarts looked lovely. Virgil was well into his, and Mattie took one eagerly. They were rich and good and covered up the flavor of the wine which was not carroty, and not anything else. Mattie drank it to please her brother and to confound the rest of the family. It was one of the greatest sacrifices she had to make. She gulped, and a trickle fell on the front of her purple silk.

Charlotte handed her a napkin. Janet scrubbed. "I'm afraid this is a job for the cleaner's," she said.

Mattie bridled. "Nothing of mine ever goes to the cleaner's. I do it all myself with OUT. It's wonderful. It's a good thing Louise sent back my bottle today. I shall use it before I go to bed."

"I hope," said Janet, "you always use it in a good draft. OUT is nothing but carbon tetrachloride. The fumes can knock you out."

"Well, of course," said Mattie, "I haven't an education like yours, Janet, but I can read labels and it doesn't say anything like that on my bottle."

"No. Because you might not be so keen to use it if it did. But if you buy the same thing from a cooperative, they warn you of the danger."

"Janet," said Virgil, "out in Minnesota aren't you a little bit socialistic?"

"Janet, dear," said Cousin Charlotte, "since you're up, will you hand me my knitting bag. On the couch. I want a fresh handkerchief."

"Shall I bring you a handkerchief or do you want the whole bag?" Janet picked up the generous bag. It had tortoise-shell handles and was embroidered with a garden scene in cross-stitch. Louise had made it.

"Janet," said Virgil, "I have known Mama for forty years and she has never let me put my fingers in any sewing bag of hers. Not me nor anyone else."

Cousin Charlotte said, "I like to find my things just as I leave them. Thank you, dear. Louise wanted me to ask you who is the Junior League member of your central committee."

"Mrs. Kingston. Shall I put the bag back?"

"Louise," said Louise's aunt with unction, "won't like that."

She saw Duncan take the bag from Janet, his hand touching hers. "Duncan," she asked, "why did you leave France?"

Duncan replied, "I wanted to see my family again."

"And," said Mattie, "a good time to do that is when your income is down. You couldn't cut the same figure now in Paris on your Grandfather Duncan's money that you could in 1920. Even your mother can't make hers go so far as she'd like."

"None of us can ever do that," said Charlotte serenely.

"It helps to be careful," said her sister-in-law. "I've got everything my father left me. That's more than Virgil can say, in spite of all your money."

Virgil cleared his throat.

Mattie went on, "Of course it would be a wonderful thing for you if the Longvale Club actually buys your house for their winter quarters. Or shouldn't I believe everything I hear?"

"No, Mattie," her brother said gently, "not everything. We've had no real offer."

"If you do," advised Mattie, "snap it up. You can always come here and live with me."

Into this enticing vision of the future, Duncan intruded suavely, "I regret, Aunt Mattie, that I am not the wastrel nephew of your dreams. I have business in the States. Real cash money."

"Are you selling something?" she asked with suspicion.

"Yes, I am happy to say."

"What? Insurance?"

"No. Art. Mine." He turned to his father and mother. "A man I met in Paris, a Californian, named Wells, saw some things I had written, plays and stories. He thought they had possibilities. Apparently he was right about one of them, anyway."

"Was that what your long-distance telephone call was about last night, son?" asked Virgil.

"Yes, Father."

"We were wondering how soon you'd tell us what it was about." The tone was old and hurt. "Why didn't you tell your mother and me that you were a writer?"

"It didn't seem a West kind of business. I wasn't sure you'd be interested."

"But you're going to make some money at it, son."

"Anything you do, dear, is interesting to me," said Charlotte.

Duncan patted her hand.

"It's simply swell," said Janet.

Mattie Peckham said, "You were a smart boy, Duncan. I told you that when you left home. A smart boy. And a wise child. There's only one thing a wise child doesn't know." She giggled.

There was no response.

"It's ten o'clock," went on Mattie. "I can't imagine what's keeping Bridie. She's never been late before. But you needn't wait any longer. Janet is here."

They all rose. Charlotte put the cards in their case, and carried out the tray. Virgil bent, puffing, to fold the card table. Duncan guided Janet from the room. Mattie smiled all to herself. She followed them. She arrived in the shadowed hall in time to hear him say, "A cousin is a person you have to kiss good night," and laugh. She saw him do it.

Mrs. Peckham put her hand in the bosom of her dress. She took out a letter.

"Duncan," she said, "please mail this for me on the way home."

He held out his hand for the letter. Janet looked toward it. Perhaps this was the letter to her mother; perhaps Bridie hadn't mailed it. There might be a loophole of escape.

"Janet," said Mattie Peckham, "you seem awfully interested in my gas bill. I have a much more interesting document to show you."

Under the high, dim light, their faces looked young to her, the girl unhappy, her nephew a little wild. She had been waiting for this. It was better than she had hoped. Janet had never entered into her plans. She was sheer gift. "Yes," she went on, "as soon as the others have gone home, you come up to my room, Janet, and I'll show you a letter you'll never forget as long as you live."

Virgil and Charlotte were with them now. The three Wests went down the steps. Virgil was saying to Duncan, "What was Aunt Mattie going to show Janet, son?"

They went down the walk. Virgil and Charlotte turned to the left and took the path through the hedge, Duncan to the right and toward the mailbox in front of the Baluta house.

Mattie closed and bolted the big front door. "Put Kitty out," she ordered Janet, "and leave the side door unlatched for Bridie. I always do. Then you come right straight to my room."

To find and eject a snarling cat was a matter of ten minutes' unpleasantness for Janet; by that much it delayed the additional dark hurt she knew Cousin Mattie was waiting to deliver. She closed the door leading to a little side porch toward the West chateau. A flight of stairs rose from a small entry. Slowly she climbed the steps and crossed the central hall to her room. Without turning on the light, she went to the window and looked down on her old home. Just one quiet moment before Cousin Mattie shrieked for her.

Directly below Janet's window was the Peckham drive, the Baluta drive and the Baluta sunroom. This room was lighted. On the settle across two windows, Helenka Baluta sat, her gold hair fluffed out in curls. Janet could see her face in profile, flushed, gay. It was turned toward a man. Only the back of his head was visible, pressed against a red cushion. The hair was black.

Ralph's hair was black. He knew the Balutas. He knew Helenka. He was not at home this evening. And all this was true of another man. Duncan had had ample time to do his last family chore and relax at Helenka Baluta's side.

"Janet, I heard you come up. I'm waiting."

Janet was almost glad. Know the worst. Things weren't altogether good now.

Mattie's bedroom was vast, but hot and very close. It had been her father's bedroom. He had furnished it and he had died in it. It still contained his Franklin stove, for Mr. West had never trusted wholly in a furnace. His daughter thought the stove was a nice cheap way to take the spring chill off a room, and it was glowing tonight.

Mattie Peckham sat on the side of the enormous black walnut bed. She still wore the purple dress. On the marble-topped table beside the bed was the bottle of OUT, and a rag. In her hand she held an envelope with a pale blue stamp. She had never looked happier.

"Come here," she said. "Now, darling, Cousin Mattie has always felt that older people ought to tell young girls what life is like."

The envelope was thin and gray. Janet could not read the postmark. In a young, unformed hand it was addressed to Mrs. Eli Peckham, 110 Elm Street, Watson, Massachusetts, Ètats-Unis,

Janet shrank back.

"Of course, you would rather not know. Cousin Mattie understands. But it is for your good."

The letter came out of the envelope. It was a single sheet of thin, foreign paper. She held it out.

"Dear Aunt Mattie," Janet could see the large scrawl. "Take it," Mattie said, her eyes black beads, her hand trembling on the sheet, her smile a dead triumph. Janet put out her hand.

Below the telephone rang.

"Answer that," commanded Mattie, "and come straight back. I shall be waiting."

Groping for unfamiliar switches, Janet stumbled down the hall to the wide front staircase. With characteristic economy, there was only one telephone in the Peckham house. It stood on a small table in the main hallway, directly behind the grizzly bear. Janet turned on a small table lamp, took off the receiver unsteadily.

"Listen, Janet," began Louise, querulous, insistent, "I've just heard that Florence Kingston has been put on your most important committee. I had to call you up right away."

It went on for three-quarters of an hour, the circumstantial account of Florence Kingston's long and, to an unprejudiced listener, peculiarly colorless career in the socially sanctioned good works of Watson. There followed a similar account of Louise's own—very righteous. With the shadow of the bear falling across the little pool of light, the great black stairwell above her, the greater foreboding of what awaited the end of all this, Janet sat and dreaded, and did not listen to Louise. She heard the stillness all about her, broken once or twice by creaks and groans that could be Bridle returning or ghosts climbing the staircase or mice, or just old house. Once she thought she heard a door close on the second floor. Probably Cousin Mattie had decided not to wait.

"You simply must see, Janet, that nothing more disastrous could possibly happen to you. Good-bye." Louise had at last hung up.

Janet turned off the light over the telephone and found herself in blackness. Cousin Mattie must have turned off the hall light from an upstairs switch. With a bruising clang she met the Japanese armor. Thereafter Janet climbed ignominiously on all fours. Utter silence above her. Cousin Mattie must be asleep. As the top came in sight she could see light, a burning crack beneath Mrs. Peckham's bedroom door.

Janet's first impulse was to slip by that hot, horrible room. No. If she evaded it tonight, tomorrow, some day, she would be forced to read the letter that a boy had written to that jolly old girl, his Aunt Mattie.

Janet knocked at Mrs. Peckham's door. There was no answer. She pushed it open.

Mattie Peckham lay on the floor beside the black walnut bed. The wig had slipped far to one side, uncovering a head bald and shiny as a brown egg. The OUT bottle, spilled empty, lay at her side, its fumes filling the room. The letter was not visible.

CHAPTER VIII
Thursday, 11 P.M.-12 P.M.

In the dark kitchen Mr. Baluta put his hand on the door. It was a hard, knotty old hand. It was trembling. He pushed open the door softly, peering around it into the lighted hall. Like a poster against the white front door two figures embraced. Mr. Baluta stared at the back of the man with head against the golden head of Mary Alden, her arms holding him close. Slowly she raised her eyes.

Mr. Baluta beckoned and slipped back through the door.

A moment later she stood beside him in the kitchen. Mr. Baluta motioned to the side windows. The Peckham house from spire to basement was glowing. Mammoth jigsaw shadows lay across the lawn at the edge of parking lights from three or four cars. Across bright windows figures passed.

Mr. Baluta gestured toward the closed door behind them. "Send him away."

She did not speak or move.

He said, "He will go to that house. Sometime he will come back and tell us what is going on."

She said, as if dreaming, "Does it matter?"

In the half-light, he looked at her. He spoke, harsh and low. "Have you forgotten?"

She stiffened. She pushed back her disordered hair. "You are right," she said and went briskly out of the room.

Alone, the old man pressed his heavy face against the window, peering, staring into the strangely illumined night.

Outside, the Peckham house looked like a black, old dead tree hung with the Christmas lights of its windows. Inside, it sounded like dry boughs creaking in a wind of indignation. The house was used to death. It was not familiar with the heavy tread of the Law.

The great front stairs groaned, the narrow east corridor moaned, and with each endless pass and repass during that long night, a loose board in Mattie's bedroom floor sent up a thin shriek. All sounded the same refrain: Why Did You Call the Police?

The first human expression of this sentiment came with Bridie's excited eruption into the hall. Bright daisies on her hat quivered with outrage and she clutched her purse to her bosom as if the man at the telephone and the man pounding up the stairs were wearing stripes instead of brass buttons.

She shouted at the slim green ghost of a girl standing at the head of the stairs, "Why've you got the police in this house, Miss Janet?"

Janet said huskily to the policeman from the squad car, now beside her in the upper hall, "The big room at the right." She came slowly down the stairs, clinging to the rail.

Alarm had superseded outrage in Bridie. She met the girl halfway up the stairs and grabbed her arm.

"There can't nothin' have happened to *her?*"

"There has."

There was the noise on the porch of men carrying something heavy. Bridie toiled up the stairs. Janet went to open the front door. Three firemen came in, carrying blankets and the pulmotor and tramped up after Bridie.

The policeman at the phone hung up and came toward Janet, notebook in hand. "I'll take your name, Miss... Are you alone here?"

Around the stairway from the side entry Virgil West waddled into view. He had pulled on a dark coat and trousers over pink flannelette pajamas. He looked both dazed and calm. Behind him trotted Louise, a raincoat slipped over an excessively lacy negligee, her wave set in a net.

"I'm Mr. Virgil West, officer. I understand my sister has had a bad accident. I'd like to go to her at once."

"Sure," said the policeman. "I'll go with you."

Janet sank down on the bottom step. Louise sat down beside her. Her voice was desperate and low, "Listen, Janet, Father says you told him on the phone that Aunt Mattie was overcome by fumes from OUT. Was it ... was it the bottle Ralph brought over this afternoon?"

Janet nodded. "She said it was the only one she had and she was glad you had sent it back. There was a spot on her dress. From the lunch after the bridge game. You know how hot and close her room is with that stove going."

From above came the heavy pulse, the struggling exhaust of the pulmotor.

Louise asked, "When did it happen?"

"Sometime between ten-fifteen and eleven."

"And you were in the room next to hers and didn't hear her fall or anything?"

Janet looked white, surprised. "You know where I was. Down here at the phone, talking to you."

"Not all that time. Just a minute or two."

"Forty-five of them."

"Nonsense," said Louise. "And how did you happen to be so interested in the exact time?"

There was a single, loud ring of the doorbell.

The competent man with a doctor's bag said, "Medical Examiner," and Janet again indicated the way to Mattie Peckham's bedroom.

Charlotte, white hair perfectly arranged, fully and sensibly clad in gray wool, came into the hall. Above them the sucking sound grew louder as the bedroom door was opened for the police doctor.

"What is that noise?" asked Charlotte.

"The pulmotor, Mother."

"Then," said Charlotte, "she isn't dead. We must hope for the best. Louise," her cool eyes rested on her disheveled daughter, "go into the dressing room and take that net off your hair." Her tone was kind. She sat down beside Janet and took her hand. "My dear, what an experience for you. You were alone with her when she was overcome?"

"No. She was all alone."

"You weren't in bed, dear?" She looked at the green crêpe dress, the smooth hair.

"Oh, no, Cousin Charlotte. I was here at the telephone, talking to Louise. From a few minutes after you left until eleven o'clock. Three-quarters of an hour." She said it carefully, defensively.

"I think," said Cousin Charlotte, "you are a little mixed. Quite naturally, after all you have been through. Louise would never use a telephone for so long a time as that. I have never allowed it."

There seemed to be no suitable answer.

"Janet, dear, why did you call the police?"

"Because," said Janet, tired but defiant, "when someone is asphyxiated, I thought one should summon a pulmotor squad. I didn't know whether the police or the fire department had one. But I was sure the police would know. So I called them."

"That wasn't really wrong. Only we have never done things that way in the Family. We would have called Dr. Taylor and he would have arranged everything. You remember Dr. Taylor, Janet?"

"I did remember. As soon as I'd called the police, I looked at the list of numbers written in the front of Cousin Mattie's phone book. Yours was there. And I saw Dr. Taylor's name. I called Cousin Virgil and then I called the doctor."

"You did very well," Cousin Charlotte patted the hand she held. "But why isn't Dr. Taylor here?"

"Perhaps," said Janet rudely, "because he doesn't take his job as seriously as the police take theirs."

"Excuse me, ma'am," said the squad car driver who came down the stairs. The two women rose.

"Have you seen my husband Mr. West?" asked Charlotte.

"Yes, ma'am, he's just outside the Room."

"I must go to him," said Charlotte, and ascended the stairs.

"Now, Miss," began the policeman, bringing out his notebook again, "Your name? Age? You live here with your grandmother?"

"Janet West Carter," she said. "Twenty-three. With my mother's cousin. Just temporarily."

"Here on a visit?"

"I'm working in town."

The policeman gave her a companionable look. He had not felt at home with the stained glass, the armor, and the bear. A working girl was more in his line. "Uh-huh," he said. "Where you working?"

Again the doorbell rang.

"I'll get it," he said.

Two men stepped into the hall. One was a stocky little Irishman who looked as if he had recently and reluctantly abandoned the wearing of derby hats.

The other man, tall, long-boned, and lean, carried himself easily and well in a light gray suit. His blue eyes, when he saw the bear and the armor, twinkled. To the girl in green leaning against the newel post, he took off his gray soft hat. His hair was the dull blond of a towhead turned thirty, his head narrow, long and high. Almost anyone would have guessed he was of Scandinavian origin, but no one had ever called him a dumb Swede.

"Good evenin', Lund," said the policeman. "H'ya, Murphy."

"Evening, Shea," said Lund. His voice was deep and pleasant. "So this is the scene of the crime!"

"No, sir," said the literal Shea. "It's upstairs. And it probably ain't a crime. Just an accident. Though, of course, that's for you to say, not me."

"Who's up there now?"

"Leary, my partner, Doc Nichols. Pulmotor squad. Cook or something. And the old lady's family."

"Sounds like quite an audience for your master mind, Lund," said Murphy affectionately.

"This here young lady," said Shea, "is the one who found the ... found Mrs. Peckham after she was knocked out. Miss Carter, meet Lootenant Lund."

"How-do-you-do," said Janet, and held out her hand.

Lund took it, looking a little surprised. He smiled at her and said, "I'll be down in a few minutes and talk to you."

She said, "Yes, Mr. Lund."

"Stay here, Shea," ordered Lund. "Answer the door and the phone. And remember that no one's accused or suspected of anything yet."

The detectives, too, went up the groaning stairs and disappeared in the upper darkness. Janet said to Shea, "Are they sure yet that she won't live?"

"No, Miss. You can hear them still trying."

She left him, then, left the police and that muffled sucking that seemed to go on forever. And for what? Mattie Peckham, lying on the floor beside the bed like a great black tombstone, had looked about as dead as anyone could be.

The little cupid-adorned reception room was the nearest refuge. Janet sank down in Mattie's red velvet chair and dropped her head against the back. Before her tired eyes wavered the cabinet with the trophies of Mattie's life. The vases, images, fans, and the snick-a-snee which, that afternoon, had given Janet a moment's thought of killing. Earlier at the Baluta house Duncan had said, "Actually no one needs to be murdered except Aunt Mattie." And last night there had been Louise. Probably the others, too.

With all that hate around her Mattie Peckham would probably die the victim of her own niggardliness.

Or was there more to all this than a whiff of carbon tetrachloride in a hot, airless room? This time it was Janet who joined the refrain of the house and the family: "Why did you call the police?" She closed her eyes and wished ardently that she had never read a book on the psychology of the unconscious.

A hard hand grasped her shoulder and she cried out. Duncan was standing over her, his eyes as hard as his hand.

"Janie, for God's sake. Tell me what all this is about. I was just going by. I saw all the lights. And cars. The policeman at the door says Aunt Mattie has been asphyxiated. Janie," his hand still held her shoulder too hard, his voice was harsh, his eyes strained, "is Aunt Mattie dead?"

Janet pulled herself free. "Sh!" she said and listened. She didn't think she could hear the pulmotor now. "We don't know yet. I think she is, Duncan. I found her."

Duncan walked to the door. Only Shea was visible. He took Janet's arm, insistent, but not now brutal, and led her away from the door as far as possible. "What," he said hoarsely, "about the letter?"

"The letter?"

"Don't pretend you have forgotten." His eyes were not pleasant.

"No."

"Did she show it to you?"

"Yes."

"You read it." It was a bitter statement.

"No, Duncan, of course not. I saw the envelope. And the heading. Then Louise called me on the phone. I went back to Cousin Mattie's room. Then I found her."

She covered her eyes for a moment, but it only made more vivid that memory of a shiny egg with a yellow mummy's face turning blue.

Duncan took down her hands roughly. "Look at me. Did you find the letter?"

She looked at his tense face. "No, Duncan. I swear it. I tried to save her. I lifted her toward the windows. I opened them. And loosened the neck of her dress. The letter wasn't in sight. It wasn't under her when I moved her. Or in the front of her dress. Duncan, is it so important?"

"It is," he said, "to me."

"I think that Cousin Mattie put it away again while I was at the telephone. I was there a long time. I think she got impatient, and decided to clean her dress and go to bed. She put out the light in the upper hall and closed her bedroom door while I was downstairs."

"I'd like to believe you." Duncan's eyes were hard on her white face. "I'd like to believe that you haven't read the letter and that you don't know where it is right now. I'd like to believe dear Aunt Mattie changed her mind for the better. And there is one more thing I should like." He stood off from her, watching for changing expression. "I'd like to know why you called the police."

Fury rose in the girl's face. That phrase had been repeated too often. "I did it," she said, "for a simple, obvious reason. I wanted technical help in an emergency. But if anyone else asks me why I did it, I shall think he is a murderer."

He left her then. She leaned back against the window, worn out by this sudden, unexpected anger. Her cheek lay on the cool glass. Her eyes half-closed. They opened, and she froze with horror. From the other side of the window, a face was retreating, distorted by light and shadow to a horrible mask. It was gone. But a moment before, it had been there, with only the glass between.

Janet fled from the room. In the hall Shea sat solid by the front door, and a figure paced light and quick, humming a tune monotonous and haunting. He turned and came toward her, a lithe little man with a dark moustache.

"Is there anything I can do for you, Miss Carter?" asked Jerry.

"I saw ... I thought I saw a face, a horrible face ... at the reception room window."

Shea and Jerry were out the door, leaving it wide open. Anything could come in there. Janet, shuddering, went to close it.

Someone spoke from the shadowy porch, unctuous and suave. Janet, swallowing a scream, remembered from long ago that bedside voice.

"Come in," she said, "Dr. Taylor."

He came in, a heavy man with a great gray pompadour, and the spats and white-piped vest of Before-World-War-I. "My child," he said, "this is a sad house tonight. My patient ... Is she still living?"

"The police," said Janet acidly, "are doing their best."

"I will join them," said Dr. Taylor, and very tenderly patted her shoulder as he passed.

There was only one more person to visit the Peckham house that night, one member of the family, strangely, persistently missing. Ralph. Ralph who was to call for Bridie. Bridie had come home an hour ago. Where was he?

It was utterly still and empty in the vast hall. There was no doubt that the pulmotor had ceased. That could mean recovery. Or death. A faint whisper came from the hall above. A door opened and there were hushed voices and approaching footsteps. The little Irish detective and Lieutenant Lund came down the stairs. They were at the foot of the stairs, and suddenly the hall was full of people. Through the front door came Shea and Jerry. With them a third man, Ralph, at last.

There was a rush from behind the stairs. Louise, pale, her hair hanging in damp curls, flung her arms about her husband's neck. "Darling," she said, "I heard you come home while the family were still playing bridge over here. You've been working in the garage ever since, haven't you? You're so clever with the car."

Ralph unwound her arms. "Thanks, Louise. I don't need an alibi. Has something happened to Mrs. Peckham?"

He looked at the two detectives. Murphy did not return the look. His eyes, narrow with suspicion, were fixed on Louise, while his fingers stroked protectively the hair, over his left ear.

Lieutenant Lund stepped forward under the chandelier. "Mrs. Peckham is dead," he said. He paused and added, slowly, "Mr. Ogden." The light brought out a fine network of scars about his lips.

CHAPTER IX
Thursday, Midnight

Lieutenant Lund turned to Louise. "Mrs. Ogden?" he asked courteously. "Dr. Taylor is with your parents and your brother in the small upstairs sitting room. He wants you to join them."

"Poor Dad. Of course." Louise went up the stairs. Ralph started to follow.

"Would you mind waiting, Mr. Ogden? In that room at the left?"

"Certainly," said Ralph. He looked puzzled.

Lund said, "I'll be with you in a minute."

Ralph sulkily took himself toward the cupids.

Lund spoke to the slim girl in green. "You've had a hard night of it. There's no reason to make it harder. The parades down this staircase during the next half-hour may be on the grim side. Will you wait somewhere until I need you?"

Janet looked up to blue eyes that seemed kind.

"The library. At the right beyond the staircase."

"O.K., Miss Carter. I won't be long." As she disappeared down the hall, he said to Jerry, "You're Mr. West's chauffeur?"

"Yes."

"All right. Go after Miss Carter. Stay with her or near her. She's had a shock. Old lady wasn't a pretty sight."

The pulmotor men, limp and disheveled came down the stairs. In their wake followed a valiant figure, and Lund and Murphy regarded it with respect. Throughout the rough struggle in Mattie Peckham's room, it was Bridie who had literally stood ready, in case her mistress gasped her way back to life, to supply the human touch. Bridie had seen it through and not without a certain horrible enjoyment. Now she had come downstairs to make coffee for the Family.

"And ye can't stop me," she told the Law.

Lund knew it. "Murphy, go along and help her." A quiet look passed between him and his partner.

"You bet I will," said Murphy.

Lund beckoned to the policeman. "Shea," he said in low tones, "stay here in the hall. Doc Nichols will probably be down soon with orders for the morgue. He'll tell you what he wants. I've deputized the Bedside Manner. Murphy and I'll get to work on the other three."

Shea grinned. "I kinda hope you don't have to get tough with the little girl, Loot. She's kinda nice."

"This," said Lund, "isn't the kind of job where you can get tough. If it's a job for us at all. As for the rest of it, Shea, I agree with you."

He crossed the hall in long, quiet strides. Ralph Ogden was slouched in a pink satin chair, nervously pulling the snick-a-snee in and out of the ivory case. Lund, lean and straight, stood over him and thought: Not quite bald, not quite gray, not quite a paunch, but there are signs of the times.

"Mr. Ogden," he said, "the doctors are pretty sure that Mrs. Peckham met with an accident. Took in too many fumes of cleaning fluid in a closed room, passed out, and then breathed in enough from the upset bottle to kill her."

Ralph nodded. "Always was dabbing at herself with the stuff. My wife does the same thing. Can't stop her. This, I should think, might."

"Would you say," asked Lund casually, "that Mrs. Peckham had seemed in her usual health lately?"

"Yes, more so if anything."

"More what?"

"More ...." Ralph chose his word carefully, "lively. There was an awful lot of life in that old girl." His face was reminiscent, not of pleasure.

"Hard to get on with?"

Ralph grew wary. "Not so bad when you were used to her."

"When did you see her last?"

"This afternoon around six. Come to think of it, she looked a little white around the gills. Though she was scrapping with the chauffeur in top form."

"Where did you see her?"

"Here, in the hall. Wait a minute. My God! So that was the stuff I brought over in the bottle.... The stuff that killed her."

"You brought it?"

Ralph eyed him suspiciously. "How many times have you been told that before tonight?"

"Not once. Why should I be? This isn't a murder case."

Ralph's face did not clear. "You never know in this family."

"You mean you expect murder?"

Ralph said, "No. Just every little thing you do is mulled over and over.

And even if this were murder, I'm not concerned in it. The bottle belonged to Mattie Peckham. She had loaned it to my wife. Louise handed it to me as I was going out the door and told me to take it over to her aunt before she yelled bloody murder ..." he stopped short.

Lund said, "So you thought Mrs. Peckham didn't look very well at six this afternoon. How did she look?"

"White and as if she were a little dizzy. She seemed to be hanging on to the banister. But I may be wrong. I'm talking an awful lot. Too much, I suppose," he smiled ruefully, "for my own good. I haven't had much experience with the police."

There was a moment's silence. Then Ralph looked up at Lund. Slack fingers playing with the yellow silk tassel on the snick-a-snee were suddenly tense.

"Thank you, Mr. Ogden," said Lund pleasantly. "Good night."

Ralph stared at the tall detective's back through narrowed eyes.

In the library where so recently the family had sat intact and solid for all its wrangling and hates, Janet Carter lay back in a Morris chair. Outside the door the slight figure of Jerry passed and repassed whistling softly. The haunting little tune crept behind the eyelids she tried to close, and forced them open, slipped under the skin that ached from Duncan's bruising hand. It was music she knew and couldn't name. Something as simple to recall as a popular song hit, but not one. Not music she would have expected Jerry to know.

Her tone was irritated and tired. "Jerry, what are you whistling?"

"I beg your pardon, Miss Carter. I was not aware ..." Jerry stood in the doorway.

"What is the name of that tune?"

"It is the *Pavane* by Ravel. *Pavane pour une Infante défunte*."

Pavane for a Dead Princess. Stately old dance for a dead princess of Spain, composed by a modern French composer and whistled by a chauffeur, origin unknown. And for the late Mrs. Mattie Peckham.

Janet giggled. "I'm s-sorry, Jerry. I so-sound a little hysterical."

He took a step into the room. "Mademoiselle, er, Miss Carter has had reason to be upset."

Janet shuddered. "It was bad enough before I saw that face at the window. Did you find him?"

Jerry came into the middle of the room. "No," he said and his voice was low and cautious. "Neither I nor the policeman. I was there first under the window. All around the house. Miss Carter, there was no one."

"I saw him."

"Miss Carter, are you sure?"

Not sure of that white face, blurred through the glass, blobby, with white forehead and upstanding hair? "Of course I'm sure."

"Did you," said Jerry, looking at her behind long lashes, "recognize this face?"

Ralph had a pompadour. Ralph, of all the family, had not entered the house before her fright. She did not like Ralph. Easy to believe that it was he. But there was another man who fitted all the features she had been able to record in her moment of horror. A big, bland face, a gray upsweep of hair. Dr. Taylor. And while Jerry and Shea were chasing around the house he could have stepped from a hiding place onto the porch. Janet had let him in while the search was going on. But why would he spy through the reception room window? Why would Ralph?

Janet met Jerry's veiled regard squarely. "I did not recognize him."

"Miss Carter," he said with careful suggestion in the tone, "you said a moment ago that perhaps because of all the very terrible things you have been through tonight, you are hysterical. One can understand that so well. Miss Carter, are you certain that you saw a face at the window? Couldn't you have imagined it?"

That clammy-looking gargoyle a hallucination? Even the shock of discovering sudden and unlovely death could not have made her mind manufacture such a horror.

"No," said Janet. "I did not imagine it."

She rose and walked over to the lone and ill-filled bookcase that gave the Peckham library its name.

Behind her Jerry shrugged. Again he strolled down the hall, began again to whistle, stopped.

"Witt," said Lieutenant Lund behind him, "when did you last see Mrs. Peckham alive?"

Jerry wheeled sharply to face him. "At six today."

"You had a little trouble?"

Lund stood six inches above Jerry, but no more straight. Their eyes met direct.

"Only the usual thing, sir."

"What's the usual?"

"Madam saw me passing her house and not in uniform. An evening off, quite clear. So she shrieks at me most painfully from a balcony to come in. And then I am told to fetch her maid in the suburbs at nine-thirty. Not so loudly, but also painfully."

"You did as she said?"

"No. I had a break. Mr. Ogden came along and offered to do it, as he would be out at that hour with the car."

"Oh! And he did that?"

Jerry hesitated. The detective's eye was clear and cold. "No," said Jerry. "I think not. Bridie came home on the bus."

"How do you know?"

"Because she and Lottie, the waitress of Mrs. West, came up the street together. I saw them." He flushed.

"When you saw Mrs. Peckham," Lund asked, "did she look well? Seem in good health?"

"Perfectly," said Jerry. The question evidently surprised and relieved him.

"Thanks," said Lund. "You can go home now. Shea has your name. You live at the Wests'?"

"Yes. Over the garage. I thank you, Lieutenant." There was the beginning of a bow, followed closely by an American "So long."

Lund walked lightly across the library where Janet still stood before the bookcase. The Peckham bibliotheca consisted mainly of old bound volumes of *Field and Stream*, but it also contained Elwell on Bridge, the complete works of Winston Churchill the Less, and a handsome brown tome stamped on the back with the gilt figure of a woman with outstretched arms and Mary Magdalene hair, and the title, *Salt Lake Fruit*.

"It was bitter, I take it," he said, "that fruit."

The girl smiled. She looked pale but alive. Unbowed. But bloody? He hoped not. As Shea had said, "kinda nice."

"If every Mormon family had two or three Cousin Matties," she said, "it couldn't have been very sweet."

"And there'd be at least one left." He watched her closely.

She shuddered. "I had forgotten. Just for a moment. That she was dead."

"Not a popular character?"

"I'm not sure. I wasn't quite used to her. I hadn't seen her since I was a child. Until yesterday. Or rather, Wednesday afternoon."

"Let's sit down and have a cigarette." Lund took the Morris chair, leaning easily back, long legs outstretched. Janet curled up on a cracked leather sofa draped with the crazy quilt made by Mattie Peckham in the year of her marriage.

"You look ..." began Janet, and stopped.

Lund encouraged her. "I don't look like a cop because I'm not Irish?"

"No. You look like home to me."

"Where is home?"

"Minneapolis."

There was a wide smile on the detective's face. Half of it was for the reason he now stated. "You and me both!" The biggest half was because the easy contact with a witness so often to be groped for, had been handed him on a silver salver. "That is, it used to be. Thirteen years ago. It's a great town."

"I love it. There's room for so much that seems squeezed out and dried up here."

"Maybe," he suggested, "you don't know the right kind of people in Watson."

Janet started to smile. He looked so like Minneapolis, the tall blond boys at the University, truck drivers, members of her father's firm, policemen. This man was a policeman. She had never had reason to know a policeman in Minneapolis or anywhere else. The smile stopped.

The policeman, watching, said, "You came to Watson on Wednesday to visit your relative?"

"No. To work here for three months. I am going to direct the International Festival. For the Fourth of July."

"That," he said genuinely, "interests me a lot. We'll talk about it sometime, I hope. Not at one-thirty A.M."

And not immediately following sudden death. That affair upstairs didn't smell quite right.

"You were staying here with Mrs. Peckham. She was your mother's cousin? You were invited to visit her?"

Janet said, less openly, "Yes."

"Coming here as you did just the other day, you wouldn't perhaps know a lot about Mrs. Peckham's health. Did she seem feeble to you? Did the other members of the family talk about her physical condition?"

"No one talked about it at all. When I first came, Cousin Mattie seemed awfully old, of course, but after the first sight, what you thought about most was how strong she was. I mean her personality. I'm not explaining it very well. She seemed to get such a kick out of life."

"And gave it back?"

Janet said cautiously, "I suppose everyone does. Now and then."

Lund said, "Miss Carter, Dr. Nichols and Dr.... er Taylor think Mrs. Peckham would not have been so quickly suffocated by those fumes if she had been in perfect health at the time she inhaled them. I know how knocked out you must feel, but I'm asking you to tell me briefly when you saw Mrs. Peckham during the day just ended, and any details about her appearance, her food, her actions that may help us to decide the cause of her death."

Janet straightened. She put out her cigarette. "Certainly." She folded her hands in her lap.

"I didn't see Cousin Mattie before I left for work this morning. Bridie told me she always had breakfast in her room. I came home soon after six. As soon as I came in the door, Cousin Mattie called to me. She was sitting in the small reception room. She wanted ...”

Janet paused. When she had started her matter-of-fact recital she had not foreseen how much there was to conceal and how soon she would arrive at it. Not concealing crime, not hiding something from the police, but covering from a stranger the dozens of little meannesses that added up to her total picture of Cousin Mattie Peckham, deceased.

“She wanted to see the dress I had just bought. She was interested in small happenings. I guess all old people are.” But not all old people will follow up an interest in an incipient romance with the delivery of a mortal blow. Not all can. They don’t have letters. She must be very careful to say nothing about the letter.

“Then I got supper. Bridie was out. I prepared exactly what Cousin Mattie ordered. She ate cold roast pork and apple sauce and bread and butter and a ... a large piece of fruit cake. And one raspberry jam tart. She drank two cups of tea, black and bitter.”

“Not what you’d call a domestic science meal.”

“Distinctly not. After supper she told me ... I washed the dishes. Cousin Mattie went upstairs and changed her dress. Soon after seven the family came over to play bridge. I gather they come every Thursday when Bridie goes out. I had gone up to my room before they arrived. I didn’t see any of them or anything of Cousin Mattie until Duncan ... until they invited me to come down and have refreshments with them. Cousin Mattie ate a tart, the same kind that she had at supper, and drank some carrot wine.”

“Some?”

“Wine. Mr. Virgil West, her brother, makes it from carrots. Cousin Mattie spilled some of it on her dress.”

“And can you blame her!”

“No one could. But it was unfortunate because that was what made her decide to use the cleaner tonight.”

“Did she talk about it when this happened?”

“I think we all did.”

“Who,” asked Lund, “was here?”

“Mr. and Mrs. West. And Duncan. Their son.”

“Do you remember just what was said?”

“Not very much was said, really,” Janet replied carefully. “Probably nothing would have been said if it hadn’t been for me. You see, I didn’t know Cousin Mattie awfully well and that she was very careful about money in little ways. So I suggested she send the dress to the cleaner’s. She hit the ceiling and began to rave about the OUT stuff. Then I went on being a fool and said you ought to be careful to use it only in a draft, even if it didn't warn you on the label. And Cousin Virgil West asked me if there wasn't a lot of socialism in Minnesota. So that was that." Lund grinned.

"The Wests went home at ten o'clock. I put out the cat and unlatched the east side door for Bridie. She was late. I went upstairs," she was speaking very slowly now. "I ...." she felt a stab of pain from a forgotten bruise, not from Duncan's hands but from that memory of a black-haired man and Helenka Baluta, golden and laughing, in the sun-room. "I went to say good night to Cousin Mattie. She was sitting on the side of her bed with the bottle of OUT on the table beside her."

"The phone rang. I came downstairs to answer. The call was for me. It was from Mrs. Ogden, my cousin Louise. She was upset about some of the members of the Festival of Nations committee. Tempest in the Junior League. She talked for about three-quarters of an hour.

"While I was at the telephone, I heard Cousin Mattie's door close. And the central hall light was turned off from the upstairs switch. Cousin Mattie was, as I said, careful about money. I didn't know where the downstairs switch was, so it took me a while to get upstairs again."

"Were you," asked Lund sympathetically, "attacked by the grizzly bear?"

"Unfortunately, no. It was the armor. When I got to the upper hall I could see a bright streak of light under Cousin Mattie's door. I knocked on the door."

"Why?"

If only she had not paused, had not given him a chance to ask what she was finding it so hard to answer plausibly.

"To ... to say good night. Cousin Mattie was ... particular about little things." Was she, if the little things weren't money?

Lund took a puff at his cigarette and said, "Considering Mrs. Peckham's alleged interest in small events, didn't it seem strange to you that she closed her door? Wouldn't she have been likely to listen to your conversation at the telephone?"

Because this was so pleasantly not what she had expected him to ask, Janet flew to the answer. Eric Lund might look like the boys back home, but she did not know him ... yet.

"I don't think Cousin Mattie was much interested in civic and social affairs. She never asked any questions about my work." It was Cousin Virgil who had put the only question with an interesting answer. "And she could have overheard a good deal in the first few minutes. The door didn't close for some time after Louise called."

Lund nodded. "So you knocked on the door."

Janet pressed her hands tightly together. There was nothing to conceal now, but so much she wished she could forget. "Cousin Mattie didn't answer. It was terribly still. I opened the door. The room was hot and full of fumes of carbon tetrachloride. I found her."

Lund said gently, "Just how was she lying?"

Janet took a deep breath. "On the floor by the bed. On her back, with the head ..." That bald and horrible head ... "toward the bed."

"Where was the bottle of OUT?"

"On the floor, too. I don't know just where. I didn't see it until I had felt it under one of my knees while I was beside her on the floor ... I ..." She shuddered. "Shall I tell you what I did?"

"Is there anything you want to add to what you told Leary when he arrived?"

"No," said Janet.

"Then we'll call this off for tonight. You've been through enough. Shea had just told me that you had another shock. Something about a face at the reception room window."

"Yes."

"No one you recognized?"

"No."

"That's that." Lund rose. "The Wests live in the big place east of here, don't they? Do you know the people who live on the west side?"

"I know their name." Caution returned to Janet. "My father sold the house to Mr. Baluta. It was our home."

"Baluta lives there alone?"

She could hear Helenka's deep, lovely voice saying, "You can ruin all this for me." She said resolutely, "Yes, he lives there alone."

She rose and went to the door. Lund, looming above her, looked down at the young eyes shadowed with fatigue. "Thank you, Miss Carter," he said. "You've been a great help. We'll get this thing cleared up soon."

Not even the eyes asked him to define "thing" more closely. "Thank *you*, Mr. Lund. You're almost the only person I've talked to tonight who hasn't asked me why I called the police."

She saw the steady clarity of the blue eyes, the straight mouth and the little scars. She could not read the expression as he said, "I did not ask you that question, Miss Carter, because I know the answer."

He motioned for her to precede him down the hall.

CHAPTER X
Thursday, Midnight, Continued

Dr. Taylor, his voice and gestures polished with the finest grade of soap, said to the Wests:

"And so, it would be of the highest advantage to us all if you could bring yourself to permit an autopsy to be performed. I myself cannot be present, but I can assure you that it will be conducted with respect."

Old Mr. West raised tired eyes to the doctor's. "Is it necessary?"

"No, no," Dr. Taylor assured him, "not *quite* necessary. I am completely confident that an unfortunate accident accounts fully for your sister's untimely end. And, I may say, the police are in accord with my diagnosis. However, they have their reports to make. Routine. And since they were called in," he spread out his hands in a gesture that laid all blame very politely elsewhere.

"You think," Charlotte, sitting beside her husband, spoke as if she, too, were almost worn out, "that was unfortunate?"

"From the point of view of the bereaved, yes, dear lady. All these rough fellows in the house. All this intrusion on your grief. But only the police or rather the firemen and their mechanical skill with the pulmotor might have saved Mrs. Peckham. They did, I believe, their best, and therefore we should perhaps cooperate a bit with them."

He turned away from the horsehair sofa where the old pair sat and said to Duncan leaning on the mantelpiece, "Don't you agree with me, my boy?"

Duncan, who had not been listening to Dr. Taylor said, safely, "Well, of course ..."

"Your opinion, my boy," went on Dr. Taylor, "will be, I am sure, of the greatest assistance to your parents in making this hard decision. For so many years you have been out of the family circle. You can view these sad matters with a certain detachment. A pity you did not know your Aunt Mattie more intimately in her closing years. A remarkable character. Formidable perhaps, but strong."

The door opened and Louise slipped in quietly. She drew up a chair beside her father and laid her hand on his arm, saying, "Dad, dear." She was not the woman who fluttered desperately around Ralph Ogden. A look of deep affection passed between father and daughter.

"Louise," he told her, "Dr. Taylor thinks there should be an autopsy performed on your Aunt Mattie. I'd like to know what you think about it. And Duncan. And Mama."

Louise's lips parted.

Her mother said, "Anything the rest of you agree upon will seem right to me."

Duncan straightened and said, "Let's get this clear. Isn't it perfectly evident that fumes from the cleaning stuff killed Aunt Mattie?"

"Well, *nearly* clear." Dr. Taylor answered him. "The fumes from carbon tetrachloride, the chief component of OUT are potentially dangerous. A healthy person breathing a high concentration in a tightly closed room might easily suffocate."

"Was Aunt Mattie a healthy person?"

"She was an ... er ... elderly person. Her heart was not a young person's heart. Now, if in addition to a heart condition which the autopsy would reveal very clearly, we should find out that some untoward circumstance had occurred today, any little deviation from the normal in eating and drinking that might add a tax upon the body, then Dr. Nichols would have, I know, no hesitation in signing the death certificate. I am quite sure this will be the case." He paused and smiled at each one in turn. "So, if you all will agree ..."

"I agree," said Duncan, "but it isn't really any affair of mine."

Old Virgil turned toward his wife. "I think it's the best thing to do, Mama," he said.

"Yes, dear," she said, patting, his hand.

"Louise?"

"Yes, Dad."

"You are so wise," Dr. Taylor told them. "It will make everything quite simple for you all. Then, while the ... er laboratory arrangements are being made, you may be asked one or two questions about Mrs. Peckham's last hours. Nothing painful. And when it is over, you are all to go home and take the sedatives that will bring you rest."

Dr. Taylor strode into the gruesome litter of the Peckham bedroom. "Nichols," he said to the medical examiner, "I've buttered up the family. You can whistle for the morgue wagon. They don't know the law well enough to realize they had no choice."

"O.K.," said Dr. Nichols.

Bridie poured out Lieutenant Murphy's second cup of coffee. "Help yourself to the cream, Mr. Murphy," she urged.

Mattie Peckham had permitted the purchase of a half-pint of cream on Tuesdays, Thursdays and Saturdays, but Bridie had already put out tickets for a full pint on Friday morning.

There is a legend believed by many families even less romantic than the Wests. It is the myth of the Old Family Servant, a being tyrannical, surly and utterly devoted to every member of the family. Except for her church, she has no other life.

Al Murphy did not know this legend. What he did know were the scores of Bridies who had grown up with him in old Ward One. He responded generously to the cream pitcher, added three lumps of sugar to his cup, and said, "This accident'll make a big change in your life, Miss Callahan."

"It will," Bridie agreed, counting out cups.

"Sit down and drink a cup of your own good coffee," urged Murphy. "Lund won't want you to serve refreshments till he's got his work done."

"This is my work." Bridie added saucers to the cups on her tray. "What's his? I'd like to know what you fellers are doin' in this house."

Murphy looked proud but patient. "We were invited," he said, "as experts."

"Experts," sniffed Bridie. "You didn't help none. My Madam's dead."

"You called us too late."

"I called nobody. I wasn't here. If I had-a been, it wouldn't have happened."

"Too bad you wasn't. Wasn't this the night of the tap-dancing contest at Hibernia Hall?"

"My niece Veronica won it. That's why I was late gettin' home for the first time in twenty long years," Bridie mourned. "If I'd a been here, I would never have let *her* have the bottle at that time o' night."

"You been here a long time?"

"Forty years."

"My God, they must of brought you to work in your baby buggy!"

"And that," retorted Bridie, "ain't the way you're goin' to get my age. I ain't goin' to read in tomorrer's paper: 'Bridget Veronica Callahan, 41, the alleged cook of the deceased.' I notice it don't ever say, 'According to Detective Murphy, 46.'"

Murphy flushed. Bridie had only overestimated his age by two years, but he had long been confident that he didn't look a day past thirty-five.

"After all that time," he went on, "the Madam should have done something handsome for you. In her will."

"Not her," Bridie said, getting out a chest of spoons. "The money'll be kept in the family."

"That don't seem fair after all the years you been here."

"Perhaps it ain't fair," said Bridie, "but it's right."

"What you going to do? Course you could get another place, I know ..."

Bridie sat down across the red-checkered table. "I dunno," she said. "I won't suffer. Mr. Virgil and Mrs. Virgil will do what's right by me. But what I can't bear to think of," the tears rose in eyes and throat, "is to leave this house."

"It's kind of different," said Murphy.

"It's the elegantest house in town." Bridie wiped her eyes. "There ain't another like it."

"Here," said Murphy, "drink some good hot coffee."

"You're very kind, Mr. Murphy. It's been a terrible shock."

He nodded. "Losing someone you'd worked for most all your life. You must have thought a lot of Mrs. Peckham."

Bridie drank a long sip of coffee. "She suited me fine," she said. "She didn't mix much in the runnin' of the house. I was here before her father died, and she wanted it to go on pretty much as was. I tell you, Mr. Murphy, they're funny, them Wests. Grown-up people all behavin' the way their fathers and mothers would have wanted them to. 'What would Father have said,'" she mimicked. "Mrs. Peckham, Mr. and Mrs. Virgil, still talking that way at their age, and Mrs. Ogden all set to carry on the same way."

"That Mrs. Ogden," said Murphy grimly. "She's a … a scavenger."

"Louise ain't so bad," Bridie said, "though she'll never have a street named after her. She's awful good to her people. And she's crazy for that husband of hers."

"Fond of her aunt, too?"

Bridie looked at him over the rim of her cup. "Yes."

"A very united family, eh?"

"Yes. They had their troubles, but who hasn't?"

"Any special ones lately that might have been preying on Mrs. Peckham's mind?"

"Her? She throve on trouble. Wait a minute. You ain't insinuatin'?"

"No, no. Doctor thought there might be something else that helped those fumes work so fast. If she was depressed. Or not up to par some way."

Bridie gazed at him fixedly. She took another swallow before she spoke. "She wasn't depressed. She was excited. Last night. You know. Wednesday, I mean."

"What was she excited about?"

"About all the things happenin' at once. Duncan, Mr. Virgil's son, comin' home after twelve years in Paris, France. And Janet Carter comin' here after most ten, and that blonde comin' to live next door. So last night she didn't sleep much and she had a headache this mornin' which made her mad."

"Mad?"

"She'd had so little sickness all her life she was fit to be tied if she had a toe-ache."

"What did she do all day?"

"I don't know after two o'clock. 'Twas my day out. She ate a good breakfast as usual, a scraped banana, oatmeal and cream, two eggs on toast, and coffee. She ate it all up good. And she fussed about Mrs. Virgil just as usual, too, but not quite so sharp. I could see she didn't feel just herself. She didn't eat much lunch. I made it kind of light, anyway, soup and pear-date salad, 'cause I know the kind of supper she always stuffs in when I'm not here. She kept on playin' solitaire most of the mornin' and lookin' out the windows, and then just before I was leavin' she found the pill."

"Huh?" said Murphy.

"When she was sick, the few times she was," explained Bridie, "she didn't want to wait to get over it. She wanted to do something to stop it right away. She was a great believer in dosin'. She would'uv killed herself that way long ago, except that she didn't want to spend the money. So she just took what medicine was left around the house after her husband's sickness. He's been dead fourteen years, so that was just about used up. What made her so mad today was because she thought there wasn't any more left. And then she found the pill."

"What kind of a pill?"

"I dunno. It was in one of them little pink boxes. She's been using the box to keep some of her earrings in for the last five years, and pushed down under the cotton she found this one pill. So she took it."

"Miss Callahan," asked Murphy, "would you know where that little pink box would be?"

"Why, right back in her top left bureau drawer, Mr. Murphy. With the earrings in it. Her jet and garnet pair. She never threw anything away."

"I hope you're right." Murphy got up. "Thanks for a swell feed." He stood listening.

From the front of the house there came the muffled sound of men walking in unison, like bearers of a stretcher. Or of a basket. The front door closed heavily.

CHAPTER XI

Thursday Night

Lund leaned lightly against the door and looked around the sitting room. "Pink Pills for Pale People," he thought. His fingers closed over the little box in his pocket.

Six people drinking coffee. All pale. With grief? With fear? Or merely with fatigue? It was two o'clock in the morning.

They had told him all that, in the nature of the case, he had the right to ask. Louise, crumpled heavily against her husband, watching him with the apologetic devotion of an unwanted dog, caught her mother's eye, blushed, sat straight. She had told the detective the facts she knew about the bottle of OUT. A day or two ago, just as she had been going out to a luncheon, she had discovered a spot on her blouse. They were out of cleaning fluid and she had sent Lottie, the waitress, to borrow Aunt Mattie's ubiquitous bottle. She had forgotten to return it until Thursday afternoon. Then, seeing Ralph about to leave for his club dinner and remembering that she was not to play bridge at her aunt's that evening, she had asked her husband to return the bottle. If she had sent it back later with the rest of her family, they would have had to listen to a lot of talk about it from Aunt Mattie. She had been on the stairs when she thought of the bottle, and Ralph was in the hall below. She had called to him to wait for it; and her mother had brought it from the shelf in Louise's bathroom. Louise had given the bottle to Ralph. There would be the fingerprints of practically the entire family on that bottle of OUT. Louise's face suggested nothing but a tedious recital, but Lund seldom accepted things as he saw them.

The three who had played bridge with Mattie Peckham agreed that she had been alert and had played an excellent game. They concurred on Mattie's announcement that as soon as she got upstairs that night she would clean her dress. They repeated Janet's list of the refreshments she had consumed.

Mr. and Mrs. West had gone directly home, where he had immediately undressed and got into bed. After prolonged preparation, Mrs. West had followed him. Her husband, she said, was then asleep. Virgil said stubbornly that he was not. Charlotte agreed with courtesy, Lund thought, rather than with conviction. Hers would be a damned difficult manner to deal with on a witness stand. Or in a family circle.

The son, by a slight sardonic stress on the carrot wine, suggested it was enough to kill anyone. Although this seemed credible, it did not impress Lund in his favor. This was Duncan, the cousin from Paris, whose name had appeared rather consciously in Miss Carter's speech. Duncan reiterated, perfunctorily, that he hadn't known his aunt well enough to be a judge of her health. After the bridge game he had, at his aunt's request, mailed a letter for her, and had then gone for a stroll. He had not seen the town since his boyhood. He was, he implied, not accustomed to an early bedtime. On his return he had seen the signs of activity around the Peckham house and had come in to investigate.

"As soon as you entered the house, Mr. West," Lund's tone was without implication, "you had a talk with Miss Carter in the small room at the right of the front door."

He ignored Duncan's stiff jerk of the head toward the shadowy corner where Janet sat, and went on, "Shea, the officer who was stationed in the hall, tells me that almost as soon as you left, Miss Carter rushed out into the hall and said she had seen someone staring in at the window."

Duncan's eyes opened wide, his brow lifted.

"Shea and the chauffeur," Lund continued, "went outside at once. They didn't find the peeper. Mr. West, can you think of anyone not in this house at the time who might have been interested in—what was going on in that room?"

Duncan's Lido tan had faded, his detachment had cracked. "No," he said quietly, but unsteadily.

Lund's blue eyes flicked across the room to Janet Carter. The question, he could see, had surprised the girl. She met his look steadily, without, he thought, fear, but her eyes turned quickly to the cousin.

Duncan said, "Some curious person going by, and seeing police cars. You didn't recognize the face, Janet?"

"No, Duncan."

What was the relationship between these two? There was, Lund was sure, something more than cousinship. Were they enemies or lovers? Both, perhaps. His opinion of Duncan did not rise.

"Was it a man or a woman?" Duncan's tone to Janet was harsh.

"A man," she began confidently. "Oh, I don't know. I took it for granted ... I suppose it could have been either."

Duncan gave a curt nod. The girl bit her lip. He said, "Sorry, Janie. It must have been a bad moment for you."

"Moderately." Her eyes turned to Lund for understanding, and got it.

"Have any of you seen this before?" Lund took his hand out of his pocket. The pill box Murphy had found, round, pink and worn, lay on the palm of his long hand. There was a printed label on the top, Elm Hill Pharmacy, decorated with the curlicues of an earlier day. The name and date were in faded ink. "Doctor: Taylor. 3-9-18."

They passed it around. They were interested. They were surprised, mildly and wearily. They were apprehensive of trouble, as people unaccustomed to the police might be. Lund could not detect recognition or fear. He didn't explain the box. He said, "Thank you. I won't have to trouble you again tonight."

Old Mr. West rose stiffly. "Isn't this all you'll ever need to ask us, officer? What further business could you have here?"

"None, probably," Lund told him. "That depends on the result of the autopsy."

Mr. West looked bewildered. Mrs. West said, "Mr. Lund, we must arrange as soon as possible for the funeral. The rest of the family must be notified. When ...?"

"Dr. Nichols is prepared to work at once. You will be notified early tomorrow morning."

"Thank you, Mr. Lund. We may go home now? It is late."

Lund thoroughly agreed. "Certainly. Unless any of you can think of further information to clear up the way Mrs. Peckham's accident happened."

No one spoke. He looked once at them all. At the bitter remembrance of an earlier meeting reflected in Ralph Ogden's face; at Louise, heavily asleep against his shoulder; at Duncan, tautly blank; at Mr. West, tired and resentful; at the royal patience of his wife. He looked last at the girl. Her lips were closed, her eyes veiled, but her whole face declared awareness. Of what, he did not know. Feeling or knowledge, there was as something she had that the others lacked. He meant to find out someday soon. It was she who had called the police.

Mrs. West was saying to her, "Janet, my child, you must come home with us."

They were all rising. Ogden roused his wife gently and helped her to her feet. The younger West was looking hard at the girl.

Lund opened the door. Someone bustled into the room. "I want my cups and saucers," said Bridie.

"I'll help you," the Carter girl said, beginning to collect them on the tray.

"Janet, aren't you coming with us?" Mrs. West repeated.

The girl stood straight and smiled. Pale from fatigue, delicate in the flimsy green dress, there was a strength about her that caught Lund for a moment. "No, thank you, Cousin Charlotte. I'll stay with Bridie."

"Come, Mama," said old Mr. West.

They went into the hall where that fussy fool Taylor was unctuously distributing sedatives. Bridie followed with her tray.

Duncan West went to the table where Janet Carter was gathering cups and teaspoons. He bent over her, laying his hand on her shoulder. She winced with a little cry. "Oh, Duncan, haven't you hurt me enough tonight?"

Her hand went to her shoulder.

"My God, Janie, I didn't know I hurt you!"

Lund could not see their faces.

"It's all right, Duncan. Please go home. I'm so tired. Such a lot has happened since ... this afternoon."

Duncan West turned his head, cautiously, and saw Lund.

"Good night, Janie," he said abruptly. "We'll talk in the morning."

"In the evening," she corrected him. "I'm going to work at nine A.M. *We* are." She smiled at the detective. "Mr. Lund and I."

After West had gone, Lund took the tray she had piled and went with her down the stairs that had borne so much tonight and protested only feebly now. At the foot waited Dr. Taylor.

"My dear child," he said. "I didn't know when I came in that you were little Janet Carter. I brought you into the world."

The girl studied his face. "Did you?" she said. "I always thought it was a stork. Or possibly, Mother."

Dr. Taylor said hastily, "How tired you must be, my dear. Get to bed at once. Bridie must find you an electric pad and bring you hot milk to take with this little pill."

"Thanks," said Janet Carter. "And then I might get up and do the same for her. She's been through as much as I have."

A door leading kitchenwards opened and Murphy came into the hall, wiping his mouth. Janet took the tray from Lund. "Thank you for a lot of things," she said. "Goodbye, Mr. Lund."

"Good night, Miss Carter."

She went through the door that Murphy still held open.

Lund looked at his assistant. "Carrot wine," he diagnosed. "My God!"

Murphy grimaced. "If I understood your meaning, I was to make some easy social contacts in the culinary regions. I did."

"Too bad," murmured Dr. Taylor, "that the trouble wasn't next door. It was old man Duncan, Charlotte West's father, who bequeathed the cellar."

"'Murder in the Wrong House'." Lund shrugged into his topcoat.

"Look here, Lieutenant," protested the doctor. "You can't mean that you think there was anything wrong here tonight?"

"Could be. You came in a taxi, Doctor? We'll take you home."

They went down the steps. "God, what a chatoo!" Murphy took a deep breath. "Anything could happen there."

"The Doc," said Lund, "doesn't agree." He opened the door of the car.

"The West family and murder. Impossible."

"No," said Lund, "they all had the opportunity. The girl and Mrs. Ogden were on the phone three-quarters of an hour and the side door was unlocked. None of them had too good an alibi, I'm betting."

"The girl," said Murphy, "had fifteen minutes of her own. Ten o'clock to ten-fifteen."

"Right."

"Opportunity, yes," said the doctor, "but can you suggest the motive?"

"I could suggest plenty. Money is always my favorite. Duncan Rifle

Works aren't doing so well. Too much damned peace; too little blessed prosperity."

"And the old woman," added Murphy, "with the first cent she ever put in her sock and not likely to leave it outside the family."

"Ye-es," said Dr. Taylor. "Yes, in theory. But I know these people. The strongest thing about them is their family feeling. Even among the remoter members. That Carter girl's mother was the biggest stooge Mattie Peckham ever had. Even Janet has been raised in the True Faith. Besides, look at the medical evidence. The fumes of carbon tetrachloride in a closed room with a temperature easily 85°, an old, enlarged heart, a diet that would kill a horse, and, on top of that, a dose of God knows what. Not," he added, "that Mattie Peckham couldn't stand any three of these. She was the toughest old bitch I've ever come across and tough old bitches are my business. You boys may think they're yours. I tell you, you don't know them till you've doctored Elm Street Hill. Mattie could have stood three of those things, but not all four."

"You aren't sure about your pill?" said Murphy.

"But I shall be. My guess is it was the last of the emetine and bismuth iodide that I gave Eli Peckham for his dysentery in 1918, and if my books and the records of the Pharmacy square with the autopsy, what have you got to say?"

Lund said, "And if there are no suspicious marks on the body, I'll have to say 'O.K.'."

"You'll say it."

"Probably. But I still won't like that old woman's death."

"In which," said Dr. Taylor, "you'll be unique."

"That's what I mean," said Lund. "Everyone seems to have hated her guts. Or been scared to hell of her."

"Uh-huh," agreed Taylor, "but why kill her tonight? Why wait all their lives and almost all her life? She wouldn't have lived much longer."

Murphy stopped the car. "You're home."

"Nichols will phone you when he's through," Lund told him as Dr. Taylor got out.

"I could tell you now what he'll say," Taylor retorted. "There won't be the slightest suspicion of murder."

"There'll be plenty," said Lund, "no matter what he finds. Plenty of suspicion. But nothing else. No evidence."

CHAPTER XII
Sunday Afternoon

There were a great many flowers at Mattie Peckham's funeral. There were not many people. Most of the social leaders of Watson, before whom Mattie had vivaciously fawned, had been older than she and were now dead. Their daughters and nieces had ordered wreaths and sprays by telephone and gone off to their bridge lunches, which, after all, were fitting memorial services to Mattie. Some old friends came; others stayed away with the comfortable rationalization that a funeral held in a mortuary chapel didn't mean so much as a house funeral.

At first, when Duncan had suggested it, the idea of holding Mattie's last rites in any place except Mattie's house had been profoundly shocking to the Wests. What would Father say, thought Virgil. We've never used an undertaker in that way, Charlotte had murmured. Pity, Ralph Ogden had grunted, to let the house go to waste; it was just made for a funeral. Louise giggled.

But thinking it over, they saw the merits of the plan. A house funeral was an appalling amount of work and they were tired. Mattie Peckham had managed to die in a way as wearing to her family as her life had been. And it wasn't as if this had been an ordinary death. The supreme sacrilege of the autopsy having been committed, why quibble now? So Bridie and the Wests' cook prepared the turkey and ham and mince pie which Grandfather West had considered essential to a funeral feast, and Virgil and his butler brought out Grandfather Duncan's funeral port. And on Sunday noon these weighted the buffet table in Mattie's dark dining room where the Family, now expanded to include fifteen or sixteen cousins, stood about and ate before the two o'clock service. Most of them ate a lot. Everybody kissed one another coldly and asked a good many questions.

Fortunately, there were no questions that could not be met. It looked that day as if the Wests had all the answers. At breakfast time on Friday, Lund had called to give them the medical examiner's verdict. Accidental death from suffocation, aided by age and other causes. An arteriosclerotic heart at seventy-five, and two-tenths of a grain of emetine and bismuth iodide. It had taken them all to kill Mattie Peckham.

So the ravens had gathered and scattered again. Now there remained only the Next of Kin, seated in the Peckham drawing room with their lawyer.

Charlotte Duncan West thought how much more men looked like a funeral nowadays than women did. It was the clothes. She and Louise in their spring suits, dark blue and gray, but the men, all in striped trousers and the formal black cutaways that only Duncan called a morning coat. There was something debonair about him, from wing collar to spats, that suggested a wedding at high noon. That was the way Charlotte wanted her son to look. Her son-in-law, Ralph, looked like what he was, the well-dressed bearer at the funeral of his wife's aunt. Mr. Gault, the lawyer, was correct, but his collar was rasping a shaving cut. Virgil's clothes were getting too tight again.

The Family was nervous. All except Charlotte. Mattie, she felt sure, would leave something to Virgil. He was her brother. Perhaps she had been fond of him, too. What she left would make him feel more independent. That would be nice for him. But even if Mattie hadn't, even with dwindling business, even with the Depression, they would be all right. Grandfather Duncan had left a lot of money twenty years ago. They were safe. Charlotte was a queen who had asked for a very small kingdom. Her husband, the gentle plump boy who had melted her uncomfortable reserve in 1892, her daughter, and her son. She smiled at each one and began to knit.

Mr. Gault cleared his throat. He put on his Oxford glasses and prepared to read the Last Will and Testament of Mathilda West Peckham. His bent gray head blended into the painting hanging behind him, a gigantic Snow Scene, incredibly dingy, that Mattie had painted when she was sixteen.

"To my beloved brother, Virgil Horatio West, all stocks, bonds, securities and other monies."

There were tears in Virgil's eyes. They sought Charlotte's.

"To my sister-in-law, Charlotte Duncan West, in remembrance of her strong feeling for it, my house at 110 Elm Street ..."

Charlotte heard Louise suppress a giggle. She did not raise her eyes from the cool blue wool. Her hands trembled a little. It was so like Mattie. She had known, indeed, how strong was Charlotte's disgust with the old yellow eyesore which reared its ugly head over her hedge. She had also known that Virgil loved his father's home. She had known how much it would hurt him to have his wife pull it down. Charlotte's horizon could never be rid of it now.

"To my niece, Mathilda Louise West, recalling her childhood affection for me ..." Mattie had some really valuable jewelry, worth a great deal of money. But Louise looked angry. It was not pleasant to remember the years before she was sixteen when Aunt Mattie with presents and flatteries and little privileges that Charlotte had withheld, had tried to steal her from her mother. When Louise began to realize, she had felt duped and dumb. And, Charlotte thought, she would probably interpret the omission of the Ogden from her name as a final insult to Ralph.

It was not the final one.

"To Ralph Henry Ogden, I bequeath the fishing equipment of my late husband, Eli Peckham, which will be found in the harness room of my carriage house ... the entire collection, excepting only the silver-mounted flask, of which article the said Ralph Henry Ogden already has a sufficient supply in his possession."

The wizened old hand had reached beyond the grave to deliver one more blow below the belt. Of his age and generation, there were few men so temperate as Ralph Ogden. Mattie had quite simply and clearly wanted to remind him and Louise and her parents that on the Christmas Eve when his foreign wife had committed suicide, he had been drunk. Charlotte thought it was a wonder that Ralph had not killed Mattie Peckham long ago.

No one looked at anyone else. Mr. Gault read on hastily the final item: "To my nephew Duncan West."

Money to Virgil, house to me, personal property to Louise. What is there left for Duncan, his mother wondered.

"To my nephew, Duncan West, I bequeath the letter postmarked Paris, France, January 1,1921, which will be found between pages 87 and 88 of the book entitled *Salt Lake Fruit* which is in the bookcase in the library of my house.... He will know what to do with it."

Duncan's father stirred. Louise looked at Ralph. Ralph looked at the floor. Duncan got to his feet. While Mr. Gault read the closing paragraph petitioning the court to appoint Virgil and Louise as executors of the estate, he stood looking out the window. Rain had begun to fall. Duncan turned back into the room.

Mr. Gault had risen. So had the family. Charlotte's eyes looked with pity for a moment at her son. The others avoided him. Mr. Gault said, "I strongly advised Mrs. Peckham against the last two provisions in the will. We always so advise our clients. Too many unforeseen eventualities.... But she was adamant."

"Or something," said Ralph. "Well, I guess we can take it."

Duncan came up to them. If he looked now like a member of a wedding party, it was an usher with a hangover.

"Would there be any legal obstacles," he asked with attempted humor, "to my obtaining my inheritance at once?"

Mr. Gault's dry face flushed with embarrassment. "If your father and your sister do not object, I should say no. I think that there is no doubt that the court will confirm their stewardship."

"Then, shall we adjourn to the library?" Duncan's brows were lifted, his mouth smiled, but there was a determined whiteness about his face.

"Well, son," said Virgil, "we might as well get it over."

He rose sorrowful and heavy from his chair. The character of his sister, which he had tried to disregard for sixty-five years, had become in a moment too plain to ignore. He did not like to add to this a suspicion concerning his son.

Into Louise's little dark eyes had come something of her Aunt Mattie's curiosity. "I'm ready, Father."

Ralph leaned back in his chair, lighting a cigarette.

"Mr. Gault," Virgil said mournfully, "I think you had better come, too."

Charlotte West put her knitting into her bag which hung over her arm and followed them. She had known since she married Virgil that nothing could stop Mattie Peckham from what she set out to do. Nothing, she had formerly phrased it, but death. The qualification had been wrong. Nothing could.

In the small, crowded room where Mattie Peckham had played her last bridge game and which she had selected as the stage for her last bit of hell with the family, the Wests grouped themselves around the bookcase. It had glass doors and twisted gilt handles. Virgil signed for Mr. Gault to stand close beside him and turned the key in the filigree lock. He pushed open the doors and stood, lower lip protruding, staring at the shelves. He wasn't much used to hunting for books. The others stood in a semi-circle behind him. The ash burned long on Duncan's cigarette. Charlotte held out an ash tray to him.

"I can't seem to see the book," said Virgil. "What did you say was the name of it, Mr. Gault? Salt Water Something?"

"*Salt Lake Fruit*, Daddy," said Louise gently. "You remember. It was about Mormons or something. Some slick salesman told Uncle Eli it was spicy. Aunt Mattie never got over it. The price, I mean. There wasn't any spice."

"And this," suggested Duncan, "was an attempt to get her money's worth out of it?"

"Son," said old Virgil, "your aunt is dead."

"I wonder," said Duncan, "if she ever will be."

His mother's eyes, watching, agreed. She moved to her husband's side. "Let me help you, dear. It's a big brown book with lots of gold on it."

She knew it well. She had always hoped the children wouldn't get hold of it when they were small. She was sure it was a very sensational book.

And that last night when they had been playing bridge she had faced the bookcase for three hours. Every time she had been dummy she had glanced idly at the wall. She could, she felt, put her hand on it at once.

The gold woman with hanging hair. Third shelf, left, about the middle. The only really full shelf in the case....

Behind her someone drew a sharp breath. Someone else sighed. If only they wouldn't take it so hard, wouldn't watch so closely. It should be such a little thing. In a minute now Duncan would have his letter and they could begin to forget. To forget something that only he and Aunt Mattie had known.

Charlotte put out her hand toward the shelf that for thirty years had held Eli Peckham's bad bargain. Then she saw the gap. Between *Elwell* and *Richard Carvel* ran a little empty alley.

Salt Lake Fruit had disappeared.

CHAPTER XIII
Sunday Afternoon, Continued

She raised her arms against the blue April sky. It was the gesture with which Mary Alden had ended *So Long as Life*, but it was only half-consciously dramatic now. In the picture, that upward sweep and flung-back head had portrayed freedom and ecstasy. It was not without joy today, the strange hidden happiness she had never expected to feel, certainly not in this place. But she was not free. For the first time in many years she was bound. Bound by fear.

Actually, she thought, the beautiful star is not raising her arms against the sky. Or the backdrop. She is raising them against the grotesque yellow barn of the old, dead witch woman. She laughed without mirth. She let her arms fall, then raised them again, as an exercise.

The exercise was not repeated. For she had seen that two people were watching her.

Janet Carter was coming toward the patch of warm sunlight between the weeping willow and the Peckham carriage house. Standing in the gap of the high hedge the dark man called Jerry, an old tweed jacket over uniform trousers, stood and stared at Janet. The girl did not see him.

"Good afternoon, Miss Baluta," Janet said.

"Life has been very hard for you. I am sorry." She put warmth into her voice.

"Oh, thank you!" Janet crossed quickly to the Baluta yard. Jerry shrugged and retreated through the hedge.

"You might like to see how my grandfather has kept your rose garden." This was really a lovely child, she thought, softly colored and graceful and not without courage. Helenka Baluta's life had been built on courage. "Although the garden runs mostly to vegetables. We are practical peasants," she smiled, well aware of the contrast between the designation and her Hollywood finish.

"I like it this way," Janet said.

"This hasn't been a gay homecoming for you." There was no indication in her tone that she was launching a program.

"No. Finding her was pretty awful. And funerals aren't so funny, even if ... Everything's almost over now. They're listening to the will now in the drawing room."

"They?"

"The Family. All the Wests and—Ralph Ogden." Janet colored at the name.

"She has been generous to them, you think, the old lady?"

"I hope so. She owes it to them. Cousin Mattie could be a pretty unpleasant person to live with."

"And now you will not have to live with her. And she cannot be unpleasant."

They were both silent. To Helenka Baluta, that unpleasantness could have been dire. Was the girl thinking the same thing? And if so? But how really little she could know.

"Miss Carter," she went on, "I know that no member of your family would talk about my, shall I say, dual personality for malicious reasons. In their present state they would probably not mention it at all. Still, many people call at a house of mourning. And movie stars are news. I live by it. I should know." She smiled with a sweet cynicism.

Janet said, "Of course Duncan won't. He could easily stop his father and mother from talking. I could remind him. Or"—the admiring eyes had become hostile—"you could. Better than I."

She would have liked to probe that hostility. It could explain so much that she needed to know. "Would you do it? I have not yet finished reading his screen story. I shall not be sending for him for a day or two."

The young eyes looked at her questioningly. "All right."

"And the others? Believe me, I am sorry to intrude my affairs, to have to ask you to take this trouble for me, a stranger. Particularly now when you have the strain of new work of your own. I work, too. I know."

The girl's eyes were more friendly now. "I'll be glad to do anything I can. Louise is the real danger. She likes to talk. And all the Junior League will come to call."

Helenka laid her hand on the girl's arm. "I must stay here a little longer. Things are not so simple as I had thought when I came. My grandfather needs me. I shall live as quietly as possible. But if I were seen, if the servants talked about the granddaughter of Mr. Baluta, it might remind your cousin of her aunt's little talk. Isn't there some way that you could stop Mrs. Ogden?"

"Yes," said Janet. "There's Mr. Ogden."

The lashes fell over Helenka's eyes. This, too, to deal with. Mrs. Ogden. Mr. Ogden. She had not heard those names for twelve long years. "What exactly do you mean?"

The girl said, "I mean that Ralph is Louise's whole life. She would do anything he asked her to."

She could not refrain from asking, "And Mrs. Ogden is the whole life of Mr. Ogden?"

"No," said Janet. "Since I have been back here, I've thought he didn't seem to have much of any life at all. I've always hated Ralph. For the same reason that you have, probably. Because of her death. The Princess Mariska. But sometimes now I'm sorry for him, a little. He seems so … oh, as if everything had stopped for him a long time ago."

Helenka Baluta took a tortoise-shell cigarette case from the pocket of her gold sweater. She offered the opened case to Janet. When the cigarettes were alight, she said, "Will you ask Mr. Ogden to request his wife to make no reference to me?"

"Oh, yes. I could easily, after Cousin Mattie's talk. You wouldn't want to do it?" Again, suspicion in the girl's eyes.

"No. I doubt that Mr. Ogden would remember the little Baluta girl and I have no desire to introduce him to Mary Alden. Whether or not he has seen me on the screen."

"He hasn't," said Janet. "It seems that he doesn't like movies. At that last dreadful dinner Cousin Mattie kept telling him what he missed. Particularly because he hadn't seen *Candle in the Night*."

Helenka Baluta looked up at the sky. It was no longer a clear spring blue. It was a rainy gray-black, also true to April over a New England river valley or over flat, bleak fields in Poland.

"Have you seen *Candle in the Night?*" she asked.

"No," said Janet. "I've only seen you in *So Long as Life*. It was wonderful. And I'm going to see *Candle in the Night*. It's being shown in the small theatres now, you know. I'm so glad I shan't miss it."

"Don't go," she said harshly.

"Why not?"

"I was a little vicious about it, wasn't I?" She laughed. "It is technically bad. It was made in 1929, in the second year of sound, the dark ages, my child. The voices are brassy. The speeches are delivered, not spoken. I am too vain to want you to see the beginnings of Mary Alden."

"Then why," asked Janet, "did Cousin Mattie Peckham ask us all to promise to go and see *Candle in the Night?*"

Helenka Baluta said, "I can't imagine." She did not have to. She raised her left hand, the extended slender white fingers, strong, shapely, ringless. "There is rain. Let us go in and have some coffee."

"Oh, I ought not...."

The rain had begun to fall. "Nonsense!" She caught Janet's arm. "Of course you will come. We must run."

There was a fire in the living room today and a small table laid before it, with sandwiches of water cress, caviar, and little sponge cakes.

She went into the kitchen where the old man was standing by the coffee pot on the stove. She said to him in Polish, "My grandfather, I have the little Miss Carter with me."

He shook his head. "Better that you talk to the girl alone. I have had my coffee."

She returned to the living room with the pot. "This is not festive, but much hotter than in the ceremonial urn. Let us be homelike. This house is, after all, more your home than mine."

Janet said, "Oh, no. I deserted it."

"And I deserted the little house down below on the riverbank. That was where I lived when you lived up here."

"And you climbed from there to the stars."

"Only to the stars of Hollywood. Even so, it was a long way."

"And awfully hard."

She took a deep breath of cigarette smoke. "Hard. Yes. But simpler than you might think. It was a straight path, amazingly straight, considering what it started from. But the journey took almost ten years."

The girl's eyes were wide. "How did it ever begin? How did you really get started?"

Helenka Baluta closed her eyes a moment. "I began," she said, "in a night school. It was a policeman who sent me there. Oh, no, my dear. Not in the way you think. I have no record. For that, thank God and all the Saints! It was the young patrolman who came to that little house on the night that the Princess Mariska died. I told him I wanted to be an American. He showed me the way. By telling me about the free night school. Without him it would have taken much longer.

"You see, we lived in isolation, my grandfather and I. To you, living up here, it seemed a neighborhood with everything in common, those shacks below that you called Polack Town. Actually, we were the only Poles living there. The rest were Czechs and Magyars. We had no common language, and quite different customs. And my grandfather had a different way of life even from the few Polish workers that he knew. He had not come from Warsaw or Lodz. He did not know town life, but neither was he quite a peasant. He had been a house servant, the slave almost of his masters, but a petty dictator to other servants and to the peasants who came begging at the kitchen door. The war broke life for him. For us all. The great estate where he had been the butler was destroyed and trampled by the invaders. He stayed on till the end. Then, when he knew his prince and his prince's heir were dead, he dug up his small savings and came to America."

"With you."

She said, "He has never really belonged here. But I belong. From the beginning, before that night, I had always meant to belong. The past should die. It has for me." Her tone was defiant.

"And at the night school you learned what you needed to know? To be an American, I mean."

"Oh, yes. Some of it. I learned English and elocution from a lady named Miss Ophelia Todd. She coached the Watson Little Theatre. And that was where the next step came. The Little Theatre was being ambitious beyond its powers. It had cast *The Swan*, Molnar, you know. And the debutante who was to play the princess, and after her the bride, and then the stenographer who tried the part, failed even in the eyes of that precious little company. So Miss Ophelia Todd drafted her humble night school student."

"And you were good."

"I was," Helenka laughed, "terrific. Not in the sense Sam Wells now uses. But I was better than anyone else in the cast. It seems that I had a natural talent for acting."

"And you had known a princess."

"Yes. I had known a princess." She lighted another cigarette. She had eaten nothing. "Oh, well, after that, I decided to be an actress. I went to Boston and hung around the Copley Theatre and walked on in plays and finally had little parts. Then I had bigger parts in stock. All over the country. And finally small parts on Broadway and a few really good notices. Then came the talkies and the need for actresses like me. Girls who could speak well and had brains enough to learn lines and drive enough to work at the whole show. Looks, too, of course, but Hollywood had enough of those by themselves. You know the rest of it. A featured role in *Candle in the Night* and then *So Long as Life*. And now," she said, "I'm all set." She wondered if it were true.

"Oh," said Janet, "it's wonderful! But all those years when you were working so hard, you must have ... why, almost starved, sometimes."

"It wasn't," Helenka remembered, "hard to keep my figure. It was harder to get rid of my foreign accent. Lessons in phonetics cost a lot.

But I always had a job besides the theatre. I have another profession, you know."

"Have you?"

"Oh, yes. I'm a first-rate soda jerk. Although I was awful at that, too, in the beginning."

The girl's cheeks flushed with sudden excitement. "Did you ever do that here? Work at a soda fountain, I mean?"

"All day. While I was at the night school."

Janet Carter said something startling. "You worked in a drugstore in Morgan Park. You wore your hair in bangs."

Helenka Baluta sat very straight in her chair. She must hold her voice low, controlled and cautious. "You recognized me?"

"Oh, no," Janet laughed. "I couldn't. I have a good memory of sorts, but only for the part of a picture that is important to me. The important thing in the picture of the Morgan Park drugstore for me was a chocolate nut sundae with cherries and whipped cream. I was fourteen years old. And I was interested in bangs, too. I wanted to cut some, and Mother wouldn't let me."

"I don't quite understand."

"It was a silly thing to bring up. It all comes back to Cousin Mattie."

"Again, I do not understand."

"Cousin Mattie was talking about the Bijou Theatre the other night. It's in Morgan Park. I haven't been in Morgan Park very often, and only once for a reason worth remembering. I was driving with Cousin Mattie in her car and she stopped at a drugstore and set me up to a concoction that Mother would never have let me eat. That was the way Cousin Mattie was lovely to children. I was sick that night. When I told her about it the other evening, she was terribly pleased because I remembered so much about it. She urged me to reproduce more details. I just wondered if the girl with the bangs could have been you."

"Could you," Helenka asked, "reproduce a few details for me?"

"Not many. You spilled a little of the cream, and Cousin Mattie laughed. She would."

Helenka said, "In that first year there were a good many ladies who made me nervous, young and old."

"And now," Janet's admiration was almost blatant, "nothing in the world could upset you."

Helenka stared beyond the window where rain made the Peckham house a blur of amber. "It could," she said. She was silent a moment. "And what does this remarkable memory of yours reproduce for you concerning ... the first Mrs. Ogden?"

"Very little, really," Janet said. "Just that she was the most beautiful woman I have ever seen. Until I saw you on the train. I knew when you went down the aisle of our car that I had never seen anyone so lovely, except, perhaps, Mariska."

"But you don't really remember her?"

"No. Just as something wonderful and a little strange. You see, she was part of a big moment for me, too, and something almost as childish as a chocolate sundae. It was my first party with a real orchestra, not a victrola dance. At Cousin Mattie's. A party for Louise. The Princess was like something out of a book, so white and gold and delicate. She was awfully nice to me. I never saw her after that night. Three months later she died. In a way, I've never forgotten her."

Helenka Baluta said softly, "I am glad you remember her. Not many people do." And added to herself, it is better so.

"Ralph remembers her."

Helenka laughed a little. "With this Louise, as you describe her, for his wife, it is not strange that he does. There are children?"

"No."

She said, as she had said on that night long ago. "A man wants his son."

Janet rose. "It's stopped raining. I must go. I've stayed dreadfully long. You've made me forget so many ugly things."

The actress smiled.

CHAPTER XIV
Late Sunday Afternoon

After the shower the Georgian brick looked washed and clean. Birds chirped purposefully on the lawn of the West chateau. The Peckham house within the gloom of its cedars looked soggy.

To Janet, loitering as slowly as possible up the irregular brick walk, those decaying towers and pinnacles, those nightmare carvings like yellow teeth hanging over a dozen miniature black caverns, the balconies and false porches, were sinister.

She had told the great Mary Alden that she had forgotten ugly things. It was not true. She had remembered them even in the midst of the life story of a movie actress. The sore feeling of secrecy when Helenka Baluta would not admit close acquaintance with either Ralph or Duncan, the hidden terror in the thought that of all those who, last Wednesday evening, could have profited most by Mattie Peckham's death, Helenka Baluta was the first. Janet was becoming increasingly aware, in spite of the verdict of the medical examiner, of why she had called the police.

Now there was an immediate fear to be faced. She must go into that house alone, up the dark groaning stairs, down the murky hallway to her room, a room that had probably been searched again. Clumsily, hastily, thoroughly searched. That, she knew, had happened when she was at work on Friday; it had happened again on Saturday morning. Why and by whom, she did not know; at the moment what she dreaded most was catching the person in the third attempt.

She turned the key in the creaking old lock, swung open the door into the empty hall. It was too still. The setting sun through the colored glass windows over the stairs sent down broken flecks of blue and scarlet and green. One rested on the nose of the grizzly bear; it was bright red.

She took a deep breath and started up the stairs. They moaned beneath her feet. She stopped. Was there an answering creak farther up? In the hall, perhaps. She went up more stairs, gripping the rail too tight. There was something in the hall. Not a noise this time. A smell. Growing stronger. Cigarette smoke. What she feared most was at hand.

In the upper hall was a thick and aged carpet which deadened all footsteps. She did not hear anyone approaching. She did not quite see anyone. Only the shadows growing thicker in one spot. Then, in one spot, paler. A human face.

She leaned against the banisters, stopped dead in her ascent. Someone sauntered into the light of the stained glass windows. Cigarette between his lips, he looked down at her. Slowly he took out the cigarette and spoke.

"Hello, Janie," said Duncan.

Anger drove out fear. "So you've been searching my room again," she said.

He came slowly down to meet her. She could see the little wrinkles in his brown skin, the mocking eyes, the sardonic mouth. She put her hand to her shoulder.

He stopped. "Janie, you're making a mistake about me." His voice was tender. "I'm not going to hurt you, now or ever. You must believe me. Look at me." He was two steps above her, gently raising her chin with his hand. "I've never been in your room in my life. Not," his eyes narrowed, the lips softened, "that I shouldn't love to come, Janie. But only when you are there."

She moved her head out of his light grasp. "Don't be silly, Duncan. Someone has been going through my room, hunting hard for something. After what you said to me, the night Cousin Mattie died—and what you did to me—is it strange that I should think you might still be looking for your letter?"

Duncan laid his hand firmly on her arm. "Come up here. In the little sitting room. I want to talk to you and I don't want to be interrupted by Bridie coming home from her Ward One broadcast of the Last Rites. Janie, you're trembling. What are you afraid of?"

"I'm not afraid," lied Janet. She obeyed the light pressure of his hand, let it lead her to the room where Lund, four nights ago, had questioned the family. She chose a small, hard rocking chair. Duncan, on the sofa opposite, hands clasped between his knees, leaned forward watching her.

"Gault read us the will this afternoon," he said. "Aunt Mattie did quite handsomely by the family. She left me something, too. A letter."

Janet gasped, "That letter? Was it so important, Duncan?"

"I can't see how it could have had any importance to her," he said carefully. "As for me, it was just kid stuff. The sort of thing that makes your ears red when you've reached man's estate. But, Janie, it involved someone else. Someone who could be hurt a great deal if this letter were found and read."

Janet returned his look steadily. She kept all feeling from her voice. "You haven't found the letter?"

"No."

"And you still think I have it, although you didn't search my room for it?"

She could not read his expression. "I did not search your room and I should like very much to know who did. If you took the letter from Aunt Mattie on Wednesday evening, I think you would have done something quite different with it. You might have put it in the stove. If you didn't do that, I think you would have taken it away with you when you went to your office on Friday morning. There's just one other possibility if you're concerned at all."

He did not go on at once.

"And what is that?" asked Janet with spirit.

"That you're wearing it next to your heart. Under your brassiere, to be technical. It would be fun to take it from you, Janie."

Hot color flooded her cheeks. In a voice quivering slightly she said, "I did not see the letter after I left Aunt Mattie's room to answer Louise's telephone call. I saw a letter in her hand before I left the room. It may not have been the letter you mean."

"It was that letter. It would have given her peculiar pleasure to show it to you that night. After she had watched our biological reactions. For we had them, Janie. You can't deny it."

She said nothing. He dropped down on the floor at her side, one hand on her knee. "We've got them still."

"No, Duncan." With relief Janet knew what she said was true. "No, we haven't. You don't have to seduce me to find out all I know about your letter."

"This," he asked, "is the straightforward American girl I have been looking forward to? She wouldn't be a hypocrite after all, would she?"

"No, Duncan." She laid a cool hand on his, still lightly pressing her knee. "I was ... thrilled the night you kissed me. But a lot of things have happened since then. Until things are normal again, can't we just call it unfinished business?"

Duncan got to his feet. "I have a hunch," he said, "that it is finished." His fingers tousled her hair, lingered a minute on her neck and withdrew. "And I could give better than a guess at the reason. However, I won't bring that up tonight. Because I'm not through with this other business. About the letter. In her will Aunt Mattie named the place where the letter would be found. It was between two pages of a book in the library of this house. She named the pages and the book. It was called *Salt Lake Fruit*."

"Good Lord!" said Janet.

"So you know the book."

"I've seen it."

"When?"

"Last Wednesday night. After Cousin Mattie ... died."

"Are you sure?"

"Positive. I was standing in front of the bookcase, looking at the titles ... they're slightly weird, you know ... when Lieutenant Lund came in. That book was the biggest thing in the case and the gaudiest. He looked at it and said, 'It was bitter, I take it, that fruit.' That's how I happen to remember the book."

Duncan's eyebrows rose slightly. "That," he said, "I can well believe. And after the great detective had polished off his epigram, you did not notice the book again?"

Janet said quietly, "I haven't been in the library since then, Duncan."

"Neither," he said, "has, perhaps, the book. At least it isn't there now. It is lost, strayed or stolen. Two executors and the legal profession, as well as the heir, can swear to that."

"Duncan," she said, "must you always accuse me of something I have not done? I have never touched *Salt Lake Fruit*. I haven't even opened the glass doors of that bookcase."

"I withdraw my insinuations, Janie, really. I didn't mean it."

"And why," she asked, "is this book important? Aunt Mattie had the letter in her room that night."

"On Wednesday night when we were having our unnecessarily violent talk in the reception room, I am certain that you said to me that while you were at the telephone Aunt Mattie might have put the letter away. Away where? There's just a chance that she put it back in the place where she seems to have kept it permanently. If she did, I want to get to it before anyone else can. That letter is mine. Morally it always was; now it is legally. Janet, is there a chance that Aunt Mattie could have come downstairs and put that letter in the book while you were at the telephone?"

She thought of the little table behind the bear, the dim light, the side hall, the stairs rising from it, the hallway crossing the rear of both floors of the house. The house had groaned and sighed while she sat at the telephone, the light had gone out, a door had closed. "Yes," she said. "She could have done it quite easily."

"Do you think she would have?"

"Yes," said Janet again. "She had said a lot of vague things to suggest to me that someone I ... liked had done something I wouldn't care a lot about. And she had dangled the letter in front of me. She might have thought that suspicion would do what she wanted to do, better than the facts."

"In which," said Duncan, "her psychology was crude but sound. And so tonight, I haven't the letter, I haven't the book, and I haven't my girl. It would be interesting to know just who took them. And if there was one thief, or two, or three."

He rose and moved to the door. "Good night, Mademoiselle *ma cousine* and nothing more. I trust you did not suffer from your encounter with the rain this afternoon."

"It was brief."

"So I saw. From the drawing room window. You are getting to be rather a pal of the Glamour Girl."

"Duncan, will you tell your father and mother not to repeat Cousin Mattie's story about her? They will understand, particularly when they know that it means a lot to you."

He nodded. "Yes, that would be wise. Louise, too."

"I thought perhaps Ralph ..."

"Right again. He's probably done it already. For his own sake. Janie, what is that old story about him and his first wife?"

"Not tonight, Duncan, please. I'm terribly tired. And we ... were talking about it this afternoon. I'd rather not go over it again."

"Would 'we' be you and Helenka Baluta?"

She was struck by something strained in his voice. "Yes."

"Do you," he asked, "know that girl well?"

"How could I? A famous movie star. And me. We've only met twice."

"That might be enough. I don't think she's the kind of woman for you to know."

Janet was on her feet. "Oh, don't you really? Do you think all movie stars have deep, dark pasts?"

"I think," he said, "that it's possible this one has."

"All writers who live in Paris are commonly believed to have them, too." The dark head on Helenka's sofa, Duncan's words at her door. (You don't know my name? So we play it that way?) "Perhaps you have a past. Perhaps it's mixed up with Miss Baluta's. You might answer that, and then I'll know whether I ought to know *you*."

He said a surprising thing. "I don't know whether our pasts were, as you put it, mixed up. Or whether they weren't. That's the hell of it. Good night, Janie."

CHAPTER XV
Tuesday Morning

"Look here, Louise," said Ralph as soon as the butler had left the breakfast room, "how about that fishing tackle of Uncle Eli's? Do you think I could have it before I go up to Moosehead?"

Louise spread honey over the thick layer of butter on her waffle. "I'm sure you could, darling," she said. She smiled at him a little sadly. It was lovely to be instrumental in adding to his piscatorial pleasures, but painful to be reminded that she had never been asked to join in them. "I'll try to locate it this morning. I began to go over things yesterday afternoon."

Ralph had stopped listening, but she went on. "I don't suppose it's necessary to make an inventory of every little thing, when Aunt Mattie left it all to me. I'm really looking for Duncan's letter."

Ralph held out his coffee cup. "Don't you really know what that letter was about?"

"No, dear. Of course, I would have told you if I did. I don't remember much about Duncan just before he left home. I didn't notice very much that fall." Not much, that September of 1919, except the handsome young captain, arrived from Europe long after all the other boys whom she knew had returned. Ralph Ogden, back from his minor and ornamental position on a military mission to Poland and bringing that Polish wife who was so ornamental and for whom his feeling was not minor.

"Well," said Ralph, "there's usually only two kinds of trouble a fellow's likely to get into at eighteen. Women or money."

"He wouldn't write to Aunt Mattie for help about money."

"Or about anything else, if he were bright."

Louise reached thoughtfully for the heavy cream. "I'm not so sure about that, Ralph. You know we were brought up to believe that she was something wonderful. Daddy wanted us to feel that way and Mother played up to it until we were old enough to see what Aunt Mattie was like. I don't know how soon Duncan found her out. One of her cute little tricks was to get me to confide in her and then intimate to Mother that she knew a lot more about me than Mother did. She could have done the same thing to Duncan."

"I don't get it." Ralph lighted a cigarette. "Why would she wait twelve years to do her hinting? Why didn't she spring it before he went away? This looks like a surprise party all around."

Louise flushed. "If you were right about the other thing besides money," she said, "I don't think Aunt Mattie would have mentioned a word of it in 1919. She wouldn't want any kind of scandal to come out about the Family. She was on top of the social ladder then. She would have helped Duncan to cover up.... But there couldn't have been anything wrong. Duncan couldn't have ... Oh, Lord, how I hate the word 'letter'!"

Ralph said nothing. She went on. "But I don't expect to find that letter."

"No?"

"No." She lowered her voice. "Ralph, I think Janet burned it."

Ralph grunted.

"For Duncan's sake. To save him. She didn't know about the will, of course. It's just what I would have done, Ralph. For you."

Ralph got up from the table. "Janet isn't that way about Duncan."

"How do you know?"

"I know. But, my dear, I'm not going to tell you what I know. There's enough you have to keep off your mind already."

Tears came into Louise's dark little eyes. Ralph put his hand on the back of her plump neck. "I shouldn't have married you," she whimpered.

Ralph's moment of contrition ended. "Your Aunt Mattie Peckham," he said, "thoroughly agreed with you. On the last afternoon of her life she commented clearly on my performance as a husband. And as a father."

Alone at the table Louise wiped her eyes, and automatically took another waffle. But she let it grow cold and limp on her plate while she thought of what Aunt Mattie had said to Ralph. The reference was doubly cruel. Not only to their childless marriage, but to those black words old Mrs. Ogden had whispered about town twelve years ago. That the baby the Princess Mariska had not lived to bear had had an unknown father.

Ralph should have killed Aunt Mattie for saying that. And then came a thought she must never have again: Had Ralph killed Aunt Mattie? If he had, she would have liked to help him, but her companionship in murder would probably be as little welcomed as it was in fishing.

So there was only the lonely boredom of Aunt Mattie's inventory to fill the day. It was a day of soft spring. Louise, pausing in the doorway to tuck back a straggling lock of hair, thought how lovely the forsythia would look against the broad green of the lawn if only the Peckham house weren't the same shade of yellow. Near the gap on the West side of the hedge, Jerry, armed with clipping shears and reluctantly, since he held them behind his back and hence as far away from the hedge as possible, was gazing upward with a fixity that could mean intense interest or entire blankness.

He seemed to be staring at one of the yellow doghouses which were tacked on at intervals to the Peckham second story. Functionally they were as reprehensible as aesthetically they were rancid. There was the peaked roof and the door at which any domestic canine would have wagged his tail, but the roof was peaked not to shed rain but to support a miniature minaret, and any pup or human passing through that door would crash to his death on the garbage cans below.

The little room within this kennel Aunt Mattie had called her den and the designation had done it no wrong. Someday, Louise knew, she would have to invade its thick air of unwashed sweaters and ancient, candied violets turned to grit.

She crossed the lawn to the hedge which Jerry began to clip with great grace and little skill. The cock of Jerry's eyebrow as he watched her somewhat ponderous progress around the Peckham house was not without compassion.

The sun made violently green the new turf on the front lawn. Louise passed it, pretending that stealing Eve, the stag, was a lot of fun she and Ralph had had together. But there was no fantasy into which she could fit Mr. Baluta sweeping his sidewalk, with his square back turned bluntly toward her. As if the old workman who had wept and prayed for the Princess Mariska could not bear to look at Mrs. Ralph Ogden. Pain was alive again as she stepped into Aunt Mattie's hall. There, on the night of the long-ago party, under the great crystal chandelier full of bulbs for once and gleaming, she had stood with Aunt Mattie to receive the guests. A radiant girl in sapphire blue with curly black hair and the blush in her cheeks that everyone had always kidded her about, suddenly burning deep when Ralph laughed and put his hand tight around her bare upper arm.

Close to his own bright cheeks, the smart little moustache, the teasing eyes, and those warm fingers, she had felt this was the most wonderful thing that had ever happened to her. Then Aunt Mattie Peckham had cackled, and Louise had looked dizzily toward the stairs. A slim white figure was coming down the stairs alone, a girl in a long Grecian gown with one gold rose at her breast. Her yellow hair was braided in a crown above a pale, oval face. Her eyes, sad and scornful, just saw Louise and turned away.

And Louise, suddenly seeing herself, a big, red-faced girl in a long-waisted dress with a too short over-draped skirt and hair stuck out over rats, had been moved forward by Ralph's hand still on her arm, but not so tight, and heard him laugh again and say, "Meet the wife."

Now Louise, for ten years the wife, felt in her sweater pocket for her handkerchief, without which one couldn't adequately cry.

From the side hall a thick familiar figure came into view. "Daddy," gasped Louise.

"Hello," said Mr. West blandly. "I was sitting in the library and I thought I heard you come in."

Louise looked at her father curiously. He smiled at her. He did not look sleepy today, nor petulant, nor even very old.

"I've come over to work on the inventory," she said, "in the reception room. Mother and I started it yesterday."

In the relative cheerfulness of the pink and gray reception room a card table had been set up to hold the contents of the prize cabinet and Louise's notebook. Old Mr. West lowered himself onto the triangular chair of pink satin and debased mahogany, and looked tenderly over the collection on the table.

"Daddy," said Louise in a low voice, "what are you going to do about Bridie and Janet?"

Her father tore his connoisseur's gaze from the little white Venus de Milo which was the exact height of the little white Leaning Tower of Pisa. "Well, Louise," he said, "I think we'll leave them right here for a while."

"Janet won't want to stay."

"Janet will stay." It was a statement of absolute certainty, calm, unstressed.

"Have you asked her, Daddy?"

"No. She will stay." He was sure. "Bridie would rather not be all alone in the house. And I don't think we will move in until the Fall."

Shock broke Louise's voice. "Did you say 'move in'? Move into this house?"

"Yes, dearie," her father said, ignoring her surprise. "That is, not you and Ralph. Just Mama and me."

She could not speak. He went on. "The Longvale Club is all ready to buy the other house, but they'll give us plenty of time to move over here comfortably."

As if it could ever be comfortable to move into Aunt Mattie's house! "Daddy, you can't. Mother hates this house. She never would do it."

Again that complete assurance in her father's usually deprecatory old voice. "She will do it."

Louise leaned toward him, hesitated. "Daddy, didn't Aunt Mattie leave you ... enough?"

"Oh, yes, daughter," said Mr. West. "Mr. Gault has given me a pretty good idea. Your Aunt Mattie was always careful. When everything is settled, I think I shall have about three hundred thousand dollars. And the house."

"Yes, the house."

He smiled gently, obstinately. "I've lived in Mama's father's house for forty years. Now she'll live in my father's house—not for so long. Mama is sixty, and it will really be her house. In view of everything that's happened, I think Mama will be glad to do it."

Could her father really believe what he was saying? She had never seen him like this before. It frightened her a little.

"So you see," her father continued, "I want to keep Bridie on and then she will be with Mama and me when we move in. Bridie, you know, came to work for my mother in 1892, two years before I was married."

Mother and Bridie. Mother and Bridie and the House. If anyone had killed Aunt Mattie—though, of course, no one had—they had wasted their time.

"Well, dearie," said Mr. West, "I guess I'd better be getting down to the Works. What are you doing with all this bric-a-brac on the table?"

"Making lists of things. Finding out what there really is in the house."

"If you find any little things you don't really care for," her father said, "you don't have to give them away. Just leave them here. They'll look homelike to me."

"Of course, Daddy. I'm taking almost nothing. I'm really looking for *Salt Lake Fruit* and Duncan's letter."

Her father paused in the doorway. "Louise," he said slowly. "I don't believe you'll ever find the letter. Goodbye."

When the front door had closed heavily behind him, Bridie clumped down the front stairs. The groan of each step accompanied the outrage in her face. Her nose was red with anger, her hair was pulled back in righteousness, and as she crossed the hall to the reception room, the arms that had so often been crossed meekly over her abdomen were belligerently akimbo. She stood for a moment, glaring at Louise's back, bent over her notebook. Mrs. Peckham had uncannily known if anything was out of place, and this writing it down was the limit. Bridie had never pilfered in her life; it is to be doubted that she would even think of it, but it had sometimes seemed to her that it would have been nice to borrow something once in a while. She would never achieve that now. Her breathing became a snort. Louise turned and saw her. And, as usual, said the wrong thing.

"Bridie, there is something missing from the cabinet."

For a moment curiosity curbed Bridie's wrath. "What's missin'?"

"It's a knife," said Louise anxiously, "a Chinese knife in a curved ivory case. With a yellow silk tassel on the end. You know, Bridie, Uncle Eli's snick-a-snee."

"I know," said Bridie, "but that's all I know. If you're insinuatin' anything at all, Miss Louise ..."

"No, no, Bridie," Louise said peevishly. "Don't be silly. I'm not asking you if you took it. But haven't you seen it out of place anywhere in the house?"

"I have not," retorted Bridie, "but if I had of, why should you worry? There's plenty in this house for all."

"I have very good reason to worry and perhaps you have, too," said Louise sharply. "A snick-a-snee is a dangerous weapon."

Bridie's eyes narrowed. "When I'm that worried," she jeered, "I'll ask Miss Janet to call in the police to protect me."

Louise's hand, straightening the ivory elephants on the ebony bridge, was trembling. Bridie, seeing it, smiled and started out of the room. In the doorway, she turned. "Miss Janet says she don't know why she called the police the night Mrs. Peckham died. You don't know either, do you, Miss Louise?"

There was no answer. Bridie went happily away.

This was the moment when Mrs. Florence Kingston, chairman of the Committee for Cultural Relations with the Foreign-born, gushed into the tiny office of her secretary. "Oh, Miss Carter, we have been so fortunate.... We've got the most wonderful new committee member representing our splendid Swedish people. Such a Viking type." She moved aside, gesturing behind her. "Do come in and meet our charming little worker."

The little worker rose politely. Then she saw the Viking and her fingers closed on the edge of her desk. Mrs. Kingston said, "This is Miss Janet Carter. Mr. Eric Lund. She will just love to tell you all about everything."

"I doubt it," said Mr. Lund.

CHAPTER XVI
Saturday Evening

Gay in rose-beige chiffon, Janet held the gardenia to her cheek. She put down the flower on the marble-topped dresser and picked up the stiff little card with one word on it which was more exciting than the heavy perfume. She murmured the word softly.

A shadow fell across the late sunlight from the doorway, and a voice said, "Janet, dear."

Charlotte West stood on the threshold, elegant, reproving. "May I come in?"

"Oh, of course, Cousin Charlotte," Janet stammered. Awful to be caught talking to oneself. And saying that. "What lovely wool."

In a very straight chair Charlotte smiled above her inevitable needles. "I'm so glad you like it, dear. I think it is a rather good shade of ecru. Duncan says it is just the color of your skin. I'm starting a sweater for you. If you think you would like it."

"I'd love it. How perfectly grand of you, Cousin Charlotte."

"I shall enjoy making it." Charlotte glanced at the glowing face now turned to the mirror, at the fingers busy with the light brown knot of hair. "Janet," she said gravely, "this is the night you and Duncan had talked about attending the dance at the Longvale Club, isn't it?"

Janet started in guilty surprise. "Yes."

"My dear," the cool blue eyes sought Janet's in the mirror, "you realize, don't you, that you can't go?"

"Uh," said Janet, selecting this moment to apply lipstick delicately.

"Because, you know, we are in mourning. Even if we don't wear black. Duncan, of course, would not go to a dance so soon after his aunt's death. She was only your cousin, Janet, so with you it would be a matter of your feeling. And your mother's feeling. Your mother was always so devoted to your Cousin Mattie." There was a pause. "We were a little surprised that your mother did not come on for the funeral."

"Uh," said Janet from the east corner of her mouth. Damn Cousin Charlotte. She had got it on crooked.

"But I don't want you and Duncan to have an unhappy evening ..." the soft, clear voice went on, "so I thought it might be a treat for you to come to our house for dinner and then you and Duncan could perhaps dance together to our victrola. I'm glad you are wearing that exquisite dress. It's new, isn't it?"

Janet put down her lipstick and turned away from the mirror. "Thank you a lot, Cousin Charlotte. It's awfully kind of you. But I hadn't thought at all about the Longvale dance. I'm sorry I can't come over for dinner with you and Cousin Virgil. And Duncan. But I've got a d … I've been invited out somewhere else."

It wasn't clear that Cousin Charlotte was surprised. After all she had the gardenia before her eyes and nose.

"That's pleasant for you, dear," she said serenely. "Is it someone we know?"

It was not simple to answer all that was implied of fine social distinctions. "You have met him," said Janet, and put the card in her evening bag. What would come next?

Bridie came. Very neat and virtuous today, the hands folded over her large, early dinner.

"Mrs. Virgil," she announced, not without drama, "the *Fruit* is back."

"What fruit is back, Bridie?" The impatience was justified.

Bridie smiled tolerantly and raised her voice. "I said it's *back*."

"I am not deaf, Bridie."

"Not very much for your age," agreed Bridie who was only fifty-eight. "I said that there *Fruit* is back. That book you was all hollerin' about."

Charlotte pushed the wool into her knitting bag and rose. "Where did you find it?" she asked.

"I didn't find it."

"Come, Bridie. Didn't you tell me that *Salt Lake Fruit* is back? Back where?"

"In the bookcase in the liberry. Just where it's always been. You can see for yourself."

"I shall," said Charlotte and swept past her.

Bridie did not follow at once. "She won't see that book in the bookcase," she seemed pleased to state. "It was there, but soon as I noticed it, I tellyphoned to Mr. Duncan, and he was yankin' it to pieces when I come upstairs. Miss Janet, your feller's just drove up."

Cursing relatives, Janet dabbed hastily at her mouth and pinned the gardenia effectively into her summer ermine wrap and into her finger, and hurried toward the stairs, praying that all Wests were buried in the library. Buried and dead.

"Ah, Love's Young Dream." Dr. Taylor's big, soft face beamed redly about him. Soft lights and music within, a moonlit garden beyond the windows, lobster thermidor on his plate, and at the dark alcove table that luscious blonde. "Ah, young love's dream. Ouch."

He moved his hip flask from a painful point and gazed in mellow content at the blonde leaning forward into the light of the candles on her table, her lovely neck bent to the flame of a match. Only the hand of her escort was out of shadow.

"Enjoying yourself, Phil?" Across the table from the doctor, dry little Judge Hawes withdrew his penetrating gaze and his steel knife from a gorgeous tenderloin. "One way or another, Toni can please us all."

"Toni Taranto's a smart wop," agreed Dr. Taylor.

"He is smart," agreed Judge Hawes, "but he is not a wop. That is, if I assume your term is limited to Italians. Toni is a Pole."

"Never heard of a Pole running a night club," grumbled the doctor. The blonde had moved into the shadows, close to her companion. "Thought all they did around here was grow onions."

"Yes," said Judge Hawes succinctly, "and Toni knows you think that. So, to you, he's from Taranto. Good evening to you, sir."

The thin, white-faced owner of the River Inn, passing their table, bowed low to Judge Hawes and went on to the alcove.

"Did he," queried Dr. Taylor, "learn to bend his back like that in an onion field?"

The blond woman held out a graceful arm, calling a greeting in a rich voice. The words were not English. Toni Taranto kissed her extended hand.

The Judge turned toward the doctor's gaze. "I've sometimes wondered," he said. "Toni's never been in any trouble."

Dr. Taylor scowled at the limber back which concealed his view of the blonde and hitched his chair about to increase his horizon. In the near foreground were too many dowagers, but three tables away, by a window, he was pleased to note a delectable little pair of shoulders only partly veiled by floating chiffon. He took a deep drink from his glass. Yes, a lovely little girl in pink. Not exactly pink, but although the waiter had poured only ginger ale into the glass, everything was looking increasingly rosy to Dr. Taylor.

The lovely little girl turned her profile toward him. It was a face he had seen before, but he wasn't quite sure where. He took a good look at the man with whom she was seated.

"Well, for God's sake!" he said to himself, and then to the Judge, "Know a police detective named Lund?"

Judge Hawes nodded. "Another smart one. He's just passed his bar examinations at the head of the list. I hear he's going into the F.B.I. Is he here celebrating tonight?"

"And how! With a certain little debutante of the West-Peckham clan. Not quite the companion you would pick for a policeman."

"I pick companions for no one," snapped Judge Hawes, who was just meeting the temporarily insoluble problem of beefsteak and a partial plate. "Lund has spent five nights a week at law school for the last five years. He can't have had much time for women."

"He has now," said Dr. Taylor wistfully. "Ah, Love's Young Dream."

Judge Hawes rose. "I am going to extend my congratulations to Attorney Lund," he said. "Will you accompany me, Phillip?"

"No," said Dr. Taylor, but not because his legs might be a little unsteady.

Through the pink haze of his mind something new was trying to penetrate. Not an idea. A cliché, but not the one he had just spoken. Love ... dream ... no, something not altogether pleasant. Something that came nearer to the atmosphere of the last time he had seen those two together. Lund's words to himself and Murphy, something about suspicion. The haze lifted a moment.

"Not," he said aloud thickly, "Love's Young Dream. I've got it now. Busman's Holiday."

They were alone again at the table by the door leading into the garden. Lund's narrow Nordic face, still a little flushed by the old Judge's compliments, turned to Janet with a deprecatory smile.

"I think it's wonderful!" She held out her hand to him.

"Routine." His fingers closed quietly over hers.

"Oh, no!"

"Not much more," said Lund honestly, but the blue eyes were pleased. "I had a year at the U before my father died. My Uncle Arvid here in Watson sent for me to live with him. He was a policeman, so for the next five years, I followed the way of least resistance. Oh, I took a few correspondence courses, enough to make up my pre-law credits. Then I got wise to myself and went to night classes at the College of Law. Everyone gets through in five years, if at all."

She drew away her hand quickly. Her fingers were tingling, although he had not pressed them. "I still think it's wonderful, Mr. Lund."

"Mr. Lund?" he mocked softly.

She looked down at her lap. Her evening bag lay there, with the white card inside, with one word written on it. The Mr. Lund of their crisp, casual meetings in her office, at the committee table. The cool, impersonal voice over the telephone saying, "This is Lund. Would you care to go out for dinner with me tomorrow night?" The word on the card was Eric, and it had changed the world for Janet. Not because she thought it meant anything to him, but because of the revelation of what it meant to her.

She looked up at him. His face was turned toward the orchestra, and then she, too, was aware of the music and what it was.

"What are they playing?" he asked.

"*The Pavane for a Dead Princess....*"

"I like it."

"Oh, so do I," and added hastily to cover too great emotion, "so does Jerry."

"Who's Jerry?" There was an edge in his tone that she would have liked to think was jealousy.

"You know. The Wests' chauffeur. He was whistling it over and over the night Mrs. Peckham died. When I was in the library. Waiting for you." And then Eric had come into the room and she had fallen in love with him. She must say something fast, no matter how silly. "Actually, the music makes me think of a real princess who is dead."

Lund's eyes said: Go on. They had said it successfully to many people who had far more to conceal than had Janet.

"She was like someone in a dream. I saw her when I was a little girl. Here in Watson. Cousin Mattie was giving a party for Louise and I was allowed to go over and watch for a little while. I had a new dress, the color of this one.

"There was a long pier glass in the dressing room with lights at each side of it. The rest of the room was dim. I was standing in front of the mirror when the door opened and I saw her reflected behind me in the glass. She was white and rather like a ghost.... She was the most beautiful thing I had ever seen.

"I stood and stared at her. She laughed, not as if she were happy, and then she said a strange thing. 'My child, I think you are feeling the same thing about me that I am feeling about you.'

"She dropped her wrap on a chair and just glanced in the mirror, and then she spoke to me again. 'Let us hope that for you this beauty will bring a little more value than it has brought to me.'

"Three months later she killed herself."

Through the rush of voices around them the *Pavane* music came close to them again, the beat, beat, beat of stately sorrow.

He said, "And you never saw the Princess again?"

Janet shook her head. "Except later that evening. I was sent home to bed early, but I sneaked into our garden to listen to the music. There was someone in the bushes near our garage. I heard giggling and ... you know. Some boy, I think, with one of the maids. And then I heard a different kind of laugh. That was dear Cousin Mattie Peckham standing up on one of those balconies of hers. She could see all over the family backyards from there. The Crow's Nest, my father called it. At first I thought she was spying on the boy and girl in the bushes. Perhaps she was. Then someone turned on a light in the house that lighted up the whole garden like a stage, and just on the edge of the dark I saw the Princess Mariska. She was standing alone with her hands over her face as if she were crying. And that, Mr. Eric Lund, is the end of my girlish tale. You see, the light came my way, too, and I didn't want a report about bad little Janet handed to Mother in Cousin Mattie's well-known style."

"Cigarette, little Janet?" He leaned forward to light it. "Why do you think the Princess committed suicide?"

A small contempt crept into Janet's voice. "She was the wife of Ralph Ogden. You've met him."

"Yes," said Lund, "and a lot like him. I have also met a lot of suicides. I can't say I've noticed any obvious connection."

"You win," Janet admitted, but did not know how much. "I really don't know at all. I was only eleven years old. All I really remember is the merry Christmas conversation it made at our family hoard."

"I'll bet you were a brat."

"At times. That was one. She died on Christmas Eve, and all of us from the three houses were having dinner together the next day. None of us had really known the Princess, and the Ogdens weren't close friends at all, but that didn't stop the talk. Cousin Charlotte was so sure that it had been dreadfully hard for old Mrs. Ogden to have a foreigner in the family. And Cousin Virgil said weren't Poles the ones who got to be princes if they owned ten horses, and Cousin Mattie said a lot of things I didn't understand or remember. Louise pretended to feel very sorry, and that made me maddest of all. The night of her party I had seen Ralph pinch her arm. Louise had fat arms, then, too. So I said pleasantly, 'Louise is glad Mrs. Ralph Ogden is dead,' and spent the rest of Christmas in my room."

Lund said, "Nice people, including you. What did your Cousin Duncan add to the good will?"

"Duncan?" Janet was astounded. "Duncan? I haven't the remotest idea. I really never noticed him very much until he came back from Paris. Just before he went away he was a horrid boy who went around with an 'I-Know-All-The-Facts-Of-Life' air."

"And now?"

"Well, he's a little in that style today," she admitted. "Oh, of course Duncan wouldn't have been at that Christmas dinner. He went to Europe in October 1919."

Lund stood up. "Shall we go out for a few minutes?"

He wrapped her in her ermine jacket and opened the French doors into the cool and quiet. It was dark except for a few bright cigarettes belonging to others like themselves. Janet, tripping on her trailing frock, swayed against Lund, and he held her there. They found a bench and sat silent. His arm was hard against her, but his hand did not press. Not like Duncan's insinuating fingers awakening feelings she had not quite wanted him to satisfy. She looked up at the lean profile outlined dimly against the night sky.

He turned his head toward her. "Janet, you're a different kind of girl."

"Different," she said, "from what?"

"I haven't had much time for women," said Lund. He did not mean by it quite what Judge Hawes had. "Most dames are dumb."

"I can be, very easily."

"Not in a lot of ways I could name."

"Name one." She could feel the warmth of his cheek just above her hair.

"Well, you haven't asked me yet if I got the scars around my mouth when I was bitten by Public Enemy Number One."

"Of course not. Because I never knew you had any," lied Janet.

Even a smart man has his duller moments. "Haven't you, really?" said Lund. "There are plenty of them. I couldn't have got them in a less heroic fashion. I was going to school one morning when I was about nine or ten and the wind on our beloved Minnesota prairie blew me into a barbed wire fence. It was twenty below, so I froze there, and when another kid pulled me loose, I left part of my face behind."

"Eric," her fingers touched his lips, feeling through the rough little network of scars the memory of that old pain.

He caught her hand, holding it hard against his mouth.

Then, very cool, he said, "Time to go home now. Policemen work on Sunday. I'll bring the car around to the side entrance."

Not quite sure how she was feeling or how she ought to be feeling, Janet opened the door of the powder room. After all, her hair was mussed a little.

Before a mirror, a young woman in silver brocade was arranging a blond coiffure much more disturbed than Janet's, and looking enormously pleased with herself. Their eyes met, startled, and there was no doubt that Helenka Baluta was annoyed to see her neighbor.

"Hello," said Janet uncertainly.

"Hello," said Miss Baluta, her smile now in the best movie manner. "That gown exactly suits you."

"Thank you," said Janet, her eyes cautious. Was Duncan, she wondered, not in such very deep mourning after all? Or Ralph? She turned her back on the glittering Miss Baluta and bent to brush imaginary grass from the hem of her dress. When she turned again, there was no one else in the room.

Nor, when she came out into the passage, was there anyone there. Lund's tall body filled the doorway to the drive.

"Did you know that blond woman?" he asked.

She could not say no. "I've met her."

"Yes," said Lund. He smiled faintly. "She came out and got into a car as soon as it drove up. However, I recognized the driver."

"Known to the police?"

"In a way."

He did not say whether or not the man was known to Janet. He did not ask the name of the woman. Obviously, because he knew it. She got into his car, painfully recalling the glibness with which Miss Carter had told Detective Lieutenant Lund that Mr. Baluta lived alone. Jerry, Bridie, every servant in the West household would have told him or Murphy that there was a glamorous granddaughter. No wonder he had smiled just now. She sat as far from him as possible.

They drove in silence.

"Come over here," said Lund. She could see him grinning at her beneath the brim of his hat. He took one hand off the wheel and drew her to his side. "Now, stay where you belong." He pressed her head on his shoulder, put his hand back on the wheel, and they drove on again, silent.

When he spoke, the car was turning up Elm Street Hill. "Janet, when are you going to get out of that house?"

"As soon as I can. Perhaps Monday." It looked an appalling black dungeon tonight. "I hate it." She shuddered against him.

"Any special reason?"

"N-no. Only someone is always prowling around. You never feel alone."

"Who prowls?" His tone was serious.

"Everyone in the family. Of course, they don't really prowl. It's their own house. Only, now that they've all got keys, I fall over them in every dark corner."

"That," he said, "is what I was afraid of."

"Afraid?" He had stopped the car beneath the porte-cochere. He made no move to kiss her.

"Yes. Get out. I'm coming in with you. Give me your key." He swung the front door wide, flashing a strong torch around the hall. "Where's the switch? Here?"

In the sudden glare the old bruin seemed to blink. Lund motioned Janet into the house. "Up the stairs," he ordered, "and into your room. Don't look so shocked. I'm going to see that you lock yourself in, and lock me out. Me and three or four other fellows."

"You're crazy," said Janet.

"I am not," said Lund without rancor. "Follow me."

At the head of the stairs, he said, "Is this your room?"

"No. That one."

Again the torch flashed around dark walls till he saw the switch.

"Perhaps," suggested Janet, "you'd like to look in the closet and under the bed."

"I am going to," he said, "and in the bathtub, too." And did it.

He came back to her, looking down into her face. "I am serious about this. You aren't going to turn out to be a dumb dame after all, are you? Don't you know why I'm doing this?"

"No," she said.

"Then I'm telling you. You've got to be careful. You know too much and you've told me too little. Now I'm going. I'm on eight hour duty tomorrow from noon on. I'll give you a ring. Plan to get out of this house as soon as you can. Lock that door and don't open it till you hear the cook around in the morning."

"Eric." There was an edge of fear in her voice. "Eric, I ..."

He came back to her side. "I did forget one thing," he said, and kissed her. "Now, for God's sake, lock that door."

CHAPTER XVII
The Second Sunday

Virgil West silently closed the door and stood listening. There was no sound except for the cold fall of rain outside. Sudden April change had taken away the spring and made the house dark at noon. All the dining room lights were being used against the gloom and he plodded toward them. He had a job to do and one that he wanted to do heartily. But, deprived of its usual Sunday morning rest between a heavy breakfast and a heavier dinner, an old heart will not respond to every call. Particularly when confronted with such powerful depressants as noon breakfast with the Sunday paper, and a female cigarette smoker, cluttering his late father's dining table.

"Janet," he said as sternly as his fat voice could sound, "aren't you making things pretty hard for Bridie?"

She flung up her head from her reading, which, he noted with concern, was neither the society page nor the funnies.

"No, Cousin Virgil," she said crisply. "I am not."

"Well, Janet," he tried to sound placating, "all this muss on the table and so near dinnertime...."

"I'm not having any dinner," she told him. "I've just got up. Bridie has gone to her sister's. I told her I'd do the dishes when I finished."

Virgil thrust out his lower lip in alarm. No Sunday dinner to be eaten by a member of his family?

"I'm sorry if it shocks you, Cousin Virgil," said Janet. "It won't happen again. I expect to leave here tomorrow."

"No, no, my dear." He had begun this all wrong and almost too late, for he now saw that the paper was open to the Classified Section. "We couldn't let you. We should all miss you. And we need you. Bridie is a little superstitious. She wouldn't stay in the house alone."

"Hasn't Bridie lots of friends and cousins who would be glad to live here?—Won't you have some coffee, Cousin Virgil?"

"Thank you. I'll just have one of those muffins with a mite of honey." He sat down and gathered strength for what might be prolonged action: He was not without ordnance. "I'm afraid that wouldn't do at all, Janet. We don't want anyone but the family here at a time like this. Your staying here with Bridle would fit in perfectly with our plans."

"But, Cousin Virgil," she said. Her manner was very polite-to-older-people. "I have plans, too." The hand which did not hold the offensive cigarette was resting on the notice of a kitchenette apartment, centrally located, where one might ask a friend to dinner when his eight-hour day was over.

Virgil West sighed. He hadn't wanted to use Other Means; that was what he called the paper in his pocket. He drew it out now, and handed it very deliberately across the butter plate. "I found this up in your Cousin Mattie's den."

The girl took the sheet of notepaper, torn to the exact size needed, in Mattie's saving way. She seemed to be reading every word that was written on it, although she must be as familiar with it as he was. The writing, except for the signature, was that of his sister.

> I, Janet West Carter, promise to reside in the house of Mattie West Peckham until July 5, 1932, and to pay the sum of twenty dollars ($20.00) per week for board and lodging. I further agree that to each weekly sum shall be added interest to the value of $1.20 for each weekly bill not paid in advance.

It was dated on the day of Mattie's death.

Janet looked up at him, not at all politely now. "Is this legal?" she asked him in a tone to match.

"I think it is," he said in his kindest voice. "My dear, in any case you have given your word."

Janet laughed. "I shall consult my lawyer."

Old Mr. West did not now feel sorry for what he had to do. "You have a lawyer, too?" He said very slowly, "A lawyer as well as a policeman?"

Her eyes did not leave his face.

"Your mother wouldn't have you going out at night with a policeman."

"What," she asked, "could be safer?"

"Janet, have you written her about it?"

"No."

"Perhaps," he went on, "I ought to tell her about it when I answer her letter about Cousin Mattie's death."

She was showing him nothing of her feelings.

"I was a little surprised that your mother didn't come on for the funeral. You say your father is doing all right in his business. It didn't seem like her to stay away."

Janet looked down at her plate. So she *had* sent some sort of message home, and he would have liked to know what it was. But the main issue now was to keep the girl here and away from that detective.

"I know you didn't mean to do anything wrong," he went on. "Nothing that would make things harder for us all in our time of sorrow. You just lost your head a little when you called the police."

She was staring full at him now.

"That policeman you were out with last night. I wouldn't quite trust him if I were you. He's trying to get something out of you."

"What could he get?" she asked. "What could he get that concerns ... the Family?"

"Well, nothing important, of course, but policemen are kind of bull-headed; they've got one-track minds. You and I know your Cousin Mattie died a perfectly natural death, but this fellow Lund would have liked to make a big case out of it for his own glory. I'm not sure he wouldn't still like to do it. You're too smart a girl, Janet, to let any man use you."

He hoped that had done it. Anyway, he was through for today. It was almost dinnertime. He got up heavily. "Think it over."

Still she did not answer and he lumbered out, not, he felt, in defeat.

And two hours later, Janet was still thinking it over. Last night had brought her two strong emotions, love and fear, both of which old Mr. West had touched off. In spite of her talk to Lund about prowling, and the search of her room, concerning which she had remained unwisely silent, she had not really been afraid of the Family or of the house. Cousin Charlotte's interfering visits, Duncan on the dark stairs, were irritations until Eric had taken them seriously; and this morning, his command to lock her door hadn't seemed as important as his good-night kiss. But the stout figure of Cousin Virgil, whom she had previously known only as curious, trivial and kind, now loomed over her as the embodiment of Lund's warning. For some reason, terrible in its vagueness, the Family wanted her to stay in this house, and so she must leave it at once. But still she sat on the old couch in the library, her hands twisting a newspaper cutting describing a small apartment where a girl wouldn't want to ask a man who was just using her, and her ears strained against the silence of the house for the strong ring of the telephone.

When sound came, it was petty and mean. Small metal prying into small metal; another tribal invader turning his key in the side door. Janet stood up, her hands clenched. The opening door let in the noise of the rain and the sound of feet, heavy, but moving faster than Cousin Virgil's ever did. Ralph Ogden, red cheeks wet with rain, spoke.

"Hullo, Janet. Hope I didn't scare you. Dark as hell. The key to the carriage house is supposed to be here. Louise says Uncle Eli's fishing tackle is out there. I never was inside the place."

He rummaged in a table drawer, exposing from the rear a thinned crest and an augmented base, not chic accessories for a movie star's Saturday night.

"Got it." Key in hand he straightened and turned toward Janet. "I've lugged over my own fishing stuff. Left it out on the porch. I'm going to check my lures with Uncle Eli's and see if he had something I haven't got. To keep the Big Ones from getting away. Always have gotten away from me."

His blunt acceptance of life as a thing in which nothing ever happened to him touched Janet slightly. She said, "You ought to come out and fish with us. All the fish in Minnesota are big ones."

"I'd like to test the truth of that," Ralph laughed, "but there's not much chance unless the rest of your family likes me better than you do. Why don't you like me, Janet? I could think of plenty of reasons if you knew me. But you don't really know very much about me, do you?"

Under the steady gaze of his dark-circled eyes, Janet flushed, silent. She would have to answer him.

From somewhere near at hand there was a creak, sharp and sudden as a shot, as if the Peckham house was complaining in its arthritic old joints.

She said, "I knew the Princess Mariska."

He turned from her and walked to the rain-lashed window. When he finally spoke, his voice was so low that she scarcely heard him. "How did you happen to know Mariska?"

She told him about the meeting before the bright mirror, in almost the same words she had used to Lund on the previous evening. The long-hidden memory was, she discovered, already less precious. Drama, in the telling, had become melodrama.

Ralph came back to the table, sank into the old Morris chair. The circles under his eyes were darker.

"Yes," he said, "she was beautiful, and it didn't get her anywhere—except a long way from home."

The silence hurt, but Janet could not break it.

Ralph spoke again, slowly, painfully. "I'll never forget that home of hers. A dark old castle. Mucky roads. Forests full of deer. Footmen in knee breeches serving dinner. Orchids and gold spoons on the table. And oil lamps. Cockroaches. And rats. And no plumbing. God, those peasants at the wedding reception! Men with long black beards, barefoot women kissing our hands and feet. A damned long way from Watson, Massachusetts."

"Is that why she—died? Because she was so homesick?"

"No. I suppose she was homesick sometimes. That's probably why she used to go down and visit those Balutas. But Mariska didn't want to go back to Poland. Our marriage had solved a big problem for her. She was an orphan with no money. The old prince, her uncle, was tickled to death to hand her over to a man who didn't even know what a dowry was. Mariska wanted to be an American.

"And how we exploited that, my late unlamented mother and I. I'm no West-Peckham, Janet. What my family said—because it was the family saying it—didn't mean a damned thing to me. But I believed what I wanted to believe. That Mother-Knows-Best stuff. She would train the ignorant foreigner to be a nice American wife for her darling boy. We had a couple of maids, but Mariska had to do dishes and clean the bathroom. On Christmas Eve my mother sent her out to buy roach tablets."

"Roach tablets? Why on earth?"

Ralph shook his head wearily. "I'd been fool enough once to think my mother might be interested in Poland. She forgot the orchids and the footmen right away, and she kept her mind on the roaches and the rats. I'm glad to say she's dead."

"Yes," said Janet.

"But don't get me wrong," he continued. "I'm not passing the buck. I knew I ought to take Mariska away from my mother. And I would have done it. I was crazy about her. But I was waiting a little while because I was having a lot of fun in Watson. I was going with a richer bunch than I had known before the war. I shut my eyes to the kind of life Mariska was having to lead. It never occurred to me that everything wouldn't come out right in the end."

He sat so long staring at the floor that Janet thought he had finished.

"So, on Christmas Eve I was at the Club and she went out to a drugstore and bought her own death. I'll show you something." He fumbled in his hip pocket, pulled out his wallet. He held a scrap of paper toward Janet. "I carry it around for the good of my soul."

She took the bit of heavy white letter paper and read the short list: 5 two-cent stamps, eau de cologne, roach tablets.

"Turn it over," he said.

The writing on the other side of the paper was the same—delicate, firm, foreign.

My husband,
Believe me this thing I am doing is the best for you and for me.
                                                                Mariska

Ralph stood up, pushing the note back into his wallet. "She had every reason to kill herself," he said, "but I would never have dreamed she'd do it. She was always so strong. And then the child—She hadn't told me about it. We'd sort of put off having one. But she expected to have one. She thought I ought to want one. She had been brought up that way. Well, Janet, I'm off."

She said gently, "Good-bye, Ralph. Come out to Minnesota and fish with Dad and me some day."

"Thanks, kid," he smiled gratefully. "I might do that.—I've got just one other thing of Mariska's I'd like to show you sometime. I keep it in my tackle box. The only place that's one hundred per cent mine."

"I'd love to see it," Janet said softly.

In the doorway he paused. "Funny thing," he said, "four people mixed up in my wife's death and now all in the neighborhood when dear Aunt Mattie departed."

"Four people?" repeated Janet.

"Yes. Myself. The two Balutas. And that smart detective."

"Eric Lund?"

"Didn't you know that, Janet?" He looked amused. "I thought he would have told you about it. Lund was the patrolman who came to the Baluta shack on the night Mariska died."

Seeing the change in her face, he was less amused. "Forget it," he said, and went away.

Alone again, Janet forgot nothing. Like ghost voices on a sound track the phrases came. "That policeman ..." "He's trying to get something out of you...." "I wouldn't quite trust him...." "I thought he would have told you...." "You know too much and you've told me too little." Then her own voice, last night, telling and telling and telling to that smart detective who hadn't needed to ask a question. Her cheeks were burning. Her cold hands twisted and tore the scrap of paper she had been holding when Ralph came into the room. That clipping. A hotter flush rose to her face.

She dashed to the wastebasket, slipped down on the floor beside it, and like a dog with a bone, buried the fragments beneath the mild debris. But she could not bury the remembrance of the hospitable reception she had given Eric's kiss.

Too dumbly absorbed in the contemplation of romance versus reality to recall an emotion that should have been stronger, too deafened by the sound of those remembered voices to hear the house door cautiously closing for the third time....

Tiptoeing steps reached the library, a figure filled the doorway. Then Janet heard, saw and was afraid.

Seated on the floor between the end of the couch and the bookcase and partially screened by the center table, she was not immediately visible to eyes searching through the gloom of the room. She closed her own eyes. She held her breath. Could he see her from where he stood? Would he come into the room? Or go away before she choked?

Minutes were black and long. Then her straining ears caught the light, wary retreat of a man who did not wish to be seen or heard.

CHAPTER XVIII
The Second Sunday, Continued

With noiseless hands Duncan opened the telephone book. Pages slipped over. The dial revolved almost without sound, and was answered by a distant, guttural "'Allo."

"I wish to speak to Miss Helenka Baluta," the voice was imperious but low.

There was a grunt and then a growl, "What iss your name?"

"Mr. Duncan West."

"So." There was a short silence. "Miss Baluta don't know you." The receiver crashed on the hook.

Duncan slipped his own receiver silently into place. It was well that he had slunk over here to the protection of Aunt Mattie's parsimony. What couldn't any inmate of the West chateau have made of that call, listening on one of the half-dozen extensions!

Actually, just what could he make of it? Was Baluta speaking for himself alone? If so, what did he know? Helenka Baluta didn't know Duncan West. Was she making a special application of the old ironic quip about what constitutes an introduction?

He stood puzzled, hearing the silence and then hearing something else. A crackle, repeated, and stopped. He strode down the hall to the right, not now bothering to tiptoe.

Janet was in the library, trying, too quietly, to fold the Sunday paper. Duncan, meeting a white stare, felt her provocation. It would be delightful to feel that cool defense yield to his arms.

"You don't look surprised to see me," he said. "Were you in this room when I stood here a few minutes ago?"

"Yes," she said. She looked frightened. Perhaps she had reason to be.

"Where the devil were you? Hiding under the couch?"

She shook her head. "Just sitting on the floor in the corner."

"Mouse hiding in her hole?"

She said carefully, "Why not? Cats prowl around this house today."

"Are you suggesting," he asked, "that my mother has been here? It's her house, you know."

"Duncan! Of course I didn't mean Cousin Charlotte. Cats come in two kinds."

"Meaning me, then."

"Not exclusively. You're the third. I think I shan't wait for Jerry and the butler to complete the list."

"Or," he suggested, "for *Monsieur le grand policier* Lund?"

Her face was not white now. He moved close to her side, taking hold of the newspaper she still held. "Where are you going without waiting for any man?"

She turned over the folded paper topped by the classified section to the back covered with announcements of local amusements. "I'm going to a movie," she said. "The rain has stopped."

"Shall we make this our date in memory of our unshared childhood on Mt. Hero? Or are you not free?"

Janet hesitated. "All right, Duncan, let's take Ralph along. He's out in the carriage house, playing with Cousin Eli's fishing tackle."

"Ralph? I understood quite clearly that he doesn't like movies. And that you don't like him. Could it be that you don't want to go out with me unchaperoned?"

Her glance and her words were direct.

"I don't feel like going anywhere with anybody alone."

So she *was* afraid. "Very well, then. Ralph goes with us. By force if necessary. Get your coat while I ring up Jerry."

"I'll be right down," she said. "Take the paper and choose your poison. Anything is all right with me."

It was, strangely, not so right with Jerry.

"The Arcade?" the chauffeur repeated over the wire. "Mr. West, that is a poor, small theatre. Very badly ventilated. Old. Not in a good part of town."

"Thank you, Jerry," Duncan told him. "You are only adding to its interest. Have the car at Mrs. Peckham's carriage house in a quarter of an hour."

"Certainly," said Jerry, and added, "sir."

"The Arcade?" Janet came down the stairs. "That's a horrible, smelly hole. What's the picture?"

The telephone bell rang.

Duncan, answering, smiled mockingly at Janet. "Oh, I'm so sorry," he spoke into the transmitter. "She's just going out."

His smile increased as Janet darted forward, then stopped.

"Well," went on Duncan kindly, "if you feel so strongly about it, I think it can be arranged. Janet, my dear, you're wanted by the police. Do you mind?"

Her voice was cool enough. It was a good thing the fellow on the other end of the wire couldn't see the color of her cheeks.

"Yes, I'm going out.... To a movie ... No, not alone ... Why? (smartly) Were you thinking of shadowing me? ... (more meekly) The Arcade ... (politely) I'm sorry, too, but I don't think I could tell you anything you didn't find out last night ... (penitently, but to an empty line) Oh, Eric, please ..."

She, too, hung up and said curtly to Duncan, "Let's go."

They went out the front door, under the porte-cochere and crunched over the gravel drive past the Georgian house. Cedars sent cold rags of rain down on their heads. Duncan, throwing a defiant glance at the Baluta windows, took Janet's arm.

"I think you'd better tell me about Ralph's first wife." He felt her muscles grow tense. "The indispensable minimum. What did Aunt Mattie mean by 'the little accident' at the Balutas'? Is she dead?"

"Yes. She killed herself."

"At the Balutas'? Down by the riverbank? What was she doing in a place like that?"

"Duncan," Janet looked up at him. "Didn't you ever see her? Don't you know who she was?"

He shook his head.

"She was a Polish princess. She used to go down there to speak her own language with old Mr. Baluta."

Before them rose the kind of carriage house best suited to the Peckham mansion. It was a less appalling building because there was in every way less of it. Even the yellow paint was of an older vintage.

"When did all this happen?"

"In 1920. Ralph brought her to Watson in the fall. She died on Christmas Eve."

Janet slipped her arm lightly out of his and ran to the door of the carriage house. It was a heavy sliding door set near the top with a diamond pane. "I'd forgotten about the window," she said. "When I was a kid I loved to jump up on my toes and get a quick look inside. My eyes are on a level with it now."

Arching fingers over brows, she peered through the dirty glass.

"Duncan!" She sprang back, clutching his arm. "There's an animal in there."

"I doubt it," said Duncan, and took her place at the door.

Through the cloudy pane wild antlers wavered, ruminant eyes returned his stare. He slid back the door.

"Come here, Janie," he said, "and meet an old friend."

The floor of the carriage house was hare and empty, except for Ralph Ogden squatting over his fishing tackle under the loft. Up in the loft and far more impressive stood a huge iron deer.

"Eve!" Janet giggled, and ran toward the foot of the loft. The deer swayed forward slightly as if in welcome. "Hey, look out!" Ralph cried out. "You'll bring the damn thing down on all of us."

Eve rocked gently back on hooves that had been made to be bolted to a pedestal. Janet drew a deep breath. "That would have been something. She must weigh a ton."

"You exaggerate," said Duncan. "Eve, we were informed, is hollow. Not over two or three hundred pounds."

"That's plenty," Ralph was sure, "to crack even a skull like mine."

Duncan looked down on his brother-in-law. Not at all the type you would expect to have a sad romantic past.

He said, "Well, let's celebrate your escape from death. Janet and I are here to drag you off to a very special cinema."

Ralph transferred a red and white plug with vicious triple hooks from a huge tackle box labeled "E. T. Peckham" to a second box, larger and newer. Compartment trays were gay and precise with spinners, plugs, trout flies. "Movies," he said, "are all spinach to me."

"I think you're right," Duncan spoke lightly, "and I don't doubt that this one will be no exception. But I am curious. You probably don't remember that Aunt Manic urged us all to see a film called *Candle in the Night?*"

Ralph glanced at Janet. Her back turned to him, she was quietly admiring Eve. "I remember it very well," he said.

"We're going to see it now. Coming?"

Ralph got up slowly. "I have a little curiosity of my own. Yes, I'll come along."

Janet turned toward them. She looked from one to the other. "Ralph— I didn't know—It was Duncan's choice." Beyond the open door gravel spattered as Jerry brought up the town car smartly. As he started toward it, something rang against Duncan's heel.

"Good lord, what's that?"

On the floor lay a metal thing like a great crawfish with spread claws. Ralph grunted. With a laugh of recognition, Janet swooped toward it and caught it up.

"You ignorant foreigner, don't you know what it is? It's a gaff. Perfect for Great Northern."

"Great Northern What?"

"Pike. Fish. You use it to lift them into the boat. Like this. See?"

She came toward him, holding out the curved blades full of teeth. Her eyes were gleaming. She pulled the crossbar toward her. Like scissors the arms were closing slowly around his throat. He felt the cold, light touch of the metal and jerked back his head.

"It's time to go," he said.

Ralph with a grin took the gaff. "Be with you in a minute. I'll just put this in my tackle box. I want to take the best of everything up north with me next month. The rainbow trout and 'lakers' had better look out for me this season."

He followed them out, slid the heavy door into place, and locked it.

"There are a number of ways a person could get hurt in there," he said, and pocketed the key.

CHAPTER XIX

The Second Sunday, Continued

As the peal of the telephone died away, Helenka Baluta opened her eyes. Muffled by distance and closed doors, she heard briefly the old man's gruff voice, and then the house was still. She did not define the sounds which seemed part of the dream from which she was waking. She stretched slowly, smiling. For the first time in her life, reality was better than any dream. She laughed and snuggled back into the pillows.

The sound of a heavy car on the drive below brought her finally to her feet. Sheer black chiffon was a haze over her body as she moved to the window.

The car had stopped in front of the old woman's barn, and the charming little Janet was getting in. Three men stood beside the car. Three black-haired men.

Helenka Baluta looked at them all. At one with a flash of quite impersonal aversion, at another with delight. The third man glanced in the direction of her window. Helenka shrank back, hands pressed over her face.

"Oh, no," she moaned. "Oh, no!"

When the car repassed the Baluta house, it was only the old man who watched.

Jerry turned to the left and down Elm Street Hill. Across the lawn of the chateau, Charlotte West, a gardening basket on her arm, was making regal progress toward her hedge. She waved her hand delicately.

The Arcade Theatre was in a dingy, run-down street. A cracked facade was splashed with raucous lithographs of *Gory Gangsters* and paler posters of the second feature, *Candle in the Night*. One look at the place and you could smell the bad air inside. Eric Lund had been looking at nothing else for ten minutes and he felt slightly sick. The real smell, though, was the Peckham case. Some fast work had been done on Janet since last night. He was no longer in doubt that there was a case. But he was as far as ever from proving it. He slanted his hat brim farther down over his eyes and moved deeper into the shadows of the tenement hallway. It would be the opposite of good to have the Captain of Detectives find out that he spent his free time tailing the scions of the Duncan Rifle Works.

They were coming now. The contrast between the slatternly Arcade and the long, slim town car with the elegant Jerry suggested something. But what? That three unalleged murderers were out to take an extension course from *Gory Gangsters?*

Lund had expected to see two of them. Duncan's tone had told him clearly with whom Janet was just going out. Ogden was a surprise, an unpleasant one.

However, he'd rather see Janet with the two of them than with either one alone. Lund's smile was sardonic at the expense of Lund. Much analysis of the lower motives of mankind had not led him to ignore his own. He knew they were now double.

Ogden was buying tickets at the box office. Janet, a neat little figure in a pink suit, was looking quickly up and down the street. For the "shadow" she had suggested? Or invited? He wanted to go to her. But not yet. He focused on Duncan West, talking to the chauffeur at the curb. If the pantomime were reliable, Jerry seemed to be offering to wait and to be getting orders to go. He got into the car and drove away. The three went into the theatre, Janet lagging, and urged on by Duncan's arm.

Lund knocked out his pipe. Let them get seated and he would follow them into the theatre. He took a step out of the hallway. And a step back. The Wests' car was stopping directly in front of him. He had misread the signs. Jerry would now settle down to wait for a couple of hours.

But that was not what Jerry did. Instead, he leaned forward against the left-hand window. He was watching the entrance to the theatre and watching closely. Philosophically, Lund refilled his pipe.

During the next quarter-hour, a few cars went by and a couple of buses bumped through. People straggled out of the Arcade and a few went in. Then a man came out alone. He stood quite still in the middle of the pavement. It was Ralph Ogden.

Jerry sprang from the car and across the street. Ogden seemed unaware of his approach. Jerry touched his arm. Ogden looked at him for a minute, then nodded slowly. The two recrossed the street. A few feet from Lund's watching-post, Jerry opened the car door, intense eyes fixed on Ogden. Ralph Ogden's shoulders were sagging. His face had a look of shock as on that evening when he and Lund had first met.

When they had driven away, Lund came out of the doorway. What the hell had happened to Ogden in the Arcade and why had Jerry been certain that something would happen? And how about those other two who were still in the theatre?

It was time he, too, was in there. He started for the curb just as Janet rushed out. Her hat was clutched in one hand. Her eyes searched up and down the street. In a moment she would have seen Lund, but in that moment one of the vehicles of the Watson City Bus Company stumbled to its stop in front of the Arcade Theatre. Lund got across the street just as the gears clashed and the bus moved away. A passenger in pink was paying her fare.

Lund's wave and shout were lost. To this frustration was now added a sudden miasmic surge, as the doors of the Arcade opened wide to let out the crowd at the end of the afternoon show. He had to take a lot of soiled elbowing before he saw emerging from the den the haughty face of the Third Murderer. Duncan West did not look ill as his brother-in-law had looked. His brows were drawn together as if in worry and bewilderment. Lund, for the first and only time, felt a touch of comradeship.

West looked sharply over the crowd, shrugged and walked on briskly in the direction opposite to that the bus had taken, and as far as possible from Elm Street Hill. His looked implied that if Janet Carter were standing in the middle of canaille, Duncan West was not going to stand there with her. If he had seen Lund, he did not seem to be concerned.

Just where did this leave Detective Lund? All alone, out on a limb, waiting for a streetcar. That about described it. Except for one thing. He was starving hungry. Desk-work which he should have finished before celebrating on Saturday night had taken him until three o'clock. He'd had no lunch. He could pick up his car around the corner and pursue

Janet's bus up Elm Street Hill, there probably to be met with the kind of reception better coped with on a full stomach. With Ogden mysteriously wilted and Duncan making tracks for the opposite end of town, it looked as if neither of his favorite suspects could do much preying on Janet before Lund could eat his dinner.

The best spaghetti joint this side of Naples was a half-block from the police station. Lund chose the darkest booth and ordered liberally. This was the exact spot he had selected for dinner that night with Janet. She would have looked good sitting on the opposite bench. With a wry grin Eric Lund raised tired feet and set them on the seat of romance.

The rich reality of minestrone had just reached his mouth when Murphy found him. The strong little Irishman planted his hands flat on the end of the table and said to Lund, "Sorry, Rik. We got to get going."

"Go away till I finish my supper," growled his partner.

"Listen, Rik," Murphy's lips barely moved. "There's been a murder."

"Can't you hold clown the corpse alone for a while?" Lund asked him in tones muffled by beans.

"I could," Murphy watched him closely, "but I thought you wouldn't want to miss out on this one. It's at 110 Elm Street."

CHAPTER XX
The Second Sunday Evening

The darkness of the house was strange. A tall smudge against the lowery sky that had brought on early twilight. When calamity falls, it is human to fight it with a futile blaze of lights. So had the Peckham house appeared ten nights ago when Lund approached it, neither knowing nor caring who was dead. Tonight he did not know the name of his second corpse.

The squad car was not in sight, but at the edge of the driveway a flashlight signaled. Patrolman Shea stepped on the running board beside Murphy.

"It's out back," he said.

"Who's dead?"

"Dunno. Leary's inside."

"Inside the house?"

"Barn. Kind of an old-fashioned carriage house. Straight ahead.... Remember that little girl, Lund?"

"What about her?"

"She found this body, too. Kind of funny, ain't it?"

"Yeah," said Murphy. He darted a quick look at Lund's profile and followed him out of the car.

Headlights made circles against the closed door of the carriage house. At the left the squad car was parked. Close to the bushes at the right four people were huddled in groups of two. Leary stood guard before the barn door. He said, sickly, to the two detectives, "I give a good look inside and shut her up to wait for you. It's hell in there."

Lund said again, "Who's dead?"

"Fellow named ...." Leary consulted his notebook in the headlights' beam, "Ralph H. Ogden."

"Family next door been notified?" Murphy jerked his thumb toward the Wests'.

"Nope. Carter girl asked us not to do a thing till you guys got here."

"O.K.," said Lund. "Be with you in a minute, Murphy."

He went over to the spot where two women stood close together.

"Eric!" Janet left Bridie and came toward him. Her face was pale and anxious. Little drops of perspiration stood out on her forehead.

"Can you tell me what happened?" he asked. Her body quivered within his steadying arm.

She said through chattering teeth. "I looked in the window, just the way I did this afternoon. And she wasn't there! Eve wasn't there!" Her eyes were glazed with remembered horror.

Lund said to Bridie, "What do you know about this?"

"Nothin', sir. That is, till I heard her callin' the police and sayin' there'd been a murder. Then I come runnin' downstairs and we been here together ever since."

"All right," said Lund. "Take her inside and make her lie down. Keep her warm. And call Dr. Taylor."

"Yes, sir."

Lund took his arm away from Janet. "Can you make it into the house?" he asked.

"Of course." Her voice was low and hoarse. "I'm sorry, Eric, to be so ... silly."

"You're behaving all right," he said. "I'll be with you when I can."

He joined Murphy and the two men by the shrubbery. Old Mr. Baluta was standing stone-still. Jerry was saying, "I drove Mr. Ogden home from the movies. I put the car away. That is all I know."

He was not his usual dapper self. Rumpled hair and open shirt gave him the appearance of one roused from his bed at midnight.

"How come you got here so quick?" Murphy asked. "Leary says your people over there haven't been told."

"I was at the Balutas'," said Jerry, "having coffee in the kitchen with Mr. Baluta."

"Don't go away from here," Lund told them. "Let's take a look at the barn, Murphy, before the rest of Homicide gets here."

Leary, his head turned away, slid back the door of Mattie Peckham's carriage house. In the weak light of one high bulb, a big black animal lay in a mess of snarled cord and bright bits of tin and feathers. From beneath its body a stream of blood had flowed and stiffened. It took a second to recognize the iron quality of the animal and to be certain that the red-smeared lump between its antlers was the head of Ralph Ogden.

Lund went over and knelt carefully by the head. Murphy felt around for a wrist.

"No pulse," he said.

Lund's fingers touched the blanched cheek. "He hasn't been dead more than an hour. He couldn't have been. I saw him downtown at five o'clock."

"Six thirty-five now."

Leary spoke from the doorway. "How'd that thing ever happen to fall on him and kill him?"

"Same way it was able to throw fishing tackle all over itself after it was lying down," Murphy told him. "Iron stags are smart."

He rose painfully, extracting a basserino hooked to the left knee. Outside in the growing dark they heard Leary's over-compensatory bark at Baluta and the chauffeur. "Stand back. Make it snappy!"

"Where?" Murphy asked Lund.

"Cut, I think. Under the blood behind the ear."

Murphy shook his head at the welter of fish lines, metal spoons, red and white plugs and spilled bottles of reel oil and pork rind frogs sprayed over the fallen stag. "Somebody want to make this look like an accident? Or just go off his nut?"

Men filled the doorway of the barn. Fingerprint man, photographer, medical examiner. "Jesus Christ!" someone said, and was echoed. Dr. Nichols went directly to Ralph's body.

Lund said to Murphy. "You want to carry on here while I start on the family?"

"O.K.," nodded Murphy.

Lund strode outdoors. Baluta and his guest had retreated to the farther side of his own driveway. Lund wondered behind which of the dark upper windows the beauteous blonde was studying the scene.

He turned left across the Peckham clothesyard and through the gap in the hedge. Where were those four—old Mr. and Mrs. West, their son and their daughter? And why hadn't their chauffeur rushed home to spread cheer?

The dark plain of the lawn was utterly quiet. No sounds of the repellent activities that Lund had left behind had reached the towered probity of the great stone house. Well, he was about to change all that. He went up to the door at the base of the donjon. Although both architectural style and the mood of the moment cried for an alarm bell, there was only a small button to press.

The ring was a long time in being answered. The door swung slowly out. Mr. Virgil West's measured words followed it. "Good evening. Why, Mr. Lund!— Were you looking for Miss Carter?"

He looked like a courteous old dodo who wasn't eager to have a policeman in his house—or in his family.

"No, Mr. West. I'm afraid I shall have to trouble you for a few minutes."

Virgil opened the door. "Come in," he said.

He tramped forward into the middle of a high, beautiful hall. Paneled walls glowed in a soft light. In the center was a vast fireplace and exquisitely carved mantel, the sort of thing that American businessmen of the Eighties paid their agents to rip out of the castles of businessmen of the Italian Renaissance. Flanking the fireplace, broad stairs rose on each side in wide curves, meeting in a landing set with mullioned windows. Virgil halted and turned a tired old face to Lund. "Is something the matter?"

"Yes. There has been an accident. Is Mrs. West at home? And Mrs. Ogden? And the servants?"

Virgil peered into Lund's poker face. "My son and daughter are not at home. Most of the servants are out. We're under-staffed these days. My wife is here. I think you'd better tell me about it right away."

Lund was only a little sorry for him. Any of these people could have killed Ralph Ogden, and almost any of them could have murdered Mattie Peckham. Of this earlier slaughter he no longer had doubts. "Tell Mrs. West I must see her," he said.

"Virgil." The voice that called down to them was as stately as the hall. "Ask the policeman to come up."

Feeling very much of the people, he followed Virgil up to the landing. The queenly Mrs. West swept ahead of them, down deep-carpeted corridors to a bright room with flowered curtains and cushions, and portraits of a little boy and a little girl somewhat sweeter than life.

Lund said, "Mr. Ogden is dead," and looked quickly from one to the other.

Mrs. West's face grew stiffer, Mr. West's more pulpy. Two old people receiving bad news according to their natures.

"Where did it happen?" she asked. "How ..."

"In his car?" the old man wanted to know.

"Mr. Ogden died in Mrs. Peckham's carriage house."

They looked at each other. They seemed stunned. Virgil spoke with difficulty. "You said ... an accident. Was it ... the stag ... that old statue ... did it fall on him?"

"It fell on him."

Charlotte gasped. "We should have made Mattie remove it long ago."

"I know," Virgil said. "I'd completely forgotten it. And no one ever went near the carriage house."

Lund said, "You needn't feel responsible, Mr. West. The iron stag didn't kill Mr. Ogden. It fell on him after he was dead. *That* was the accident."

Virgil's lips were forming "suicide" and "heart attack" but his eyes were round with another fear. His wife said, "You had better tell us."

"Ralph Ogden was murdered."

Old Virgil's mouth worked wordlessly. Charlotte raised an elegant hand to her face.

Lund went on quickly. "I can't give you the details yet. The medical examiner is still with the body. I'm afraid I must ask your help. Is there anything I can get for you?"

What did you do in a house like this? Should he ring for the butler to bring a double carrot wine? Was he a good enough detective to find them a glass of water all by himself? Thank God, neither of them looked very faint. An admirable pair. Or a tough one.

Charlotte West's hands lay quiet against her gray lace gown. "What do you want us to tell you?"

"Do either of you know of any reason why Mr. Ogden might have been killed?"

They didn't know. No reason for the killing. No imaginable killer. No reason even for being in that derelict carriage house.

"When did you last see Mr. Ogden?"

"It was in the middle of the afternoon," Charlotte West replied. "After the rain. I went out to look at the garden. Our car went by, going down the hill toward the center of town. Ralph was in the car with my son and Janet Carter. All the young people waved to me. My husband was sitting in the window of the angle tower above the garden. I don't suppose he saw the car go by. He was ... reading."

"I saw it perfectly," said Virgil testily.

"Did you see Mr. Ogden return?"

He shook his head. "I sat up there all the time my wife was on the lawn. I heard the car come back. No one came into the house. My son isn't back yet. Is he ... over there?"

"No. Did you see the car come back, Mrs. West?"

"I had come into the house before that. To take a rest. My husband was also resting."

This was evidently Elm Street propriety for the Sunday afternoon nap.

"What kind of man," Lund asked, "was Mr. Ogden?"

Charlotte said, "He was my daughter's husband."

Virgil added, "He was a good son to us."

They seemed to think they had covered it all.

"You told me," Lund went on, "that no one ever went near that carriage house. Can you give me any possible reason why Mr. Ogden should do so, and on this particular day?"

Virgil thrust out his lower lip. "No, we can't," he said. "Mr. Lund, isn't that what you ought to find out and tell us? And also the person who killed Ralph? Haven't you the slightest idea who the murderer was?"

Lund stood up. "I could guess," he said. He watched their faces. "I could guess it was the same person who killed Mrs. Peckham."

He heard them gasp, saw their expressions change, but not for him. They were gazing at the doorway.

Louise, in too fluffy furs, was standing there. She spoke, flushed and cheerful, "Who's dead now, Mr. Lund?"

Charlotte West moved swiftly past him to her daughter's side. She put a firm arm around her. "Louise, dear, we have bad news for you."

Louise cried out sharply, the only word that could mean disaster for her. "Ralph?"

Her mother said, "Ralph is dead."

Pallor covered Louise's bright face. She looked at Lund. "Was he murdered, too?"

He nodded.

Her hands came up to her breast, pressed hard. "The snick-a-snee," she moaned. "Someone stole the snick-a-snee."

Then she fainted.

CHAPTER XXI

The Second Sunday Evening, Continued

The body of Ralph Ogden, now cleared of wreckage, lay under the center light. From a shadowy corner Eve, erect, stared out over the corpse to which she had dealt heavy, but quite unnecessary blows. Dr. Nichols pointed to the ugly dark stain around the left and front of the corpse's neck. "Severed jugular," he said. "Easy to do from the rear and above. If he was sitting on the floor. But why the hell would he be doing that?"

"What kind of blade?" Lund thought he knew the answer.

"Can't be sure yet. Thin and smooth. I'd say it was curved. Let you know later."

Murphy beckoned to a table, commandeered from Bridie, on which fishing tackle was laid out neatly. Small, innocent stuff, although in the present circumstances one might take a fish's view of those vicious hooks and barbs. The only knife was a thick, strong blade with one edge deeply serrated.

"She must have taken the weapon away with her," Murphy said.

"So you've picked your suspect?"

"Well," Murphy's broad fingers found his temple. "She's pretty handy with sharp blades, Mrs. Ralph Ogden is."

"You wouldn't have a personal bias, would you?" asked Lund.

Murphy grinned. "Not much of a one." He looked steadily at his tall partner. "Haven't you got a little personal problem of your own, Rik?"

Lund put his hand on Murphy's shoulder. "I've got to talk to her now, and you're coming with me."

In the door of Janet Carter's bedroom Bridie stood guard.

"Huh," she said to Murphy, "come back to finish your job?"

"And for another cup of your su-per-lative coffee, Miss Callahan. How about it?"

"Well," agreed Bridie, "I wouldn't mind a cup meself. As long as you fellers are here. I wasn't leavin' her alone with that one."

Her retreat revealed Dr. Taylor being very soothing to Janet who looked tired, but not otherwise ill. She also looked very pretty and glad to see Eric Lund. She smiled at Murphy.

Dr. Taylor said, "Hail to the Knights of the Rubber Hose!" His stomach didn't feel quite right today. He got up from the bedside chair and beamed at Lund. "Young man bound to succeed. That's what I said to myself when I saw you two at Toni's last night. Lovely girl, lovely little scene, but it didn't fool me. Clear case of Busman's Holiday."

Silence surrounded his departure. Janet said to Murphy, "Won't you sit down? You want to ask me ... things, don't you?"

"Thanks, Miss Carter. We're sorry to have to bother you after what you've just been through." This was true, but he was sorrier for Eric, sitting with his hands in his pockets and an expressionless face.

The girl was mad or hurt or both. If she had fallen for Rik, the doc had made everything just dandy.

Right now she forced her attention on the job in hand and answered his questions straight. She told him why Ralph Ogden had gone to the carriage house that rainy Sunday afternoon, and how she had happened to know about it. No, he hadn't seemed depressed, worried, or frightened.

What had they talked about? Fishing in Minnesota. Later, her cousin, Duncan West, had come in, and they had decided to see a movie and take Ralph along.

"Any special reason for asking him to go?"

The girl glanced toward Lund. "I thought he might like to go."

"Who chose the show, you or West?" Lund asked her.

Janet answered him coolly. "Duncan chose it. *Gory Gangsters.*"

Murphy continued. "So then you went out to the carriage house to invite Ogden. What was he doing?"

She described the tackle boxes and Ralph kneeling in front of them sorting the contents. She told, shuddering, about Eve's forward movement. About Jerry's arrival and the departure for the Arcade.

"Anything special happen in the theatre?" asked Murphy.

"N-no." The directness was gone. She was thinking out her answer. Lund stirred in his chair.

Murphy waited. The silence bothered the girl. She looked at Lund, met his fixed stare and said defiantly, "Ralph left after a little while."

"Why?"

"I … I'm not sure. He wasn't sitting with us. The place was crowded … When I saw he wasn't in his seat, I … left, too."

"Why?"

"I … I thought he had been taken sick. It was awfully stuffy in the theatre. I didn't feel well either."

"Did you find Ogden outside?"

"No. He wasn't in sight. You see, 1 don't know just when he left."

"Did you go back to the show?"

"No. An Elm Hill bus came along just then and I got on."

"How about Mr. West?"

She seemed to remember him for the first time. "I don't know," she said. "I haven't seen him since I left the Arcade."

Lund spoke. "What picture were you seeing when Ogden walked out?"

Janet's tone was all childlike honesty. "I told you. *Gory Gangsters.*"

Lund nodded. The girl let out held breath. Lie number one. Or two or three?

Murphy went on. "You came directly home on the bus?"

"Yes."

"What time did you get here?"

"I'm not sure. Sometime before six."

"Go right in the house?"

"No."

"Why not?"

"It was so dark," she said. "I ... I promised Eric—Mr. Lund."

Lund said, "I told her she knew too much for her own good and she ought to be careful."

"I thought Bridie wouldn't have come home yet. I wandered around the lawn and the garden. And after a while I went up to the carriage house just as I had this afternoon—to see if I could see Eve. And," again she spoke in horror, "Eve wasn't there."

"What did you do then?"

"I opened the door. You know—what I saw."

"You went in?"

"I had to. I had to see if I could help Ralph. I ... there wasn't any pulse. There wasn't any breath. I knew he was dead."

"What did you do then?"

"I came here to the house and—called you. Bridie was at home after all. She heard me. We came out here and waited for the squad car."

"Afraid that someone in the neighborhood might have been the murderer?"

She didn't answer.

"Miss Carter, while walking round the house and the yard, all that time from six o'clock till you called Headquarters at 6:27, did you see anything? Hear anything?"

"Nothing," she said. "Absolutely nothing."

"What happened while you and Bridie were waiting for the squad car?"

"Nothing then, either. As soon as the policemen came, Mr. Baluta came out of his back door and asked us what was wrong. Jerry came out of the Balutas', too, but not right away."

Lund stood up. "Janet—do you know who killed Ralph?"

"No," she said. "Oh, no!"

"You do know, don't you, that this murder of Ogden reopens the question of how Mrs. Peckham died?"

"I know."

"And that we may have to go back even further?"

The girl was pale. She put her hands behind her back. Murphy could see how tightly they were pressed together.

Lund said to her quietly, "I'll come back to see you, Janet. As soon as I can."

As they went downstairs together, Murphy said, "We'd better get hold of the operator at the Arcade Theatre and find out what was on the screen between five and five-thirty. Those third-run spots always have a double feature and a newsreel."

"Right," agreed Lund.

Kind of tough to have to check up on his own girl, but Rik was the guy who would do it. It wouldn't improve his disposition, though. There at the foot of the stairs was Shea with young West. It was Murphy's bet that Rik would now get back a little of his own.

"In here, West," Lund gestured toward the reception room. Behind Duncan's angry back, he raised his eyebrows at Shea and received a shake of the head and a slight wink.

"We'll sit down and talk."

"Will we?" Duncan continued to stand over the seated Lund. "What about?"

"About where you've been since you left the Arcade Theatre at 5:30. You were alone, Mr. West."

Duncan said fiercely, "Suppose you tell me what's going on here. Why are you and your men in this house?"

Lund said, "Sorry, Mr. West. Didn't Shea tell you?" He paused, measuring the apprehension of his victim. "Your brother-in-law, Ralph Ogden, has been murdered."

Duncan sat down then. "Oh, God!"

"He was found in the carriage house in the backyard. That big iron stag had fallen on top of him." Did Duncan look relieved? "Fallen or been pushed."

Duncan said, "It would be easy. Janet almost brought that monster down on us all."

"It wasn't the stag that killed him."

Duncan said, "That big crab with the horrible teeth. It choked him."

Lund said, "You saw it happen?"

"I? God, no! I know nothing about what happened to Ralph. It ... I was thinking of something that almost happened to me. Not important, comparatively."

"I might think differently, Mr. West."

"You seem to know we all went to the cinema this afternoon. Ralph. Janet Carter and I. As we were leaving the carriage house to get into the car, Janet picked up a hideous scissor-like affair quaintly called a gaff and pretended to choke me with it. Of course, it was all in fun, but in the wrong hands ..."

"About this movie you saw. Who suggested going today?"

"Miss Carter."

"She chose the picture, too?"

Duncan hesitated. "No, I did. *Gory Gangsters.*"

"The Arcade," suggested Lund, "isn't a very attractive theatre."

"That's an interesting comment," said Duncan. "My chauffeur made a similar remark when I told him where we were going. Frightful snobs, upper servants."

Lund merely looked more interested. "Did you also suggest Mr. Ogden's going with you?"

"That," said Duncan, "was my cousin's idea."

"Did you object?"

"I did not. But I found it odd."

"Why?"

"Because I had been told two things on my first evening in Watson. One, Miss Carter did not like Mr. Ogden. Two, Mr. Ogden did not like the cinema."

"Who told you that Miss Carter did not like your brother-in-law?"

"Mr. Ogden."

"Did you," asked Lund, "like your brother-in-law?"

Duncan said, "I neither liked nor disliked him. I didn't know him."

"Yes. Mr. West, why did Mr. Ogden leave the Arcade Theatre twenty minutes after he entered it?"

"I—don't know." Duncan's uncertain tone grew firmer as he added, "I didn't know he had gone until after Miss Carter got up and dashed out."

"And you stayed to the end of the show and came out alone. You turned north with the crowd. Where did you go then, Mr. West?"

"An alibi," said Duncan, "would be good to have, wouldn't it? Even though I had nothing against my brother-in-law."

Lund didn't bother to nod.

"I have an alibi," said Duncan. "A perfect one. From 5:45 to ... oh, perhaps 6:30, I was in the periodical room of the Carnegie Library. I am quite sure the not-so-young lady at the desk will remember."

"Probably you were quite a treat to her."

Duncan went on blackly, "From there I came directly—home."

Lund stood up and looked squarely at Duncan. "You realize, don't you, that you've made out a rather good case against one person?"

"I do not."

"Motive, means, and we already know she had the opportunity. It all points to Miss Carter, doesn't it?"

Duncan, too, was on his feet. "Not to me. But I haven't your— professional—bias."

"Mr. West," Lund's tone admitted no more than did his face, "speaking professionally, where were you between ten-fifteen and eleven P.M. on the night of April first?"

"That," Duncan wanted to know, "would be another good time to have an alibi? Yes. Mr. Lund, I have none. I regret it deeply. However, since I can prove that I did not participate in the assassination of my unfamiliar brother-in-law, may I not hope that constitutes exoneration from the alleged destruction of an aunt scarcely less remote?"

Lund said, "How well did you know Mrs. Ogden?"

"How well did I know—my sister?"

Lund looked hard at a suddenly taut face. "Sorry. I should have said the first Mrs. Ogden."

Duncan took a deep breath. "I did not know her at all." He did not question this surprising non sequitur.

"O.K." Lund strode out into the hall where Murphy stood beckoning.

Duncan said, "I should like to see my cousin, Miss Carter. Or are you holding her incommunicado?"

Murphy answered him. "She's up in her room. Go right ahead. And," he added in a low voice to Lund, "Shea's on guard outside the door. Look, Rik, Mrs. Ogden just phoned. She wants you to come over as soon as you can."

CHAPTER XXII
The Second Sunday Evening, Continued

"I'm not very bright," Louise Ogden explained gratuitously, "but you are. *Awfully* bright. So I want to help you *all* I can."

Eric Lund said gently. "Just what do you want to help me to do, Mrs. Ogden?"

"Why, to find out who murdered Ralph."

"Do you know who it was?"

"Yes," she said, "oh, yes! It was the person who killed Aunt Mattie. Don't you think so, Mr. Lund?"

"It could be," he said, "if your Aunt was murdered."

"You know she was." Louise did not look stupid now. "And it wasn't any *queer* person that killed her. Not any tramp or burglar or ... or homicidal maniac. Mr. Lund, you've got to find out, *whoever* it was."

"You don't know who killed Mrs. Peckham?"

Louise's fingers twisted and untwisted together. "I've thought and thought. There were so many reasons why ... Almost anybody could have.... even thought for a while that Ralph might have done it." Tears rose in her throat. "But, now, of course he didn't. He must have been killed because he knew *who* did it. Don't you think so, Mr. Lund?"

He said again, "It could be. Why did you think that Mr. Ogden had killed Mrs. Peckham?"

"Because," she choked, "I would have done it if it had been me, and made no bones about it."

"Yes, Mrs. Ogden?"

She wiped her eyes and went on. "Aunt Mattie was so *mean*. So terribly mean and unfair to Ralph. She was always insinuating that he drank. That was cruel, Mr. Lund. Ralph hardly touched liquor and Aunt Mattie knew why. Because of the night Mariska died. He ..."

"I know, Mrs. Ogden."

She looked up at his pitying face. "How did you know?"

He told her.

"Oh! Then you know about the baby. Mariska was going to have one. The day Aunt Mattie died, she taunted Ralph about it. That maybe it wasn't *his* baby."

"Wasn't it?"

"Oh, it must have been," Louise began positively, but ended, "I—I don't really know. Mr. Lund, all that happened a *long* time ago. I thought you'd ask me a lot of questions about—what you need to know about Aunt Mattie and Ralph, and I could *really* help you."

"I will," he said kindly. "Mrs. Ogden, why do you think your husband was killed with the snick-a-snee?"

"Because," she said, "it was a dangerous weapon. And it had disappeared."

"You mean the Chinese knife that was on the little table in Mrs. Peckham's reception room? The one in the ivory case with a yellow tassel?"

Louise nodded. "It was there on Monday afternoon. I was making an inventory. On Tuesday morning it was gone. Anybody could have taken it."

"Who would have known about it, Mrs. Ogden? Known that it existed and known that it had a sharp blade?"

"Anybody. That is, anybody in—the family. Was that what killed—Ralph?"

"He was killed with a sharp blade. Death must have been instantaneous."

"I'm glad," she said through tears. "Ralph! I ... I'm sorry. Go on, Mr. Lund."

"Have you," he asked, "ever seen a peculiar sort of gaff that your husband kept in his tackle box? Shaped like ice tongs?"

"No," she said sadly. "Ralph never showed me *anything* connected with fishing, Mr. Lund. He kept everything locked in an old tool chest in Daddy's garage. I'm sure he was out there fussing with it, the night Aunt Mattie was killed. After he came back from hunting for Bridie. I saw the light there before I telephoned Janet. I think that during that time ... Janet says it was three-quarters of an hour and I guess she's right, but

Mother wouldn't agree because she doesn't think it's nice to talk so long. But it was really an *extremely* important call ... Well, I think that while I was at the telephone and Aunt Mattie was getting killed, or rather, after she *was* killed, Ralph came out of the garage and ... somehow or other, saw the murderer."

"You had been at home alone all evening. Why did you wait until 10:15 to call your cousin, Mrs. Ogden?"

Louise thought a moment. "Oh, I remember. It was after Daddy and Mother came home from playing contract at Aunt Mattie's and I found out that Florence Kingston was chairman of the committee that's running Janet's pageant. You may think she's a wonderful person, Mr. Lund. I know you're on her committee. But I *know* what she's like. She's ... well, no matter now. I felt I had to warn Janet *right* away. Before she went to work the next morning."

"I understand, Mrs. Ogden. Now you say your husband kept his fishing equipment in your garage. Why, then, did he take it to Mrs. Peckham's carriage house this afternoon?"

"His inheritance. That awful will. Aunt Mattie left it to him. And it killed him." Sobs shook her. "Aunt Mattie killed Ralph even after she was dead. And Duncan's letter! She'll never, never be dead."

It came then in a flood, a whirlpool of tears and free association. When it was over, Louise knew that the bright Mr. Lund was very kind. Mr. Lund knew all about the reading of the will, the search for *Salt Lake Fruit* and its useless return, about the letter that Janet said she hadn't burned; what Ralph had said about its contents, and why Louise thought Duncan, aged eighteen, might have confided in his Aunt Mattie Peckham. And in gratitude for the detective's kindness, Louise added, "Ralph said he knew Janet didn't burn the letter to help Duncan, because she isn't in love with him, Mr. Lund. She likes you a lot better, I'm sure."

Lund, looking as if he would have been glad to exchange a lot of Janet's hypothetical love for a little frankness, said, "Did you know that your husband, between two visits to Mrs. Peckham's carriage house, made a trip to the Arcade Theatre this afternoon?"

"To the ..." Louise gasped. "To the movies? Ralph? Why, he never went near them."

"He went today, with your brother and Janet Carter."

Understanding came to her face. She cried out angrily, "He went to see that girl!"

"I don't understand..."

"I do. Aunt Mattie again. She wanted everybody to promise ... M-Mary Alden. *Candle in the Night*. And he said he didn't know her. That

Polack girl. Helenka Baluta."

It took longer to get that story straight, but Lund did it. Mattie's dinner party, the fellow travelers on the train, the warning to tell no one about the identity of Mary Alden.

"Mrs. Ogden, was it your husband who asked you to remain silent about this or was it your brother?"

"I think it was both," she sobbed, "but Janet was mixed up in it, too. I suppose I shouldn't have told you, but nothing really matters now that Ralph is dead."

Before he left, Lund asked one more question. "Can you tell me how Mrs. Peckham got hold of this rather special information about the identity of the Baluta girl and the movie star, Mary Alden?"

Louise shook her head. "Aunt Mattie always knew everything we wouldn't want her to know," she said.

"Murder," said Bridie Callahan, "is bad." She blew sententiously on the coffee in her saucer.

"So you're agin it?" Murphy asked solemnly. "Well, some feller round here takes a different view. Got any ideas?"

Bridie lowered her saucer and her voice. "Furrin spies!"

"Aren't you sort of seeing things in the night?"

"I am not." Bridie jerked her head angrily. "We had spy talk all over this place for years. Ain't you ever heard of what they make in the Duncan Rifle Works? Lots of people can tell just from the name."

"Yeah, but the war's been over for fourteen years."

"There'll be another along soon," said Bridie.

"Maybe so. I was just kidding you. A sensible woman like you wouldn't dream up spies. You must have someone in mind."

"I sure have," Bridie whispered. "It's that furriner. The chauffeur that calls himself Jerry Witt."

"That's not his real name?"

"Listen, Mr. Murphy. I clean his room every day. Over Mr. West's garage. In that room he's got a black box and it's locked. Decent, honest people don't have to lock up their things. Why, it could have been a pistol in that box and we could all have died in our beds."

"Wasn't it a pistol?"

"It was not. Well, that is ..."

"You thought it was your duty as a citizen," murmured Murphy, withdrawing speculative eyes from the versatile wire pins that skewered Bridie's hard knot of hair.

"Faith and I did! He's got a paper in there covered with a lot of heathen-lookin' words and a gob o' red sealin' wax. And his photygraph pasted in the bottom left-hand corner. And the name written under it ain't Jerry Witt."

"You don't say. What was it?"

"Well, I can't tell you exact. The first word looks kind o' like 'Jerry,' but it's got more o' those letters with tails on 'em. And the last name starts out like Witt, but it's got another yard tacked on, too."

"Say! Anything else in the box?"

"A lot of old jewelry. Dark and kind of junky lookin'. And a picture. A picture of a big stone buildin'. Know what I think? I think it was a prison he was shut up in somewhere in the old country."

Murphy nodded admiringly. "What old country would you guess that to be, Miss Callahan?"

Bridie was positive. "Poland. Just like them Balutas. They're all in it together. Mr. Murphy, we're surrounded by spies."

"So Witt is thick with the Balutas?"

"He's hung around there ever since the old man bought the house. And where did the old man get the money for a house like that? Not from sweatin' in the mill. And that girl and her glad rags. Spyin' is the kindest thing you could say about where *they* come from."

"She could have earned them," suggested Murphy.

"That's what I'm tellin' you. But not by bein' a waitress for Mrs. Johnson. You know. Her that used to have the swell caterin' business right after the war."

"And the Baluta girl used to work for her?"

"Eyah. I don't remember the kid, but my madam did. The very day she died she pointed out the window to where that blonde was struttin' round the backyard in negligee, and she says, 'Bridie, do you remember the little Polish girl who used to pass around the frappé at my big parties?' Funny, I ain't hardly seen the Baluta girl outside the house since. How 'bout more coffee, Mr. Murphy?"

"O.K. by me.... You been expecting more trouble ever since Mrs. Peckham died, haven't you?"

Bridie raised the coffee pot slowly from the stove. "How do you know that?"

Murphy shrugged.

"Well, with things disappearin' right and left from this house."

"Someone's at the door," Murphy said. "I'll go. Oh, it's the Master Mind!"

Eric Lund stepped into the kitchen, sniffing. "Master Nose. How about a cup for me, Bridie?"

"She was just telling me some highly significant facts, Rik," Murphy announced. "We were right in the middle of discussing some mysterious disappearances from the murder mansion."

"Just little things," said Bridie modestly.

"Takes keen eyes to see details," Lund assured her. "What sort of things?"

Bridie licked her lips over the tale of Miss Louise and the snick-a-snee.

"Wasn't there a letter lost, too?" Lund suggested.

"They didn't say so," Bridie told him, "but they was always huntin' in any place where there was papers."

"Duncan was hunting?"

"Not when I was around. It was mostly," she added with reluctance, "Mr. Virgil."

"What about the book?" asked Lund.

Bridie grew scarlet. "What book?"

Lund said, "A book about Mormons. The name is *Salt Lake Fruit*."

"Oh, that!" Bridie was defiant. "Maybe that was gone, but it come back. You can see it right now in the liberry."

Lund glanced at Murphy who winked and improvised. "You wouldn't have been reading it under the covers, would you? If it wasn't stolen, seems as if someone borrowed it."

Bridie's back was flat to him. There was no answer. Murphy nodded slowly at Lund.

Now Bridie eyed them guiltily. "How do we know there ain't been a lot of other things taken, too? Do you fellers know 'twasn't a thief killed Ogden?"

"Poachers, maybe," Murphy suggested, "looking for venison."

"Bridie's serious about this," Lund encouraged.

"I am that! What valuables was he tellin' Miss Janet about this afternoon?"

"So the Carter girl didn't give you your Sunday afternoon off," sympathized Murphy.

"She did and more of it than any member of that family ever did before. And no dinner to get. She's a fine girl. I thought she was kind of queer when she snuk off to call her father long distance before six o'clock on the morning after my madam died. Told him to keep her mother at home from the funeral, she did. Said she couldn't take it, and she'd explain when she saw him. But she's been awful good to me, and I don't like the way people are always pokin' around her room and all over the house. Most every one of them has done it sometime or other. So after I went out on Sunday, I got to thinkin' over how she was alone, and I come back. She didn't hear me. I got a back-door key nowadays."

"And you heard her talking to Ralph Ogden?"

"In the liberry. He was sayin' that he knew she didn't like him much, and then the stair I was on creaked somethin' awful and I had to go farther up where I couldn't hear good. They was talkin' kind of solemn for a while, and then he come over near the door and he says, 'I got something I'd like to show you sometime. I keep it in my tackle box,' he says. 'It's the only place that's one hundred per cent mine.' Them snooping Wests! Ogden could of seen me then if he'd looked the right way, so I had to go upstairs and down the hall where I couldn't hear no more."

Lund put down his empty cup. "What you did hear may be extremely important."

"Maybe so," Bridie admitted modestly, "but you better keep your eyes on that Jerry."

CHAPTER XXIII
The Second Sunday Evening, Continued

The hypnotic quiet of a New England Sunday evening had settled down on Elm Street Hill. Under the Norman towers, Dr. Taylor, having competently dispatched Louise from some hours of sorrow, was urging Charlotte West to abandon her puritanical attitude toward his nice little powders. He was wasting no blandishments on old Virgil, who, he was certain, had always slept through everything. Beyond the hedge a long point of light pierced the Judas window of what had recently been Eve's prison, where Murphy sought painfully for an enigmatic object among the fishhooks. Where the shrubbery was thickest on Mattie's lawn, a plain-clothes man had just taken up his eight-hour stand, and on the opposite side of Elm Street, a second man was preparing to stroll till dawn. Eric Lund looked up at the bright window in the Peckham house, in the room where, last night, he had kissed Janet. Then he rang the Baluta doorbell.

The door opened and the old man stood before him, impassive and stony.

"Sorry to have to disturb you," Lund told him crisply. "I'm a detective of police, investigating the death of Mr. Ogden."

"Yes, sir. You will come in." He gestured heavily toward the sitting room.

Lund glanced appraisingly at a cheap, bright lithograph of a saint with a bleeding heart tacked above a carved chest that only a Hollywood income could buy. He sat down on a hard chair. "That's a bad business next door," he said.

"Yes." It was polite.

"Where were you, Mr. Baluta, when Mr. Ogden was murdered?"

"I stay in house all day." He was patient. "When cops drive into yard, I was in kitchen like I told officer."

"You weren't alone?"

He shook his head. "All day—my granddaughter is in house, too. A friend comes to see us 'bout six o'clock, maybe a little sooner."

"You mean the West chauffeur, Jerry Witt."

"Sure. We drink coffee in kitchen."

"And your granddaughter? Was she in the kitchen with you, too?"

Baluta said slowly, "Yes."

Lund held out his tobacco pouch to the old man. "Do you remember the night Mrs. Peckham died?"

"Sure."

"What do you remember?"

"Big lights. Lots of cars. I call my granddaughter and we look out of kitchen window. Next morning we read in paper old woman is dead."

"Was anyone else with you that evening?"

Baluta seemed to think it over. "No."

"The old woman," Lund encouraged, "wasn't the kind of neighbor you'd be likely to miss very much."

"I do not know her." Baluta's eyes seemed to sink deeper under his rough brows.

"Mr. Baluta," said Lund, "I'd like to talk with your granddaughter alone."

"I get her." He pulled himself up heavily.

"I am here." There was drama in the voice, but it was tired. When the old man had disappeared through the kitchen door, she came toward Lund. "You are little Janet Carter's escort," she said.

Lund rose. Was it only last night that he had seen her rich, shining beauty? Now she was ravaged. Pale, composed, in a straight dark gown, lips smiling, hair lusterless, eyes dead.

"That's a flattering description," said Lund. "I'm usually called a cop."

She said, "Let us sit down."

"The first time we met," he said, "I was in uniform."

"The first time?" She was staring at him. In a minute she would probably recognize the scars.

"Down on River Street. The night that Mrs. Ogden died."

"You!" she said, deep and low.

"Tonight, it is Mr. Ogden who is dead."

"I know."

She had set her chair in shadow. Lund could not read her face. That first death had broken the old man and left her cold. Tonight the reverse seemed true.

"You've come a long way from that night—Miss Alden."

"You know that!" Her tone sharpened. "Someone in that family told you. They promised they would tell no one."

"I'm not concerned with Hollywood publicity," Lund told her. "Miss Baluta—if you prefer—I'm working on a murder case."

Again she said, "I know."

"Miss Baluta, the murder of Mr. Ogden may tie up closely with the death of Mrs. Peckham. With your worry about adverse publicity, Mrs. Peckham's death was rather fortunate for you."

"Mrs. Peckham was also—murdered?"

"I have no evidence of it. Miss Baluta, have you seen Ralph Ogden frequently since your return to Watson?"

Her voice was cold. "I have not. Nor any other member of that household."

Lund smiled. "Aren't you forgetting that we met last evening at Toni Taranto's?" She did not speak and he went on. "Did you know that Ralph Ogden spent this, the last afternoon of his life, seeing a movie called *Candle in the Night?*"

Through tense silence, Lund heard pounding feet on the steps. Before he could reach the door, it was flung open by Shea.

"You're wanted, Loot," he said. His face was flushed.

"O.K." Lund turned to Helenka Baluta. She was standing now, looking frightened. "We'll talk again. You are not to leave town."

"I do not wish to," she replied, her head lifted proudly.

Lund did not need Shea to guide him to the latest scene of violence. In the corner formed by the turn of the driveway toward the Peckham porte-cochere where lilac bushes were thickly clumped, torches burned across the turf. Several figures knelt or stood over a prone body.

Murphy was there and one of the plain-clothes men, and as Lund reached the spot, Janet came from the rear of the house, her arms straining around blankets.

They had turned the man slightly off his face. Above his left ear a spot shone dark red in the torchlight. Blood had meandered down his neck and into his shirt collar and dried.

"Pete's gone for Doc Taylor," Murphy said, "and to tell his folks. Doc's over at their house."

"Who found him?" asked Lund.

"The little girl," Shea answered him, "but I was right behind her."

Janet, kneeling to spread her blankets, looked up at Lund appealingly. "He isn't dead, Eric."

"Knocked cold," Murphy explained. "He seems to be breathing pretty good. He must have been lying here quite a while."

"Bridie's filling hot water bottles." Janet tucked the blankets beneath the body as Murphy and Shea skillfully raised it. "Thank heaven, the kettle was boiling."

Three more people now rounded the house. Dr. Taylor, puffing slightly, the second plain-clothes man like a shadow, and Charlotte West.

"Who did this?" Charlotte's voice was sharp with hate. "Who did this to my son?" She pushed Janet aside and reached for the bruised head. "Duncan, darling. Mother is here."

"Don't do that, Mrs. West." Dr. Taylor was not suave. "Do you want to finish the job? He may have a skull fracture. We must get him to the hospital at once."

"I've phoned Watson General," said Murphy. "Ambulance will be right along."

"Good!" Dr. Taylor put down Duncan's limp wrist. "Pulse not too bad. Ah, just what we need." He took hot water bottles from Bridie, and slipped them under the blankets.

Lund said to Shea, "Shoot."

"It happened like this, Loot. Miss Carter wanted to take a walk. She went out the front door and around the drive here and then across the grass toward the backyard. There was that light in the carriage house and I figured she was lookin' for you."

"Stick to the facts."

"Well, then she saw him—Duncan West—lyin' in her path and she stopped sudden, and I did, too. I sent her for Murphy and stood by till he come. Then he took charge and I come for you."

"Right. What happened when West went upstairs to talk to Miss Carter? That was about 8:20."

"Just 8:20. It's ten o'clock now. Plenty happened, but it was all over in a few minutes."

"I'm listening."

"Well, see Loot, he come up past me, very snotty—I was sittin' almost at the head of the stairs—as if to say, 'Try to stop me.' I didn't, but when he got close to the girl's door, I moved in. Her door was open and she was lookin' at a book. She got up quick. He went right up to her and sez, 'I know why you left the theatre.' She just looked at him. He took hold of her shoulder and she cried out that he wasn't goin' to hurt her after every family murder, and then I took hold of him, and I sez, 'On your way, buddy,' and he didn't linger."

Lund looked grim. From the valley below, the approaching siren rose to them.

"Mr. Lund." Charlotte West spoke from the darkness. "I shall, of course, accompany my son to the hospital."

"Certainly, Mrs. West. I'll drive you in my car."

"I should prefer ..." The noisy arrival of the ambulance cut her short. She moved over to the stretcher on which Dr. Taylor and a young interne were loading the unconscious Duncan. Old Virgil West waddled across the yard to her side. Sorrowfully, he looked down at his son.

Murphy said to Lund, "I suppose you're going to go along to roll the guy. O.K., I'll carry on here with the alibi stuff. See you when you get back. I think I got a little something."

The ambulance passed down the drive. Dr. Taylor, with Virgil West, went off toward the chateau where the doctor had left his car. Murphy, Shea, and the two plain-clothes men stood in a dark knot. Lund seated Mrs. West in his car. At the rim of its lights, a little apart from the faithful Bridie, stood Janet alone. Eric went over to her. For a moment he looked down at the young face. Her eyes were asking him something, but he had no time to find out what it was. He laid his hand awkwardly on her shoulder. "I'll come back," he said.

She managed to smile. "I'll try to save all the bodies I find till you get here."

It was after eleven when Lund returned. Murphy met him under the porte-cochere. Duncan West could have been struck down by almost any member of the three households, wielding almost any weapon of reasonable bluntness and weight. Or none of them could have done it. It all depended on whom you trusted. Jerry reading in his room. The Balutas having supper together in their kitchen. The Wests drinking tea in front of their morning-room fire. Louise, who had been talking to Lund; Bridie, serving coffee to Murphy; and Janet, watched by Shea, were obviously not involved. The only possible time was between eight-thirty, when Leary made a final round of the Peckham grounds before leaving for the night, and nine o'clock, when Pete Hogan, the plain-clothes man, took up his place in the shrubbery beside the carriage house. Duncan had lain deep in the shadow of the lilacs near the house for more than an hour.

"Well, so long, Rik. Here's the little something I promised you. Found it in the biggest bait box, Ogden's own. Hope it gives you ideas. I'm stumped."

He drove away, and Shea opened the front door for Lund.

"Gals are in the kitchen," he announced. "You look all in."

"Thanks. Same to you."

"The Cap's sendin' a relief for me at twelve."

Lund nodded. Suddenly he felt the way Shea said he looked. It wasn't really late. What was wrong with him? He started toward the kitchen, turned instead to the right of the golden oak stairs, and followed the short corridor to the library. Better take a look at the bookcase and see if *Salt Lake Fruit* was really there. He switched on the light and it fell full on the dingy sofa. He sat down on it. It was lumpy and uneven and smelled of old people. Eric Lund raised his feet. The headrest was built to break necks. His neck fell back against it. He was asleep.

Suddenly he was smothering. A mass of soft fibers was filling his nostrils, blinding his eyes. A warm weight was pressed on his chest. Fool, he thought, as he struggled to wake. To expose himself to this in the middle of a murder case! With a mighty effort he raised sleep-paralyzed arms and pushed at the danger.

The weight was gone and the darkness from before his face. He sat erect and stared. On the floor by the sofa, hair awry and eyes blazing, Janet Carter was inelegantly-sprawled.

"I could kill you," she said.

"Too bad," he said, "that I woke up in time to frustrate you."

"Eric Lund." She stared at him, more fearful now than angry. "You don't really think that!"

"Why not? What the hell *were* you doing?"

"I—I hate you," she sobbed. "I—you know very well what I was doing."

He was wide-awake now. "Show me," he said. He held out his arms. Again her loosened hair fell across his face.

"This is pretty nice," he said when she sat up, "but we shouldn't overlook the possibility of that door opening."

Janet got off his knees. "It won't," she said. "I locked it."

"My girl." He reached for her, but she evaded his arms.

"Eat your supper."

"God, what a gal! I'd forgotten I hadn't eaten since breakfast. So that was what was wrong with me. Partly, that is. You have everything."

"Only soup and ham sandwiches and a glass of milk."

"And one more kiss for papa?"

She sat down on the rug at his feet and asked seriously, "How is Duncan?"

"Not bad. There's no fracture, probably not even concussion. He'll be all right when he comes to, except for a headache."

"I'm glad. Eric, did the same person try to kill him, too?"

"I don't know. I want to show you something." He drew an envelope from his pocket. "Do you recognize the handwriting?"

The heavy paper, now yellowed, had a blue Theodore Roosevelt in the corner. It had been posted in Watson on May 11, 1921, to Mr. Duncan West at the Hotel Lutetia in Paris, and the handwriting was that in which the West family had been insulted for sixty years.

"Cousin Mattie Peckham wrote that," said Janet.

He held out his hand for it. "It was in Duncan's pocket."

"But that's not ..." Janet stopped.

"Not the letter she left him in her will. The one she showed you the night she died."

"You know!"

"Everything Louise knows."

"Eric, that's all I know, too. I saw the envelope and just the top of the letter. It was mailed in Paris and the writing looked like a boy's."

"Then what do you make of this?"

Janet took a small square case in her hands. White leather, gold edges, a gold clasp. She pressed the catch. White satin in the left-hand square, white velvet at the right, flattened and blackened in an empty oval.

"What do you think was in that case?" Lund asked her. "A brooch?"

Janet shook her head. "There are no pinholes. The depression and the marks at the rim could be made by a gold setting. It might have been a picture, a miniature on ivory."

"Thanks." He returned it very carefully to his wallet. He saw her face pale.

"You've been through too much, dear."

She took the empty soup dish from the tray on his knees, her face bent over the work. "It's been pretty terrible sometimes, waiting for something to happen."

"You were always sure Mrs. Peckham was murdered, weren't you, Janet? Why were you so sure?"

She looked at him frankly. "It was because of the door. The door and the light. While I was at the telephone. First Cousin Mattie's door closed and *then* the light was turned out in the hall. There was no sound after that. Sometimes I tried to believe that it had happened the other way around, the light out and then the closed door. But I'm sure now."

"And you thought you couldn't hide your fear from your mother? That's why you telephoned your father to keep her at home?"

She nodded. "Bridie heard me?"

"Janet," he got up and put the tray on the table. "Do you know who killed Mrs. Peckham?"

Her eyes did not leave his face. "No."

"Can't you tell me who you suspect?"

"Eric, I can't. I can't, because I ... I suspect everybody."

He walked to the window and stood with his back to her.

"Don't *you* know who did it?"

He turned to her. "From the beginning I was playing a hunch. Years ago, there was a queer case. It seemed simple, but it never smelled right to me. This affair of Mrs. Peckham's didn't look quite right either. There was one man involved, more or less, in both cases. Ralph Ogden was my hunch."

"I know that." Janet's tone was stiff and sharp. "Ralph told me. He said you were a smart policeman. You still are, aren't you?"

He came close to her, the mouth with the little scars set hard. "So that's what they all told you, is it? That I was using you to get the low-down on the family?"

"Detective Lund!" she said.

His arms went around her. "Don't fight me, Janet."

She clung to him, shuddering. "If I hadn't been so—personal about everything," she whispered, "and so suspicious and proud, I would have waited for you to telephone me this afternoon. And Ralph would be alive tonight."

He looked down at the head buried against his shoulder, stroking her light brown hair, wondering if he could probe deeper for the truth tonight.

"It wasn't your fault, Janet," he said finally. "The thing back of all this local hell has been going on too long. Too many knew too much for their own good. Don't forget that you do, too. I'm going now and I'm not coming back till I get to the bottom of it. I'm taking you and the dishes to Bridie." He raised her chin. "Promise me you won't let either her or a policeman out of your sight until the murderer is caught."

CHAPTER XXIV
The Last Day

Al Murphy was leading a scavenger hunt on Elm Street Hill. Hat rammed down on the scalp locks whose desecration had permanently soured him on the tribe of West, he watched his men sift and poke their way through the refuse of the rich. Virgil West watched, too, lower lip thrust out dolefully. Jerry clipped the hedge and hummed his favorite tune, blandly unaware that his black box had again been opened to the public. In a turret Charlotte West knitted beige wool.

Bridie, trotting out coffee and doughnuts, reported that Lund's girl was sleeping late. Not a curl of the blonde's head showed at the Baluta windows. The charwoman was hanging out a big wash and the old man was spading up his potato patch.

It was a dull hunt and not hopeful. For a scrap of paper gone twelve days ago. For a carved ivory case holding a weapon designed for cutting and thrusting and possibly used for same. For a gaff shaped like a giant crab. For an enigmatic object which might have been a miniature and might have been nothing at all. And what houses to grub through. One like a museum, the other like a wastebasket.

Duncan's room had yielded nothing. Ralph's suite was as bare of clues as was his downtown office. From vitrine to ash can, the search must go on and on.

In the heart of town Eric Lund was also hunting. When the door of the Carnegie Library opened in the morning, he was there, smiling at a dry little lady and asking her if it wasn't hard to start the early shift.

It was, she said, and it wasn't. That is, she liked it except when she'd been the last person to leave the night before. Like yesterday. She smiled in response to the gleam in his eye that she thought was sympathy. He had very nice blue eyes, and though he wasn't so fine looking as the dark young gentleman of the previous evening, he was an unusual visitor. The scars around his mouth were really quite dashing.

Without realizing how it happened, she was telling him about the dark young man, very gentlemanly, but a little wild, too, and with such an odd request for a Sunday afternoon. Their staff, of course, was greatly reduced—the Depression—really she didn't have the time to do what he asked, but she had done it. Down in that dirty vault. Hunting for an hour and a half. Of course, he had offered to help, but she couldn't allow anyone in the stacks without a written request from a property owner.... Yes, the papers, she was afraid, were still lying on the periodical room table. She hadn't had time... the library closed at 7:30 on Sunday. The gentleman was the last to leave. Except, of course, herself.

Lund asked to see the last Sunday's *New York Times* and was shown to the table still cumbered with Duncan's research. Whatever had driven West from the dingy Arcade to this equally odd spot, he had not bothered to conceal a motive. The dusty bound volume of the *Watson World-Democrat* for the year 1920 had been left open at the issue for December 25. There could be no doubt as to which front-page story Duncan had been reading. SOCIETY BRIDE A SUICIDE.

"The book isn't in my way. Please don't move it. I'm sure a page boy will do it for you later." And Lund was left alone.

That old story. Almost his first day as a rookie cop. He could still see the little room as if it were a tableau on a stage. All centered around the dead girl with diamonds and sables and a *risus sardonicus*. And her epitaph was the cautious gentility of the *Watson World-Democrat*. "It is said she was a princess in her own country. She was about to become a mother."

Lund thanked the librarian and walked out. He got into his car, glanced at an address in his notebook and drove north. Duncan's alibi for the hour of Ralph Ogden's death was clear. Nothing else about him was. Frowning, Lund turned into a bungalow neighborhood, and stopped before a Cape Cod cottage.

Mrs. Lyle Swanson was plump and pink-cheeked. Owing to a recent satisfactory experience involving the recovery of a stolen Spitz, she was inclined to view the police as human beings.

"And it's nice to see a Scandinavian boy doing so good. The Irish are all right, but, you know ..."

Lund did, thinking of Janet and her hopeful pageant. "We are trying to locate a girl who lived here about twelve years ago. We don't know very much about her, except that she worked for a cateress named Mrs. Florence Johnson. I understand that you were working for Mrs. Johnson about that time, Mrs. Swanson."

"Yes, I was," Mrs. Swanson replied, looking important and serious, "but not much longer. In 1921, I got married and Mrs. Johnson, she died that next spring."

"Did you know most of the girls who worked for Mrs. Johnson?"

"Oh, I knew them all real well. There weren't more than six or seven of us, except for awful big parties. Mrs. Johnson would only hire the best."

"She had the finest trade in town," Lund suggested.

"That's right. I guess everybody knew that."

"Well, then," said Lund leaning easily back in an overstuffed plush chair, "you can probably tell me something about a young girl named Baluta."

"Baluta?" She wrinkled her very white forehead. "Baluta? Oh, the Polack girl. Helen ... no ... well, something like that. Helen with something crazy tacked on to the end. She was a foreigner."

"Helenka Baluta."

"Oh, sure. That's it. You know, we girls all thought it was funny that Mrs. Johnson would hire a Polack. But you know, the girl did real well. Her grandfather or something had worked for higher-ups in the old country, and she had learned a lot from him, I guess."

"What sort of girl was she?"

Mrs. Swanson thought this over. "She was a quiet little thing. Of course, she couldn't talk so good. She was kind of hard to understand sometimes."

"Light or dark?"

"She was a blonde. The last few times I saw her she looked kind of washed out. You know," she lowered her voice, "we all thought she was in the family way."

"Do you remember when you saw her last, Mrs. Swanson?"

"Well, no, I don't. She was still working with us in the fall ... that is, in 1920, but I kind of think she dropped out before Thanksgiving. I remember we were awful short-handed that season—But, say, I've just remembered something about Helenka. Maybe this will really help you. I don't just know the details, but she got in with some rich people and had her picture in the paper. I think it was the next spring after we was all working together. So she couldn't have been going to have a baby."

Lund took an envelope from his breast pocket, the same envelope he had handed to Janet Carter. Inside was a newspaper clipping. He took it out and handed it to Mrs. Swanson.

"That's her." She looked closely at the smudged picture of Miss Helenka Baluta who played the lead in *The Swan*, presented by the Watson Little Theatre. "May 15, 1921," she read from the top of the clipping. "My, that's a long time ago."

"Is this a good picture of Miss Baluta?" Lund wanted to know.

"Well, it's as good as any you see in the papers. I hope Helenka ain't in trouble...."

Lund put the clipping back in the envelope that had carried it to Paris, twelve years ago. "We're just interested in getting a little information about her work-record in Watson. You've been very helpful."

"Well, I'm glad to hear it. Seems as if I hadn't had much to tell you."

In the doorway he paused. "Mrs. Swanson, were you surprised to read that Helenka Baluta was starring in a play?"

"You know," she said, "I was. I'd always figured her to be kind of dumb. I guess she must have been a good actress all the time."

The morning went on and Lund proceeded through the schedule in his notebook. He drove to the Watson General Hospital where Duncan West lay, slowly regaining consciousness but not yet able to talk to the police. He saw a copy of Mattie Peckham's will. He sat for an hour while Judge Hawes, in windy fashion, discoursed on the financial condition of the West family. It wasn't good, but with the assured sale of the chateau to the Longvale Club for a fair price and for cash, it didn't look as though either Virgil or Charlotte would have been driven to murder. Not that pair. Ralph's insurance business was doing well and he had a modest income from the estates of his parents. The trust fund provided for Louise and Duncan by their Grandfather Duncan, although diminished in value by the Depression, was still paying each of them five thousand dollars a year. Lund had to admit that in this case his favorite motive for murder was pretty weak.

Back at the police station Lund lit his pipe, tilted back his chair and did some thinking. He knew the danger of playing his hunches, but he also knew their value. Suppose for the moment that everything he knew about all the people in those three houses really made one case. How could you link them all together? Twelve years ago there had been two girls with no bond between them except their national origin. Neither girl apparently had any vital relationship to the West-Peckham clan. Helenka Baluta had worked once or twice in their kitchens; the Princess Mariska had been a guest at a dance. But there was another thing those two blondes had had in common. They were both said to be pregnant. Those children had fathers. Fathers from the West-Peckham clan? Well, Mariska's husband had later married into the family. How about Helenka's lover?

There was an obvious choice for the part, and the obvious is frequently right. In September 1920, Duncan West, aged eighteen, "a horrid boy with an I-Know-The-Facts-Of-Life air," had been in some kind of trouble. From her Crow's Nest overlooking the whole neighborhood, Mattie Peckham could easily have spied on him taking a stroll with Helenka among the hillside daisies. Well, Duncan had confided something to his dear Aunt Mattie Peckham, and she had probably advised him to leave town. He had gone to Paris, liked it, and stayed. But sometime, probably soon after his departure, he had written her a letter, a clear, incriminating, boyish letter. The old lady kept it. Her answer might well have been the clipping in the envelope addressed in her hand, which Lund had removed from Duncan's pocket in the hospital. Whoever had knocked him out had not searched him. In contrast to the deaths of Mattie and Ralph Ogden, nothing seemed to have disappeared with the assailant.

Old Mattie would have had the time of her life, following the career of Helenka and hanging on to that letter. Helenka comes home a movie star, Duncan comes home the same day. Both of them would have been glad to see her dead.

But how did Ralph come into the picture? His unhappy wife had been "about to become a mother." The mother of a child unreliably reported not to have been his. Was Duncan the father of Mariska's child? Not likely. A raw kid and that cold, white beauty. The descriptions, though, were Janet's, the impressions of a child of ten or eleven years. There was another possibility: that Ralph was the father of Helenka's child. There had been something wrong in the atmosphere of the Baluta house on the night Mariska died. Ralph might well have ignored Helenka in his grief. And the girl had a talent for acting.

Whatever the mess was, whoever the fathers were, you could bet that Mattie Peckham had known all about it and that it had been the death of her. Two fathers, three murders or murderous assaults. And why not a fourth? Why not the murder of the Princess Mariska by her husband

and his mistress? No, the police wouldn't have been that dumb—he hoped.

Lund banged the front feet of his chair flat on the floor and went to work. There were ten people in the three houses who might conceivably have wanted to murder Mattie Peckham. Of these, two were definitely out. One was Bridie who was known to have watched her niece win a tap-dancing contest at Hibernia Hall and to have reached the Peckham house in the company of the West waitress after the police had arrived. The other was Louise with her forty-five-minute telephone call beginning too soon after her parents' return home to have permitted her to commit murder and come back. Janet, Lund admitted, had had fifteen minutes in which to operate before Louise phoned. Duncan and Ralph were without alibis. Taking a walk, fussing with fishing tackle at night in an empty garage. Jerry, according to Murphy's latest report, had offered the archaic excuse that he was with a lady; the truth would have to be sweated out of him and he, Murphy, would be glad to do it. Then came the two pairs who offered mutual alibis. Virgil and Charlotte, Helenka and her grandfather. Together, they said, on the night Mattie was killed, at the hour when Ralph was stabbed, when Duncan had been knocked senseless and left in the bushes.

O.K. Eight people could have done it, alone or in pairs, trios, or quartets. Who had the strongest urge to do so? Not Janet, unless she were desperately in love with Duncan. Lund thought he had evidence to refute that one. Not Jerry, unless he was in league with "them spies." It would, of course, have been common knowledge among the servants that the Peckham side door was always unlocked on Thursday evenings.

Duncan's motive was strong. How strong would depend on the contents of the letter. It looked as if Mrs. Peckham's visitor had intended to secure the letter, and murder had been done impulsively. However, the opposite could have been true; the letter could have been a bonus to murder.

Ralph Ogden's motive was not so clear, but there had been bad blood between him and the old woman. And, again, how many people beside himself had Duncan involved in the letter? Ralph might well have struck to save the honor of a dead wife.

Virgil and Charlotte would be suspects only if the contents of the letter exposed their son to disgrace. One would think that a little lechery twelve years gone would not have come in that category. For those other two with the ambiguous alibi, the case was different. The broadcast of a delinquent girlhood could be fatal to the career of a movie star now featured as a pure New England lady. In the twenty-four hours between Mattie's dinner party and her death, Duncan—or Ralph—could have informed Helenka of the letter, and Grandpa could have gone along to help her. Jerry's knowledge of the family habits would have been useful at this point.

Eight suspects, two murders, or three or four. One murderer? Two or three? Hell, Lund was sick of speculation. He wanted more facts. He was going after them now.

The telephone rang on his desk.

"Hey, Loot," said the policeman at the PBX, "there's a guy here says you asked him to meet you for lunch. Name's *Mr.* Toni Taranto."

CHAPTER XXV
The Last Day, 5 P.M.-6 P.M.

Before a pier glass lighted at each side by long romantic tapers, a girl regarded her image with wide, steady eyes. Fair braids lying on her slim shoulders gave her a childish air. She raised a braid in each hand, crossed them at the top of her head, pinned them there. Her face, beneath the shining crown, was beautiful and strong.

She opened lovely lips. Creak, grate, rasp. Some of the katzenjammer resembled human speech.

Lund looked at the luminous dial on his wrist, and left the Arcade Theatre.

The Baluta front door was ajar. Two people standing just inside were not glad to see Eric Lund. The woman looked at him as if he were a collector to whom she owed very little. Silent, she led the way into the living room. Jerry followed, whistling softly.

"Nice tune," commented Lund.

"You know the *Pavane* of Ravel?" Jerry's eyebrows suggested that music appreciation was not taught in police schools.

"I know it. A dance for a dead princess." Lund sat down in the hard chair facing those two on the settee. "I know the tune. I know why you go around whistling it. Of course, you may not know yourself. It could all be in your subconscious."

Jerry's eyes were brilliant, his cheeks red. The actress was utterly quiet. The white narcissus at her breast was too heavily sweet.

"You can't get that tune out of your mind, can you?" said Lund. "Because the princess is not dead."

She looked as if her heart had ceased to beat.

Lund let her sit that way for a while before he said, "Did you think you could get away with it forever, Mrs. Ogden?"

She moved her blond head wearily. Her voice was husky. "I thought it was possible. I've had bad luck."

"So," said Lund, "had Mr. Ogden."

Her face twisted. "I know. I know." She did not look like a film star now.

Jerry sprang up. "You will stop this!"

Lund's quiet tone was a command. "Sit down—Prince Jerzy Witkowski!"

The jet moustache seemed painted on the man's white face. "You have been going through my private papers."

"Certainly. It happens to lie within my rights. Following a couple of murders. I have also been talking with one of your friends."

"I trust that you gathered much valuable information?"

"I learned," said Lund calmly, "that you are the younger son of an impoverished family. That you had your way to make and not much training or business ability to help you out. That you're quite sensibly earning your living in the way you're best fitted."

"Toni told you that!"

"Yes. You needn't be so hot about it. After all, *he's* a smart businessman."

"Your prohibition laws are absurd."

"Would you like to say the same thing about our laws against murder?"

Witkowski sat down again beside the woman. "Of whose murder do you accuse me?"

"I'm not accusing you." Lund looked at Mariska Ogden and back at Witkowski. "You two are in love. You come from the same kind of family. Assuming that you might like to marry, Ralph Ogden stood in the way. I think an illegal marriage would not appeal to Mrs. Ogden. She has been very careful during the past twelve years."

Mariska answered him with dignity. "You are right. Mr. Lund, how did you know about that Christmas Eve?"

"Something was wrong about the picture," Lund told her. "At the time I didn't know what it was. I do now. It was your hair."

Her hand went to the shining blond locks hanging today on her shoulders. "My—hair?"

"You were wearing it in braids," he said, "down your back. A girl of twenty who wanted to be a hundred per cent American wouldn't have gone around looking like a peasant."

There was respect in her rueful smile.

"And now I know why you did it. You used to wear your hair in braids pinned up around your head like a crown, didn't you? The night Helenka died there wasn't much time to fix up a disguise. So you took the pins out of your hair."

She nodded. "How could you know that, after all these years?"

"I saw a movie today," said Lund. "*Candle in the Night*. A girl stood in front of a mirror and pinned up her pigtails. What goes up can come down."

Witkowski reached for Mariska's hand and clasped it. He said defiantly, "Are these petty details of the slightest significance?"

Lund ignored him. "You don't remember the first time you met Janet Carter. She hasn't forgotten it. No, she didn't recognize you when you met again, not consciously, anyway. But she kept thinking about the dead Princess Mariska, and she told me the story of her first glimpse of you. In a mirror. With lights burning at each side. Janet described that scene on Saturday night. On Sunday afternoon, she saw *Candle in the Night*. She and Ralph Ogden."

The woman's teeth bit deep into her lower lip.

"It wasn't strange that old Baluta was harder hit than you were by that girl's death. I suppose you got him to play along with you because in the old country he'd practically been owned by people like you."

"You know a great deal, don't you?" The Prince Witkowski still tried insolence.

"What I know," said Lund, "is no more dangerous to Mrs. Ogden than what Mrs. Peckham knew. Mrs. Peckham was murdered."

"Mr. Lund ..."

"Wait a minute. Your husband"—He saw her wince—"Your husband went to see *Candle in the Night*. He came home and was stabbed to death. What did Duncan West know about you," Mrs. Ogden?"

She turned to Jerzy Witkowski. Between them silent conference took place. And in that silence the doorbell rang.

The door leading to the kitchen swung open. Old Baluta, without a glance at the group in the living room, trudged across the white hall and opened the front door. A man flung him aside and came wildly into the living room. It wasn't immediately easy to recognize him as Duncan West. He had no tie and his shoestrings were dangling. His unshaven, tanned skin no longer suggested Riviera sun. Ragged hair stood up on his head, away from the white patch with a dark, bloody center. His eyes were fixed on Mariska Ogden. She rose slowly. Duncan halted six feet from her. He spoke quietly.

"You murderess."

She did not move or speak. Sickening fumes drifted through the room from the dressing on his head and from the flowers crushed at her breast.

Duncan said, "You killed Helenka."

"I did not kill her." Mariska's voice was clear and cold. "I have not killed her or anyone else. It was you who killed Helenka Baluta."

"That's a lie. I was in Paris. I have never actually known that she was dead until you told me now."

"Helenka committed suicide," said Mariska. "You were the cause."

Duncan swayed. He sank into the chair that Lund pushed forward, and bowed his head in his hands.

Old Baluta watched him, immovable in the doorway. Witkowski slid the handkerchief from his cuff and touched his forehead. Lund said to Mariska, "This is where you tell a straight story about December 24, 1920."

She sat down. "I think you know most of that story. My marriage was not happy. The main cause, other than my own ignorance and immaturity, was my mother-in-law. My husband was ... oh, I suppose not very grown-up. America, the land of freedom, seemed a prison to me. For one of my religion, there can be no divorce. On that evening, my husband went out to celebrate alone. That gave his mother a chance for the final insult. She sent me to a drugstore to buy poison for rats. Rats would naturally move into any house occupied by foreigners. She always made everything quite clear.

"I bought it. The errand gave me an excuse to get away from the house and visit—my grandfather."

She smiled at the old workman. "For twelve years I have conditioned myself to think so of Mr. Baluta. Even in my dreams. I have been proud to do so."

Steve Baluta did not look at her.

"He was at home. And Helenka. She looked sick and pale and was huddled in a shawl. But I was too full of my troubles, too unused to thinking of people except in relation to myself, to wonder about her. I told my story. About the poison, and that it was mainly strychnine, that there was enough to kill a herd of wild horses. —Her grandfather was shocked by such treatment of a princess. Neither of us saw Helenka pick up my purse and leave the room ... We heard one scream from the bedroom and a fall. She was dead when we picked her up.

"There was nothing I could do for her. There was something I could do for myself.... I could try for freedom .... I did it ... I and Helenka's grandfather."

Lund said dryly. "You could easily have failed. Your mother-in-law might have come to River Street. Your husband might have been sober."

"But what of that?" she smiled. "The family scene would have been unattractive, but my husband would finally have been convinced that I was desperately unhappy. Something would have been done."

"You had bought poison," said Lund. "You had tampered with a body. It's unattractive to be suspected of murder, Mrs. Ogden. Weren't you even afraid of that?"

Her face, older than it had ever looked before, was still beautiful and proud. "I was afraid of only one thing. One thing I did not know existed until I heard you tell Ralph about it. The father of Helenka's child. The unknown man who could come back and expose me."

"And when you finally met him, you tried to kill him with a blow on the head."

She hesitated. "I ..."

Witkowski came back to her side.

"I done it." Baluta moved into the center of the room. "I wait twelve years."

Duncan raised his head. "I wish to God you had finished the job."

The eyes under the shaggy brows were fixed on Duncan's wound. "I don't bring Helenka to America to live like in old country. Masters from castle, peasant girls ... Helenka don't know no boys. She was good girl. But up here on hill ... Same thing as old country. I never know about her till she's dead. I never see you. I wait. I get old. I think I like to live in house right here."

"Was it Mrs. Peckham who told you about Mr. West and your granddaughter?" Lund asked.

"Old witch woman don't tell me nottin'. But when she stop talkin', I know. I wait for Mr. Duncan West. Day after that, man come to my house. *She*," he glanced at Mariska, "don't know him. He tink he know her. I don't have to wait no more."

"Was that the day Mrs. Peckham died?"

"Yah. I got good look at the feller in front window of her house. Girl get scared and cop come out to chase me. *He* was wit'." He gestured toward Witkowski. "He give me time to get away. I wait for good chance."

"You got your chance last night. What a night!" Duncan said. "That afternoon Janet Carter had told me that Ralph's first wife had killed herself in the Baluta shack down by the riverbank. On Christmas Eve, 1920. When we got to the theatre *Candle in the Night* was on the screen. The film my malignant aunt had wanted us all to see. Well, I saw it, and knew that Mary Alden had never been Helenka Baluta. Who she was I didn't know, but when Ralph staggered out and Janet rushed after him, I had most of the answer.

"The proof was in that old newspaper." Duncan quoted bitterly. "'She was about to become a mother.' ... God, she was only a child herself.... I headed straight for this house. I had a score to settle with the famous Miss Mary Alden. Then the police stopped me. Not for long. You," he said to Baluta, "were more effective. It took me another day to escape from the hospital."

"I am just comin' from garden. I forget and leave spade out there. I see you. I don't wait no more."

"Why didn't you hit hard enough to finish the job?" Duncan asked pleasantly.

Baluta shook his heavy old head. "Too long ago. T'ings don't seem to matter so much no more."

Duncan nodded. "I know. As for you," his tone to Mariska was scornful, "I was stupid enough to accept you at first. I should have known at once that you were not Helenka. She could never have been anything but generous and kind."

"Mr. West," said Lund, "do you want to charge Baluta with assault?"

"God, no!"

"That clears up a small part of the mess. Helenka Baluta killed herself. As for the assumption of her identity by Mrs. Ogden, that is no particular concern of the police."

Mariska drew a deep breath. She leaned back against a red cushion. Jerzy Witkowski murmured into her gold hair.

"So you *were* afraid?" Lund went on. "The deception harmed no one. That is, legally. That, I assume, is what you are concerned with.... Well, I'm still very much concerned with two unsolved murders in which all of you should have a certain interest. Would any of you care to revise or amplify your statements concerning your whereabouts on Thursday, April first, from 10 to 11 P.M.? And on Sunday afternoon, April eleventh, from five-thirty to six o'clock?"

"I would," Duncan said in a tired voice.

"O.K. Then I'll have a police car rush you back to the hospital. I gather you left without a release."

"Quite." Duncan's hand scraped over his rough chin, touched a bare path of scalp shaven wide behind the stained and odorous bandage. "When I left the house next door at ten o'clock, my aunt had just informed me that she was about to show a letter to Janet Carter that I had written to her during my first winter in France. The letter concerned Helenka. You can guess the story: My aunt had seen us together more than once. The last time was the night of a party at her house. Helenka was one of the waitresses. We went into the garden.... Aunt Mattie was most sympathetic. I was being unfair to the poor little girl, et cetera. I ought to go away while I had the chance.

"I knew I had been behaving badly, but I thought I'd been careful enough so that there was no danger for Helenka. After I had been in Paris for a while, I knew better. I began to worry about her." He looked at the old man. "Believe me, I hadn't set out to seduce Helenka. She was the sweetest person I have ever known. She couldn't speak English very well. We had a hard time talking.... It happened.

"I wrote to my aunt and asked her to find out whether Helenka was going to have a child. If so, I'd come home and marry her. That was the letter Aunt Mattie was planning to show the only other girl I have thought of marrying."

His look at Lund was hostile. "I suppose you have the answer I received to my letter. It would have been easy to get under the somewhat unsportsmanlike circumstances. Miss Alden," he addressed her mockingly, "it might interest you to know that my aunt sent me a newspaper clipping concerning a play at the local Little Theatre which starred Helenka Baluta. The accompanying picture did justice neither to you nor to—her. I accepted it as authentic, however, which made it easy for you to deceive me for a little while after we both returned to Watson."

He turned back to the detective. "This started out to be my alibi for the Peckham murder, didn't it? I really haven't one. I carried out my aunt's ironic errand to mail another letter. There was a light in the sunroom of this house and I saw the glamorous Mary Alden playing a rather thorough love-scene with my father's chauffeur.... I tramped the town for an hour or more with lots of jolly things to think about."

Mariska held a restraining hand firmly on Witkowski's shoulder. "We were together," she said, "at ten and at eleven."

"Right," said Jerzy Witkowski.

"And where were you, Mr. Baluta?"

"In kitchen all the time. When cars come next door, I tell *her* to send *him* to see what goes on."

"Now, Mr. Baluta, what about yesterday afternoon between five-thirty and six o'clock?"

He said doggedly, "We drink coffee in kitchen like I told."

Lund said, "You agree, Witkowski?"

It was Mariska's proud voice that answered. "We were together. In my room."

"Thank you." Lund's tone expressed civility. "We'll be on our way, West."

Duncan, hot with fever, did not refuse the detective's arm. They went out to the Peckham driveway where a police car was parked.

"For the love of ..." Murphy spoke to them from the front seat. "If you haven't caught Fugitive Freddy. Me, I haven't caged a fly all day. Listen, Rik, I've got to pull out of here in a hurry. There's been a hold-up in South Watson. Cap's sending me out and Hogan, too. Be back as soon as I can make it."

"O.K.," said Lund. "You have to go by the General. Leave Mr. West there, will you? Let him do the explaining. What goes on next door?"

"Nothing." Murphy was disgusted. "Louise Ogden went out an hour ago. To the undertakers, and then to the hospital. Sullivan's tailing her. Mrs. and Mr. West were in their sitting room all day till we started to give it a going-over, and then they came over to this house."

"Shea in the house?"

"Nope. We're too short of men now, Rik. He comes to the back door every half hour and Bridie reports to him. Here he is now. Be seeing you."

He drove away with Hogan and Duncan West.

Lund looked at his watch. Six-thirty. Twenty-four hours since he had looked down at Ralph Ogden's crushed and wounded body. Shea fell into step beside him, his torch cutting a path in the early April dusk.

Behind the house the lighted kitchen window sent out blazing squares. Shea climbed the back steps and knocked on the glass of the door. No step answered him. The faint tick of the kitchen clock was the only sound.

Shea rattled the knob and beat a tattoo. Lund mounted a bulkhead under the farther kitchen window and peered in.

"Get busy on the door," he ordered Shea. "Bridie's in there. With her head down on the table. Can't tell whether she's dead or alive."

A minute later they stepped over shattered glass into Mattie Peckham's cavernous kitchen. The warm smell of baking meat filled the neat room. Lund bent over Bridie. He raised the head from her arms, folded on the red-checked table cloth. No blood, no bruises, no soft wet spots beneath the tightly combed hair. She muttered slightly without opening her eyes.

"Drugged, ain't she?" asked Shea.

Lund nodded. "Sleeping pills, probably. Dr. Taylor has been handing them out right and left. Call the Department doctor, and get some coffee started. I'm going to look farther."

The grotesque hall, dim in the light of one small lamp on the table behind the grizzly, was empty and soundless. There was no one in the drawing room or the small reception room. Without noise Lund slipped along the dark corridor leading to the side entrance and the library. Then he heard the steps. Slow, heavy steps, muffled by old carpet. Rising steps. They stopped. Then came a shuffling.

Someone had reached the top of the first flight of stairs and was proceeding down the second-floor corridor. Lund leaped up the stairs. Weak light came distantly from the front of the house. There was no one in sight. But he could hear the steps. Mounting, mounting again. Somewhere in this devil-designed house there must be a staircase to higher floors.

Lund turned a darker corner and found it. A short flight of stairs, very steep, leading to a closed door. Light showed beneath the door. A voice murmured behind the black panels. The heavy old man had reached the top step. His right hand went into his coat pocket, drew out a gun, leveled it. His left hand slowly turned the knob of the door.

CHAPTER XXVI
The Last Hour

When tea was over in the library, Cousin Charlotte folded her knitting. She smiled at her husband and said, "Don't you want to look at the paper?"

Cousin Virgil's answer, measured even by his standard of velocity, came forth very slowly. "Well, no, Mama. I think I might like to take a little nap."

"Virgil West!" Charlotte slipped the knitting into her bag and hung the bag on her arm. "I don't see how you can. After drinking that bitter tea of Bridie's. I don't expect to close my eyes all night." She rose and picked up the tray with the three cups and Mattie's squat, ugly silver service. "No, no, Janet, I'll take it out to the kitchen. You sit here and have a nice little visit with Cousin Virgil."

She passed from the room, a silver figure delicately wafting the fragrance of mignonette.

Janet got up from the couch. Cousin Virgil, his lower lip sagging toward his chin, watched her through half-closed eyes. He was changed in the day since Ralph had died. Yesterday morning he had seemed to menace her. Tonight he looked broken and very old. She had never heard him admit before that he ever napped. Could he be playing a part? Not likely. But, as she had told Eric, she suspected all the family.

Cousin Virgil picked up the *World-Democrat* from the center table, and lowered his glasses on his nose. Janet walked over to the bookcase and looked at the unpalatable titles. Behind her there was a soft swish. The newspaper was on the floor. Cousin Virgil was manifestly asleep.

Janet tiptoed to the door. She would join Bridie in the kitchen.

"Darling," softly Cousin Charlotte called down the black well of the stairs, "come up here just a moment. I've found the best light for measuring your sweater."

Janet looked up into the ugly dark. Well, just for a minute. She went up the stairs and along the corridor at the end of which Cousin Charlotte stood smiling.

"Up here," she said. The short flight of stairs led to the nonfunctional doghouse overlooking the family hedge. In the cluttered little room a student lamp with a strong bulb stood on the desk where Cousin Mattie Peckham had added up her accounts. A low chair with its back to the door was at the left of the lamp.

Cousin Charlotte sat down in the chair. She took out her knitting, the sweater of soft beige wool that Duncan had said was the color of Janet's skin. It was almost finished.

"Sit down on the floor here in front of me, dear," said Cousin Charlotte. "No, with your back to me. Closer to me. I want to fit it across your chest."

The soft wool tickling her chin was pleasanter than Cousin Charlotte's dry fingers.

"Janet," said Cousin Charlotte, "are you going to marry Duncan?"

There was only one possible answer. "No, Cousin Charlotte."

"Are you going to marry that policeman?"

"I—I don't know."

The hands on Janet's shoulders were not gentle. "You are intimate with him. You have told him everything you know, haven't you?"

The sweater slipped to Janet's lap. One of Cousin Charlotte's hands held her shoulder. The other held something before her eyes.

"Have you told him about this? Take it."

Janet obeyed. An ivory oval framed in gold. The image of her childhood dream. The Princess Mariska at twenty. The girl Ralph Ogden had loved. She started to turn to Cousin Charlotte.

She could not turn. Something held her neck like a vise. Cold points pressed forward and inward toward her throat. Teeth dug into the nape.

There was laughter in Cousin Charlotte's voice. "Did you think you could look at that picture and live?"

Janet stared dizzily ahead. There was a door. The door, locked since the house was built, that opened on nothing.

"Ralph was looking at the picture, too.—I heard Duncan telephone Jerry that you and he were going to the Arcade. When I saw Ralph in the car with you, I knew something would have to be done. Anything would be better for Louise than the knowledge that his first wife was still alive. Ralph couldn't have kept away from that woman. Luckily, he came home alone, and went straight to the carriage house. For that picture. It was easy to settle everything with the snick-a-snee. He was sitting on the floor just as you are now."

Janet moved cramped toes toward the door. The door began to move slowly outwards.

"I have oiled it," Cousin Charlotte explained. "It is a long way down to the brick walk. I am sorry, Janet. I am sorry about the others, too. But it all had to happen. When you all came home and Mattie told us about the letter. It was very simple to get the letter. I have it here in my bag. I thought it unwise to burn it that night, in case something was suspected and the stove was searched. Then I found out that Duncan would never be at peace until he knew where it was. The day the will was read, I planned to slip it into *Salt Lake Fruit*. But the book was gone and I had no other opportunity."

For the first time there was real regret in her voice. Janet moved her neck ever so slightly. The pressure increased chokingly.

"I am sure you know enough about this instrument to remain quite still," said Cousin Charlotte. "It is really very clever. I am glad to have a chance to use it."

How many Great Northern pike, unconquerable warriors a moment before, had Janet seen impotent in those aluminum teeth and jaws? She wondered if, when the last pressure had been made and released, there would be scraps of her skin mixed with the fish scales embedded in those cruel fangs.

"Of course," Cousin Charlotte explained, "it was unnecessary to kill Mattie because of the letter. It was easy to take. I am fifteen years younger than she was. After I had it, she smiled at me. She said that I might think that I had protected my son, but she could still tell my daughter that she was a bigamist. She told me what she knew. She knew more about my children than I did. I could count on Louise's regrettably loquacious telephone habits, but I did not need so long a time. Mattie died quickly."

The points clutched, relaxed again. Cousin Charlotte's free hand pulled the miniature from Janet's weakened grasp.

"She's a pretty girl, isn't she? She won't talk. Duncan won't talk. Virgil won't talk. You would talk. To that policeman. So you are going to die."

The points crept in deeper, pressing Janet into blackness. She could feel herself being edged toward the door that was creeping open at the pressure of her struggling feet. The air was cold. Everything was growing cold and dark.

Lightning blazed through the darkness. The world exploded.

A fire glowed and crackled on the hearth. Rosy-colored curtains blew gently to and fro at a window looking out on a starry sky. Over the walls of the room Goldilocks flirted with three vaudeville bears.

Janet Carter looked around in horror. This was the kind of thing you learned in Abnormal Psych. Flight from reality. The person who can't take it retreats into the safety of childhood reverie. Here she was, back in her nursery. At any moment now she would have the illusion of her mother bending over her.

Something was being lifted from the stiff region between her chest and chin. Janet looked up. Not at her mother. It was the beautiful blond woman she had known under many guises. The Princess Mariska, Mary Alden the star, Helenka Baluta the girl who made good, Mrs. Ralph Ogden. She smiled at Janet and put a cold compress around her throat.

Janet laughed. It hurt, but not too much. Of course, she was in her nursery in her father's house on Elm Street. Later, it must have been the tenants' nursery, and Mr. Baluta had left the walls unchanged. The paper in her day had told a different story, Red Riding Hood and the Wolf. She knew how she had come here. More or less. And why she was wrapped in voluptuous silk and fur smelling of lilies of the valley. Mariska had taken away the clothes drenched with blood from Cousin Charlotte's shattered shoulder.

Eric Lund came into the room and stood looking down at Janet. "You saved me," she said.

"Not I. I had my gun out, but I didn't fire the shot that saved your life. It was old Mr. West."

"Cousin Virgil!" Tears of weakness formed in her eyes.

Eric spoke lightly. "That isn't all he's done for you. Look." He pulled a bottle from his pocket. "He sent you this. And it isn't carrot wine."

Mariska brought glasses and Janet sipped mellow old port slowly and not too painfully.

"Tell me," she asked, "about everything. And light your pipe."

"Old Virgil West," Lund obeyed, "was hard to figure out. Were those naps of his at the time of both murders real or imaginary? Anyway, he evidently suspected that his wife had killed his sister. He hasn't talked about that. I gather he was letting well enough alone. But Ralph Ogden's death was a different matter. Also, this time he had proof. He says that just after Jerry returned with the car yesterday afternoon he 'happened to be' in the turret room belonging to his son. From the window he could see beyond the hedge and across the whole Peckham property. He saw Mrs. West go into the carriage house and he saw her come out again.

"Today he has watched her constantly as she sat knitting. He tasted the tea, and suspected that she had put Nembutal in the bottom of the cup. He was more certain when Mrs. West insisted on pouring tea for Bridie and sending her back to the kitchen with a brimming cup…. He had drunk very little of the tea, but he was tired. He hasn't slept much in the last ten nights. So he really dropped off for a few minutes. Then he did the only thing he could."

"Bridie? How is Bridie?"

"Coming along fine. She'll be Louise's right-hand man in the morning."

"Mr. Lund," Mariska asked, "how is Duncan West?"

"All right, too. His temperature is down. And he has his letter. You'll soon be working together in Hollywood."

He drew a white leather case from his pocket and handed it to Mariska. "This is yours, Miss Alden."

"Thank you." Her gratitude was for the name. She opened the case. Her hands trembled and she let it fall.

"Mrs. West had everything in her knitting bag," Lund went on hastily. "The letter, the miniature, gaff, snick-a-snee. It would have been searched before tea-time if Murphy hadn't been called away."

"And after all Cousin Charlotte did, she didn't save her children from scandal. It will all come out now, won't it?"

"No. She's a remarkable old girl," said Lund. "She will plead guilty to the murder of Mattie Peckham. And of Ralph Ogden. The court will probably find her of unsound mind. If she is, it is an insanity that protects her children. She lies in the hospital, saying over and over to the police woman and the nurses, 'I killed her. We had to have the money. And Ralph knew'."

"And Louise will never know why Ralph died. But how will she live? And poor old Cousin Virgil?"

"They will live together in Mattie Peckham's lovely old home," Lund said, working for a smile. "Those two could survive everything. They are made of tough material."

Mariska had risen to her feet. For a moment she and the tall man looked at each other in hard appraisal. He said, "You also will survive."

She lifted her golden head. From the depths of strength and art that had made her what she was, she drew into her face luminous beauty. Mary Alden, the movie star, went out of the room.

Eric sat down on the bed beside Janet. "You aren't tough." One hand smoothed the brown hair lying loose on the pillow, the other touched her cheek. "You still need police protection. Like this."

THE END

ERIC LUND AFTERWORD
By Curtis Evans

Lizzie Borden took an ax
And gave her mother forty whacks.
When she saw what she had done
She gave her father forty-one.

The author of the first Eric Lund mystery, *No Bones About It*, was born Ruth Sawtell in Springfield, Massachusetts, in 1895 and lived out her years as an adolescent in that city, departing only in 1913 when she enrolled at Vassar College in Poughkeepsie, New York. (She later transferred to Radcliffe College in Cambridge, Massachusetts, whence she launched her successful academic career.) Located about one hundred miles southeast of Springfield, in the lowest corner of Massachusetts, is the city of Fall River. There, three years previous to Ruth's birth, prominent citizens Andrew and Abby Borden were horribly done to death in their home by an unknown assailant wielding a hatchet or some similar implement. Shockingly to Victorian sensibilities, Lizzie Borden, the thirty-two year old daughter of Andrew and stepdaughter of Abby, was arrested and charged with the crimes—only to be acquitted a few months later in one of the most publicized murder trials in American history. Lizzie would live out the rest of her life in Fall River, dying in 1927 with a cloud of suspicion still hanging over her, in spite of her legal vindication, which had only darkened with the years.

At bottom Lizzie Borden was acquitted of murdering her father and stepmother by "a jury of her peers" largely because these twelve good men and true (evidently all local farmers) could not conceive that a genteel woman such as Miss Borden could possibly have committed such a monstrously brutal crime. Surely a lady, one gathers their thoughts must have run, would have fastidiously employed poison to get rid of a pair of unwanted relations. (And, indeed, Lizzie had tried to purchase strychnine from a local pharmacist a few days before the murders—evidence which was excluded from the trial.) I sense a similar attitude to those jurors on the part of some of the critics of *No Bones About It*, who in their notices have faulted as implausible the tale's denouement, in which painfully genteel Charlotte Duncan West attempts to bump off Janet Carter, the young heroine of the novel, with a pike gaff, after having previously successfully dispatched Ralph Ogden with a wickedly curved blade known as a snick-a-snee (or snickersnee). However, I cannot help wondering whether the author had in mind, when she was devising *No Bones About It*, the Fall River tragedy from a half-century earlier. The whole case, in which murder and attempted murder are committed by a ladylike woman (not only with poison but with edged weapons) within an insular genteel family decorously seething with acrimony, seems to me to recall the Borden case in spirit. Although Mattie Peckham is the first murder victim, not its perpetrator, her name recalls that of Lizzie Borden; and I note as well that Aunt Mattie's Irish maid Bridie's full first name is actually the same as that of the Bordens' Irish maid, the chief witness in the Borden case: *Bridget*. Moreover, Bridie came to work for Mattie Peckham's family in *1892*, the year of the Borden murders. If Lizzie Borden could have delivered dual deaths with a hatchet, why might Charlotte West not have administered quietus by means of a snickersnee?

The lead defense attorney in the Borden trial, former Massachusetts governor George Robinson, had his law office in Springfield, where he returned after Lizzie's acquittal and passed away suddenly from apoplexy a few years later in 1896. His papers on the case remain locked away "on the sixteenth floor of an unremarkable building on Main Street," still protected, nearly 130 years later, by lawyer-client privilege—a tantalizing remnant for modern-day devotees of the Borden enigma. Fall River had no Eric Lund to resolve all of the questions for us.

—August 2021
Germantown, Tennessee

COLD BED IN THE CLAY

RUTH SAWTELL WALLIS

Why weariest thou this day,
  Wild heart for the bed abhorrèd,
The cold bed in the clay?
Death cometh though no man pray,
  Ungarlanded, un-adorèd.
  Call him not thou.

CHAPTER I

Seated high on a cement ledge, the man with the scars around his mouth looked down, down into the enormous blue eye.

An eye without white sclerotic; with no black pupil. Blind, vast, mateless and adrift. At intervals a tattered upper lid gave a gross wink.

To the left and to the right of the Brobdingnagian optic a classic colosseum loomed. Where a retina should have been there sprouted a field of corn. At the center of the lower lid a circus band waved brass trumpets, with red arms tasseled in gilt. Across a green plain, a thin endless line of tiny black marionettes splotched with scarlet, purple and blue were being drawn toward the gigantic iris.

The man with the scars jerked up his head, slanted a jaunty Panama lower against the rays of a descending sun. He took another long look at the scene below him. Surrealist nightmare? He grinned. Not now. The ingredients were the same but he no longer saw them as a fantastic picture. It was all real enough. A football stadium in mid-June; he and thousands of people around him and below him, facing the open end which met farmland. In the center of the gridiron stood a grandstand, its crescent-shaped shell lined in deep blue over which a fold of canvas flapped down in the river breeze. To the blare of a young and gaudy band, four hundred men and women, two by two, in professorial costume were marching. A State University was holding its annual commencement.

Well, let it, and more power to it. He was no Yale man. His so-called higher education had been earned by propping open heavy eyes in a dingy night school. And this spot was no hillside in ancient Greece. Flat in the middle of the U. S. A., a college campus ought to meet a cornfield. Corn paid taxes and taxes paid for the pomp and circumstance which the student band was demanding for the boys and girls.

The boys and girls. Fifteen hundred agitated black gowns on the cement seats directly over the field which their professors were parading. From mortar-boards cocked at impertinent angles, bright thin tassels of a dozen hues twisted and swung over masses of hair, more or less blond, more or less curled, covering the necks of the girls. In June, 1945, less than one in ten of these graduating seniors was male.

Behind them and on all sides sat the ten thousand people you would expect to see. Fathers who for four years had worked harder in the garage, the drugstore, the small law office, and played less at club, lodge, tavern, so that the kid could go through the "U." Mothers in rayon prints, pretty but not new, trying to pick out Joanie or Marlys. Beaming grandparents, critical aunts, clusters of girl friends (more hair), here and there the uniform of a boy friend unpredictably returned from the violent world indicated on his left breast. Small brothers and sisters, few and audible, wanted to go home now.

The man with the scars, Eric Lund, cast a professional glance around the stadium. Busman's holiday? No day for him was ever quite that. In this singularly homogeneous crowd, could he spot the person who didn't quite belong, the man or woman only a little off-center? Not easy to do. Those three, for instance, ten rows in front. The lank, long-trunked elderly woman in the middle, whose rose-burdened hat loomed above the hunched shoulders of the man with the overlong hair which suggested but did not prove the conscious artist or the absent-minded professor. On the lady's left, a much younger woman showed a pale profile topped by curls like dwarf bananas, and ending above cascades of lace frills in a chin like a spade.

How many, Lund wondered, could spot the trio as slightly different from the people around them? Who could place them in the right occupations, the correct relationship to each other? He could. And for a good reason. He knew the name of one, the addresses of all three.

But those two across the aisle. There could be no doubt of their difference. The careless, expensive sport clothes, the deep tan that only leisure could produce in this latitude so early in June, and the strange quiet intentness with which they watched the robed figures advancing toward the stage. They were young, the girl not more than twenty-three, the man a few years older. He sat on the aisle, a little below Lund, his narrow, close-cropped head bent forward. His nose was thin, with pinched nostrils; he had a puffed and peevish mouth. Between his knees thin brown hands were pressed lightly together.

You would notice them both. It was the girl you would not forget. Not merely because of face and figure which were better than all right; not only for the striking color of aquamarine sleeveless, backless dress and rose-brown skin. It was the peculiar impression of softness and strength, not completely blended, as if a young and simple nature had been forced into fortitude before its time. Her face, like her arms and neck, was rounded, her mouth full, not painted. A draped turban of blue silk banded forehead and temples and severely covered her hair.

Boom! Tzing! From the band there rose a new tune, shrill, mock heroic. The girl laughed and said something to her companion. Lund could not see his face but the vicious jerk of his head toward and away from the girl was clear.

So was the change in her. Her eyes widened, the whites prominent against her tanned skin. With her mouth stiff and hard she gazed straight ahead. At short intervals, however, her eyes shifted quickly to the man.

Eric Lund knew fear when he saw it. It was useful in his business. There was no doubt that this girl was deeply afraid.

At the moment when the first of four hundred professors stepped from grass to cinder track for the last lap of their parade, the band dropped *Pomp and Circumstance* and took up the *Procession of Peers*. Two stout, decent teachers of, respectively, archeology and dairy husbandry, transformed by their own marshal's wands into self-trundled tubs overlaid with old red portières, led off to the apt strains of

> Loudly let the trumpet bray!
> Tantantara!
> Proudly bang the sounding brasses!
> Tzing! Boom!
> As upon its lordly way
> This unique procession passes
> Tantantara! Tzing! Boom!

Halfway down the line a professor of lyric poetry whose wife wrote horror stories stumbled over the raveled hem of his doctor's gown. And high up in the stadium Audrey Adriance, her eyes suddenly bright with fun, sang silently with the band,

> Bow, bow, ye lower middle classes!
> Bow, bow, ye tradesmen, bow ye masses!
> Tantantara! Tzing! Boom!

She put her hand lightly on Don's sleeve. "Do I hear what I think I hear?"

His arm flung off her touch. Contempt was the one expression in his voice. The curly girlish lashes closed over his eyes.

"For God's sake! Is everything so damned funny to you? Don't you know enough to recognize something good when you've got it?"

Again! Audrey thought, again! She felt her eyes and mouth stiffen into the old lines. She sat very still, gazing into a sky touched with the first streaks of sunset. She did not hear the band now. What have I done? What will Don do? She knew she must not look at him. It seemed a long time before she dared to turn her eyes slightly, fearfully, seeking his hands. She saw them resting quietly between his knees, brown hands, not very strong.

Good? The University, these people, the river breeze, the cornfield, the sky? Oh, yes, she recognized their quality so well that for a moment five years had fallen away, and something had seemed really funny once more. Good, yes, but not yet hers. Probably it never could be.

During the few remaining minutes of the *Procession of Peers* she did not realize how many times she looked at her husband's hands.

Professor Alfred Dexter marched with Professor Beulah Briggs Cox. March is a verb of many meanings, each of which was being employed at that moment by someone in his immediate vicinity. Only the most indulgent definition could be said to include Alfred's trot-and-skip and Beulah's bulldozer plow through the gravel. It was hard work for little round Alfred to keep anything resembling step with the power generated by her great hips and bosom which even the folds of a doctor's gown could not weaken. Particularly when he was panting from excitement. In a minute or two they would be too near the band for conversation and there was something he had to know.

He turned his flat-nosed face up to hers and demanded through his beard: "Beulah, do you think it's right for a state employee to buy things in New York?"

Through the thick lenses of her pince-nez, her eyes glared down at him. Malevolently? Stupidly?

"Alfred," elegant accents came from the depths of the stupendous diaphragm, "I wonder what is behind that remark!"

A man less strong for learning would have been shattered by the charge from this great dreadnought gone battleship gray. Alfred Dexter did not even suffer shock.

"I mean," he barked, "that box!"

The gleam behind the glass might have been humor; it might not. "You saw the package from Lane Bryant?"

Alfred's beard quivered. "Yes, Beulah? You have something to tell me?"

"Alfred," she was smiling in the way he feared, as if she weren't really going to tell him the thing he wanted most to know; even after twenty neighborly years, he didn't really understand Beulah, such a peculiar woman with her white hair and big midriff and that fresh young complexion. "Alfred," she repeated, "I shall confess to you."

"Yes, Beulah?"

The last low rays of the sun were hitting her glasses. "Recently, as you are aware, I have indulged in ... an act I had never before perpetrated."

His cheeks and nose were scarlet now, inside and out, a pleasing sensation.

"Alfred, I shall not repeat the performance. The result was—disastrous." The glasses blazed down on his avidity. "Alfred, I am telling you the terrible truth—it does not pay to select by mail. The article did not fit!"

Tantantara! Zing! Boom!

"Your bride is walking with my husband." From a hard stadium seat Rachel Dexter pointed bony red knuckles, like buds strayed from the cabbage-roses on her hat, down to the steps of the grandstand on the green. Professional pairs were tripping up them and not lightly. "A faculty *husband*." Rachel's wrinkled dimples were kind. "That's so unusual, Mr. Cox."

Reluctantly Clifford Cox on her right withdrew from the prettiest section of girl graduates the pale popped grapes that he used for eyes. "What does pink mean?" he asked.

"Pink?" Rachel blinked. "Pink? Oh, the tassels on their caps? Pink is ..." She raised the thick commencement program closer to her steel-rimmed glasses.

"Music, dear." The young woman at her left smoothed the three fruity curls that topped her long face. Her tiny over-red mouth minced the words. "Pink for music and quite without significance."

"But lots of the colleges have such appropriate colors, Edna. Look, Mr. Cox." Rachel had found the place. "On page seven. College of Agriculture: Colors, maize and blue ... College of Commerce: Drab."

"What about this one?" Mr. Cox laid a thick finger on the page. "Nursing Education: Salmon pink and green."

"My husband," Edna Gray looked prim, "would say it suggests the kind of dinner that hospitals serve to expectant fathers."

"Thornton," said Mrs. Dexter, frowning at the damp spot Mr. Cox's thumb had left on her program, "is a very clever man."

Mr. Cox, wiping a hand over his bulging forehead, said to either or both of them, "I wouldn't know."

"And Thornton's so fine-looking, too." Rachel's metacarpals again waved downward. "The only one of the marshals who looks like one. So tall and dark and handsome."

"'Handsome is as—' you know," Edna spoke with becoming modesty. "Let us hope he remembers that he's to meet us right here."

Mr. Cox gave his forehead another good scrub, inspected his palm and returned to the contemplation of pink tassels and adjacent parts.

Thornton Gray walked alone. Swinging his yellow stick, kicking his red velvet gown, he still, as Rachel Dexter had suggested, filled the office as those who valued it did not. He had accepted the assignment because the University was almost entirely decent about asking a teacher to do things other than the main job. And a man ought to be enough of a man to stand looking like a monkey once a year. If it weren't for the damned caps. Like a streetcar conductor's but without the dignified shade of a visor. Anyway, he was the only marshal whose necktie wasn't crooked.

Huge, dark, heavy, still young, he strode over the grass close to the rear of the robed and hooded procession, brandishing his wand. Teacher's ruler, herdsman's stick? Spare the rod and spoil the sheep! I can take it, I can take, I can take it!

For months, for years, he had marched daily to that self-command. I can take it? Yes, I can!

What he had once quietly believed, he had recently been telling himself defiantly. Today, for the first time he added honestly: But for how long?

Sunset flamed over the field, vast, riotous, uninhibited as one sees it only over prairie and sea. The gray stadium walls shrank; the lighted, blue-lined platform became a pinpoint on the dulled green gridiron. The voice of the University president rose deep and dignified through the amplifiers.

"By the authority imposed in me by the Regents, I now confer upon you the degree for which you have been recommended, with all the rights and privileges which it admits you to, here and elsewhere. As evidence of this I hand you this diploma."

Lilac and white banners advanced, black gowns floated out from the girls' white dresses. To the accompaniment of a fluttery waltz, the first group of candidates went up to the platform. Eric Lund looked at his program. "Lilac and white: Dental Hygienists." The girls who hold the bowls when you spit. Fifty graduates down, fourteen hundred and fifty to come. No wonder the president sat and extended a diploma in each hand to the bifurcated line.

College now followed college, each preceded by gonfalons and the president's tired tones: "... the degree for which you have been recommended ... rights and privileges which it admits you to ..."

The band went boldly and unsuitably on. *The Robin Hood Suite* ushered the College of Commerce; a handful of very 4-F lawyers straggled to *My Hero: Concert Marche Militaire*. Graduates in Agriculture and Forestry, it is true, were heralded by *Country Gardens*, but *Wine, Women and Song* unkindly stressed the impression that the second commodity would always be surplus in the College of Education.

Mr. Lund was having a good time. The tanned young man across the aisle was still tense but the girl had relaxed. Lund would like to find out what she laughed at and what she feared.

The great sky faded, darkened, and floodlights swept down, making the field a gray-walled world. Within the hot, bright shell, the professors stirred in their thick gowns and their heavy boredom. Seated four deep behind the front row of officials, they could see only an endless passing of student mortar-boards. They didn't want to see anything, anyway. During the first half-hour they had glanced over the hundred-page program, passing one now and then to a neighbor with a quip. Professors of humanities had felt themselves particularly witty about the titles of theses prepared in the more vocational fields. Now, programs were rolled, limp, pocketed, fallen underfoot.

Only Alfred Dexter still pored over the pages sadly. It was a bad year for him. Young scholars of biology and gynecology were ironically serving the forces of destruction; prospective doctors of literature and the fine arts had ignored Alfred's personal interests. Under the quite horrid beam of Beulah Cox's teeth and glasses he had, it is true, unearthed two pallid items, which held his attention though not for long. A Master of Child Welfare offered "A Study of Choice of Companions According to Sex and Facial Expression by Pre-school Children of Climax, Nebraska," and a somewhat more considerate Doctor of Zoology supplied a dissertation on "The Mating Habits of Amphibians and Reptiles with Special Reference to the Black-banded Skink." However, the sex life of kindergartens and skinks was a little immature, even for Alfred.

There was a moment of silence in the arena. Two men stood very straight at the front of the platform, facing the president; an Army colonel, a Navy captain were presenting, not students for degrees, but cadet officers for commissions. The voices of the three aging men ceased, the band blared *Stars and Stripes Forever*, and for the first time that evening a group marched smartly to the platform. It was a good performance. Thornton Gray knew they had sweated at it. For these boys in brown or blue uniforms were not primarily soldiers or sailors. These were the doctors of peacetime, all medical officers now. Whether war lasted for years as many feared or ended in a few weeks, as all hoped, these men wouldn't be unemployed for a long time. They would grow tired, patching broken bodies and minds, grow old watching men die. Many would go where he, Thornton, had thought it was his job to go. He had been wrong about that. The strong wide mouth hardened. It seemed that what he had got during his year in Japan he was not going to lose in a lifetime.

Rachel Dexter said to Edna Gray, "Look, the marshals are pushing that clotheshorse with the doctor's hoods out to the front of the platform. I always think this is the one really lovely moment of Commencement. Hadn't I better wake up Mr. Cox?"

Edna leaned forward and inspected the bent, rather greasy head and the two chins pressed into Mr. Cox's shirtfront. "Perhaps," she said gently. "He has such scholarly interests."

Not a good decision. Mr. Cox was hard to rouse and unesthetic when half-awake, and the moment on the platform was not completely beautiful. It was ten o'clock and everyone was tired to death. The young Ph.D.'s entered "the ancient and honorable company of scholars" most often by stumbling up the steps, and at least half the hoods, instead of slipping over their heads, stuck on the corners of their caps. The president did his best for them, but after three hours, "the rights and privileges" faded into "witchi-mitchi-tou" as if he were bestowing degrees upon the aborigines of the State in their native tongue.

Eric Lund stood in the aisle, lighting a cigarette. The band was still, the field turned dark, the grandstand empty. When school was out, the professors had bundled up their gowns and left in a hurry. It was taking a while for the stadium crowd to descend through the exits. Those three whom Lund had recognized were hanging around ten rows below him not too patiently, particularly Fatty Long-Hair and the young woman with the yellow éclairs on her head; both of them kept twisting and turning and looking in all directions.

Across the aisle from Lund the thin, tanned young fellow in the sports jacket was rising to his feet. The girl still sat with her blue-bound head tilted upward, looking at the stars. The man paused before stepping into the aisle and for the first time Lund saw his full face. Too-pretty lashes fluttered nervously. The fellow didn't look well.

"Oh, Mister Lund! Oh, yoo-hoo!"

Mrs. Dexter was waving her bones at him. He nodded and waved back. The young woman with her smirked modestly; the fat slob stared.

When Lund glanced back across the aisle the man was not there. Nor was he descending the concrete steps to the exit opening fifteen rows below. It didn't take Lund long to locate him, a short, slight figure slipping out of the far end of the row behind which he had been sitting, and down the opposite aisle toward the corresponding exit. If not running, he was definitely walking out on somebody.

On the girl? She had just discovered that she was alone. She stood, looking down to the nearest exit, around the crowd, across the aisle. Lund saw that her full lips were slightly parted, her eyes again wide and white in fear. Too late she turned toward the opening through which her companion had just vanished. She remained in her place for a moment, quite still. As she walked to the aisle, once more her face had relaxed into young, quiet curves. Control? Relief? Or was she used to having things turn out badly?

She began the descent and Lund followed, a dozen steps behind her. She moved slowly, lightly, a tall girl with a beautiful back. They had just passed Madam Dexter and friends when she stopped in her tracks and for good reason.

A tall man in a light gray suit had burst out of the exit, dark, strong-featured, with a big impatient-looking mouth. Over his arm hung a scarlet velvet gown. The man halted and looked up at the girl. The long narrow eyes deep beneath black brows told nothing, but his mouth softened. He bowed and stood aside to let her pass.

Down the steps to the ground beneath the stadium, across the crowded parking lot toward the bus stop on the river road, the girl walked steadily, never glancing about her. Whatever fear she had concerning the abrupt departure of her companion, she would not search for him that night.

But what had he run away from? What or who had motivated flight? Something growing in his mind as he had sat for hours, apparently intent on the ceremony below him? Something in his relationship to the girl who had watched him with nervous eyes? Or had he seen suddenly a face in the crowd that reminded him of dishonor or warned him of danger?

Quite possibly, Eric Lund thought, the guy was making a getaway from me.

CHAPTER II

Audrey Adriance was listening. Thud, muffled scrape, what did they mean? Within the depths of the room sound was as vague and dim as the morning light. It was not in character for Don to be unpacking; even the emptying of his sacred briefcase was a major though dedicated chore. But if he were driven by a sudden desire to get away, he might just possibly be repacking the books and clothes she had removed yesterday.

Not that! Don't let it be that. She wanted so desperately to stay, even in the horrible humor of this house.

What kind of people had thought up this dusky well? Well of loneliness, Pussy's well, Aunt Eliza's ...

> In the drinking-well
> (Which the plumber built her)
> Aunt Eliza fell
> We must buy a filter.

That was it. Plumbers' Gothic, two stories high. Mullions like drain pipes upright between the three-glassed window, each section crisscrossed and rosetted in the manner of lavatory tiles. Where Early English prototypes had blazoned coats of arms, here left- and right-hand medallions sprouted a sort of Tudor petunia, while the central panel bore a pale amorphous disgrace that might have been a crown of thorns, an open book, or a fried oyster. Even on a bright June morning, not a great deal of light got through, suggesting suitability to a comfort station situated above a street. That bay, butting into the left-hand wall of the room, what did it resemble if not an oversize medicine cabinet with glass doors?

To comfortable people, those who don't believe that accidents will happen, this could be a funny room. They would not fear as Audrey feared, a stumble on the polished drop down from the foyer; nor dread a trip over the two steps from floor to cushioned bench under the mullions. They would never wake at midnight, as she might sometime wake, to hear a fatal fall from the oriel into the well.

Again she listened. Somewhere high in the poor, squeezed functional portion of the house, there was a dull thump. Audrey started for the hall.

She stopped. Let Don alone. Fifteen minutes ago, at breakfast, he was O.K., wasn't he? And last night, after his queer departure from the stadium, she had found him in bed and sound asleep when she got home. On his own, remember, he must be on his own.

Suddenly she seemed to smell the dusk of the room, to feel its petty pretense stirring the toast and marmalade under her sternum. She crossed quickly to the rear of the room and flung open French doors on air and light.

She took a deep breath. She staggered. She could not have done otherwise.

The tenancy of a mock Elizabethan house does not inevitably entail the discovery that heraldic devices live in the backyard.

Such being the exceptional case, a savor of tomb might reasonably be prognosticated, but the stench that retched Audrey was composed of old melons, coffee grounds and Camembert cheese.

At opposite sides of the Adriance garbage can, two beasts rampant reared up in accepted heraldic manner, heads in profile, one foreleg raised above the other. The pair had much in common. Both were gray about the muzzle, with full, elderly bellies. Each open mouth expressed the same quiet avidity. And from somewhere about the person of each, a bit of metal clinked softly against the can.

However, this last attribute had a slightly different origin. He on the dexter side of the shield wore a dog-tag; he on the sinister a Phi Beta Kappa key.

Life had prepared Audrey for a good deal. She advanced, noiselessly, over the grass and spoke. "My good man, I had no idea that times were so hard."

On the right the Black Labrador held the pose, but the left-hand figure turned a full irate face upon her.

"Mrs. Adriance, I presume. I am *Professor* Dexter."

He was a round little man with a nose like an isosceles triangle out of which sprouted another triangle like a hula-hula skirt. His uplifted left hand waved the top to the garbage can.

"I'm glad to meet you," Audrey said. "At least, I think I shall be if you'll cover up my garbage again."

"Cover up again! Cover up again!" The words issued testily from the hardly visible slit in his beard. "Mrs. Adriance, I came down my stairs and out of my house and across your yard just to put the cover on tightly for the first time since you've lived here."

"Since yesterday. Please, Mr. Dexter, put it on now."

He banged down the lid.

"Ki-yi." Down on the paws of his tranced opposite number.

"Mrs. Adriance," Mr. Dexter cried, "you've made me hurt him. Here, Cadwallader."

With a total misjudgment of social climate, the big black retriever headed for Audrey Adriance.

"What did you call him?" Audrey bent and stroked the dense hard hair of the dog's head.

"Cadwallader," his christener repeated clearly and belligerently. "Cadwallader, from the Welsh, meaning 'Battle-Arranger.' He is a very clever strategist."

"He's very nice." Audrey dodged the affection of Cadwallader's Camembert-tainted tongue. "You've had him a long time, haven't you?"

"Yes; how did you know?"

Audrey withdrew her gaze from the middle-aged sag and graying jowls of Cadwallader. "I just guessed it," she said, "because he seems so fond of you."

"Mrs. Adriance," Professor Dexter's tone was fatuously parental, "you know, I really think he is."

"Woof," said Cadwallader. "Bow, wow, wow."

Thus addressed, a man came through a gap in the hedge, carrying in a sink strainer what seemed to be a perfect cantaloupe. His forehead, as bulbous as the melon, was white and specked with freckles like a cake of oatmeal soap.

"Hello, little girl." He popped his eyes toward Audrey who, for the first time, became uncomfortably aware of her pinafore, hanging braids and bare legs.

"Good morning," said Alfred Dexter in the manner of a neighbor, good if a trifle stiff. "I am delighted to see that you now assist Beulah with the domestic arrangements. Mrs. Adriance, may I present Mr. Cox, resident in the Cape Cod cottage behind the hedge? Mrs. Adriance is an excellent judge of dogs."

Mr. Cox leered at Cadwallader now licking Audrey's ankle. "Lucky dog. Ha, ha!"

Luckier, anyway, than Mr. Cox was at that moment.

There now advanced behind his left shoulder one of the most formidable women that Audrey had ever seen. An aging Valkyrie who had given up her riding without reducing her diet.

From the depths of her heroic bosom came forth a single, elegant sound, "Clifford."

Mr. Cox jumped and the melon bounced to the ground and Cadwallader.

"My dear," said the lady, "thank you for this little practice run with the garbage. Since it is your first, I will overlook the fact that in your haste to combine duty with pleasure, you selected the one sound melon in the house." She laughed in a way she doubtless found extremely gay. "Pick it up."

Mr. Cox, red and puffy, bent to retrieve. Cadwallader gave a last gulp, sneezed and pattered away.

"Mrs. Adriance, isn't it?" the enunciation became even more refined, "it is a pleasure to meet you even in this unlovesome spot. I am *Mrs.* Cox."

The italicized tone implied pride. Why? It is easy to marry strange things but it should be hard to boast about it.

"You arrived only yesterday, did you not?" the Valkyrie continued. "And did you by chance attend our barbaric ceremony in our classic arena?"

"Commencement in the stadium? I thought it was fun," said Audrey.

"What an incredibly loyal little neighborhood we were last night. Your next door neighbor, Alfred Dexter, marching dutifully with me while our mates admired us from on high. Together with Edna Gray from the house yonder, keeping, one may be certain, a fixed eye on her good, parading Thornton. And you and Mr. Adriance being merry about it all!"

Audrey felt a small shudder of memory. Don flinging off her hand in repellent contempt, sneaking off for some dark reason, leaving her alone in the crowd. No, merry was never the word for the Adriances.

"So now you have become quite one of us. No one is a member of our circle until Alfred Dexter has inspected the offal." Mrs. Cox turned her gleaming pince-nez on the spluttering little man.

"Ha, ha, ha!" shouted Mr. Cox without much mirth and gave his wife a slap equal to the mass of her back. "I'll bet your garbage pail is full of caviar and champagne, huh, Mrs. Adriance?"

"Ask Cadwallader," said Audrey. "I think he's being sick behind the garage."

Little Mr. Dexter found words. Pointing his beard toward Mrs. Cox, he said with great distinction, "Beulah, are you certain that *you* feel quite well at this hour of the morning?" He paused, not without drama, and then scurried off toward the echo of unembarrassed emesis.

Mrs. Cox reared her white head and declaimed to Audrey, Clifford and the June morning, "I wonder what is behind that remark?"

In the silence that followed, Audrey returned Mr. Cox's leer with a long straight stare. She saw a pudgy body of medium height, topped by reddish hair, overcompensating at the neck for what it had lost at temples and moist forehead and much in need of a good shampoo. Under her gaze his bulging eyes shifted. He passed his hand slowly over his forehead and examined the palm.

A cold spot formed inside Audrey. I've seen him before, and in no pleasant place. Did she show fear or only interest? Both the Coxes, she saw, were now regarding her with peculiar attention. In Mr. Cox's face there was a new expression that might be hope or might be the same sort of shadowy recognition as her own. Mrs. Cox put her hand strongly on her mate's mussed shirt sleeve.

"Mrs. Adriance," she oozed essence of venom, "if your poor husband is going through the long strain of summer school registration today, I should think there might be a few little things you could do to help him get off comfortably."

Audrey felt herself getting hot and mad. "There might be, but Dr. Adriance is an extremely capable man."

"By-by," said Mr. Cox as he was propelled through the hedge.

Audrey stamped angrily back through French doors. The anger was for herself. It was justifiable, though not wise, to be annoyed with the jealous old witch, but she didn't have to lie. And that unprecedented use of inferior-college etiquette, *Doctor* Adriance! Her subconscious memory of Mr. Clifford Cox must be very untoothsome indeed.

In her emotional state she did not pause to listen in the deep living room but sped across it, half tripped on the rising step to the foyer, and ran up the stairs. All that the lofty pretensions of the Tudor Great Hall had spared for the second floor were a bath—with stained-glass window—and two bedrooms, one of these a hot little crib over the kitchen. From the larger front room came a soft plump and a sharp self-satisfied command.

"Audrey. Come here."

She drew a quick relieved breath. Too quick. She stepped into the room.

In the hour since she had left it, bedroom had become bedlam.

Take it easy. Don't show how you feel. Look it over before you speak.

Clothes lay bunched on chaise-longue and floor, books and papers strewed the fringes of open luggage, little boxes spilled powder and pins. Clear dusty spots in the green carpet marked the former position of bed and desk, now shifted where they could best catch the breeze and the light from the casement windows.

Don Adriance spoke with deep content. "I've worked it out perfectly, Audrey."

He hadn't gone suddenly mad. Audrey's cooling-off period made one thing quite clear. His had been no disorganized devastation. The clothes and books and minutiae all had one characteristic in common: they were hers. Through the yawning closet door she could see his suits hanging, his shoes beneath. His papers and books stood precisely on the desk and on what she had thought was her dressing-table.

Don was smiling, impersonal, absorbed. "There was only one problem about this damned house. My study. How in hell I was going to get a good place to work. Now I've got it."

She answered quietly, avoiding the cold eyes which suited the thin tan cheeks better than the childish mouth and fancy eyelashes. "I'm awfully glad, Don."

"While I'm at the campus, will you get that thing out of here?" He pointed to the chaise-longue from which her one good dress, evidently his last ejection, now slid to the floor. "You can put it somewhere in the back room with the rest of your stuff."

"Yes, Don. Of course."

"It's wonderful," he said. "A big study all my own. I'll probably have to share an office on campus with three or four others. After all, I'm only an instructor in Freshman English. But I can work here alone half the night."

She nodded.

Excitement colored his tone. "I'm going to start some work of my own. I don't care if I have to read two hundred themes a week. This is my chance. I'm going to dig right into my study of the poetry of primitive peoples."

She wet her lips. Did he really know enough about it? Was it just another evasion?

He answered her, "What I need right away is a good contact with the anthropology department."

"Yes, that would be fine." She felt her voice was steady and normal now.

He picked up his briefcase from the bed. "I looked through the catalogue and found a course in primitive mythology. It's being offered by a man who took his doctorate at Berkeley. This morning I'm going to register you for Anthropology 112."

"Don, I'm afraid ... Do you really think I could make it? After all, it's five years since I left school. I've never done any college work. If I flunked, I wouldn't be a great help to you."

He appraised her and turned away. "You'll do all right. You're bright enough. And—you know how you look. Only," his lips thrust out peevishly, "pin up those damned pigtails."

"I do look silly." A desperate control kept her fingers gripping the folds of her green pinafore. "War-time hairpins are so scarce and poor."

Halfway down the stairs Don paused. "Well, for God's sake, don't give the neighbors the impression I've seduced a minor."

She managed to smile as she said, "We needn't worry. They wouldn't think of it. They're such nice people."

She hoped it was true.

CHAPTER III

When she was alone, she picked her way through the litter to the dressing-table. Stooping to retrieve the hairpins that Don had brushed to the floor, she said aloud, "A wife cannot show irritation over normal things. Any domestic discord, however slight ..."

Bending over the mirror, fastening light brown braids that matched the deep crescent brows, she noted with faint derision that her tone had something of the masculine impersonality in which the words had been spoken to her. Wise words, not always easy to remember, along with other things, such as Don's intense absorption in the work it had recently been impossible to carry on. In large part, that explained her exile to the back room. There was, however, something more, allied to that crack about pigtails. Don was not seducing anybody just now.

Once—a hundred times—long ago she would have added: "Poor Don." And there had been hours of self-pity when "Poor Audrey" was the theme. Not now. Was it easier when she no longer cared very much about either of them? It wasn't a question of easy or of hard. It was her life. Lots of people didn't have a very good kind. This was her kind.

She crossed to the small latticed windows at the side of the house and flung them open. She was looking at what seemed the exact replica of her own house, a meretricious erection of half-timbered top and brick base, broken at four regular intervals by windows, those of the upper story with leaded diamond panes, the lower rear fitted with the clear glass and checked curtains denoting a kitchen. The nail-studded, brass-knockered main door faced hers across a common driveway, and above it leered a pale yellow circle with an empty red lozenge in the center which Audrey knew was the bathroom window. At the corner nearest the street the plan did not quite accord with the Adriances' latticed dining-room. The opposite window, directly below her was plain, clean and shining, and at each side of it two gray Dexter heads were honestly bent back to afford a good look at Audrey.

Little did they realize, Audrey thought grimly, the type and size of reward that such concentration would almost certainly bring them. Sooner or later—not late enough.

Don had dragged the desk toward the big front window, leaving a space behind it for a chair with its back to the light. Better begin the tidying job there, the spot he would care most about. She pulled pajamas from the wastebasket, slid the rose-flowered drapes into even folds.

What a view to turn one's back upon. No horrid little human dwellings crowded here. Roadway, cliff, blue river, and on the farther bluff, under light clouds, she could see first cornfields, then the medley of University towers. To the east the sun blinked on roofs and chimneys where the town centered at the river's edge. Low hills lay behind. Downstream there was only the green of trees and flat fields.

Through her mind ran a line of poetry too often recalled in the last five years: "Nay, daughter: take the morning to thine heart."

It had not always been a comfort.

Apart from the campus steeples and domes stood the gray semicircle of the stadium where that sprawling, funny, endearing pageant had taken place last night. Something unusual in her scheme of things had happened there. Not Don sneaking off. She was prepared for things like that. This memory was small, warm, personal. A big dark man with scarlet hanging from his arm. The way he had looked at her. The way, just for a moment, it had made her feel.

Two doors up the street, a yellow taxi stopped, full of squealing small fry, obviously bound for Nursery School. A little girl in blue jeans with an enormous pink bow on her black curls hustled out to join them.

Out of the driveway next door a tall, lean man, his face hidden by a slanted Panama, strode off briskly eastward toward the bridge.

Audrey went to work. Back and forth over the carpet, bending, pulling, straightening; across the hallway, again and again, past the dim, religious bathroom and up the nasty little step into her room whose possibilities for living were one-quarter diminished by the inner surface of the bay window, the oriel. A cot, a small dresser without a mirror, a night table were quite enough without a chaise-longue. Someday it might be all right to ask Don to carry it downstairs but that was more than she could do by herself. She'd have to drag the old animal in here and park it across the oriel.

Even that wasn't easy. It was heavy. She was hot. Get it over with quickly. She eased it through the bedroom door, minding the landlord's paint, but there patience ended. She seized the raised headpiece and yanked, backing toward the second door. She had forgotten the trick step. Out went her feet and she fell flat on her back, her head on the doorsill. Cushions smacked her face, wicker scratched her arms, crushed her chest.

When she had got her breath and shoved the heavy chair away, she was sobbing.

At that moment of misery, impertinence entered. The doorbell rang.

Go on. Ring and ring and ring! thought Audrey. I won't get up. I won't go down. But of course she would. Already she was scrambling to her feet. Those nice, nice people, the Dexters, next door knew quite well she was at home. Patting her head to be sure that the braids were pinned securely, she went down the stairs.

Two ladies stood on the doorstep. The tall, slat-sided older one with kind eyes and steel-rimmed glasses said, "I'm Mrs. Dexter." The much younger patted hard yellow rolls on top of her head and minced, "Mrs. Thornton Gray."

In the Tudor Great Hall they sat side by side on the bench beneath the mullioned window. Mrs. Gray modestly crossed plump knees and folded her hands on a white crepe skirt. Mrs. Dexter planted her bony hands flat on her thighs and beamed at Audrey. From time to time her eyes strayed lovingly to a green leather animal pinned near the shoulder of her printed housedress.

Hearty and shrill Mrs. Dexter apologized for a morning call and on Audrey's first day, explained that tomorrow evening, when University registration was over, she always gave a party, a neighborhood supper.

She wanted Don and Audrey to come.

For a moment too long Audrey did not speak. This was something she had not prepared for. What ought she to do? She said, at last,

"It's terribly nice of you, Mrs. Dexter. Thanks ever so much. But you all have known each other for a long time. I think we'd better not ..."

"Oh, but you're quite wrong, my dear," Rachel Dexter broke in. "There are going to be at least two people who haven't come in other years and one of them is just as strange as you. Well, of course, I don't mean there's anything queer about *you*. But there is about him. A little, anyway."

"It's awfully good of you to want us," said Audrey, "but it's so hard to entertain nowadays, and it sounds as if you were having a pretty big party without us."

"Only two more than in other years. Mr. Lund and Clifford Cox. But you and your husband wouldn't be extra. You'd be in place of your landlords, the Kings. The Adriances *have* to come, don't they, Edna?"

Mrs. Gray looked from Mrs. Dexter to Audrey with a little cat-smile. "Perhaps they don't want to," she said.

Bewilderment clouded Mrs. Dexter's open face. "Don't you?"

"Of course we do," Audrey rushed to the childlike appeal. "We'd like to very much indeed." Maybe Don would. Damn Mrs. Gray.

"I'm afraid it won't be a very exciting party for you and Mr. Adriance," Mrs. Dexter went on. "It will be very early and very temperate. Everybody will have eight-o'clock classes in the morning."

"We like that kind of party," Audrey told her, staring down Mrs. Gray's doubting eye. Did temperate, she wondered, equal total abstinence? Well, they were in for it now.

"I think it will be quite wonderful to have four newcomers," Mrs. Dexter declared. "Last year, I felt for the first time that our parties were getting just the least little bit dull. Did you, Edna?"

Mrs. Gray demurely shook her head.

"Maybe not. Anyway, tomorrow night we'll have you and your husband, and we all think you're so good-looking and we want to know all about you!"

Yes, thought Audrey. And given the usual bad luck, you will.

"And then there's Mr. Cox. He's been here three months but he's still quite the bridegroom. And the man I just started to tell you about. Mr. Lund. He's at the University just for a week to give some sort of memorial lecture on crime and they couldn't find a room in town for him, so he's staying at our house. He's got some title or other I read in the University paper, but, my dear, he's really a detective!"

"How frightening," said Edna Gray.

"Well, you know it ought to be," agreed Mrs. Dexter. "I suppose he's got all those things you hear about on the radio—keen brain, penetrating eye—but he seems just folksy to me."

Which, to Audrey, seemed very keen-brained indeed. How long would it take a smart policeman to classify her case? Hers and Don's?

"Mrs. Adriance, how do you like your house?" Mrs. Gray offered her first independent contribution.

"It's different," Audrey suggested.

"Not from ours. All three houses are exactly alike."

"Oh," said Audrey.

"Of course, they aren't very functional," agreed Mrs. Gray, "but they're really quite amusing."

"And they have lots of atmosphere," said Mrs. Dexter. "Mr. King built them. He isn't a member of the faculty, you know. He's a businessman. He can sell you anything. He sold us our cars, too. They're all alike. That is, he sold them to himself and to us and to Beulah Briggs and then she sold hers to Mr. and Mrs. Gray. These aren't perfectly convenient houses, but the view is lovely. But some of the features are wasted on Alfred and me. Now that oriel window up there. It would be perfect for a balcony scene on a rainy night. You and your husband are the first Romeo and Juliet types who've ever lived in one of these houses."

"Once," said Mrs. Gray to Mrs. Dexter, "when I stood at the oriel and looked down on Thornton, he said I was like one of the queens of Henry VIII."

"Which one?" demanded Rachel Dexter.

"He was sitting by the fire reading, and I called and called to him before he turned around and looked up." Edna Gray was all dreamy sweetness.

"Were you a divorced queen or a beheaded one?" persisted Rachel.

"Neither. He said I was like Jane Seymour. She was the mother of King Henry's only son."

But, of course, thought Audrey. She's really a lot like the Holbein portrait. Meek eyes, long face, minikin mouth, the chin like a spade. A husband of some years' standing, who had to put down a good book and turn completely around to crane up at that absurd bay window, might be justified in a spot of candor.

"Mrs. Adriance," she heard Mrs. Gray repeat, "have you any children?"

"No," said Audrey, and added devoutly to herself, Thank God.

"Mrs. Gray has the dearest little girl," Rachel told Audrey. "Everybody calls her Sister."

Well, thought Audrey, we can keep that topic going for a while. "And are your other children boys or girls?"

"I have no others," said Edna acidly, and that was that.

Rachel Dexter rushed kindly to the rescue. "I do hope it won't be dull here for you, Mrs. Adriance. The Faculty Women's Club doesn't meet in the summer. You could have belonged to the Brides' Section."

"The ...?"

"For the young wives. Those who haven't been married five years."

"Oh. I wouldn't be eligible."

"My dear, I don't believe it! How old are you? Oh, I didn't mean to ask that."

"I'm twenty-three."

"Oh, how funny. You and Beulah Briggs. She's ... well, I can't be sure ... but she's almost fifty. And she could be in the Brides' Section and you couldn't. Isn't it funny, Edna?"

Mrs. Gray controlled excellently any mirth she might feel. "There are a lot of other sections you could join in the Faculty Women's Club," she explained to Audrey. "Music and Drama and Gardening and International Affairs."

"And Edna Gray does wonderful work in almost every one of them," boasted Edna's friend. "You know, Edna, we all think your activities had a lot to do with Thornton being chosen a University marshal. It was a fine tribute to you both."

Edna smiled.

"Now let's see what we can concoct for you to do this summer, Mrs. Adriance," Mrs. Dexter continued. "Surgical Dressings, of course, and Home Canning. We can give you lots of things out of our Victory Garden. And, of course, there's always Bridge. And we girls must get together at each other's houses often for a good gossip."

No, Audrey thought with an old alarm, oh, no! "I'm going to be awfully busy. I'm taking a course in summer school. In anthropology."

"My husband," said Mrs. Gray, "is the professor of anthropology."

"Oh, is he?" said Audrey. One of those tubby leaders of the Unique Procession.

"That's the way Thornton and Edna met. Through anthropology. Do tell her about it, Edna. I think it was so romantic."

"It was, rather," again dreamy sweetness overflowed. "We met in Japan. When the cherry trees were in bloom. I suppose I should hate Japan now, but I can't quite. Everything is so little and sweet. Of course, we lived all the time in a nice European house in Tokyo. Papa was a Presbyterian missionary in Japan for twenty years. In 1940, he went on a sort of inspection tour of the provinces and took me with him. And there in the dearest little village was Thornton, trying to make a study of the people. Of course, he didn't understand them very well, so I could help him a little. Even though he was years older than I, and though I didn't know any anthropology."

A lonely, middle-aged professor, a young American girl. Audrey guessed Edna Gray's present age as twenty-eight. And don't forget the cherry blossoms. She said sincerely, "How wonderful for Mr. Gray."

"Wasn't it?" agreed Mrs. Dexter. "I do think the way people meet is the most interesting thing. Look at Beulah and Clifford Cox, Edna."

Mrs. Gray pressed her little lips together as if she would rather not, and Audrey felt complete sympathy.

"It all started with Beulah giving an extension course in Borden. Mr. Cox happened to be in town and heard her and wrote such an appreciative note. So the next week after her lecture they met in a cocktail lounge or something like that, and the week after they met again and he had a license and they were married that night. Oh, dear, it would have seemed a little unsettling to me when I was Beulah's age, particularly if I'd never been married before. And Mr. Cox is such a different type."

Mrs. Gray stirred uneasily. "Not altogether, Rachel, when one knows him well."

"That's true. I forget the work you're doing together. It sounds so hard I can't understand a thing about it."

"Japanese isn't an easy language," Edna said. "Mr. Cox knows it more thoroughly than I do. His people were missionaries, too," she explained to Audrey. "He was brought up on Shikoku. We are translating some documents we think may be useful to the government. It's dull work and rather slow. I don't get much time for it, with a house to run in wartime. And with Sister. Even though she goes to Nursery School."

"Well, marry in haste doesn't always mean repent at leisure, I guess." Mrs. Dexter sounded hope for the Cox future. "How did you meet *your* husband, Mrs. Adriance?"

"Just in the normal way. At a dance."

"I'm sure he fell in love with you at first sight and married you the next day."

"Not quite. How did you meet *your* husband, Mrs. Dexter?"

The worn lines that had once been dimples appeared at the corners of Rachel's mouth. "It was very characteristic. I was on a streetcar. I was a senior in high school, such a big gawky girl, not a bit pretty. But I was carrying a little box, the kind violets used to come in. With a picture of a bouquet in colors. And inside was a dead kitten I had run over on my bicycle. In front of a florists' shop ... I was taking it home to bury in our garden.

"Alfred was sitting across the aisle. And he could tell from the way the cardboard bulged that there was something heavier than flowers in it.

He couldn't figure out what it was. So he had to come over and ask me. He was very gentlemanly about it, but he never can quite restrain his interest in—containers."

"Rachel, we must go," Edna Gray, looking prim, rose abruptly. "Mrs. Adriance must have so many things to do."

"Goodness, yes," agreed Rachel. "I must apologize for gabbing on and on."

"I liked it," said Audrey.

"How nice you are." She came close to Audrey. "I must just show you this and then I'll run off." Her big bony fingers lifted the little leather horse a bit away from her dress. "Look. Just squeeze his tail."

Audrey obediently grasped the tiny silver appendage. Immediately the glass eye glowed. "Wonderful!" she said and ignored Edna Gray's smirk. Mrs. Dexter was nice.

"He has a Gleam in his Eye, just as the advertisement said. See, there's a little battery. I just couldn't resist him."

Audrey thought of the right question. "Has he got a name?"

"Oh, yes," the owner was delighted. "He has two. I call him Grane. He came in the mail the very day that the Metropolitan was broadcasting *Götterdammerung*. My husband calls him Gremlin. Of course, Alfred didn't mind my getting him. I have a tiny little income of my own. All through the war I've given every bit of it to the Red Cross, of course. But I just couldn't resist Grane."

"You deserved him," said Audrey.

"Maybe not. But, anyway, he was only two-fifty, prepaid. I do think it's nice when a wife has a little money of her own. To buy her husband's Christmas present and things like that."

"Thornton won't let me spend mine," said Edna crossly, "except for myself. He's quite firm about my buying anything for him or even for Sister."

"Thornton is a very proud man," Rachel had got to the front door at last, "and he's an awfully smart one."

"I know," said Thornton's wife. She favored Audrey with a farewell social smile. "We shall all meet tomorrow at 6:30."

Shutting out the problems these obviously good ladies had made for her, Audrey returned to physical struggle with the chaise-longue, by contrast a warm old friend. When force and strategy had maneuvered it through the door and against the only wall not previously buttressed with furniture, she flung herself down upon it. Her chin resting on the elevated headpiece was also almost on the sill of the little window overlooking the backyards. Not quite so good a view as the one Don would doubtless disregard, but green and pleasant. Small lawns, the

Dexters' sprouting carrots and kohlrabi, the Adriances' grass, ended in spirea bushes and honest little wooden garages definitely without caste.

Directly back of her own yard and facing on the next street stood a Cape Cod cottage, presumably the abode of the Cox family. It looked much too small for Big Beulah and too trim for the person now leaving its rear door.

En plein tailleur, Mr. Cox could not be described as smooth. In red and yellow striped shorts he was obscene in the manner of a cookie man who needs to be put in the oven right away. Mr. Cox, however, did not share Audrey's idea about concealment. On ankleless legs he padded barefoot across the grass to a lawn chair. Mr. Cox was evidently going to sun-bathe. But not immediately. He drew close to his side of the spirea, inspected the verdure, seemed to pluck a spray.

The possibility of Mr. Cox picking a posy for the only buttonhole with which he was at present equipped fascinated Audrey to an extent temporarily overcoming her distaste for the display of human dough. He now seated himself in the chair. Tearing at the greenery, bit by bit he threw it away—all but one leaf. This, with infinite care, he fitted over his nose, then leaned back and closed his eyes. Mr. Cox would now sun-bathe all features except one.

Too much of that sun was beginning to enter into Audrey's little room. She reached forward to close the casement. The frame, needing oil, protested. Mr. Cox opened his eyes. Raising a fat hand, he shifted the leaf from nose to lips and waved it at Audrey.

She closed the window with a bang and pulled curtains across it. His face seen from above ... Pudgy fingers blowing a kiss ... Now, in repulsion and in dread, she knew exactly where she had first seen Clifford Cox.

CHAPTER IV

Don came down the stairs. Well-groomed, pressed, smelling of lavender soap. A year ago he had given up cologne. He said combatively, "I assume you told our charming hostess about my allergies."

"No, Don." She had told no one anything. Her mouth had never been so dry.

He stood silently at her side. They were the same height. His cold eyes appraised the light brown coronet of hair, the broad forehead nearly matching in hue, the soft lime-colored frock cut to fit the base of her round neck. This was known as a jewel neckline, but Audrey wore no ornaments.

"You look all right. But, for God's sake, remember not to bat your eyes. It's getting to be quite a mannerism."

"Don, we'd better go. I'm almost certain the Dexters have their eyes glued to our screen door."

"O.K."

They crossed the narrow drive, mounted low rounded steps.

"Look out, look out!" Rachel came squealing to the door. "There's a loose brick you might trip on. I always have to warn ..."

"Pay no attention to her!" yelled Alfred. "I fixed it this morning."

"Come in, come in," Rachel glowed with cordiality. "It's such a pleasure to have you both in our house. We're so glad to meet *you*, Mr. Adriance? *Dr*. Adriance?"

"At Harvard," Don told her, "one says 'Mister.'"

"Here, too." Alfred pumped their hands to the rhythm of the big, old-fashioned Phi Beta Kappa key swinging against his round little belly.

Don, Audrey saw, knew he had been caught out. Not a good beginning. She glanced nervously around the room which was a mirror image of her own. There were differences. Of course, nothing could be done about oriels and mullions, but homely objects seemed to make it lighter, more livable. In front of the fireplace a large china animal sat on a round hooked rug which stated properly that "The Cat is on the Mat." On the dais beneath the lozenged window stood a table laden with plates, glasses, food. She looked away from it quickly. Had she been "batting" her eyes?

"Oh, Mrs. Adriance, this is Mr. Lund." The man whom she had seen stride down the river road on the previous morning came toward her, holding out his hand. Mrs. Dexter's detective.

She looked up at a tall, lean man with the dull, slightly graying hair of a towhead turned forty, at a narrow Nordic face with a fine network of scars around thin lips.

"Behold, Mrs. Adriance," Rachel laughed heartily, "the horrors of having a detective in the house. I don't dare to taste a thing I'm cooking and put the spoon back in the dish without washing it. I know Mr. Lund would find out. It's an awful strain."

"Don't you dare to wash the spoon you made that swell chocolate frosting with or the bowl either till I have a chance to lick them," responded Mr. Lund.

"You see," Alfred was explaining to Don, "the houses are just exactly alike. Only we don't use them in quite the same way. Your landlords, the Kings, filled that room at the right of your front door with massive dining-room furniture. Thornton Gray uses *his* for a study and a ... a study. Mine, here on the *left* of the door is also a study."

"Among other things," said Rachel without malice. "I sit at the window a lot, too, with my Red Cross knitting. Of course, Thornton has to study more than Alfred does; he hasn't been at it so many years, and then I guess Anthropology is sort of different from Education. Alfred worked his courses out beautifully years and years ago, and now they go on and on so smoothly." She said, to Don alone, "My husband teaches the Philosophy of Education, the Evolution of Education, and the Sociology of Education. I think they're all a little alike."

"I'm sure they are," Don agreed, and Audrey saw that Rachel was pleased.

Alfred, she noted with relief, was already in the foyer.

"It's the Grays," shouted Rachel and scurried after him, calling, "Look out, look out ... a loose brick ..."

"Pay no attention ..." the rest of Alfred's speech was lost in a murmur of four voices.

Mr. Lund smiled at Audrey and she smiled back. He, too, evidently liked the Dexters. Don had strolled over to the fireplace to examine titles in a small bookcase. No one had a more supercilious nose than Don.

Edna Gray came into the room, swishing ruffles, patting harsh curls. Rachel loped after her calling, "Now, everybody must meet everybody else. Oh, Mrs. Adriance, here's your teacher."

Alfred pattered in first, then Dr. Thornton Gray. Audrey looked up, and drew a quick breath—this shouldn't have happened. There was already far too much to take. Not a stocky, middle-aged professor. Here was the dark young man she had met on the stadium stairs ... Something scarlet had hung on his arm. Of course, a marshal's gown. He was looking at her the way he had last night. She was feeling the way she had.

He did not cross the room. He bowed and said in a deep voice, "How do you do, Mrs. Adriance."

She murmured something, she spoke to Edna. Probably she was behaving beautifully. Anyway, Mr. Lund, who was looking at her, didn't seem to be at all surprised. In a minute this silliness would end.

Mercifully, perhaps, she was still emotionally blurred when Beulah Briggs Cox pushed her way through the Dexter duet, leaving splinters of "loose brick" and "I fixed it, fixed it" to fall upon her husband.

She managed to make "Good evening" sound so like "Ho-yo-to-ho" that everyone rallied round like a Wagnerian chorus, and in the weaving of the ensemble and the tingling of her own nerves, Audrey missed the moment she had dreaded for thirty hours.

She had not seen the meeting between Don and Mr. Clifford Cox.

Thinking of this, her nerves were steady enough. Fear was familiar, real. The other feeling belonged to daydreams, not to her life. Below the high hum of all other voices she was aware of Thornton Gray's but now it was less important.

Mrs. Dexter was leading Cox around the room. They had passed Don, which meant that the two men had already met. Yet Don looked only normally and unpleasingly arrogant, as, hands in pockets, he watched Cox's sluglike fingers on Mrs. Gray's arm.

Now Mr. Cox was holding out a moist hand to Audrey. She saw little drops of sweat on his protuberant forehead. The room was very warm.

"Good evening, Mr. Cox." She tried to be cordial, not to wrench her fingers away. "May I introduce Mr. Lund?"

"And won't you present me, too, Mrs. Adriance?" Beulah's arrival in the group hastened her husband's reluctant drift toward the detective. "Everyone says you're here to give the Schultz Memorial Lectures on Social Disintegration, Mr. Lund, but I am sure there is something behind that."

Audrey turned away from them. For the moment she was alone. Edna Gray had managed to make Don sit beside her in front of the fireplace. His back was to Audrey, his head inclined toward the young woman whose long face was flushed with sudden emotion and who played viciously with the lace jabot much too fluffy for a girl with a big chin.

On the far side of the room next to the front door Thornton Gray stood beside Rachel and obligingly pinched Grane's tail. He's kind, Audrey thought, although he looks stern. Proud, his wife had called him. Perhaps. The tall, broad-shouldered body lightly carried, the wiry black hair brushed back from the wide, high forehead, the large cleanly defined nose and mouth gave the impression of strength controlled. Years older than his wife? Well, yes, three or four.

The door from the kitchen swung open and Alfred backed into the room, gripping a tray of filled sherry glasses. He stopped for a moment under the oriel, smirking through his brushy beard and then trotted toward the fireplace.

There was a small love seat behind Audrey. She sat down quickly and studied her folded hands. Look happy and gay, look natural and don't look at Don.

"May I join you, Mrs. Adriance?" Thornton Gray stood over her, a glass of sherry in each hand.

"Of course." She took the glass in her right hand, clasped the left hand over the right to steady it.

He sat down at her side. The seat was so small that he had to be close. "I received a class roll card this afternoon with your name on it. That is, if you're 'Audrey?'"

"I am." Don't think of anything. Don't feel anything. And don't bat your eyes. Just concentrate on holding the glass and saying a few simple words. "I shall be awfully dumb. I've never had any University work."

"You've hardly had time," he said.

"Oh, yes, I should have graduated a year ago. That is, if I had entered …"

"But instead you married."

"Yes, I married." She couldn't say it lightly but she tried to smile. He was looking at her gravely. His eyes were long and narrow and deeply set under black brows.

"Yes," he said, "one does." When he smiled, she saw that the lines from nose to mouth were too deep for a man of his age. "Your husband is in the English Department?"

"Yes, for the summer."

"We hope he'll stay longer than that. I happened to see Wilkins, the department chairman, before he left for the summer. He told me a little about your husband and said we were fortunate to have him here."

Then he didn't tell you much, Audrey thought. "Don did his thesis under Professor Wilkins when he was at Harvard."

Thornton Gray looked at her over his raised glass. "You have a beautiful tan. I envy you the hours in the sun."

"We were in Florida most of the winter. My husband was ill. He's fine now." Is he? Don't look.

Gray emptied his glass. "Shall I take yours if you aren't going to drink?" He held out his hand.

She felt pressure on her left shoulder. Don, standing behind her, was gripping it and saying, "For God's sake, Audrey, drink your sherry."

She lifted the glass to her lips and drank, looking down at the glass.

"I want to talk to you," she heard Don say. He pulled up a chair beside Thornton Gray. His voice had the intensity it always had now when he spoke about his work.

"Me, too," Edna, simpering, was dragging a chair from the fireplace, hesitating between their group and the corner where the Coxes talked with Lund.

All the men rose except Mr. Cox. "Here, here." Rachel brought another chair forward. "Alfred will give us some more sherry and we'll all sit in one nice big circle."

Shielding her half-filled glass from the hovering decanter, Audrey tried to relax. At her side Thornton Gray was leaning far forward, listening to Don. "No," she heard him say, "I don't get a chance to do any research these days. As a matter of fact, the course in primitive myths I'm giving this summer is the first straight anthropology I've taught since the spring of 1943."

"But Thornton is doing such a wonderful job for the Army," Rachel interposed. "Training real leaders for Japan."

"That's perhaps a little strong." He smiled at her and said perfunctorily to Don, "We have a group of CATS here. You know, Civil Affairs Training for the Far Eastern Area. I give the men background courses in Japanese customs and social life." He leaned back as if the subject were exhausted.

"You're deferred for this?" Don asked.

"Unfortunately, I was assigned to the work when the Army made its contract with the University and something known as 'courtesy' keeps me here. Of course, if anyone with enough Brass on his knuckles wanted to reach down for me, I could be taken. Apparently no one does."

Rachel said with kindly interest, "Have you been deferred, Mr. Adriance?"

Audrey felt every muscle grow tense. Then Don's voice came, calm and even. "Permanently. Allergy." He spread his hands slightly apart, indicating that they held no glass.

"You've been in Japan ... quite a lot, haven't you?" Audrey spoke rapidly, looking at no one.

"I have." Mr. Clifford Cox was giving her a soft fat smile. "I was born there and lived there with my dear parents for the first twenty years of my life."

"But that does not interest our Army or Government," deplored Beulah. "No, they have as little use for experts as one often hears."

Edna Gray's little blue eyes, high up in her long face, shifted from her husband to the Coxes, as if she were trying to decide between family and friendship. "Oh," she put forth inanely, "I know it's awful not to hate Japan just now, but I can't really. It's such a cute country. Everything's so *little*."

"Little food," said her husband.

"Ah," Mr. Cox held up a lump of a thumb, "but lots to drink."

"Let me fill your glass." Alfred Dexter advanced with the decanter.

Audrey stole a quick glance at Don. His lip was thrust out slightly like an unhappy child's. His right hand lying on his knee was quivering. She looked up hastily and met the clear impersonal gaze of Eric Lund.

"The Japanese have some charming customs," Edna resumed, "and they write delightful poetry. I don't want to lose the *best* of what they have. I want to hand it on to Sister. That's why I'm so glad to work at the language again with Mr. Cox. I'm teaching Sister a few words now."

"How nice!" said Rachel. "Has she learned to say 'Mother' in Japanese?"

"Ha Ha!" proclaimed Clifford Cox.

Beulah turned the gleam of her pince-nez upon him. Everyone else looked away.

Thornton Gray spoke dryly. "In Japanese, 'Ha Ha' is the equivalent of Mother."

He leaned back on the love seat but Audrey could feel the tensity of his shoulder as it touched hers. These people—these nice people—had their troubles, too, but she didn't have to deal with them. She relaxed, half closing her eyes. Voices murmured around her. Alfred Dexter was saying something about kimonos and being answered in various degrees of feminine raillery, but she did not really listen. And in the moment of quiet that she had created for herself, she became too conscious of Thornton Gray's nearness.

Abruptly she sat forward, listening as if avid to Alfred's words to Beulah Briggs Cox.

"The most revolting advertising," he was sputtering gleefully. "It's unbelievable. 'Blessed Event' dresses, it called them. I'm amazed that you would purchase a ... that is, that you would deal with such people, Beulah."

"You should be, Alfred." Mrs. Cox offered him only an enigma.

"Would you buy a dress at a store that used such language, Edna? Would you, Mrs. Adriance?" Alfred whisked his beard from Mrs. Gray's modestly downcast eyes to Audrey.

"Probably," said Audrey vaguely and saw his eyes brighten. "That is, if there was a marked-down sale."

Alfred's bright button eyes slid up and down Audrey. "Do you mean—" It wasn't the look of a satyr nor yet that of an obstetrician looking for customers, but it was certainly keen. "Harrumph." He cleared his throat and then, "Cadwallader!"

Through the swing door the elderly black dog trotted across the room and into the middle of the circle. He would have looked very sleek and handsome had his mouth not been encumbered with a copy of *Crime Mirror*.

"Did you send him to the corner on an errand, Mr. Lund?" Audrey asked the detective.

"It looks that way. Here, old fellow." Cadwallader advanced toward the call but at the first touch on his burden he backed away, growling.

"Well, I'd like a detective to tell me how that dog got in here," Rachel wanted to know. "I shut the screen door and the inside door tight. Here, Caddy, get out." She slapped at him. "Look at him duck and I've never really hit him in my life. That dog is the worst coward."

"He is not." Alfred beamed at his pet. "He's a very clever strategist. He gets all the other dogs into a fight and then withdraws."

"You mean," said his mistress, "he runs home with his tail between his legs. You go out, Caddy. Shoo! Shoo!" She flapped him in front of her toward the French doors opening on the garden.

"What interests me," said Thornton Gray, "is the source of his material. Who in our Tudor-towered neighborhood will own to *Crime Mirror*? Certainly not the FBI?" He smiled at Mr. Lund.

"It's not required reading for the Department of Justice," Eric Lund took the pipe out of his mouth, "but we sometimes find it useful."

"Cut up in pieces and hung on a nail?" This was Cox.

"That kind of magazine," Lund ignored him, "runs a page of photographs and life histories of wanted criminals. Reward for information leading to the capture of these fugitives from justice, and so on. The Department occasionally supplies photographs of impostors, bigamists, confidence men, the sort that use a lot of different aliases. We've had good success."

"Oh, my, I'm going to get that magazine from Caddy and start informing right away," Edna Gray giggled. "I'm just crazy to have a new fur coat and Thornton doesn't think it's right to buy one in war time. Not even with my own money."

She glanced quickly toward her husband who returned the look with rocklike impassivity.

It was Don who answered her. "If I were you, Mrs. Gray, I wouldn't buy *that*—either."

The self-righteous tone, the oddly stressed words stirred a wasp of anger in Edna Gray's dull face. "You wouldn't? Meaning the reward is too small for your consideration? Or are you—afraid?"

"One hears," Don's thin lips formed a supercilious curve, "that the amount does not exceed a hundred dollars. One might assume that a lady with her own money might consider this a rather paltry award for turning in her friends."

She fixed him with a pale glower, did the same for her husband and for Mr. Cox. "My friends or my neighbors or my own family. No, it really wouldn't be worth it and it wouldn't be patriotic when there's such a labor shortage. Even at the University." She laughed, but no one else did.

"There." Rachel returned from the eviction of Cadwallader. "Come, everyone, and eat. You'll find trays at this end of the table. Everyone must help himself."

All rose hastily, gratefully. Audrey felt Thornton Gray's hand close over hers and take away her half-filled glass. He raised it in a silent toast and drank. She met his eyes and started hastily for the buffet.

On the dais the High Table was covered with pink glass plates, heart-shaped and each bearing three objects that could have been formed only with a high degree of dexterity and that could be eaten with relish by any refugee.

"Oh, how lovely," Edna crooned. "A real bouquet of salads."

"My dear Rachel," Beulah pronounced, "quite like color photographs in the *Ladies' Home Journal*. Each confection, I am certain, has an appropriate appellation."

"Here is the sugar, Mr. Cox. You take yours black, I know, Thornton. So manly. Well, yes, Beulah. That one is Puffed Tomato. The dark green sticking in it all over? Oh, those are slices of cucumber. Unpeeled."

The man close behind Audrey said quietly in her ear, "If my wife were here, she'd begin to quote Ogden Nash. Something like 'My dear, how did you ever think of this delicious salad?'"

With a mixture of relief and disappointment, Audrey saw that the speaker was Eric Lund.

"The recipe," Rachel was explaining, "called that one a macarooned pear. But mine is a little different. It's a Wheatied pear."

Audrey looked fearfully for Don. Now would be a nice moment for him to say, "My God." Luckily he was concentrating on placing himself next to the professor of anthropology.

"What," asked Clifford Cox with a snicker, "is the fat pink one?" He ran his finger over the third artifact on each of the plates still left on the buffet table.

Rachel smiled innocently at an obscene roll of boiled ham, with a stem at one end and at the other a heavy burgeoning of potato salad. "They call it Cornucopia Surprise."

Alone at the opposite end of the long table Audrey said to Eric Lund, "It looks to me like 'Night in Old Vienna' when Freud's favorite pupils brought around their symbols for supper."

"In my own uneducated way, Mrs. Adriance, I would have said, 'spare parts from the autopsy room.' But we're seeing the same thing. Let's sit over here by the door."

Through the wide-opened French doors, the Victory Garden looked cool in the early evening light. Opposite Audrey, Rachel Dexter sat and admired her guests. Next to her Don's narrow head was turned to Thornton Gray, listening, talking intently, fork suspended in steady fingers. So far, not bad. But—what about Mr. Cox? Seeking him between his wife and Mrs. Gray, Audrey met sudden hostility in Edna's tightened little mouth as she reached out a sudden possessive hand to her unresponsive husband.

"My dear Rachel," Beulah exclaimed, "your damask napkins in war time. And you have no laundress. How generously you fortify our morale."

"I detest paper," Alfred announced, "and it is much scarcer than soap."

"Or than my labor," said Rachel good-naturedly. "Are any of you going to join the Bach Chorus?"

Clifford Cox had been staring pop-eyed for some minutes. At Don or at Thornton Gray? Audrey tried not to look at anything but a pear smeared with cream cheese and Wheaties. Her stomach felt a little queer.

"Bach," said Mr. Cox. He repeated it juicily. "Say, I heard once that that fellow wrote a piece called *Air on a G-String*. Hee, hee, hee!"

In the ensuing silence he raised his napkin and mopped his bulging brow. And to ascertain that effort had not been wasted, he lowered his hand and inspected the best grade of damask.

Audrey struggled to her feet. As Mr. Lund took her plate from her, she saw in a gathering haze that Don was looking hard at Clifford Cox. In disgust at an uncouth gesture, or in recognition?

Eric Lund held open the door for her and she passed dizzily into the garden.

"Thanks," she murmured. "Please don't come out. I'll be all right when I'm alone."

CHAPTER V

She was better in the garden. Her stomach no longer moved in response to the psychological stimuli of sherry and Cornucopia Surprise; her ears and eyes were cleared from the nastiness of Clifford Cox.

But she was not all right. Unfortunately, when one feels less, one can think more. Mr. Cox was not merely smut. Within his flabby fat lay threat and menace to Don and to her. He could tell what he knew about them, tell almost anyone and it would spread insidiously in the tight little academic community, making it impossible for Professor Wilkins to continue Don's last chance. But perhaps Cox would not talk; for if he did, Don might retaliate with data that would alienate Cox's wife's income from him forever. If Don had such information. She, Audrey, had none.

Out of sight from the Dexter household, almost out of sound of their voices, she stood by the Grays' spirea hedge, feeling a wave of cool shadow, facing the more certain danger to the flimsy structure of their new life.

The destruction of Donald Adriance would need no single word spoken by Clifford Cox. Mere recognition of a man who might know too much about him, coupled with that incomprehensible hostility toward Mrs. Gray, could upset the delicate emotional balance that held Don erect. Already, in the few moments since Audrey had left the supper party, he could have slipped.

Should she go back at once? Learn the worst, help Don see it through? No, not yet. He must be left on his own, poor and weak as it often was. That way and that way only, could he hope to win.

Something loped across her field of vision. Cadwallader, still carrying the magazine in his mouth, rounded the corner of the Grays' house and aimed for Audrey.

"Hello," she said to him. "Want your head scratched? You do?"

He stood against her, wagging his heavy tail gratefully enough, but when her other hand tugged at the magazine an increased grip and a growl stated clearly that as colporteur of crime he demanded a higher price.

"Oh, please, Cadwallader," she begged, "let the lady see the nice pretty pictures."

With a gulp that anchored a further half-inch of newsprint, Cadwallader made off in the direction he had come, and there he met his match.

It was a small thing that stopped him, with black curls and red polka-dot pajamas, and it is doubtful that anything more businesslike than the slap she delivered could have been developed in four years' growth. Straight across his nose fell the efficient little hand and out of his jaws fell *Crime Mirror*.

"Naughty bad Caddy!" She hugged the damp pages to her miniature bosom. "Running off with my mag-a-zine!" She scowled ferociously at the grinning beast now reclined at her bare feet. She was not unaware of audience.

"You were much better at getting it away from Cadwallader than I was." Audrey went over to her. "Everybody in the house tried to take it but he was too quick for them."

"I saw them." The little girl had merry eyes. "Through the door in the kitchen. I peeked."

"So that's how Cadwallader got into the house. You let him in."

"Um-hum." She looked up cautiously for censure. Audrey smiled down at the incongruous urchin and her treasure. "And that's your magazine?"

"Not exac'ly mine. It's my sitter's. She keeps it at our house to read when my Mommy goes out. I haven't got any sitter tonight. I'm sitting with my own self."

"Not exactly, are you?"

The young lady switched subjects. "What's your name?"

"Audrey. What is yours?"

"Mar-gar-et." She said it carefully, defiantly, as if she expected to be disputed. "Mar-gar-et Gray."

"I like your name."

"My Daddy calls me Mar-gar-et. I don't like 'Sister,'" the child said earnestly. "All the kids at school ask me if I've got a brother or a sister or something. They ask me and ask me. We haven't even got a baby. Where do you live?"

"In the house back there. Next to Mr. Dexter's."

"In Mrs. King's house? Did you come here in an auto-mo-bile?"

"No. On a train."

"On a really truly train? I've never rided—rode—on a train in my whole life. My Daddy takes me to see trains sometimes. Some day my Daddy's going to take me to ride on a train and I'm going to eat inside it and go to bed inside it and everything."

"I like trains, too," Audrey told Thornton Gray's daughter. "Hadn't you better go in your house now?"

"Um-hum," she agreed. "Will you come with me?"

"I'll walk over to the door with you."

"It's awful dark in the big room now."

"No, it isn't. Look, Margaret, I'll pick you up and toss you in the door and then I'll stand on the doorstep and watch you go all the way upstairs. All right?"

"Um-hum." She held up her arms, the small right paw clutched tight around *Crime Mirror*.

Holding her, Audrey felt something of what it could mean to have a little girl like Margaret. A little girl with a father like Thornton Gray.

"See me! See me!" Margaret bounced and laughed in her arms. "See me! Da-addy!"

Thornton Gray towered over them, standing close to take Margaret. The child, reaching toward him, suddenly turned with a teasing giggle and wound both arms around Audrey's neck. "You can't get me, Daddy."

For a moment the three blended. A very tender expression came over Thornton's face as he looked down at the child; it did not change as he looked at Audrey.

"You like Mrs. Adriance, don't you?" he said gently.

"Mrs. Adriance?" The little girl laid her black curls against Audrey's neck. "That's Audrey. Don't you know?"

"I know." A flush appeared along his cheeks. Abruptly he pulled the child from Audrey. "I'll take her up to bed. Thanks for being with her. It's the first time we've left her alone."

The screen door slammed behind Mr. Gray, his daughter, and a copy of *Crime Mirror*.

Quickly, before she could feel anything—tenderness, loneliness, fear—Audrey went across the grass and into the Dexters' house.

The group had shifted since her departure. Based near the fireplace and with the others in an irregular semicircle before him, Mr. Lund was giving a little talk on homicide.

"Oh, yes, there are a few cases of ingenious weapons, odd poisons," he was saying, "but ninety-five per cent of all murders are by shooting, stabbing or assault."

Audrey slipped into a chair next to Don. It was the one empty seat in the circle—Thornton's. Only Edna Gray made something of her return by an ostentatious regard of the door, as if expecting a second person.

Beulah, smiling and drawing up her big bosom in the manner of a clubwoman about to question the speaker of the day, produced in a combination of chest tone and high girlish laughter,

"May I inquire of our expert with what one assaults?"

"Anything handy," Lund told her, "fists, feet, club, iron pipe, gun butt."

"Oh, Mr. Lund," Edna fluttered, "I don't understand ... about feet."

"Kicks. What did you think?" Rachel Dexter unobtrusively put a plate with ice cream and hot coffee into Audrey's lap. "It's a good way."

"Rachel, really!'

From Beulah, "Poor dear Alfred."

"Weren't you ever a child?" asked Rachel serenely. "I was and in a tough neighborhood, too."

"*Sister* would never ..." murmured her mother.

"I'm not so sure," snapped Alfred Dexter. "She has been quite strenuous with Cadwallader."

Drinking the hot coffee, finding it good, Audrey summoned courage to look at Don and Clifford Cox. Her first impression was that they were unchanged, her second that they were too carefully not looking at each other.

When her attention came back to the group, Alfred Dexter was finishing a speech.

"But with all the scientific method and all the modern inventions and all the brilliant personnel you have described, I want to know just one thing: Why do so many criminals get away?"

Eric Lund waited a moment. To control temper? Or didn't a man like that have personal feelings about his job? Audrey admired the easy, not too easy, smile he summoned for the irate taxpayer. "As you say, most of the fault is ours. But there's another cause that operates seriously from time to time. That's the unwillingness, often, of good citizens to give law enforcement officers information about criminals who live next door to them. That's because they're sure these men and women we're after are all right. Sure, they know what crooks look like. They've seen plenty of movies and photographs from the line-up. But what dangerous criminals really look like ..." He paused as the garden door opened. "Dangerous criminals look like people, like you and me."

Thornton Gray came into the room and sat down behind his wife.

"The good neighbors," Lund lit his pipe and went on, "think they know everything that goes on next door or across the hall. Usually they don't. Even with people you know well—have been around with for years—there are likely to be gaps that two friends have never bothered to fill in for each other. One of those gaps might just possibly have been filled by criminal activities."

"Take the case of you four men," he added lightly. "If you were all past fifteen or sixteen when you met the wife, there may be a spot of time she hasn't yet landed on. When you were a kidnapper or a bank robber or a car thief."

"Oh," Rachel Dexter cried out gaily, "now I know what you were doing, Alfred, the month I spent at Mother's, in 1913. You take the loot right out of your safe deposit box in the morning and turn it over to Mr. Lund and me."

Audrey did not see how Alfred received this jest. She kept her eyes on Eric Lund. It seemed to her that his narrow face had become a shade too impersonal.

"My dear wife and I," the unction was Mr. Cox's, "would be obvious suspects for each other. We married on faith."

"Well, I'm sure that for all I know, Thornton could be all kinds of a crook." Spite enlivened Edna's usual monotone. "I've always thought it was just as well that he's never going to be a great man, because after his death I could never write his biography. There's too much I don't know up to the last six years."

Audrey said nothing. Of all the wives, she alone knew that she knew the worst about her husband.

Don was rising now and so was everyone else. Farewells to the hosts came fast; they had already stayed too long. At the door little groups formed for last words. Don, with his absorbed professional air, talked eagerly to Thornton Gray. Edna Gray said something social to inattentive Mr. Cox, who for once seemed to want to join his waiting wife. Beulah, outside in the driveway with Audrey, audibly attached her standard suspicions to Mr. Lund. Silently Audrey, too, wondered "what was behind all that," as she waited for Don, ready to meet collapse, defeat, whatever came.

The door opened. Clifford Cox came out. Everything about him—suit, flesh, features—sagged. He stumbled on the step, caught at his wife's heroic arm and pushed her toward the gap in their hedge. Audrey scarcely heard their "Good night." Just inside the screen door she saw Don. He was saying something to Edna Gray. Edna said something to him. Audrey could see moving lips, catch the tones that distinguished each voice. No words reached her, no facial expressions that could have told her what she dreaded to know. She couldn't see whether Don's hands trembled. Her own teeth were chattering.

"Good night," Don called to Mrs. Dexter, "and thanks again for a lovely party."

She saw him clearly now as he opened the door. He was lighting a cigarette and in the flame she noted the long lashes against his thin cheeks with a rare pang of pity for the boy she had met at a dance when she was seventeen.

He crossed the driveway and came up to her. He did not speak. When they had entered their house and climbed the stairs, Don paused at the door of his room. The muscles of his face were taut but the hand that held the cigarette was as steady as the self-satisfied tone in which he said, "I shall be able to get everything I want from Thornton Gray. It was a good evening, Audrey."

CHAPTER VI

He was not steady in the morning. His hands shook so that he could scarcely tie his bow. He slammed in and out of the bathroom, drank glass after glass of water. One glass slopped over, fell to the tiles and broke.

Carrying the fragments to the basement, Audrey shuddered. How could Don ever make it through the day that must follow this fantastic morning? The morning after nothing at all. Very slowly she emptied jagged particles into a trash can, keeping herself away from the pointless, causeless sounds of Don's distress.

"Audrey, come here!" He was ordering her. Not begging or pleading. It was a good sign.

"Yes, Don." She raced up the stairs.

"Audrey—" His grooming was perfect and he stood very straight, briefcase in hand, his face tense with a purpose which she was, quite impersonally, to serve. "Audrey," he repeated, "what in hell was that girl's name?"

She tried not to stare, tried to read his need.

"That girl I brought home. Oh, for God's sake, don't ask what girl. I know as well as you do there was more than one. When we were in Hartford. The girl you helped."

"Her name was Hilda Hill."

"Right." It was what he wanted to know. He pushed open the swing door.

Audrey followed him into the Tudor gloom. "Don," she asked gently, "are you coming home to lunch?"

He answered her from the foyer, without kindness and without hate. "I have a great deal to do today. I'll be home when it's done and not before."

"Yes, Don," she said. "Good-by."

What next? Always before Audrey had known the answer to that. one. Don was thoroughly unreliable but quite predictable. She had seldom been able to forecast the moment of returning trouble, but when it came, the sequence was uniform. Now his quick fluctuations of mood baffled her. She would have to be ready for anything.

Such as dinner at any hour Don might return. Chicken en casserole? He liked that, and it bore waiting well. On a hot day like this, when the oven had been on for two or three hours, the dinette would be unbearable. She'd use the dining-room tonight and dust it right away.

Brushing, polishing, scrubbing the Kings' mock heroic walnut, bruising her outlying parts against false knobs and machine carving. Audrey considered Don's inconsistencies. The early morning fantasy climaxed by broken glass didn't fit with his amazing control of the Cox menace. Or had he simply not recognized the man at all? And there was the irrelevant intrusion of Hilda Hill. As Don had admitted, there had been more than one woman. They had come and they had gone, and afterwards Don had never mentioned their names. Sometimes he hadn't known the names.

Except as elements in the whole shameful pattern of their lives, Audrey hadn't cared much about the women. Probably because for a long time she had not cared about Don or about any man. She had been sure she never would....

She heard the click of the opening house door and steps over the foyer carpet. She turned from the window, smiling.

In the dining-room door stood Clifford Cox.

"The Lady Audrey looks beautiful this morning, and kind of glad to see me." His fatuous smirk included his own appearance as well as hers.

He had certainly tried to do something about it. His bright blue slack suit was stiffly new and he had left the neck unbuttoned to a point that would disclose a seductive expanse of fat, sun-reddened chest. He had even washed his hair.

"Good morning," said Audrey and waited.

"You're even lovelier than you were the first time I saw you. You'll have to pardon me for not recognizing you right away. Why didn't you say something when we met out here in the yard?" There was bravado in the last question.

When he got no answer, he went on cautiously, "How long did it take Don to remember an old pal?"

"I don't know," said Audrey. "Does he remember? He has not mentioned you to me in any way."

The cold honesty of her tone seemed to reassure him. "Don's doin' all right here. Glad to see it." He advanced toward her. "You'd do a lot for Don, wouldn't you?"

She could feel the sunny air against her back and hear the clip, clip of gardening shears not far off.

"Honey," he was close beside her, fat fingers playing with the curtain at her shoulder, "you aren't having much home life right now, are you? Our situation is a little bit the same. How about our getting together for a little fun? Just between two old friends?"

His shoulder touched hers. He smelled like lard.

"We are not old friends. You saw me only once." She twitched her shoulder away.

"But, zowie, what a lot I saw! You have to admit, sweetheart, the circumstances were kind of intimate."

Clip. Snip. The sound seemed to be in her ear. And it was, nearly. Through the screen she could see that the Adriance ivy was being cut to the bone. She raised her voice. "But you're quite wrong, Mr. Cox. I love it here because we have such fine neighbors. Particularly Professor Dexter. He is a most courteous gentleman."

The clipping stopped. When it rose again from a considerable distance, Clifford Cox tiptoed to the door. "I get it, but remember, honey," he gave a last threatening leer, "I could do a lot for you. Think it over."

Think! In the first minutes alone Audrey could only feel. Anger, disgust shook the fingers performing the now supererogatory turn of the key in the house door. Here in this secure University world she had again to make the old choice between degradation and isolation.

The old choice, the old social problem, but this time with something new. The thing Clifford Cox wanted from her was—face it—akin with what she felt for Thornton Gray.

Shock of recognition momentarily dizzied her. She grasped the newel post, put her head down on her hands. I can't—

Can't what? She raised her head. Everything looked clear now. There was something she could do.

Quickly up the stairs, unbuttoning her pinafore as she ran. The aquamarine dress from her Florida vigil, the blue scarf twisted around her hair like a sibylline turban. Speed to the bus stop. Then relax, let the bus do the work. The cooler air crossing the river, maples climbing the hill to the campus, the long stone steps of the Administration Hall, a pink slip of paper given, a green slip received. Mrs. Audrey Adriance, having cancelled her registration for Anthropology 112S, is now entitled to a refund of fees which Dr. Donald Adriance can invest in some good books on primitive mythology, titles of which he can obtain, along with everything else he wants, from Professor T. Gray. And what will Mrs. Adriance get? A simpler life, it is to be hoped, and to that, since she is next door to the University library, she might add a little knowledge to her own field of study.

Noon of this first day of summer school was a quiet hour in the Medical-Biological reading room. Few readers sat at the long tables beside the open shelves where misery, shame and death stood bound in blue and red, in austere statistics purged of the personal: *The Journal of Abnormal Psychology, the American Journal of Diseases of Children, Quarterly Journal of Studies in Alcohol, the Anatomical Record*. Here, the physician's measured hope ("your husband has a good chance to make it from now on") becomes the prognosis that under the most favorable conditions sixty-four per cent of cases had not lapsed within four years.

Audrey closed the book. It had not been merry reading but she felt something of the relief of a burden shared, an impersonal group kinship. On her way to the librarian's desk a man seated at the end of a table glanced up at her. Light from above fell strongly on the white scars about his mouth. Instinctively she shifted the book to conceal the title and flushed at the stupidity of the motion. Nothing could have made it clearer that she had something to hide. And Mr. Lund, perhaps already aware of her trouble, was the one person in their present environment who would find it nothing but commonplace.

Outside, over the green campus girls strolled or lolled. Pastel dirndls, flowered peasant skirts were few among the sloppy shirt tails and rolled jeans of a generation whose boy friends in filthy fatigues fought through the third month on Okinawa. Small-town school superintendents, thin-haired and sweaty, lugged briefcases along shady walks, and close to passing feet a gray squirrel licked chocolate from a discarded wrapper. A platoon of AST, marching in ragged formation to a fifth hour class, sighted Audrey and broke into: "Hubba, hubba, hubba!"

"My dear Mrs. Adriance, what an accolade!" A large lady, alighting from a car at the curb, planted herself in the middle of Audrey's path. "It must make you feel quite young."

"Oh, Mrs. Cox." Audrey, thinking compassionately of the girls without boys, and feeling not at all young, was unaware of military honors. To the rear of Mrs. Cox's acreage of starched white blouse and black accordion pleats, Edna Gray locked the door of her car.

"If your husband had seen the effect you made on those little G.I.'s, he would be verdant with jealousy. One could see how he suffered last evening whenever a man spoke to you."

"I couldn't," said Audrey.

Beulah Briggs Cox let forth a light treble of false laughter. "No one would believe you. I suppose you are meeting your husband for lunch?"

"Beulah," Edna Gray arriving at her side admonished, "what an embarrassingly naïve question. Women sometimes meet other women's husbands for lunch."

"I'm not meeting Don," Audrey answered Beulah Cox. "I'm on my way home. Don has a class this next hour. In this building, I think." She indicated the architectural confection of white-frosted gamboge on her right. "That is, if it's Abbott Hall."

"Alas, it is and I also have a class there in twelve minutes. Farewell." The *objet d'art* legs that took her slowly up the steps were obviously a structural weakness.

"I might go home, too." Edna looked vaguely ill, an effect unconsciously created or enhanced by crude make-up. Little smudges of mascara lay below baby-blue eyes and patches of violent pink across naturally white cheeks matched nail polish, and a jumper dress too tight over the breast and with a most uneven hem line. "There's a Red Cross lunch at the Campus Club, but I've got the car full of strawberries for jam. We've been out to a farmer's on County Road D. Thornton's going to pick up the car in a few minutes and take the berries home. I was planning to drive home with Rachel Dexter after lunch. But I don't know ... I might wait for Thornton and he could take you and me both ... Oh, I just remembered, why aren't you in Thornton's anthropology class this hour?"

"I've dropped the course," Audrey explained carefully. "When I registered I thought it might help my husband. He's terribly interested in a problem in mythology, but he can really get what he needs much more efficiently from books and directly from Professor Gray. My head isn't so good but my hands aren't bad. I can be a lot more use to Don as a typist and a cook."

Edna nodded absently. "I suppose I'd better go to the lunch. I promised

Rachel. She'll probably be late. You never know what she may have hit en route. She's an appalling driver. If you wait here by the car, Mrs. Adriance, Thornton can give you a lift home."

"Thanks a lot. But I have to stop for groceries. Good-by."

Audrey left Edna standing by the car, running a finger in and out of harsh yellow curls, and at a pace too brisk for the day she descended University Hill.

When her shopping was over, she was miserably hot. The sun outside the super-market burned her neck and beneath the binding blue scarf she could feel acid trickles down her forehead. The big sack of groceries needing both arms for support constantly reminded her that it had cost too much. Unless, by chance, it was just what Don wanted. Wasn't the bus ever coming? Except for a single elderly car, the road down the hill was empty. She leaned against the pole labeled "Bus Stop," shifting the weight to her hip. Would this be a night when Don would devour peppers or would he sit picking the minced green bits from the gravy and counting them in Middle English and Old High German?

The car stopped at the curb directly in front of her. The door opened. Scarcely looking at it, she stepped aside to give clear passage to the market.

"Audrey."

Even before she saw the driver, her name in that deep voice brought flush to her cheeks.

"Get in."

"I've got all this ..."

"Get in. This car is nothing but a huckster's truck anyway. Put it down anywhere in back. On top of anything. That door isn't shut tight. This old car ..." His arm, slamming the door, lay for a moment across her knees. "There."

Along the river flats the business section of the town ran from good to bad. Past the banks, the dress shops, the dime stores, the National Tea, the Heartland Café, Audrey concentrated on each scene. Opposite the soiled red station there was a grubby little square where dingy, sick-looking old men fed pigeons or just sat in the sun. No one seemed to talk to anyone. Audrey turned her head from their despair. For the first time she looked at Thornton.

He was driving slowly, watching the road. He was bare-headed. The thick black hair matched the curious brows that curved up suddenly and then slanted downward nearly to the outer corners of his deep-set eyes. The sharp oblique wings of his nose gave the profile a slight air of ferocity. Without turning to her, he said,

"Our Bowery. The hangout of homeless men. Men who have always been homeless. The old casual laborers who can't work anymore. This was the hiring center for the wheat fields and the lumber camps and for tile laying when they were in their prime. So now they drift back and stay. Sorry I can't take you out of it quicker. But it's well to drive carefully here and watch out for the drunks."

She turned away from him. She too watched the road.

"We're almost at the bridge." He paused. "Why did you drop the anthropology course?"

"The University certainly must give super-service." Her voice sounded silly to her. "I didn't sign the slip till eleven o'clock."

He said crossly, "I happened to go into the Registrar's office soon after you left." He stopped for the last red light before the bridge.

"Audrey!"

She turned to him.

"Why did you drop my course?"

Five years of evasion, rationalization, falsehood did her no good now. In the moment that she and Thornton looked at each other, she knew that she had told him everything she had meant to hide.

Red light became green. Thornton swung the car sharply away from the bridge. Now small factories bordered the river, poor houses straggled out toward open country. They left the pavement, climbed a dusty hill. At the top, fields lay open around them. Green bushes pushed up on the shoulder of the buff clay road dragged smooth and hard as concrete; weeds flowered blue in the ditches. On the right, between rough bluffs, the St. Cloud flowed through a channel choked with little wild islands.

The car stopped. Thornton opened the door at his side, leaned over and opened Audrey's.

"Get out."

He walked around to the car and stood beside her. "Get out," he repeated, looking down at her. Humor tempered the demand in his tone. "I want to put my arms around you."

She sat motionless, gazing through the windshield at the road, at the fine network of cracks in the buff clay. Then she got out of the car.

CHAPTER VII

The storm began at midnight. First, flames of lightning that seemed to add heat to the hot air; then, slowly and from a great distance, thunder approached, arrived, dominated the world. Last came cold rain. On County Road D hard drops beat up the clay and poured into the ditches. In the Stadium discarded commencement programs became pulp. Water raced down the gutters of University Hill, showered the bums on the Bowery, banged on the roofs of the Tudor toy village.

At a window of the Dexters' torrid oriel room Eric Lund sat with his pipe. Thunder and lightning were nothing to him except when they complicated his work. Tonight he had no job but the dull way in which he had spent the evening left him wakeful, over-stimulated. Mr. Lund could trap a killer and sleep the instant sleep of Cadwallader, but after delivering a lecture to two hundred good citizens, his nerves quivered for hours.

At such rare times he had a sure escape to reason and repose. A very simple, sentimental method for such a hard realist. Eric Lund would sit quietly and think about his wife. Tonight, however, Janet herself was his chief worry, and drawing slowly at his pipe, he tried to refrain from thought about what he couldn't help.

During lulls in the barrage he could hear the small sounds of the Dexters going to bed. Between minor ablutions Alfred seemed to patter from bathroom to bedroom to sputter at good old Rachel. Theirs might not be a meeting of very bright minds but it was safe to bet it was the most satisfactory alliance in the near neighborhood. Eric Lund did not indorse homicide but if this town needed a murder to meet the predicted death rate for 1945, a Grade A girl to throttle would be Edna Gray. Her husband might not express open gratitude to the executioner, but he would have a hard time producing credible grief. As for the other pairs ...

Lightning now and then gave glimpses of the white walls and dark windows of the Cape Cod cottage where Clifford Cox might now be making his one repulsive contribution toward earning his keep.

There were lights in the house next door. Their location changed. Full illumination in the kitchen or in the small upstairs room corresponding to Lund's, or a dim glow through the bedroom oriel when someone was using the Great Hall. The bedroom at the front and the bathroom stayed dark. Sometimes a figure was visible, and always the same. Mrs. Adriance, taking dishes out of the oven; picking up a book in the room above; once, just before she turned out a light staring wide-eyed into the storm.

Not the first night she's spent like this, Lund was certain. As certain as he was that it wouldn't be the last.

"I don't like it, Rachel, I don't like it at all."

Alfred Dexter removed a toothbrush from the middle of his beard and waved it at the bed where his wife sat up, knitting. The brush had a royal purple handle which matched Alfred's rayon satin pajamas.

"Close the door," said Rachel. "Mr. Lund will hear you or"—she looked at him over her spectacles—"see you."

Alfred shut off his secret vice from the eyes of the police and went on. "Out all night. I've stood it for years. But this is too much."

"It's his nature."

"I know, I know." He folded his hands behind his back. "But in a thunderstorm! At his age!"

"He isn't too old," said Rachel. "He's a male. You wouldn't have cared a bit, Alfred, if he were a lady and entertained all his gentlemen at home. Then you could have at least guessed who was the father of his puppies. Her puppies ... Caddy's, if he were a lady. Oh, dear, I'm all mixed up." She counted khaki stitches.

Alfred drew himself up one impressive inch. "Cadwallader," he announced, "is not the only putative father in this neighborhood."

Rachel glanced at him sharply. He was bending painfully to reinstate a slipper dislocated in the stretching process. "You wait," he murmured breathlessly. "You'll see."

She was only pretending to knit now.

"Don't you want to know who ...?"

She waited an exasperating while. "Do *you*, Alfred? Do you know?"

"W-ell," he was a little cautious. Once or twice in a long and specialized career he had been wrong. "Mrs. Adriance hasn't a very strong stomach right now."

"Neither have I," Rachel rolled up her knitting, "when Mr. Clifford Cox ... Oh, dear, where is my spectacle case?"

"Rachel!" Alfred stood by the bed, "when Clifford Cox does what? You tell me this instant!"

"Oh, here it is. Why, when Mr. Cox mops his greasy forehead on my table napkin. What did you think ... Oh, Alfred." She began to giggle.

"Give me those things." Alfred seized needles, wool, spectacles, sock, flung them on the floor, and trotted over to the wall switch.

Then the room was dark and quiet except for the thunder and lightning. Mr. Dexter climbed cozily into bed.

"Zowie! Look at that lightning!" Clifford Cox wadded curtain ruffles in his damp hand to give his wife a better view of the horrors of nature.

Thunder burst through the dark room. Silence, then an echo, as Beulah turned over in her twin bed.

"Some storm, I'm tellin' you." A brighter flash illumined his slack white belly. He freed the tortured organdy curtain and padded over to her.

"Listen, Sugar Mama," he drew a finger along the nape of her neck, "you goin' to be sweet to your baby?"

"Clifford," she reached back a hand and gently pushed off his touch,

"I am not going to give you five hundred dollars. Nor three nor two nor one. Nothing you have told me convinces me that you need to leave this place. You say it isn't healthy for you. You are quite wrong."

"If anything happened to me," he suggested, "you might be kind of sorry."

"Yes, I should. But nothing will."

He stood by the bed, shivering slightly as the first cold rain blew into the room. After a minute she said,

"When summer school is over we'll go on a trip. Anywhere you like."

He slammed the window shut and came back to her, clenching and releasing his soft fists. Thunder drowned the rattling rain.

"Mommy." He lifted up the sheet. "Baby's afraid of thunder."

"Clifford," she sighed, "please go to bed."

At first, Audrey hadn't minded the lightning. It was something to watch while she waited. And there was nothing else to do. Long ago, on nights like this, she had done lots of active things, mostly with a telephone. They had brought attention, unwelcome pity, but they had not brought Don home. But in the end he always came. He always would.

Shuddering, she picked up a book from the chaise-longue. Better read. But not up here where she might miss the sound of a car. Or of footsteps on the drive. By the window she paused, staring out into alternate darkness and glare. Whatever happened tonight would in a way make little difference to her. If Don somehow came through, kept this job, attained comparative security, she would have more food, more clothes, more self-respect, but she would not be free. Don didn't love her, didn't even like her very much, but she was the most important thing in his life because, no matter what he had done, she had stayed. She was his one stability, his one achievement. Everyone had told her that. They said that if he later became a great success in his profession, it would all be destroyed if she left him, if she took away the basis on which he had built. She had believed this, accepted the fact that she would be Don's wife as long as she lived.

Or until Don died. If Don were to die … She must have thought of this often but not so clearly, never before with a conscious wish.

She snapped off the bedroom light and ran downstairs, away from self-horror. The hot dank air of the Tudor well closed around her. Lightning taunted her from three sides, dancing across the mullions of the window above the dais, shooting through the French doors at the rear, winking dim and high from the oriel. She crouched in a wing chair facing the fireplace and opened her book.

> Up from Agean caverns, pool by pool
> Of blue salt sea, where feet most beautiful
> Of Nereid maidens weave beneath the foam
> Their long sea-dances ...

She didn't know what had first led her to *The Trojan Women*, but once found, their sorrow filled with dignity and beauty had often been an escape from her own sordid life. Sometimes, as tonight, she read without thought, the music lulling her.

> What is there that I fear to say?
> And yet, what help? ... Ah, well-a-day,
> This ache of lying comfortless
> And haunted!

This ache. For Thornton, for one brief moment which they would not repeat. She flung down the book. Was that a sound at the door? She listened, opened it on darkness and thunder. Don might not come for hours. Was it her fault that he was gone tonight? Had she been irritable with him or too obviously patient? Had she shown the resentment she couldn't always stifle, knowing that even if he someday grew up, it would be for his own sake and not for hers? They told her that whatever happened she was not to blame herself, all those wise people, in the same breath that they said there must never be a divorce. Did they know?

Now there was a new sound. She ran up the two steps to the dais. Yes, hard rain.

Rain meant a respite. Don hated wet; he wouldn't come home now till it was over. No one would bring him while torrents fell like this. Perhaps she could sleep a little.

On the cushioned bench she lay flat, head on arm. Comfortless and haunted!

The thin high wail rang through the house.

"Thornton! Oh, Thornton!"

He pulled on a flannel robe, opened his door, blinked in strong light.

"What's the matter?"

Halfway down the stairs Edna leaned against the wall with her hands covering her face.

"What's wrong?" He stood at the foot of the staircase.

"Oh, Thornton, I can't bear it!" She lowered her hands and the black chiffon night gown slipped off one shoulder.

"Can't bear what?"

Her voice rose. "The thunder! The lightning! The rain!" She started down the stairs.

"Get into your bed." He mounted the bottom step. "You'll catch cold in that thing."

She started up the stairs, turned her head over a bare shoulder. "You'll come? You won't leave me?"

"I'm coming up to see if you've waked Margaret."

When she had gone into her room, he opened the child's door and tiptoed to her bed. A moment later he came out and closed the door.

"Thornton, is Sister really all right?"

"Yes, perfectly."

"Thornton, please come here. I can't hear you." Her voice rose again. "Is Sister ...?"

He came toward the bed. "She's sound asleep."

"I'm glad," she said sweetly. "Dear little Sister."

"Edna, you'd better drop that name. The child hates it."

"You know why."

"Certainly. It makes her feel like a fool."

"Whose fault ... Oh! Thornton, it doesn't have to be that way." The lightning flash showed her sitting on the edge of the bed, holding out her arms. "Thornton—dear."

He turned to the stairs.

"Thornton, don't leave me. I'm afraid. I can't sleep. You haven't been asleep either!"

"I'll heat some milk for you," he said. "It won't take long."

After he had poured the boiled milk into a cup he carried it into the room where he slept. There was nothing in the room but a cot, a desk, books, and a few cushions covered with something durable which Edna frequently referred to as monk's cloth. From behind a row of books he took a yellow bottle and shook a large white tablet into the milk. He hesitated a moment, then shook in a second, and stirred a spoon carefully round and round in the cup. Then he went back to Edna.

A rose-shaded lamp was lighted above her bed. Wrapped modestly in a pale blue bed jacket, she lay on heaped pillows.

"Oh, Thornie, you're sweet to me."

"Drink it while it's hot."

"You'll stay till I go to sleep?"

"Yes." Her clothing lay on every chair. He took the bench from her rose-skirted dressing table and set it down by the window.

"You aren't very comfortable there."

He didn't answer.

She drank. "It tastes good. Don't you want a little? Just a sip? Oh, Thornie, don't you remember when we ..." She yawned.

"I remember upsetting the damned stuff all over me one night, if that's what you mean." He smiled faintly.

She yawned again. "I—guess—it—was. I'm so sleepy. You'd better take the cup."

He stood over her. "Are you all right?"

"Perfectly," she smiled up at him. "You won't go till I'm really asleep?"

"No," he promised, "I'll wait, Edna."

He went back to the bench and sat staring out the window. She did not speak again. After a while, when he turned around, her eyes were closed. He went over to the bed and looked at her anxiously, putting his hand on her arm. She stirred, settled deeper in the pillows. Her small mouth opened.

He snapped off the light. Gray dawn crept into the room. The storm was over and as he went downstairs he could hear the sharp clean notes of birds.

The birds may have wakened Lund. What kept his eyes open after he had consulted his watch in the clear early light of five o'clock was a determined scratching at the back door.

Wide awake now, Lund slipped on his pajama jacket, pulled cigarettes from the pocket, and went down to stop the noise. At the first scent of his feet across the kitchen, woofs reinforced the scrape. He opened the door and Cadwallader pushed past him, headed for the range, stretched out beneath it, and slept.

Lund, giving him a sympathetic grin, stepped out of the stuffy house. Outside a small breeze blew over wet flowers; it also carried a better smell to a hungry man who had not slept well. Coffee was brewing in the Adriance kitchen.

So the fellow was at home. God help that girl! Cleaning up after him, cursed for it probably, tiptoeing around all day.

A whirring sound came from the house next door, stopped, went on and on. Lund took his cigarette into the driveway. Yes, distinctly now, the hum of a vacuum cleaner at 5:00 A.M. Adriance was certainly not at home.

At the end of the drive a car stopped, a small sedan painted white. A bulky man with a good deal of gold braid got out and started slowly up the walk next door.

It looked as if God at the moment was not doing a great deal for Audrey Adriance.

CHAPTER VIII

Here in the kitchen dimmed by the wet green vines across the windows, early light of Central war time lay pale on blank white surfaces. The room still held the heat of the night. High over the stove Audrey could see the ivory shield of the doorbell. In the dusky hall the telephone table was a shadow. From one of these a sound would come to shatter the sick twilight.

The last hours of waiting were always like this. After everything had been done, the house set in ironic order, decorous hat and gloves laid out beside the shabby purse that hoarded a thin roll of bills for such exigency, then nausea crept through her.

She snapped off the current under the coffee and stood still, taking long breaths, counting them. Her fingers tested the security of her tightly coiled hair, smoothed down the brown-striped seersucker dress. She had learned a lot since the night she had rushed out in a flimsy night-robe to meet trouble, and had first met Clifford Cox. Two years ago or three? She wasn't even sure of the town or of the house. Just a staircase and his fat upturned face.

This is the hardest morning, she thought, because I've grown soft.

A bell rang.

Vibrations blended with her rapid heartbeat. Outside, a foot scraped heavily on stone.

She went quickly to the front door and opened it on a wide policeman wholly absorbed in wiping his boots on the step. Obviously he had not expected so prompt a response, for he stared at her abashed, his undershot jaw reaching up to gnaw a scraggy red mustache.

"Good morning," said Audrey.

Still chewing bristles, he pulled off a heavily begilted cap. His bald dome was red with embarrassment.

"Please come in." She managed to smile.

When she had closed the hall door, he announced in a hoarse rumble, "Chief of Police Peterson. This the residence of Mr. Donald Adriance?"

"Yes. I am Mrs. Adriance."

"You, ma'am? Are you alone here?"

"Yes."

"Mrs. Adriance, I've got some kind of bad news for you." He hesitated.

"Yes?" She knew she must be very pleasant with the police, but she had waited all night for the answer.

"Your husband," he said slowly, "your husband has had a bad accident."

"What kind of accident?" A fall downstairs, cuts from broken glass, bruises from a fight?

"He was hit by an automobile."

"An—automobile?" But Don never went out in the street; he was as careful about that as he was about carrying full identification.

"I don't understand."

The chief was looking at her as if she had said something wrong. "The wheels ran over him. He's dead."

The bald head seemed to revolve before her like a pinwheel. Instinctively she leaned forward.

"That's right," she heard him say from a long distance, "keep your head down like that. I'll get you some water. Or you want a drink?"

"No! Water, please. I'll be all right in a minute. I'll get it …"

He took her elbow awkwardly, steering her into the kitchen. She said, very low, "There's coffee." She managed to get cups and saucers safely off the cupboard shelf, cream for him from the refrigerator, and to the dinette table.

"Here. Drink it slow."

She sat down at the table, sipping tepid water and staring at the police cap like a strange vase in the exact middle of the rose-linen cover. Peterson lumbered over from the stove and filled the coffee cups. He sat down opposite her at the table.

"Thank you." She spread her cold fingers around the warm cup. "I'm all right now. Tell me—what I have to do."

"Got some folks you'd like to have with you? I can call 'em up."

"No, we just came here five days ago. Where did—it happen?"

"Out on the edge of town." Through numbness she felt the faint prickle of his hostility. "You probably ain't familiar enough around here to know the place. 'Bout three miles east of the bridge on the other side of the river. Where Main Street meets County Road D."

"In the country?" County Road D. It ought to mean something.

"Um-hum. All open fields out there. The bod— He was lyin' in a ditch. Thrown there by the car. Looks like a hit-run driver all right."

"Are you sure," she asked, "that it was my husband?"

"I'm afraid 'tis, Lady." He pulled a crumpled notebook from his breast pocket. "'Course we ain't got fingerprints yet nor your identification. Coroner's in charge of his effects but I'll read you the list: 'One draft card issued to Donald Hale Adriance, 18 Woodland Road, Rivington, Massachusetts. Race, white; height, 5' 7"; weight, 130; complexion, light; hair, brown; eyes, gray. Other physical characteristics that will aid in identification: None.' It checked with—him."

"Yes."

He resumed his reading: "'Gray gabardine suit ... paisley bow tie ... keys ... matches ... no watch. Small notebook with black cover, diary type.' You recognize all those things?"

She nodded. "When did it ...?"

"That," he said, "is what we don't know. Some time before the rain last night. Ain't much traffic over that road. All clay around there. Road's got a surface hard as cement in dry weather but after a hard rain it's soft and full of puddles. Only tire tracks are those from Harry Willis's truck. Farmer haulin' strawberries to market. He found Mr. Adriance 'bout an hour ago."

Her lips parted ... Something Edna Gray had said. Berries in Thornton's car. Fine cracks through hard buff clay—she could feel her eyes widening in the way Don hated. Funny to think it didn't matter now.

"... and we'll have to have help from you."

"Help?" Had she missed something the chief had said?

"So we can get hold of the driver who hit him. We got to fix the time of the accident. We have to get things straight before we have a good case to bring into court."

"Court?" She spoke sharply. "Into court? Why?"

Peterson took a long drink of coffee. "Mrs. Adriance," his voice was gruff, "don't you want to find out who caused your husband's death? Don't you want him brought to justice?"

She should have answered at once. But what could she say? How phrase the conflict between the wish to protect Don for this last time and to see that through his death no innocent person should suffer? Much too late, she said, "Yes, I do."

There was no belief in Chief Peterson's red-veined face. The elongated jaw worked busily at ragged sprouts on his upper lip.

"When did you last see your husband, Mrs. Adriance?"

"Yesterday morning. About 8:30 when he left for the University to teach a 9:30 class."

"Talk to him after that?"

"No. No, I didn't."

"When did you expect him to come home?"

"I didn't know. He said he had a lot of work to do. He'd come when he had finished."

"Expect him to dinner?"

"Yes. I kept it hot for him till midnight."

"What were his plans for the day? What was he workin' at?"

"I don't know anything about it except that he had another class from 12:30 to 1:30 in Abbott Hall. After that I suppose he would have been working in his office or in the library."

"Was your husband," he asked suddenly, "in good health?"

"Yes, he was." She hoped she had answered quickly.

He picked up his notebook. "Now can you give me the names of any people who would have seen Mr. Adriance durin' the day? People that might know when he left the campus and why?"

She told him the name of Don's office mate, of the head of the English department.

"And you was out all day so your husband couldn't of reached you by phone?"

"I was here all day. That is, after 1:30. I came back then from shopping."

"And when he didn't come home to dinner, you called up his office on the campus and didn't get any answer?"

"I didn't call." She could see that she'd have to explain. "Don, my husband, was working very hard on a piece of research. He intensely disliked being interrupted. So I didn't call."

"And you weren't worried or afraid somethin' had gone wrong?"

"Yes, I was terribly worried."

"You didn't call the Station." He knew that. "Call the hospital?"

"No." He probably knew that, too.

"It must of been a hell of a night for you."

She nodded.

"Well, I won't have to bother you much longer. What was your husband's classification with the draft board?"

She said faintly, "4-F."

"What was the general nature of his disability?"

"Anemia, I think, was the most serious," she answered carefully. "And allergy."

"Well," he said, "Doc Ellison may be able to tell us somethin'. In all cases of violent death, Mrs. Adriance, the coroner performs an autopsy. It's the law. We got to be sure there was no physical condition of the deceased that could explain alleged negligent behavior on his part if the other side brought it up in court."

"Yes." Why couldn't they let Don lie in peace? Lying in a clay ditch with the rain pouring down.

"Mrs. Adriance, I got to trouble you with one more question."

"Of course. Excuse me." She met his steady eyes. He was holding a stub of pencil poised over his notebook.

"Do you know anyone named Dexter? Or T. Gray?"

"They are our neighbors. Mr. Dexter lives next door, across the drive. Mr. Gray in the house beyond."

"Why I ast," he said, "in that diary your husband carried he had written down for yesterday," he consulted his notes, "'Dexter 6954' and under that, like an appointment, '2:30 T. Gray.' And then there's a word I couldn't figger out. Looked like l-y-c-a-n-t-h-r-o-p-e. That mean anythin' to you?"

"No."

"Well, I'll ask this Mr. Gray. He a perfessor, too? Sounds like it. Now, Mrs. Adriance, you ain't got any idea why your husband would be out on County Road D at any time yesterday or last night?"

"No." It was good to speak without reservation. "I can't imagine why he'd be there. He had a lot to do on the campus. We don't have a car. He hated to take walks, particularly in the country."

Peterson shook his heavy egg of a head. "It's goin' to be tough to find that hit-run driver. There wasn't a trace of the car at the scene of the accident. No glass nor nuthin'."

"That makes it hard for you, I'm sure."

He stared at her suspiciously. "For me? Yayer, well, that's my job. But it'll be kind of hard for you, too. To collect damages."

Go away! Go away! She answered him silently and he evidently didn't like the answer.

He got heavily to his feet and picked up his cap. "Mrs. Adriance," he enunciated in a new and honeyed tone, "maybe later in the day you could tell me somethin' helpful?"

"Mr. Peterson," she too stood up, steadying weakness with her hand against the wall, "I've told you ev—all I can."

He stood irresolute, scratching his bald head with the hand that held the cap. "Like I told you, we're pretty sure it's your husband was killed, but law's law. You say you and Mr. Adriance been here only five days and aren't well acquainted with anybody, so I'll have to ask you to identify the body. Would you feel like doin' it this mornin'?"

"Now."

"We-ell," he was looking as if she were a little too cooperative, "I can't take you right away. I want to get hold of these two fellers, Dexter and Gray, before they leave for work to see if they can help fix the time of the accident. I'll be back for you within an hour."

"All right," she said.

He tramped over to the back door and slid the bolt. "Good-by, Mrs. Adriance. I'll be seein' you." He shut the door behind him.

Audrey leaned against the wall, staring down at the rose-colored cloth. It looked quite pretty without a police cap in the center. It would look really lovely if it weren't for the dirty cups. I'll wash the cups. I must hurry and get it done before Don comes—

The mist of shock lifted. Don was not coming, and what she had to do for him was not housework. Slowly, as if she were terribly tired, she crossed the kitchen and the entrance hall to the small table where, an hour ago, she had laid hat, gloves and purse, ready for anything but this.

CHAPTER IX

"The man to thank is Cadwallader," Eric Lund settled his shoulders between the scrolls rising from the back of Mrs. King's Gothic oak throne, "and once I was on my big feet and saw a squad car, I was the old fire horse."

"I'm still grateful," said Audrey.

Curled up in a wing chair, she looked to him as if an eraser had been rubbed lightly over her. The rose was gone from her skin, leaving it yellow-brown; today the full, lovely mouth that she had been smart to keep unpainted was too pale.

"O.K. We'll go over to the Medical School whenever Peterson shows up. I think you'll like Dr. Ellison. It's unusual to have a man of his type elected coroner. The law in this state, you know, doesn't require candidates to have any medical knowledge at all. Ellison is a pathologist and he teaches a course in legal medicine. I've seen him at criminology meetings in Washington. He's mainly responsible for my coming here to lecture."

He set down his cup on the coffee table and picked up a plate of fruit. "Have you thought about the funeral arrangements? I might be able to help you."

"I'd like to have cremation," she sat straight, "and no service here where we are strangers. Then later, I could do what Don's mother wants. I'm certain she wouldn't want to come here. She lives in Tarrytown."

"Do you want to telephone to her now? It's after seven in New York."

"Yes," she said uncertainly. "I'll have to do it." Her eyes widened, showing white against her sun-touched skin in the way he had first seen her. She glanced toward the table with the telephone and her worn purse.

"I can get her for you. Shall I reverse the charges?"

"Oh, no, Mr. Lund. She would refuse ... She has before ... She feels that Don—was irresponsible about—things like that."

"Do you want to give me Mrs. Adriance's name and address?"

"It's Mrs. Austin Carr. Don's father died when he was a baby. Mr. Lund, please don't think I'm being mean about money when I hesitated about the call. It's just that—well, we have hardly any right now. I'll be all right. I'm an experienced stenographer. I've worked most of the time since I was married. Isn't it awfully expensive when—people die like this? If it were anything I could do for Don ..."

He said, "You have done everything for him. How about his mother? Can't she take over the finances now?"

"She could," for a moment the soft face hardened, "but I'm not sure she would. She spoiled Don terribly and gave him everything he wanted till he was twenty. Then the trouble began. And when he married me, Mrs. Carr decided he was to be just my responsibility. We've made it pretty well. There was a little money I inherited from my grandfather that took care of this last year. Anyway Don had that—I'm talking too much, Mr. Lund. It's shock, isn't it?"

"No," he said, "it's natural. You've been shut up inside yourself for years."

"It almost seemed as if he were going to be all right," she said. "He was so absorbed in his work and in some ways sure of himself. That was the most important thing, Mr. Lund."

"He was like that when he left here yesterday morning?"

"Yes."

For the first time he caught the note of evasion.

"Do you want to get in touch with some of your own people?"

Her face softened. "I'll write to Mother and Father. I can't bother them with a telegram. They'd feel so terribly because there's nothing they can do. They're neither of them well and they're poor, too."

"But when it's all over, you'd like to go home?"

"Yes. They've always tried to understand about Don and why I ... why we stayed together. No, please, let me take the dishes to the kitchen. It's better to do normal things, isn't it?"

Lund followed her across the room. She moved quickly, steadily, but the light grace he had noted the night her husband had deserted her in the Stadium, was gone from her step. Why had Adriance sneaked away? Lund was glad he didn't need the answer to that one because he'd never get it. He picked up the telephone receiver and dialed for Long Distance.

"But I can't conceive why he would be calling this house." Alfred Dexter scratched his green bedroom slipper absently across Cadwallader's proffered belly.

Beside him on the love seat, Peterson, Chief of Police, puffed a gift cigar. "Well, whatever was on Mr. Adriance's mind, he seems to of changed it. Like your wife said, either you or her was near the phone all day."

"When he was our guest on Wednesday night, he hardly spoke to my wife or to me and I don't think he even bowed to Mr. Lund."

"Yay-er, that's what the FBI feller was tellin' me just now out in the yard."

"Adriance was a very arrogant young man. Shortly after he was introduced to Mrs. Thornton Gray, I approached them with wine and I heard him say to her in a most peculiar tone, 'I wouldn't buy that, if I were you.' And he was not at all convivial. He even refused a small glass of sherry."

"He might of wanted to make a date to pick a bone with the dog." Peterson glared at Cadwallader's corpse-colored underside. Dogs were all right but not in a house. "So long as he didn't get him on the wire, it don't help us to find out the time of the accident. I better move on."

He hoisted himself to his feet. "Quite some place you got here, Mr. Dexter." His eyes wandered from oriel to mullions to beard and rested on the shiny purple pajamas lurking behind Alfred's respectable raincoat. "Kind of unique."

"It is a distinctive house," explained Alfred, "it is not unique. Surely you have seen Mrs. Adriance's. No, Cadwallader, I shall not further indulge your sensuous nature."

"I was only in the kitchen next door. Mrs. Adriance had some coffee made. Kind of funny."

Whisk-broom beard thrusting up toward the walrus mustache. "How did she take it?"

"Good. Didn't go to pieces or cry."

Alfred glanced toward the kitchen door. "How," he asked in conspiratorial whisper, "was her stomach?"

"Huh?"

"She's going to have a baby," breathed Alfred.

"The poor girl; say, that's tough. She said they didn't know a soul out here."

"Oh, did she?" There was a new gleam in the little old eyes. "I fear she exaggerated, at least, as far as she herself is concerned. There is someone here that she knew very well indeed."

"You mean a man?—Oh, ain't you a nice lady, Mrs. Dexter!" Red to the top of the dome with the knowledge that this last question was not dictated by professional purpose, Peterson took a glass of orange juice from Rachel Dexter and drank the contents at a gulp. "I gotta get along now and talk to this Mr. Gray."

"I think *he* may be helpful." Mrs. Dexter's tone disposed of her husband as witness. "Mr. Adriance had a great deal to say to him when they were both here on Wednesday evening."

"Thank you for your cooperation. Sorry I had to get you folks up so early."

"I'm glad we knew so soon," Rachel Dexter told him. "I'm going over as soon as I'm dressed to do all I can for that poor girl. Look out when you go down our steps, Mr. Peterson. There's a loose brick."

"Pay no attention. I fixed it long ago."

On the controversial security of the doorstep the chief pulled out his notebook. "Say, Perfessor, I got one more question. You know anythin' about l-y-c-a-n-t-h-r-o-p-e?"

"Lycanthrope?" Alfred's flat nose twitched with curiosity.

"Yay-er. You know what it means?"

"Certainly I do. A lycanthrope is a man who assumes the form or traits of a wolf."

"Thank you," said Mr. Peterson and went.

It was 6:30 when the chief crossed the third version of the unique threshold. The door was opened with notable promptness by a big, sleepy-looking young man.

"Perfessor Gray?"

"Yes, come in."

A tumbled bed in the room at the right explained how he had got to the door so fast.

"Watch out for the step down into the living-room," Gray warned. "This is the damnedest house."

He sat down on the arm of a chair and ran a hand over his bristling chin. "What can I do for you, sir?"

"Mr. Gray, there was an accident, last night or earlier. Across the river, out on the edge of town. Body of a man was found a couple of hours ago in a ditch alongside County Road D. Looks like a hit-run case. Accordin' to the draft card we found in his pocket, the man was a new neighbor of yours named Donald H. Adriance."

"God!" The look of sleep was gone. He got up and walked over to the fireplace.

"You know anythin' about this accident, Mr. Gray?"

"No." He rested an elbow on the mantel and stared down at the floor. "Has Mrs. Adriance been told?"

"I just come from tellin' her. She says she's got no idea when it happened. That's what we got to know in order to find the driver and the car that did it."

Thornton Gray did not look up. "Is she all right?"

On the basis of a five-day acquaintance, he seemed a little too upset.

"Mrs. Adriance? She's O.K. She's a tough one. Mr. Gray, Adriance had your name written in a diary we found in his pocket. Under yesterday's date."

"Yes," Gray, hands in the pockets of his dressing-gown, came slowly back to the policeman, "I had an appointment with him for 2:30."

"O.K., Perfessor." Peterson drew out the tired notebook. "What time did he leave you?"

"He didn't come." Gray sat down heavily. "He made the appointment Wednesday evening, but he didn't appear and didn't phone. I was in my office or around the campus from two to six."

"Were you surprised when he didn't show up?" Peterson laid the notebook open on his knee.

"Not particularly. It was the first day of the summer session. Anyone is likely to get held up by students coming in for conference. He wanted to talk about some work he was doing. It was nothing pressing."

"Uh. When was the last time you saw him?"

"Wednesday night. At the Dexters'. The family next door."

Peterson worked silently at the right-hand corner of his mustache. Gray watched, pushing a hand through his thick, unbrushed hair.

"Perfessor Gray," the chief had bitten off as much as he cared to chew, "does the word l-y-c-a-n-t-h-r-o-p-e mean anythin' to you?"

"What the—the meaning, yes. Werewolf. But it has no significance for me."

Peterson bent uncomfortably over the notebook, sucking the pencil stub.

"W-e-r-e," spelled Thornton, "and then add 'wolf.' Are you giving me a word association test?"

"W-e- ... No, sir, I am not. That wolf stuff was written under your name in Mr. Adriance's diary. How would you like to tell me why it was there?"

"I don't know." Thornton Gray's voice expressed no pleasure. "Adriance was interested in folklore. Stories about people turning into wolves might have been part of it."

"Perfessor," a gleam of dangerous doubt brightened the chief's heavy red face, "do you expect me to believe that another perfessor was plannin' on comin' over to your office at 2:30 P.M. to tell you a bedtime story?"

"No, sir," said Thornton Gray, "I do not expect you to believe it and I told you that I don't know whether or not it were so. But it could be. Professors are sometimes like that, Mr. Peterson." He yawned.

"Dad-dee," a small voice complained from the doorway, "Dad-dee, why are you talking to the p'liceman?"

The big man said gently to the child, "Please go upstairs to Mother now."

She clutched slipping polka-dot pants with each hand. "Mommy won't wake up. I tried and tried."

"I'll wake her up." He was frowning. "Excuse me, Chief."

Peterson looked at him hard. "Ask your wife what was the last time she saw Mr. Adriance."

Thornton led the child out by the hand and did not reply.

Mr. Peterson resumed rumination. This house was funnier than the last one. The same kind of a church or a liberry look like at the Dexters' and all these foreign things lying around. Take that little platform or whatever in the middle of the east wall. Low table like a doll's on it with some kind of a game like checkers set up, and setting beside it, right on the floor, a vase of old weeds. And that long piece of paper hanging on the wall was daubed all over with what looked like Japanese writing. Nice stuff to have around in war time. These people could stand watching.

Upstairs he could hear heavy steps, door opening, door closing, water running. It was taking quite a while to get a little information. Once the child called, "Daddy, is Mommy ...?" and then another door was shut.

How long this continued was never to be known to the police. When the chief woke up Professor Gray was standing in front of him.

"My wife," he said, "hasn't seen Mr. Adriance since the party at the Dexters'. She says that Mrs. Cox who lives at 25 Green Lane, just around the block, had a class in Abbott Hall from 12:30 to 1:30 yesterday. Mr. Adriance had a class in the same building at the same hour. This probably won't help you very much. Adriance had been here a short time and so few people knew him by sight that it might be worthwhile to ask Mrs. Cox whether she saw him leave the building or talked to him on the campus. She met him at the Dexters' supper."

"O.K. Thanks." He lumbered over to the door. Behind him Gray asked, "Is Mrs. Adriance alone?"

"No, lady next door's goin' over to sit with her and the FBI feller that's givin' talks at the 'U' went in right after I left." Outside on the walk he turned bed and looked up through the screen at Thornton. "Mrs. Adriance," he said, "has got plenty of company, Perfessor Gray."

Through pink organdy curtains, Mr. Cox bulged his eyes at the white police car. It was a hot morning but Clifford felt very cold.

A bell rang loudly and for the third time. He scuffed over to his bed and perched quivering on the edge.

"Holy mackerel, Beulah, what'm I goin' to do now? You said I'd be all right. Why didn't you give me that five hundred dollars?"

"Clifford," immense tones rose from the bosom now heaving out of the covering sheet, "nothing will happen if you don't make a fool of yourself." She felt blindly for her pince-nez on the night table. "I'll manage everything."

She set the glasses precisely on her elegant nose and left her bed. Even in this moment of panic Clifford was aware of the truly awful mass rising before him. She wrapped it in a cerise crêpe tent of circus dimensions and ploughed through the door. "You will not stir out of this room," she decreed and descended to meet the screaming bell.

Clifford Cox climbed into his bed, swathed his chill suet in a sheet, and hid his head under a pillow.

But fearful curiosity would not let him escape, so presently he crawled out and across the floor. Just outside the door, stairs led to the living-room whence rose the voice that could push his always teetering life right over the cliff. He set his sweaty back against a white wall and his tender buttocks on a prickly rug and listened.

"To think, Mr. Peterson, that I shall never see him again." The voice was Beulah's best. "I left my classroom quite a bit after 1:30. I don't know why it is but I always seem to have dozens of students waiting to ask me such stimulating, eager questions. And when I came out into the hall I saw Mr. Adriance in his classroom opposite mine. One or two students had stayed to talk to him. One of them was Amy Angel who has taken so much work from me. I waved to her and to Mr. Adriance, too, of course. He was a handsome boy in a sickly sort of way. And then I went across the campus and ate my lunch in the Botanical Gardens. It was a lovely day, Mr. Peterson. Not at all a day to die." Tears seeped delicately into her tone. "Forgive me. I hardly knew him but I am a woman of a great deal of feeling."

Silence.

"I guess I got that all down straight," said Peterson. "That's a big help. Now at least we know he was alive till 1:30. 'Course the students in his class would know that, too."

"When," Beulah raised a sepulchral quaver, "was he found?"

"'Bout four o'clock this mornin'. You know Harry Willis, man that raises strawberries? He found him in a ditch out near County Road D. Hit-and-run job all right. The car didn't leave a trace. *He* might of left some kind of marks on the car, but unless we get the car, that won't be no help."

"His poor wife. This will shatter her."

"I dunno. She seemed to me like a fairly tough specimen. Ready for anythin'." He repeated, "Ready for anythin'."

"I wonder," said Beulah, "what is back of *that* remark?"

Mr. Peterson let her wonder.

"Tell me, Chief. This is my first encounter with the law. I am so interested in the way you do your work. Have you a large force here? As a citizen, I should say 'have we,' should I not?"

"There's eight of us—chief, night captain, six patrolmen. The dog catcher's only on part time."

"You, as chief, must have very heavy duties?"

"Kind of. I have to do all the expert stuff myself. Keep the records and do the fingerprintin' and I'm the photographer. I got some dandy shots this mornin' of the deceased. And I do the vice squad work besides the routine."

"On the silly radio programs one gets now and then by chance, one hears so much talk about detectives. Do you have one of those?"

"I do the detectin', too. In plain clothes. When I'm off duty."

"I imagine you find a good deal to detect in the taverns." Now she was very sweet. "Do you have many exciting, thrilling cases?"

"Naw. We average 'bout one-eighty a year, mostly traffic violations. We ain't had a murder in the last ten years."

They were speaking at the foot of the stairs now. "But if you ever do have one," Beulah said, "you would do a superb job of detection, Chief. The skill with which you put your questions! Amazing."

"I generally come out pretty good," Peterson agreed. "Tell you how I do it. Just by followin' the old sayin', 'You can get more with honey than you can with vinegar.'"

When his wife had closed the door firmly on the police, Clifford Cox padded to the head of the stairs. "Holy Jumping Jupiter!" he called, rubbing his nettled rear. "I'll say you're good!"

"Yes," said Mrs. Cox.

"Mrs. Adriance, the chief is here."

She put on the wide-brimmed brown hat and the light doeskin gloves. Eric Lund thought: The girl will make a good impression on Ellison. She has dignity.

"This isn't going to be easy." He handed her the thin purse. "There's one thing to keep in mind. It's said to everybody, but in your case, it's true. Sudden death is not the worst thing that could have happened to your husband."

"I know," said Audrey quietly. "I'm ready, Mr. Lund."

CHAPTER X

Whenever she opened her drugged eyes, she saw red roses. Everything else, color and sound alike, was gray and cool green. She would close her eyes and feel light air steal over her, the freshness of linen beneath her cheek, the clean wide peace of a bed she had not lain in before.

After each drowse, the details of the room were clearer: the silver hum of the high fan swirling like water, the moss-colored carpet, the close carmine folds of the flowers. Later, she was aware of silk, pale violet, which was draped over a chair near the bed. Its strangeness bothered her. She turned away from it, and through the fine mist of the window screen looked out on trees beyond the river. Again she slept, and then really woke and sat up.

She remembered now that in the numb moments, while undressing after her return from the morgue, she had half noticed that Don's desk no longer blocked the front window. Then, as the hypnotic claimed her, she yielded to Mrs. Dexter's big kind hands and was led to bed. Now things were arranged as they had been when she first saw the room.

Against the left wall, only the roses stood on the desk, and objects from the oriel room—her Lucite brush, a small clock, powder in a pasteboard box—had displaced the books once piled on the dressing-table.

My room. A small pleasant feeling ran through Audrey's weakness. My roses. My—? She reached out for the unfamiliar silk, violet sprinkled with silver bow-knots, a robe, delicate and new. "Oh!" she said softly.

"You look as if you like your negligee." Rachel stood in the doorway.

"Mine?" quavered Audrey. "It can't be. I never had anything so nice."

"Well, you have now. Alfred will be so pleased that it suits you. I gave him the general idea but he picked it out all by himself. He got a big kick out of it, although at the last minute he lost his courage and asked Thornton Gray to go to the lingerie department with him. Thornton wouldn't, of course. Go right along and cry. It's what you need." She went downstairs.

Audrey cried quietly. All these things done for her, even a box of facial tissues ready by her pillow to take care of weak, grateful tears. In the performance of kindness, Mrs. Dexter had entered closets whose skeletons were their emptiness, but that didn't matter now. Soon Audrey would go away, and in the next place there would be nothing to conceal. The five-year pattern was ended at last. She blotted tears, and enjoyed red roses that only one person would have sent.

"Aren't they gorgeous?" Rachel came in with a tray. "Beulah Cox brought them! Are you all right? Do you want to eat?"

Audrey choked a hysterical gurgle. "Yes. Oh, thank you. You are so good to me. You and your husband. And Mrs. Cox."

"I hope it's what you like." Rachel gave her the tray and heaped pillows high at Audrey's back. "I fixed some of that lovely chicken broth you had in your refrigerator."

The bouillon spoon was shaking. Tremor like Don's ... outside the supermarket ... fine lines wrinkling a buff road ... skin rolled back from bone.

"Beulah wanted me to tell you how much she felt for you." Rachel Dexter drew a boudoir chair near the bed. "She cried more than you have. It's her age. You get emotional then. When I was that way I used to feel so angry all of a sudden, and I could cry over the silliest books. Oh, dear, I don't mean that Beulah wasn't sincere about you. How I talk."

Audrey smiled. She had managed to raise the cup and drink.

"I'm sure Beulah can't know how you feel. It must be very trying for her to live with Mr. Cox. Of course she wanted to marry. Single women have pretty lonely evenings in a little town like this. People don't ask them to dinner very often. It makes things come out uneven, or else you have to beg a young instructor who will come if he's hungry enough or realizes that he can eat your dinner and save enough to take a girl out the next night. Of course a guest like that is a complete waste because he'll never ask you back. You look as if you were enjoying your soup. The toast is under that dish.

"Beulah's been invited out a great deal since she was married, but not twice to the same house. That is, not if Mr. Cox took his table manners with him. The first time he did that with the napkin, I thought it was a special insult he'd thought up just for me. It was a comfort to find out that he had done it in at least five other faculty houses. It not only makes everybody feel sick—the hostess has to keep the napkin apart to boil the next day. Does this talk bother you?"

"Please go on. It's easier to eat when I have nice company."

"No matter how fond she may be of him, Beulah must really suffer. She's such a fastidious woman. And so is Edna Gray. I said something about how did she stand it, and she said that when they study Japanese together, they just drink tea and use paper napkins. Let me pour out the coffee for you.

"Of course, I think the whole Japanese business is just to annoy Thornton. When he started to teach this course to the soldiers, Edna wanted to give some of the lectures and Beulah begged him to give Mr. Cox a job. He refused and I'm sure he was right. Of course, they both lived in Japan for years, but you can know something well and not be able to talk about it on a platform. I don't think either Edna or Mr. Cox is really brilliant. And until lately, Edna used to be so against anything Japanese. Thornton is trying to keep the training as objective as he can. However she's feeling about something, it's sure to be very personal with Edna."

She rose to take the empty dishes from Audrey's tray. "You remember the way she spoke to your husband that night at our house. She acted as if they had been picking the same bone for years, though I don't suppose they had met more than ten minutes before. Edna hadn't met your husband before he came here, had she, Mrs. Adriance?"

Audrey said very slowly, "I don't know."

"Of course she hadn't. Thornton probably seems hard to you. He isn't always perfectly patient with Edna, I have to admit, but I know he has tried to understand her and I don't suppose she's ever thought of what he wants to get out of life. Wouldn't you like to smoke with your coffee?"

Audrey shook her head. "I've stopped smoking since cigarettes were scarce. It's hard to get enough for two, and it meant a lot more to Don."

"There are two cartons in the bottom desk drawer. I saw them when I put some papers out of sight. Won't that change your mind?"

"Yes," said Audrey, watching Rachel's knobby fingers opening the package. After today, no one going through her house in kindness or curiosity would find hidden things.

"Don was rather selfish sometimes," she said. "His mother spoiled him when he was a child and he never really grew up. Lately, when he was so unhappy about being turned down for the Army, little comforts meant a lot to him. I'm glad he had a few before— Mrs. Dexter, has anyone telephoned? About when the accident happened?"

"No one official has," Rachel held a match to Audrey's cigarette, "but eight faculty wives have called me up to tell me that they've each had a visit from the police. They didn't know what it was all about and they were highly annoyed because every one of them was in the midst of making jam from strawberries they had bought at Harry Willis's farm. Beulah Cox explained it to Edna and me. She says the police chief told her that sometimes after a fatal accident there are marks on the car that did it, even if the car isn't damaged. There isn't much traffic even in peacetime along County Road D, and it's about limited now to people driving out to the Willises', and probably a few still get out there at night for a little love-making." Then she flushed to the rims of her spectacles. "Poor child. We shouldn't be talking about that place."

"It's all right, really." Here she was back at the basic problem, the mystery of motive that placed Don on a country road. His hostility to the odor of home canning had always been as pronounced as was his present apathy to dalliance. Neither police nor coroner had suggested that Don had been taken for a ride but it was easier to imagine than that he had voluntarily gone for a walk.

"What time is it, Mrs. Dexter?"

"Almost six. Will you be all right alone while I go home and get dinner?"

"I'll be all right all the time. I'm used to being alone, really I am. I'm going to get up soon. The lunch was wonderful. And I wouldn't have eaten it if you hadn't been here."

"Well, then ... I'll put the tray in the kitchen and don't you touch those dishes. I'll be very angry when I come back if I find you've washed them. I'll run in about eight o'clock to see how you are. Shall I leave the door unlocked so you won't have to come down?"

"Please do," said Audrey. "It sounds so—neighborly."

Alone, she lay flat, blowing smoke toward the beautiful expensive roses Thornton Gray had not sent her. From now on she could have neighbors, friends, make and keep dates for lunch or movies with other women. There was something better, hardly realized, that could not be hers, but Don had lost everything. Could I have saved him? In spite of what the doctors said, is it my fault? Oh, Don.

No use to lie here, thinking of the long lashes curled back from his wide-open dead eyes. She stood unsteadily by the bed. Then she wrapped the silvery elegance of Alfred Dexter's choice over her faded nightgown. It was the quiet hour of the day, so still that she could hear the tinkle of Cadwallader's dog-tag as he loped home to supper. She bathed cold water over her face. It looked a little dim but not too bad. The little back room from which Rachel had rescued her was seething with late sun, bringing momentary faintness as she bent over the bureau, looking for the address book she kept in her writing portfolio. She'd have to send notes to a few of their old friends, remote cousins. The book was not there.

Of course it's here, she told herself; you're dazed and can't see something right in front of your face. She picked up the objects, one by one, saying over their names. Stamps, fountain pen, notes ... The book was gone. What of it? Unconsciously she must have picked it up and dropped it into a drawer. Or she had left it on the bureau and Mrs. Dexter had found it and put it away as she had Don's papers and books.

Why be alarmed, anyway? She was in no great need of the addresses. Mrs. Dexter could probably tell her where it was. And there was nothing private in it and even less anything that another person would want.

But someone had wanted it. She was frighteningly sure. She could recall with photographic clarity the moment when she had last seen the book.

It had happened on Wednesday evening, just before they left for the Dexters' supper. She had dressed early and sat down on the chaise-longue to write to Mrs. Hinton, the latest of their many impatient landladies, that in two weeks she would receive everything owed her by the Adriance family. From the bathroom Don had called to her to fetch the saddle soap he had put in the kitchen cupboard. The little open book had slid to the floor. When she came back upstairs, Don had picked it up and was reading a page.

"Here," he handed it to her, "you have a genius for dropping things."

She remembered that her fingers had been awkward with anger and she had been a long time fitting the address book into the portfolio so that she could fasten the zipper.

The book was not among the things from Don's pockets, each grimly ticketed, which the coroner had shown her, saying, "We'll have to keep these for a short time."

What if it were not found? How nice were these people around her? How, exactly, had Don died?

She sank down on the chaise-longue and closed her eyes. Against the dark she had created she saw face after face: Clifford Cox's fat leer, the gleaming lenses that masked Mrs. Cox's eyes, Edna Gray's mean little mouth, Alfred Dexter's flat, snooping nose, Thornton's hardness, Rachel's bony hands.

A soft sound came from below. The front door closing? Or something manufactured by her nerves? Were there stealthy footsteps? Someone was in the room beneath.

She knelt on the chaise-longue and as quietly as she could, pushed open the casement of the oriel. The living-room was in deep dusk. Over the mullioned windows drapes had been drawn close and the screened French doors were shut.

She heard a hoarse masculine whisper: "Rachel, where are you?" Reasonless fear shook her as she leaned out of the oriel and looked down on Thornton Gray.

For a criminal or a lover the suitable accouterment is not a large cake covered with seven-minute frosting. Holding it at arm's length and swearing at it induces in the spectator a mood neither of terror nor of romance.

Close to laughter, Audrey called, "Mrs. Dexter isn't here."

He looked up savagely, bringing the cake closer to his chest.

"Audrey! May I come up?"

"Of course."

She shut the oriel and stood up, tightening the silver sash. Thornton and his cake crowded the cramped room. "Edna sent it."

Portfolio and contents covered the bureau, books the night table. She took the sticky mound and put it on the bed. "You've got frosting on your coat."

He glared at the white smear on new gray flannel. "That's nice! I'm leaving for Washington in an hour!"

"Take your coat off and give it to me."

"No, of course not."

"Take it off!" She brushed past him. "I'll get a damp cloth."

When she came back he was putting the coat on the cot. "Give me that." He flung the rag behind him and put his arms around her. Clinging close to him, she felt sobs rise and then die down at the touch of his hand pushing her hair gently back from her temple. Close in his arms on the chaise-longue, she saw tears in the deep-set eyes.

"Audrey," he said unsteadily, "are you all right? I couldn't come to you. You knew that. All day I've thought of nothing but you."

She drew fingers over his cheek, traced the outline of his wide, strong lips.

He reached for her hand and took it from his face. "Don't drive me crazy."

She sat up straight on his knees. "You're going away tonight?"

"Yes, on the eight-o'clock plane for Washington. I had a call this afternoon from the State Department. Nothing definite yet, but I think I'll be crossing the Pacific soon."

Her hands tightened round his wrists. "You want to awfully, don't you?"

"I did. It's still my job. And the best thing for you and me, dear."

She nodded slowly. "When will you be back? From Washington, I mean?"

"By Tuesday, I think. You'll still be here, won't you?"

"Yes. Now I'll clean your coat."

She brought coat and rag back to the chair and sat on the footrest to scrub.

"This is one hell of a funny situation," said Thornton.

"There. It's clean. Put it on. You'll have to hurry."

He stood up and held out his hand for the coat.

A bell rang below, and someone stepped heavily into the hall. "Mrs. Adriance?"

"Yes?"

"Chief Peterson," he was following his voice over the stairs. "All right for me to come up?"

He was already up, rubbing a handkerchief over his bald head, surveying the scene of what he evidently thought was a crime. A man putting on his coat, a woman in a negligee, a pillow on the floor, mussed cushions on the chaise-longue, it all fitted. Then his eyes lighted on the piece that didn't belong.

"Good-by, Mr. Gray," said Audrey. "Please thank your wife very much for the cake."

CHAPTER XI

A bit of metal glistened in the moonlight. Pacing, sleepless, at midnight through the dark rooms, Audrey caught the minute glitter on the floor. Each time her course begun at her bed, ended at the threshold of the oriel room. The small spark teased her eyes. One of the casters of the cot? She would identify it, and turn back, seek oblivion of fact and feeling in slow, monotonous motion.

On the tenth round she entered the little bedroom and stepped on the bright spot. Under her bare foot she felt something cool. She stooped and picked up a flat key. Tied through the head was a small tag. Snapping on the light, she read tiny printing: "T. Gray. Front Door. Extra."

In renewed darkness Audrey slipped the key into the pocket of her robe. It must have fallen from Thornton's coat when he flung it on the cot. Luckily she, not Chief Peterson, had found it. She imagined him standing up in a law court, cinema version, and saying, "Mrs. Adriance had a key to his apartment."

She knew how she appeared to Mr. Peterson. A widow entertaining a married lover before her husband's body was cold. Mr. Lund might have understood. Perhaps she could talk to him tomorrow when he came back from addressing the State Bar Association in Barton. The accident, she knew, was nothing to the FBI, but he had already been so kind. Or hadn't he? Was he, subtly, trying to get her to tell him something? And had she told it?

I'm crazy, she thought. What is there to tell? Peterson must think there was something. For tonight he had brought her nothing, just wandered over the same track he had taken that morning. And he had carried away quite a load—a scandal, and half of a frosted cake. It ought to take him most of the night to suck the seven-minute frosting off his mustache.

She leaned against the window frame and looked down on huge shadows across the moonlit lawn. That clump of wild black rags was the unclipped hedge between their yard and Green Lane. The slight overhang of the garage roof was exaggerated to something by Frank Lloyd Wright, and the three garbage cans were giant cylinders beyond even Alfred Dexter's capacity to probe.

Three cans? But there were only two standing between the garages, hers and the Dexters'. Surely three similar shapes lay across the bright turf. Similar, not identical. Wasn't the one in the center less regular in outline? Did it narrow toward the near end? Or was that a trick effect of the small night breeze across the grass?

Bow, wow, wow! Cadwallader and his shadow trotted out into the moonlight and headed for the three silhouettes.

Bow, wow! Canines blended with cans. The barking ceased and Caddy, wagging his tail, circled the yard and made off for the river road. Again the scene was without sound and motion, but it was not quite as before. Only two garbage cans cast shadows.

Out there at the edge of the moonlight someone had been crouching, someone the Labrador knew. From deeper darkness eyes might now be staring up at her. Chill shook Audrey. Then from around the house Cadwallader broke into prolonged barks.

She sped to the front window. The dog at the edge of the curb under an arc light directed his howl toward the middle of the street. A body lay flat on the road. Belly on the ground, it moved in slow circles as if bewildered by pain.

Hit-and-run. That was what had happened to Don. Like that, through the rain, he must have crawled over the muddy clay. She stumbled down the stairs and out to the street. Other shapes ran parallel to her, converging at the curb. Over the river a siren shrieked disaster.

Alfred Dexter reached the man first, with Audrey close behind. Cadwallader tagged prudently.

"Are you hurt?" inquired Alfred. He and Audrey bent over the slowly writhing body.

A head fitted neatly with a cloth cap and spectacles rose from the man's outstretched arm. "I am not," he announced in a competent, middle-aged voice, "but if you don't start minding your own business, somebody's going to have a busted nose."

He wriggled in a sudden half-circle, snuffing loudly.

"He's drunk!" Beulah Cox's shriek rose shrill.

"No, he isn't." Audrey went back to the curb.

"He's insane!" Edna Gray clutched at the nearest support which happened to be Clifford Cox, already staggered by the burden of his own leaning mate.

The man in the street, nose to the pavement, crept round and round, heeled by Cadwallader's master.

"Alfred, take care!" Beulah called. "He may have a knife."

"Nonsense!" this was a new voice—Rachel's. "He's probably just a nice harmless old man."

"Here come the police."

From the white sedan a thin, uniformed figure walked into the middle of the street. With a joyous yelp the crawler swung round on his belly and, nose to the ground, steered steadily toward the policeman's legs. A yard from big boot tips he stopped and reared up his respectable head.

"Get out of the way!" he commanded. "What the hell do you mean by confusing the smell?"

The patrolman turned to the group on the curb. "What'd he say?"

"If you would get down to his level," suggested Alfred, "you would hear him perfectly."

"Say, listen," said the thin patrolman, "I'll do my job any day within limits, but I don't crawl till I have to. City buys the coats for us, we pay for the pants."

"Oh, for God's sake!" The creeper rose to his feet. "Why can't you people mind your own business? I'd just got a hot scent when you come plunkin' along. Now I got a good hour's work to do all over again."

"Listen, feller." The patrolman laid a hand on the blue-denimed shoulder. "How would you like to take a ride with me out to my place? We got a swell garden where you can just crawl around and smell the roses all day long."

"My God! This is some town. I don't expect nothing of ordinary people but you might think the police could tell the difference between a nut and an expert."

The hand of the law silently tightened, but Alfred Dexter, tilting his beard, asked eagerly, "What sort of expert?"

"I'm a sniffer," said the man proudly. "Service man for the Gas Company. Got the best nose on the squad."

Weak with laughter piled on the day's unshed tears, Audrey leaned against a tree while Edna, Rachel and the Coxes swarmed into the street and ringed around the specialist. She was the only one to hear the little wail coming over the lawn, "Mom-mee!"

She sat down on the damp grass and put her arms around Margaret Gray. "It's Audrey," she said. "Mother is over there with those people. She'll be here in a minute."

The child nestled close to her. "Did he get runned over?"

"No, dear. The man is hunting for a leak in the gas pipes so it won't get out and make a bad smell."

"A squirrel got run—ranned over in front of our house. His tummy was outside," said the realistic little voice. "It was in the winter time and he didn't smell a single bit."

"Here comes Mommy. Run and meet her."

"You're shivering all over. Are you cold, Audrey?"

"A little bit. Good night, honey."

"My daddy flew away in a plane. Did you know? Can I come to your house tomorrow? Will you invite me?"

"Yes, Margaret. Now run to your mother."

Fatigue had fallen on her so heavily that she could hardly drag herself to her steps. The neighbors were coming up the walk now, scattering to their homes. She didn't want to talk to anyone tonight. Better to huddle in this dark corner, rather than risk the sound of her opening door till all of them were housed. Through the blur of exhaustion words floated to her. The pinched tone of Thornton's wife saying, "Sister!" to her only child; and "Lambie Pie, of course, I'm coming home to beddie with you," a choice of expression that only Clifford Cox would make.

Rachel Dexter said to the sniffer, "But how wonderful to smell gas on Front Street and find the source way over here. Why, that's at least a quarter of a mile. You must have to know lots about geology and meteorology!"

"Yes, ma'am."

"I'll skip ahead into the house. Alfred, you give him a nice glass of sherry while I make some sandwiches."

"I apologize for summoning the police," old Alfred said mounting the stoop. "But, you know, when I saw you back of my house, I was afraid someone was stealing my victory vegetables."

"Professor, you didn't see me back of your house nor anybody else's house. The Gas Company don't lay pipes in gardens." The Dexter door closed on the positive statement of an expert.

CHAPTER XII

"There, that's all over, my dear." Rachel Dexter's eyes turned from the roadway to Audrey, while the right rear wheel of her car cut a cruel gouge from the turf of the Funeral Home. "It amazes me how a girl of your age can make decisions so quickly. It isn't an hour since the coroner called you and now you've got everything arranged."

"Because you helped me, Mrs. Dexter." Audrey took off the wide-brimmed hat that pressed too heavily on her forehead. "I feel dreadful about all the gas you're using for me. You and Mr. Dexter—"

"I can't let you think we are better than we are." Rachel swung too widely round a corner. "I must tell you the truth, even though I promised ... Last night, before he went away, Thornton Gray came over and gave me a coupon to use taking you anywhere you needed to go. So you just tell me if you have any other errands and we'll go do them now. Or this afternoon, if you'd rather."

"That's awfully nice of Mr. Gray. And you. There really isn't anything I can do today, except write letters. Mrs. Dexter"—she hesitated—"when you were putting my bedroom in order, did you see a small address book lying around anywhere?"

"No, I didn't. I'll ask the other girls if they did."

"Other girls?"

"Beulah and Edna. They were both of them upstairs yesterday while you were asleep. Beulah brought the roses and went right away again, but Edna stayed long enough to help me strip the cot and fold up the sheets. She sent Thornton over to find out how you were and then she came over after him to tell him Washington was calling him on the phone. Oh, dear, I think this is the most depressing street in the United States."

They had come to the dirty square flanked by decayed hotels which Thornton had called the Bowery. In the speckled window of a Rescue Mission pink paper streamers dangled above crazy letters: PREPARE TO MEET THY GOD.

"Not," said Rachel, "that I've traveled much. Have you?"

"No. Just moved."

An old man in overalls and a broken derby hat lurched toward the curb. He's going to be sick, thought Audrey, and closed her eyes.

Instantly the car jerked violently and filled with the screech of brakes. As her head snapped forward she saw another head strike the window beside her. Glass shattered as the body bounced off. There was a thump to the rear. Then all was still except for Rachel's anguished moan, "Oh, dear, oh, dear!"

The door beside Audrey wouldn't open. Steadying her whirling head with both hands she looked out through the cracked pane. In the gutter lay a heavy heap of overalls with a bright piece of metal protruding from it. The door handle had broken off in the old man's back.

It was never clear to Audrey whether she actually heard voices accusing, sympathizing, cursing; whether she saw faces crowding in upon her through the shattered glass, a police car arrive, an ambulance depart. It was all gray like a remembered movie. From the accident sequence of a dozen films she could have selected each detail. Whether it happened or whether she dreamed it, she did not care. It was as if her nerves had said: "We've had enough. We'll skip this one."

All the rest of the long June day she spent on a white island far from everything but one small phase of her life. She lay for hours with closed eyes, not sleeping, summoning again and again images of her brief moments alone with Thornton Gray. His figure appeared like a small, floodlighted cutout, motionless against a constantly moving background of brown, shapeless masses. In each picture one spot of color glowed. The crimson velvet over his arm; sherry in the glass he lifted for a silent toast; blue flowers at his feet when he had said, "I want to put my arms around you." Faint and diffused now, she felt the warmth of that direct, adult embrace. "Get out." By this command he had told her he was not a man who necked coeds in parked cars, that his love was as new, intrusive, and undeniable as hers.

Somewhere behind the shifting brown bulks lay reality. There, for today, she had pushed Edna and "Sister," the body of the old man hurtling past her, the clay ditch where blue flowers had grown and where Don had lain dead in the rain.

Night followed, black and dreamless, and in the morning she awoke hungry and aware, ready with the impatience of the healthy to get up and walk out of this white hospital room.

Eric Lund came to her at ten, accompanied by a brisk young woman with white coat and dangling stethoscope, and a half hour later he was sitting beside Audrey in a taxi and saying, "Mrs. Adriance, you're a wonder; you can pull yourself through anything."

"Myself, but not anyone else. Tell me about Mrs. Dexter."

"She's still at the hospital," Lund held out cigarettes, "but she's coming along all right, too. She'll probably be at home this afternoon. I think we've finally made her realize that the accident—the old man—wasn't her fault. She kept on saying that she was a terrible driver, which could be true. But this time she did the right things. The skid marks show that she couldn't have been going over twenty-five and that she must have slammed on the brakes just about as she hit him."

"He walked right out into the street. That much I remember clearly."

"Yes. There were several witnesses who said the same thing. The fellow had a record of over fifty arrests for drunkenness and he'd been sideswiped by a couple of cars in the last three years."

She said, "I know it was horrible, Mr. Lund, but I can't seem to feel very much about it."

"You shouldn't. You've taken enough and subconsciously you're reacting in the right way to protect yourself from unnecessary hurt. *This* accident wasn't your business."

The emphasis on *this* startled her. "No," she agreed, "not this one." The island of isolation was far behind her now. Blue flowers were gone; the ditch remained. "Was he instantly killed?"

"The old man? Yes. We're here." He paid off the taxi and followed her up the walk to her house. "May I come in for a minute?"

"Certainly," she questioned the cool, lightly scarred face. He put his Panama on the telephone table and helped her to open the mullioned windows and push back the doors leading to the garden.

"Shall we sit here, Mrs. Adriance?" He placed chairs by the doors, backs to the gloomy room. Three chairs.

She sat down and folded her hands, waiting. Waiting for what?

"When you asked me just now whether the old man died at once, you were thinking about Mr. Adriance, too, weren't you?"

She nodded. "It's terrible to think that Don lay there for hours, suffering. Did he, Mr. Lund?"

"No," he said, watching her, "there is almost no chance that he did. Dr. Ellison found a line of fracture running across the base of the skull. Breaks like that occur when a car wheel grinds a head into the roadway. Death from shock is instantaneous."

"I'm glad," she whispered.

"As you know," Lund said, "I have nothing to do with the case. Ellison talked to me about what he found after he had informed the Chief of Police. Peterson knows that I'm telling you. No trace of alcohol was found in your husband's body."

She drew a quick breath and turned away from the steady gaze.

"And there was no trace of poison," she heard Lund say. "Nothing that indicated negligent behavior on the part of Mr. Adriance."

Don had not suffered. Nor had Don caused anyone—no innocent driver—to suffer as had Rachel Dexter. The taut hidden fear of the last two days left Audrey and all she felt now was relief. Through tears of weakness, not of grief, she saw a stocky man in a bright green business suit stumping toward her across the turf.

"Chief Peterson is here," said Mr. Lund.

"Why?" Every nerve and muscle drew tight again. "What does he want now, Mr. Lund?"

"How are you, Chief?" Without looking at Audrey, Lund opened the screen door.

"Sorry to disturb you again, Mrs. Adriance." Peterson pulled a hard and very yellow straw hat from his bald head. "I'll try not to keep you too long from your Sunday dinner."

He took the third chair, so thoughtfully provided by the FBI, and cleared his throat. In the long, nervous silence, Audrey noted that his mustache was fluffy and quite clean.

"Mrs. Adriance," at last he spoke, "I think I got hold of the car that ran over your husband."

"Yes?"

"Well, we ain't quite sure but it certainly looks that way. Now, Mrs. Adriance, you remember I was askin' you Friday mornin' 'bout the last time you saw or heard from your husband?"

"Yes."

"And I was tellin' you that maybe the coroner'd find out somethin' about the time of death. Well, it appears that the last meal your husband ate was breakfast, some five—six hours before he died. We know he was in Abbott Hall till around 1:25 or 1:30 P.M. and that he didn't have lunch. That give you any ideas about when the accident could of happened?"

"No."

"Where were you, Mrs. Adriance, at the time?"

"Where?" she repeated, bewildered. "Where was *I?* But at what time? When do you mean, Mr. Peterson?"

She could feel Lund's blue Scandinavian eyes on her. "Well," said Peterson, "all the time from one o'clock on."

"I was here. At home. I told you. And Don didn't come and he didn't phone."

"You didn't go out all day on Thursday?"

"Yes; yes, I did. I went to the University campus in the morning. No, not to my husband's office. I didn't see him after he left home at half-past eight. I was in the Registrar's office and in the library, in the medical-biological reading room. You saw me there, Mr. Lund."

The FBI man said to Peterson, "She left, I think, at a little after twelve. Neither of us, I assume, was preparing an alibi, so we can't be certain of the minutes. I can't."

"I think that's about right," said Audrey. "Just as the bells rang for the end of the class hour—that's 12:20—I was in front of Abbott Hall, talking to Mrs. Cox and Mrs. Gray. After that, I walked down the hill to the supermarket and did the shopping and when I was waiting for the bus in front of the store"—without her volition the words came more slowly—"Mr. Gray drove past and saw me and took me—home in his car."

"Oh, he did? Know when you got back here?"

Suddenly she realized that she didn't know. "About one. Ten minutes past, perhaps." The chief's face told her how falteringly she had spoken.

"But you aren't too sure?"

"Does it matter?" She should have kept temper from her tone. "After that I was here alone, and no one saw me or spoke to me or telephoned me till you came at five o'clock the next morning—or ten minutes past." The chief shoved his chair nearer to hers and fumbled in his breast pocket. "Take a look at this, Mrs. Adriance."

In his extended hand he held a miniature pocket diary opened at two pages for June. "Do you recognize the handwritin' under Thursday?"

"It's Don's." There in the studied, over-fine letters he had affected she read *Dexter 6954*, and at the bottom of the page *lycanthrope*. Between, a quick bold hand had jotted *2:30 T. Gray, III Welles*.

"Think your husband wrote all of it?"

"No, just the first line and the last. I never saw the other writing."

"Oh."

She glanced toward Lund. Long legs stretched out, he was smoking, with half-closed eyes.

"Mrs. Adriance," Peterson smiled, "when did Mr. Adriance last have his hair cut?"

"W-what?" She saw his pleasure at the stutter. "Wednesday afternoon."

"You sure?"

"Quite. It was too long when he left in the morning and very short when he came home to dress for the Dexters' party."

"Who did you tell me were your friends here in town, Mrs. Adriance?" The chief did not look at Lund. "People you knew before you came out here?"

"But I told you we knew no one." Fear and anger struggled to get into her voice. "That is, no one who is here now. My husband knew Professor Wilkins, the head of the English department. He recommended Don's appointment. But Dr. Wilkins isn't in town this summer."

"But you, Mrs. Adriance? Isn't there an old friend of yours here?"

"No," she said defiantly. No friend, just a fat face seen for a moment, where and when she didn't know.

"Mrs. Adriance, did your husband have any enemies?"

"I don't know."

"You don't know?" Palms flat on his knees, Peterson bent toward her. "And are you just as sure that you know all his friends?"

Again Audrey turned to Lund and again got nothing. She said, "I really didn't know a great deal about my husband's associates."

"Oh. You and your husband weren't very close to each other?"

She didn't know what to say. Too close? But that wouldn't be a good answer.

"You and your husband didn't get along very well?" Again she did not answer. She could feel her nails pinching deep into the flesh of her folded arms.

"Did you have a little trouble with your husband before he left the house last Thursday morning?"

"No." She was on her feet, facing the two men. "Why do you ask me such questions? I've tried to help you as much as I can. But why do you have to ask me all these personal questions when my husband was killed in an accident?"

"Mrs. Adriance," the chief got up heavily and came to her side, "I didn't mean to rile you. But the way things are, I'll have to ask you a lot more questions than what I've done. About this accident business ..." He paused. "Right now we ain't so sure. Kinda looks as if it might not of been an accident after all."

"Not an accident?" Cold ran through her. "What do you mean? What else could ..."

The Chief of Police stared hard at her before he answered, "It could have been homicide."

CHAPTER XIII

"He was murdered?" Audrey heard a small distant voice saying. "Someone meant to kill Don?"

"I said it could be murder."

"Or voluntary manslaughter." For the first time since Peterson's arrival Eric Lund spoke. He drew back his long legs and sat erect. Eyes at once keen and impassive were fixed on Audrey.

She shifted her own to the chief whose lower central incisors were groping upward for their prey. "I don't—I can't believe it," she said.

"But accidental death seemed O.K. to you, didn't it, Mrs. Adriance?"

"You mean it seemed possible? But it was strange, too. Don hated the country. He didn't take walks. Not ever. And on a day when he was so ..."

"Maybe," Peterson said, "it don't seem possible now, but, Mrs. Adriance, last Friday morning when I come here at 5:00 A.M., you was expectin' somethin' to happen to your husband. You say you wasn't lookin' for an accident. That's probably true. Accidents are what people ain't prepared for. You better sit down and take it easy."

She sank back into the chair. "I wasn't expecting my husband to die."

She looked down at the brown hands clasped in her lap to hide tremor. Often she had watched Don's hands like this. The silver hearts and orange blossoms entwined on the wedding ring had slipped round to the palm. This silence was too long. Why didn't the policeman say something?

"Mrs. Adriance," Peterson's voice had become brisk. He had opened the limp notebook on his knee, "where was your husband workin' before he come here?"

"In Cambridge, Massachusetts."

"Can you give me his employer's name?"

"He didn't have any. He was working by himself, studying in the Harvard libraries, preparing for the work here."

"How long'd he been doin' that?"

"During April and May."

"Um-hum. And who was he workin' for before April?"

"We were in Florida," she said, "at Clearwater. Don had been sick. We went there in December."

"December to April," the chief was writing. "And before that?"

She tried to keep her hands quiet, not too tightly clasped. "He was in a hospital for six months. Near New York."

He wet a thumb in his mouth and slipped over pages, found what he sought. "Durin' the six months," he said, "in that hospital near New York was your husband bein' treated for anemia and allergy?"

She took a deep breath. For the first time in five years she was going to tell the truth. She opened her lips. The words wouldn't come. She looked toward Lund, saw him nod encouragement.

"He was being treated at Bloomingdale," she could say it now, steady and clear, "for chronic alcoholism."

Mr. Peterson wrote.

"Now you know what I was ready for on Thursday morning. Don had been doing wonderfully. He hadn't had a drink since he left the hospital, not in seven months, but I knew—and the doctors had told me—it could begin again any time."

"Yayer, that's a tough thing," Peterson nodded. "Then you wasn't surprised that your husband had been run down by a car. Just that it happened in a place he wasn't likely to be in?"

"I was terribly surprised. Don was always amazingly cautious. He had a number of falls in hotels or at home, but however bad he was, he never went out alone when he'd been drinking. Someone always brought him home—a policeman or people he had been drinking with. Or they sent for me and I went to the police station or wherever he was. Two or three times I went to hospitals."

"You didn't ever go out with your husband?"

"No. Not for five years."

He looked at her curiously. "How long you been married? Golly, you done quite a stretch, I'll say. Why didn't you tell me this, Friday mornin'? We could have avoided quite a few misunderstandin's."

She answered earnestly: "Don was dead and I wanted him to be remembered as—pleasantly as he could be. I thought, of course, that he had begun to drink, though it was unlike him to step in front of a car. If the driver was found and held responsible, I would have told at once. Or I guess it wouldn't have been necessary. There are tests, aren't there?

But you see, Don wasn't just an alcoholic, a sick person ... He was brilliant in his profession. He'd shown so much promise when he was awfully young that a man like Professor Wilkins, who had been one of his teachers in the Harvard Graduate School, had given him a chance here at the University. Even though he, Professor Wilkins, knew Don's history."

"O.K. I can see what you had in mind. You've had a pretty tough time, Mrs. Adriance. It must be kind of a relief to know it's all over."

She met his eyes and gave a small, honest nod.

"Of course, I can understand now why you don't know many of your husband's associates. You didn't care to hang around taverns with a bunch like that. What was your husband like when he was drinkin'? Was he quarrelsome? Likely to pick a fight? Do things that someone might remember for a long while?"

"He didn't get into physical fights. Usually he was very quiet. Sometimes he was—bad-tempered."

"Was he ever abusive?"

"Not except to ... The police never told me that he was."

"But he did knock you around?"

"Not really."

"This don't give much of an idea why someone should want to do violence to your husband the first few days he came to a new town. Specially since he hadn't been drinkin'. Looks as though whoever tried to kill him—if somebody did—must of known him some place before. You don't know anybody who would of had any reason to follow him here?"

"No."

"Are you perfectly sure there's no one here in town that knew your husband? Or," he added pointedly, "someone that knew you?"

She hesitated too long.

"There is someone, isn't there?"

He didn't, she thought, have that idea all by himself. Had Mr. Cox told? The clipping shears outside the window ... Alfred Dexter, of course. And how much had he heard?

"There is a man in the neighborhood," she explained carefully, "who seemed to recognize us. His name is Clifford Cox. I remember him vaguely as someone who brought Don home one night in rather bad shape. I don't know where it was or just when. Two or three years ago. Mr. Cox said something to me about it. I'm not at all sure Don recognized Mr. Cox. It would be surprising if he did. And Don didn't mention him to me, even after we had spent an evening with the Coxes at Mr. Dexter's house."

"Um-hum." Peterson was looking at her as if the best was yet to come. "Mrs. Adriance, when and where did you used to know Perfessor Gray?"

She could feel heat flooding to her face. All her strength steadied the tone in which she said, "I met him for the first time on Wednesday evening."

"Yayer? Quite a party the Dexters must of had. Everybody there but me. You there, Mr. Lund?"

"Sure." Lund got up. "Does anybody eat today?"

"Golly," the chief looked at his watch. "Quarter past one. Wife'll be after me if I don't run." He looked down at the green suit. "This is my Sunday off. I'm comin' back at two clock to see Mr. Dexter. You be round, Mr. Lund? O.K. Swell. Good-by, Mrs. Adriance, for now."

Audrey looked up at Eric Lund. She liked the long, narrow face, the blond, slightly thinning hair, the mouth with the faint, adventurous scars. I can trust him, she thought. I've got to trust someone.

"Mr. Lund," she begged for truth, "why do the police think that Don was murdered?"

"I honestly don't know. If I did, it would probably be in confidence. And remember, Mrs. Adriance," his smile erased half his words, "I'm not to be trusted. I haven't any professional interest in your case but if it developed an angle for me, I'd sell you short every time."

"I don't believe you would."

"I would. However, even my wife says I'm quite trustworthy in a kitchen. I'm going to cook our dinner."

While he rummaged effectively for chicken and the remains of Edna's cake, she sat at the dinette table where Peterson had drunk the suspiciously ready coffee, too tired to protest Lund's efforts.

"You really do know your way around," she offered gratefully. "Is Mrs. Lund a cook, too, or just you?"

"Janet? She can do everything. And I didn't deserve to get anything at all. I fell in love with her because she was the only girl I'd ever met who didn't ask me if I got these scars in a romantic way."

"You didn't?"

"God, no! I blew into a barbed-wire fence when I was a kid. Twenty below on a Minnesota prairie. A helpful older sister pulled me off and some skin too. I'd frozen on the wire. Will this cream whip?"

"Yes. The beater's in that drawer. The vanilla's on the second shelf. Not very tasty vanilla. Strictly non-alcoholic."

"O.K. And I assume you didn't go in for perfume around the house, either." His matter-of-fact approach to things long hidden was enormously comforting.

"I'll say not. And no cologne. There are a lot of other little things the

Adriances lack, too." She held out her left hand. "This is not the ring with which I was wed. Ten small diamonds won't buy a lot of Scotch but they'll buy a little."

"All this began when you were seventeen?" He dumped the chicken from casserole to skillet.

"More or less. The first two years it wasn't bad. I was too dumb to know what was ahead. Don was twenty-one, just graduating from college and ready to enter the Harvard Graduate School in the fall. Because he was four years older than I, I thought he was terribly grown up and knew everything. And when he said he couldn't get along without me, I married him. It took me a year to find out that what he really couldn't get along without was whiskey and that I would have to grow up right away so that there would be one adult in the Adriance family."

"He was a heavy drinker then?"

"Well, at times. Once in a while he would do something pretty hard to take. We lost quite a few friends during that time. And he spent too much money for liquor. But he kept up his work during the three years before he got his doctor's degree, so he was positive he could go on the way he was. Of course he couldn't."

"What did the war do to him?" Lund sliced bread.

"That was the final push over the edge. He had been getting worse. During the summer of '42, as soon as he'd taken his degree, he started drinking in the mornings. He was beginning to realize that he couldn't stop when he wanted to. Oh, well, you know how it goes. Don thought that the Army would straighten him out in a minute. But the draft board called him in the midst of a week's bout, so that was that."

"He lost job after job. You moved from place to place, etc. Vinegar or lemon juice in your French dressing, madam?"

"Lemon juice, thank you, even though it's more trouble. Don didn't lose many jobs because he didn't take many. I took a business course the first year we were married, so I usually earned enough to keep us going."

"But now and then he showed up at your office drunk and you got fired."

"Mr. Lund, you don't know what a relief it is to talk about it at last. With someone who knows all the answers."

"I only know that there isn't much of an answer to chronic alcoholism except the one you were given on Thursday."

"That isn't always quite true, is it, Mr. Lund? The article I was reading when you saw me in the library, in the *Quarterly Journal for Studies on Alcohol*, said that among cases that had had the best care as private patients in a sanitarium, sixty-four per cent hadn't lapsed in four years. Don had that kind of treatment, Mr. Lund. He might have made it all right for the rest of his life. He was terribly intense about anything that touched on academic things—his classes or research or any of the things he hadn't been able to do for the last three years."

"How about the last day? I guess we can begin to eat now. Have one of your own radishes."

"Thursday morning? That was a little mixed. He didn't drink at the Dexters' the night before. I was simply sick with fright, that evening, but we had to go. Don's doctor had said again and again that he could succeed only through himself, by being mature and not rationalizing and not depending on me to keep him out of trouble. Part of the therapy was inviting patients to cocktail parties so they would lose self-consciousness. But I expected Don either to be a kill-joy, or to drink."

"And he didn't do either?"

"No. His hands shook part of the time. They always did when he was sorry for himself. And the next morning when he got up, he went through all the motions of a hangover."

"Without having drunk a drop?"

"I'm sure of it, even without the coroner's tests. Don's psychiatrist told me it might happen. He kept it up for an hour or so. Then he snapped out of it and went off to the University full of that same deadly drive that he'd been showing for weeks. He said he had a lot to do and he'd be at home when it was done and not before. It didn't get done."

"But your job is ended."

"Yes, almost."

Lund looked at her quickly. "Mrs. Adriance, I'm going to ask you a damned rude and indelicate question. Are you going to have a child?"

She put down her water glass. "That's almost funny, Mr. Lund. There hasn't been a possibility of that for at least two years. Don was still going through ..."

"Impotence following alcoholic exhaustion?"

"And before that, there had been—other women. At the worst, he used to bring them home. Mr. Lund, I had forgotten! The last morning, last Thursday, he said something about one of them."

"One of the women he brought home?"

"Well, not really. This girl was in trouble. Don and I were both working in a defense plant in Hartford then and Don had been doing fairly well for a few weeks. The girl and a man she had married in Providence had been sitting around the taverns with Don, although the girl was definitely not a tavern type. Rather a droop but awfully nice and just a little cross-eyed. I never knew the details, but, anyway, the man left her without a cent. I think she had had a few hundred dollars and he had got it all. Then he just told her he was already married and walked out. And Don had practically his only Boy Scout moment and brought her home to me."

"And you saw it through?"

"What there was of it. All she needed was a decent bed to sleep in—which the Adriance ménage miraculously had at the moment—and the loan of her fare home. She sent back the money, too, and wrote that her father and mother had been wonderful to her. We didn't hear from her again."

"But Don asked you about her?"

"The last time I saw him. I don't understand it. I've told you what she was like."

Lund, admiring the whipped cream he was arranging tastefully on the cake, asked abstractedly, "What did he say?"

"I'm trying to remember. I'm almost certain that he asked me the name of the girl he brought home in Hartford. I told him. It was Hilda Hill. He said 'Right' and that ended it. Don was very irritable, as you can imagine. I didn't ever question anything he said."

"She was from Providence?"

"I think so. Some Rhode Island town. I kept her address in my ... Mr. Lund, I've lost my address book. It's hardly a loss to take up with the police or the FBI." But encouraged by his friendliness and his good coffee, Audrey told him.

"And you conclude," he tamped tobacco into his pipe, "that Mrs. Dexter, the two Grays, Mrs. Cox, or possibly the whole neighborhood could have walked off with the book, but that no one would want to."

"Yes. It contained practically nothing but the names of people we owed for rent and groceries during the last few years. They're all paid but one and I've promised that for the near future."

"The FBI," he said, "will take the case under consideration. How about a little dish washing?"

"No, please. I need an occupation. If you want to do something for me, go and keep Mr. Dexter from telling the Chief of Police that I am about to become a mother."

Some time after Lund had gone, she remembered his warning: I am not to be trusted.

CHAPTER XIV

Chief of Police Peterson in plain but gaudy clothes struggled with the untidy problem of his mustache and a stub of cigar. Beside him in the parked sedan Eric Lund silently played the part of a man waiting.

"Yay-er," Peterson spat the last wet eighth-inch out of the window, "it explains why the girl was expectin' trouble and got the house ready and the coffee and all that. I can see why she wouldn't be burstin' into tears, and why she wasn't so anxious to apprehend the driver if she thought Adriance was responsible. But seems to me that his bein' a steady drunk gives her a big motive for bumpin' him off. Particularly now."

Lund nodded. "She had the motive. It looks as if she had the opportunity. But it's an awkward way to murder anyone and not too likely to be successful. She's had better chances during the six years they've been married. Why now?"

"Well, I donno, Mr. Lund. I ain't a big FBI man. I'm just a local cop, but seems to me she's got two or three awful good reasons as of today. She could be havin' a kid that wasn't her husband's and he might of found it out and threatened her. Although I s'pose you could tell she wasn't lyin' to you. But she and that Perfessor Gray are carryin' on. You noticed that?"

Lund nodded. "I'd say it hadn't gone on long or far."

"If it ain't," said Peterson, "it will. I told you what I butted into Friday night. And when I was talkin' to him early that mornin' he was a hell of a lot too concerned about Mrs. Adriance—was she all right, was she alone—Well, she was alone with him before night. It could be O.K. but it don't look good. You're tellin' me what she said about her and her husband. Well, I know from direct personal observation that Gray's got his own bedroom. Human nature is ..."

"Human nature," agreed Eric Lund.

"You're damned right it is. Have a cigar?"

"Thanks, I'll stick to this." Lund waved his pipe. "It wouldn't do any harm to check up on Gray since 1939 and see if his path crossed the Adriances'."

"Yay-er. That's what I think. Only," he scratched his head, "it would be kinda hard for us to do with our limited facilities."

Lund drew slowly at his pipe. "Look here, Peterson," he said, "this is your case and it's none of my Department's business. You aren't in need of help anyway. You and Ellison and the University laboratories can do a swell job. But I've just run into an angle. It may not have a thing to do with Adriance's death. I doubt that it has. I was going to pull out in the morning but now I think I'll stick around a day or two and see what I can pick up. I'll need help from you, Chief, so if I can return it by having the Department do a little checking for you on Gray or any of the others ..."

Mr. Peterson registered dignified relief. "That would be swell, especially if there's Jap spy stuff to run down. I gotta go now and give the neighbors a goin' over. You meet me at Headquarters around four o'clock. I can show you somethin' pretty, Mr. Lund."

"Strawberries," sniffed Alfred Dexter, "gallons and long tons and whatever colossal quantities my wife buys them in. From 12:30 to 4:00 P.M., all those hours that so esoterically concern you, and while she was gallivanting at her war work, I was washing and culling and hulling. Except for one extremely short nap. I find it very hard, these days, Mr. Peterson, to get adequate sleep. What with jam in the kitchen and prowlers in the garden ..."

The chief turned the sedan toward the St. Cloud bridge. "You didn't get a real good look at the prowler, did you, Mr. Dexter?"

"Most unfortunately I did not. I had already gone to bed, I had to get up for a perfectly natural reason. The moon was very bright, I happened to look out the back window and saw a shadow moving in a very strange manner between my garage and Mr. King's—the Adriances'. I immediately summoned your department and then released my dog. He is a big Black Labrador, quite savage, though very gentle with children."

"I've met the brute," said Mr. Peterson.

"Oh? I'd forgotten. Well, almost at once he broke into fierce barks, and then, not unnaturally confused by a multiplicity of scents, he chose what well may have been the strongest, which led me and the rest of the neighborhood to the scientist from the Gas Company."

"Did you notice who got there first?"

"I did. With the possible exception of Mrs. Adriance. Then everybody seemed to come at once. Mrs. Gray and the Coxes and families farther up the river road and from behind us in Green Lane. Cadwallader had wakened them all. They may have heard the police siren, too."

"It's possible. Can't keep Bill Doolittle from soundin' it the minute he leaves headquarters. He don't get a chance to use it often enough for the novelty to wear off. Didn't Mrs. Dexter come out to see the show?"

"Oh, yes, she got there finally."

"And Mrs. Adriance was the first? That poor woman's had a lot goin' on lately."

"'Goin' on' is right. I'm sure, as my wife says, that she's a very good girl at heart."

"Referrin' to Perfessor Gray?"

"To Thornton Gray? Most certainly not. If there is a man in the case, it is indubitably Clifford Cox."

"So?" said Mr. Peterson with the sceptical note most likely to tap the Dexter keg.

"I do not wish to gossip," lied Alfred, "but I cannot sit here mute to an aspersion of my friend Thornton Gray. Mr. Peterson, on the very morning of the day her husband died, Mr. Cox made a secret call on Mrs. Adriance. At 8:50 A.M."

"He sneaked in the back way?"

"No, he went to the front door, or rather to the side, but I am quite sure he entered without ringing."

"You mean he had a key?"

"N-no," Alfred reluctantly admitted, "but it was after Donald Adriance had left home for the day."

"And for good. You have a chance to observe anything further, Mr. Dexter?"

"Yes; yes, I did." Alfred's beard bobbed gaily. "I just happened to be clipping the ivy, a few minutes later, and I couldn't help overhearing a very little of what went on."

"What did?"

"I couldn't *see* anything," regretted Alfred, "nor hear half of what was said. In fact, I didn't catch a word of hers. Her back was toward the window. But I very distinctly heard him call her honey and I shall not soon forget one sentence. 'Zowie, what a lot I saw of you. Sweetheart, we were pretty intimate.' Something very close to that."

"Huh!" said Mr. Peterson.

"I agree with you. And just when his wife may be going to have a baby."

"You mean Mrs. Adriance?"

"I am rather certain that she is, but I was now referring to Mrs. Cox."

"Ain't she a little older than that?"

"I would have thought so, but I have clues pointing in that direction. And she has practically told me so herself."

"I'll be damned." He stopped the car in front of the hospital. "Say, Mr. Dexter, you must have wonderful hearin' for a man of your age. And I don't mean you're old, either. How come you could hear all that talk between Cox and Mrs. A. when you was clippin' the ivy on your house?"

"The ivy," said Alfred, "was not on my house. I knew the moment I saw the Adriances that they were not the type to think of such things. At the hour we were discussing, I was performing a small service for my good neighbor, Mrs. King."

"My keys? Last Thursday afternoon? Did I leave them in the car, or didn't I? I'm not a bit sure." To Peterson, sitting beside her hospital bed, Rachel Dexter's face looked full of tired bones. Grane, the leather horse, was pinned gallantly to her bed jacket. "You see, I so often do leave them. It's important, isn't it, Mr. Peterson?"

"Yes, ma'am, 'tis," he nodded solemnly.

"Oh, dear," she said, "oh, dear." Large tears oozed from under her spectacles. "I make such terrible trouble for everyone. That poor old man! And I'm not a bit brave like Audrey Adriance. She's such a wonderful girl and so lovely in every way."

"You ain't got a thing to worry you now. You done all right from beginnin' to end. Now if you could remember about those keys."

"Wait a minute. I'll try." Rachel blew her nose efficiently. "I remember parking the car there at the end of the Student Union at half-past twelve. I said to myself, 'You must take out the keys,' and when I got up to the Red Cross Rooms, I thought, 'Oh, dear, I've left them again,' and I couldn't feel them in my bag, but it was awfully full and I didn't empty it out. Then I forgot all about it till Edna Gray and I were in the elevator going home. That was at four o'clock. I said to Edna that I had left the keys in the car and I certainly hoped it hadn't been stolen. Though, of course, it wouldn't have been. Everything is so safe on the campus."

"Yay-er?" encouraged the chief.

"And the keys *were* in my bag. They must have been there all the time, Mr. Peterson. I remember laughing with Edna about how stupid I was. Wait a minute—this might all have happened on a different Thursday. My weeks are pretty much alike, Mr. Peterson."

Peterson sighed and wrote something in his notebook. "And then you drove straight home and put the car up and nobody took it out till yesterday morning?"

"Well, I didn't quite put it up. I sometimes get a little mixed with the kohlrabi patch. Alfred drove the car from the street into the garage. I had quite a time waking him up to go do it. Poor man, I left him with strawberries to hull, and I think he must have slept all afternoon. A kind of lie-down strike. Anyway he hadn't done much about the berries. I had to sit right down and do it. The kitchen was so hot! I took the jam down to the laundry stove. I was just finishing it at midnight when we had that little excitement."

"And you rushed right out and let it burn, I bet."

"Oh, no, I didn't. I waited till it was all done. I don't lose my head *all* the time, Mr. Peterson."

"I'll say you don't. I'm much obliged to you for all this. And now I'll go tell your good husband to come in and keep you company."

"He is a good husband," said Rachel. "He's told me I can stay here till tomorrow noon and just rest. I know it's selfish of me when there are sicker people wanting my bed, but it is so lovely to be waited on."

He left her, happily operating the Gleam in the Eye of Grane.

Edna Gray said with gentle insistence, "Mrs. Dexter doesn't forget things. She only thinks she does. She is a very responsible person. Of course, it was this week Thursday and the keys were in her bag."

"Did you drive over to the Student Union with her or just drive home?" The chief admired the tight pink dress; she couldn't have looked better in a sweater.

"I drove to the campus in my own car and left it for my husband. In front of Abbott Hall. Then I walked over to the Union."

"You didn't happen to notice whether the Dexters' car was parked anywhere around?"

"I hardly think it was." She poked a curl. "Mrs. Dexter arrived quite a few minutes after I did."

"Mrs. Dexter leave the place at all, do you know, before four o'clock?"

The light blue eyes were very patient. "I couldn't be sure, Mr. Peterson. We were working at different tables. I was there all the time except for half an hour when I went to the Quiet Room to lie down. Walking across the campus in the heat had been a little too much for me." She didn't look too well now. Pale around the edges of her paint.

"Mr. Peterson," she spoke timidly, "is it all right to ask you why you want to know these things?"

"Sure it's all right but I don't know too much myself. Just kind of checkin' up on everythin', important or not. You never know." He held out the diary. "Do you recognize any of this handwritin', Mrs. Gray?"

She was quite a time looking at it, while he bit up at his mustache, watching her.

"I do. A part of it. All of the middle line is my husband's." For the first time the chief noticed that her mouth was too small for her chin.

"Does that bottom word mean anythin' special?"

She pursed her thin little mouth. "Lycanthrope refers to wolves."

"Mrs. Gray," this was going to be good, "what was your husband's relationship to Adriance?"

"Mr. Adriance," she said deliberately, "was obviously a very jealous person."

"You mean of his wife?"

"It was quite noticeable. On Wednesday evening at the Dexters', Thornton—Mr. Gray—sat down on the love seat beside Mrs. Adriance and at once Mr. Adriance, who was talking to me at the time, dashed across the room and broke up—well, the conversation."

Mr. Peterson hesitated. He was getting what he wanted but he was enjoying it less than he had expected. The woman's eyes were too far up in her face.

"Mrs. Gray, hadn't you met Mr. Adriance some place before he came to this town?"

She answered in pinched hauteur: "Neither Mr. nor Mrs. Adriance was the type of person I would be likely to meet anywhere."

"Did Mr. Gray know either of the Adriances before they came here?"

The tip of her tongue licked her upper lip, like a little cat. "If one's husband is older than fifteen or sixteen when one first meets him, there may be spots in his past that one never learns, no matter how much interest one shows. He might have done anything or known anybody."

Peterson said nothing and she went on, "Since we were married, in 1940, Mr. Gray has spent two summers away from me and our little girl. He was teaching anthropology at different summer schools. In 1942, he was at Columbia and in 1943, he was at Brown."

"Where is this Brown?"

"In Providence, Rhode Island." Her tone suggested that he was an ignorant man.

He stood up. "When you expect your husband back from Washington?"

"On Tuesday, but, of course, I can never be quite sure."

"Huh." He was beginning to think that if he was Gray, he'd take his time. "You got a lot of unusual things in your house, Mrs. Gray."

She smiled at the game board, and the old weeds in the jar. "I was born in Tokyo. I think everything the Japanese do is so lovely."

The chief's face grew violently red. "I think different!" he said and slammed the Grays' screen door in memory of a young private named Pete Peterson, Jr., who on the afternoon of December 7, 1941, no longer served at Hickham Field.

"I thought I'd seen him some place before," Clifford Cox's hyperthyroid eyes met Peterson squarely, "but, you know, you see a lot of guys that look like that. He wasn't an unusual type. Same with his wife. If I hadn't seen the two of them together, I'd never have recognized either one. I was in a bar in Tarrytown, New York, back in 1941. I forget just when. Adriance had a car out front and he wasn't fit to drive it, so I drove him home. The wife got out of bed and came down in her nightie and took him in. "Thursday? Zowie, that was a hot one! I lay around most all day with my clothes off. Yes, I was out a little while in the afternoon, round one and two. You get a little restless in a burg like this. Nice little town but I'm used to something really big, so I took the bus down to the Low Jinks Bar and had a sandwich and three or four beers. Bartender probably would know me. I've been there before. Whoa! Here we are back at the old stand. Coming in to interrogate the madam?"

"I kinda had that in mind," said Mr. Peterson.

Beulah Cox had tried to rest. For the first time in years she had that morning directed her fagged spirit to church and her erratically aching body to a Sunday afternoon nap. Neither muscles nor central nervous system had responded; each still protested the exigencies of her hormones and her husband.

"I left Abbott Hall, as I told you, at 1:30, and walked over to the Student Union." She felt too tired to elaborate. "I bought a sandwich there and a carton of milk and took them over to the Botanical Garden. I suppose I left the Union about 1:40. One of my students, one I think I mentioned to you the other day, Amy Angel who was a member of Mr. Adriance's 12:30 class, came past the bench where I was sitting, and we shared the lunch and chatted until it was time to go back to Abbott Hall. Amy was with me, I should say, from two o'clock until my class began at 2:30. The English Department faculty then held a meeting which ended at four-fifteen."

"Thank you very much," said Mr. Peterson. "I got that all down good and clear."

It was four o'clock in the basement of the City Hall. At a scarred table in the chief's damp sanctum, Eric Lund was looking at pictures. Behind a wooden door that had left the mill in 1894 and received a new tacking of sheet iron in 1900, the Saturday night souses slept it off in what Mr. Peterson had once described on a questionnaire as "6 Sells."

Before Lund were two photographs, suggesting strange dark realms of the universe. The first was like a wild, bright-haired comet streaking through night; the second, an arc of light above blackened earth made horrible by sparse, twisted limbs of vegetation.

"Remarkable," Lund meant it. "Wonderful photography. Do your own enlargements?"

"Yay-er." Mr. Peterson tried not to sound proud. "The first one is the close-up of this spot right here." He pointed to the picture of a sedan. "The old man was sideswiped in the leg by the right fender, bounced up and hit the window frame, and broke the glass like you see. Then the body hit the rear fender and left this dent." He pushed another photograph toward Lund who nodded and returned to the contemplation of the comet-like apparition.

"And this is the old man's hair?"

"Yay-er, stuck on the upper right-hand corner of the window frame. Matched the hair on the body. Coarse and white and wavy. Ends rounded like it hadn't been cut for a long time, and his hadn't."

"O.K. Now this one?" He bent over the image of dawn in a devastated area.

"That," Mr. Peterson said slowly, "is the underside of the left-hand runnin' board."

"Hairs standing up from the edge? Glued on with blood?"

"Yes, sir. Light brown, fine, and almost straight. Ends angular like when they've just been cut. They match swell, Mr. Lund."

"I'll be damned. How did you happen to look there?"

"I thought I might as well do a good job. Had the car taken over to the Southside Garage and used their greasin' rack."

"Damned good, Peterson. Not one in a million in a town this size would have done it."

"Maybe I wouldn't of under ordinary circumstances." Peterson was proud red to the top of the dome. "I guess I was just showin' off to myself because the FBI was in town."

"Whatever the reason ... Go ahead, Chief, how do you reconstruct the first accident?"

"Just the physical part of it is all I've got clear in my mind yet. Somethin' like this: Adriance is walkin' along the road on the left-hand side fairly near the ditch. Car came along and hit him with the bumper. He falls down with his feet in the ditch. Front wheel goes over his head and breaks the skull. Head bounces up and scrapes the bottom of the runnin' board and leaves this here hair and enough blood to glue it on. Then the rear wheel pushes the body the rest of the way into the ditch, like we found him. I got plenty of shots of that, too."

Eric Lund said, "Of course the evidence of hair is never anything but circumstantial. Which doesn't mean that it isn't valuable and damned impressive to a jury. Now, leaving aside the reason or reasons why Adriance was walking along an open road three miles from the campus, last Thursday afternoon, an act, according to his wife, completely out of character, just how did he happen to get hit? The car presumably came up behind him or he would have seen it and got out of the way. We know he wasn't drunk or otherwise incapacitated."

"So then the car came up behind him on the wrong side of the road."

"O.K. And you say it happened before the rain which would have wiped out all skid marks, but on the other hand, what would cause skidding on that dry clay road?"

"There's plenty of freak accidents, Mr. Lund, but still ..."

"An automobile isn't a handy weapon for assault. But it's been used more than once."

"If 'twas an accident, somebody's keepin' awful quiet. So we got the old hit-run case anyhow. Me and the boys've got a nice little list of check-ups to make. Supermarket, 'U' Red Cross, Low Jinks, Angel. And maybe a quiet reception at the airport for Perfessor T. Gray?"

"I'll hear from Washington when he leaves."

"Swell. Now, you want to say somethin' about your angle?"

"Yes," said Eric Lund.

CHAPTER XV

Audrey woke in terror. Strange throbs seemed to come from deep in her body, grinding, not beating like a heart. Am I dying? she wondered, and sat up in the bed.

At once the sensation ceased. Still dazed with sleep she blinked toward the bureau where fallen rose petals lay like ink blots on white linen. The clock dial dimly registered five. Nice nightmare I must have had. But she couldn't recall it and that frightened her.

The grinding began again, external, not feeling but sound. The telephone.

Three days ago Audrey had been ready for any trouble. Now, disorganized by one wild fear, she ran down the stairs. Thornton. Something had happened to him. The receiver shook in her hand. In the second before she spoke, sense returned to tell her that whatever was wrong with him she would not be the first to know.

A woman's voice, dry and flat, said, "This is Edna Gray."

Panic cramped her. "Yes?"

"Are you alone in the house?"

"Yes." Was that a prudent answer?

"Go to your back door and open it as quietly as you can."

"Mrs. Gray, I don't see why ..."

"Please. You must do it." She was pleading. "I'll be over at once."

The receiver clicked.

Guilt shook Audrey. For the first time she realized fully that this was not just a rather mean young woman named Edna Gray. She was about to encounter Thornton's wife. However things stood between the Grays, however brief and transient was her own relationship to Thornton, Audrey knew that she had done Edna a wrong. Now she would have to face it.

She took Don's old raincoat from the hall closet and wrapped it over a cold shivering that was not entirely of the mind. Hadn't Peterson suggested that violence had already been their neighbor?

Are you afraid? Edna Gray had said that, little wasp lips stinging the words at Don. And Don, smiling, taunting, had not answered her question. Not then. But later, on that clay road beyond the town ...?

Now I am mad, thought Audrey. Edna Gray could have no reason to kill him. It was ridiculous to tiptoe like this across her own locked kitchen. She pushed back the muslin curtaining the glass in the door.

Outside it was now quite light. The neat little garages, the two garbage cans, the hedge, stood clear and shadow-less. Audrey slipped the bolt back from the door and opened it slowly. Now, as she leaned out, she could see Edna Gray staggering across the Dexter yard. Her right arm clasped a heavy burden wrapped in a pink blanket; from her left hand a small suitcase bumped her knee. Even at this strange hour each yellow curl had been strained into perfect place.

Audrey held the door wider as Edna stepped soundlessly over the grass beneath the window of the room presumably Mr. Lund's. Evidently she feared Alfred Dexter's curiosity more than she did the nationally professed sleeplessness of the FBI. Her face was sickly white.

At the doorstep she stumbled against Audrey's arm outstretched for the suitcase, righted herself silently and passed into the kitchen. The bundled blanket slipped from Edna's arm and unwrapped itself.

"Just a minute, Sister." Edna knelt beside the sleepy little girl who was hugging something tightly, and arranged black curls that the blanket had mussed. She might have been giving her a last touch before a birthday party. "Now, come."

Without a word or look for Audrey she led the child through the swinging door that opened into the Tudor living room. Almost at once she came back alone. She was wearing a tweed suit of pastel blue and the blouse with too many ruffles. She gave Audrey a short, tense look, then turned away and called softly through the door, "Good-by—Margaret."

"Mrs. Adriance," she crossed the kitchen quickly, "my mother is very ill. In Iowa. I have had a telephone call. I am catching the five-thirty bus." Her voice recited, her eyes were blank. "All the things Sister will need are in the bag. She's had her orange juice. Give her any kind of cereal and a soft-boiled egg. The Nursery School won't let her come today because she's getting over the sniffles. Take her over to our door for the school car tomorrow at quarter of nine."

"But, Mrs. Gray ..."

Edna's hand was on the doorknob. "Her father will be home some time tomorrow."

Still no feeling appeared in her tone nor in the high-placed eyes. Between the pinched, slightly parted lips her teeth seemed to be holding up the weight of her chin. She spoke again, now with the note of plea that Audrey had heard over the wire. "Promise that you will stay with Sister here in the back of the house for the next few minutes. I don't want her to be upset by seeing the taxi."

Before Audrey could answer she had opened the door, closed it behind her, and was gone.

Audrey brushed the hair back from her forehead. This, she thought, is something! But what? It could be, it must be, what it seemed. An emergency had arisen; time was pressing, Rachel Dexter still at the hospital. Even so ...

"Audrey," an anxious little girl clutching a battered magazine as if it were her last link to home peeped through the swing door, "can I come in here with you?"

"Hello, Margaret." Audrey made her voice brisk and gay. "I invited you and you came, didn't you? Let's get our breakfast. Will you help me find a pitcher for your milk? There's one with a doggie on it. Like Cadwallader."

The child came slowly into the middle of the room. She looked perplexed rather than tearful. "Mommy called me Mar-gar-et."

"Climb up on the stool and we'll hunt for the doggie." The stiff raincoat was in Audrey's way but she couldn't risk going upstairs to dress till the taxi was out of sight of incipient howls.

"O.K." Margaret clambered up on the stool. "You take this."

Audrey, steadying the stool with one hand, stuffed into her coat pocket what was obviously the sitter's choice of current literature, and began a typical day with a four-year-old.

In midafternoon, when her invention was running low while Margaret's activity approached an all-time high, Audrey thought of trains. With a great deal of feminine consultation about color of socks and angle of hair bows, they dressed themselves and took a bus to the station. Margaret begged to feed the pigeons in Bowery Square and Audrey, buying and plying peanuts, struggled against the memory of one old man not now present and probably not missed.

They then crossed to the station and admired three trains. It was the engineer of the beautiful silver streamliner who had waved to the flattered Margaret, and she was dancing along, propelling Audrey beneath the windows of the car that you could eat inside of, when they saw Mr. Clifford Cox. Pale gray hat on the side of his fat head, soapy forehead shining, pop-eyes, and slack lips smiling, he passed them, oblivious to all save his own happy thoughts, and climbed into the first coach of the train.

Even four-year-olds can tire. On the homebound bus Margaret spoke only once. "I showed the picture to Mommy." She yawned and leaned against Audrey, almost asleep.

At eight, when she was settled for the night, Audrey sank into the big chair by the fireplace. Yes, she was tired, but in an awfully good way. I'll get used to it in a few days, she thought. No, she mustn't get used to taking care of a little girl, because she couldn't have this one or any other so long as she loved Thornton Gray. Tomorrow when he returned, he would view with more embarrassment than pleasure her involuntary guardianship of his child.

The doorbell rang and a man's voice called through the screen, "Hello, Mrs. Adriance. Lund."

When he had settled down opposite her with his pipe, he said, "The FBI has fulfilled your assignment. Here's your address book."

"Where did you find it?"

"Peterson found it in your husband's briefcase at the University office. When the murder possibility arose the police gave the place a thorough going over. Mrs. Adriance, have you any idea why your husband would have a particular interest in this book near the time of his death?"

"Could I see it, Mr. Lund?"

"Certainly." He handed it to her with a glance that she no longer assessed as casual.

Probably, she thought, turning to the H's, every page has been fingerprinted. Here she had left the book open when she had gone to the kitchen for Don's saddle soap. "Mrs. Mary E. Hinton," she read to herself, and then, with widening eyes, the name above.

"On the afternoon before he died, I found him reading this. I've already told you." With fingers that shook she held out the open book.

He nodded. "Thanks for telling me this, too. It may help Peterson. Before I return the book to him, would you like to copy out any addresses?"

"Yes, thanks. There are one or two cousins of Don's that I ought to write to, even if his mother notifies them."

"You've heard from her again since you phoned?"

"Yes, she's been very good about the financial arrangements. She will pay for the cremation and for my trip to Tarrytown."

"That was Don's old home?"

"Yes, he lived there till he went to college. Since then he's been there only once. We were there together in 1940. That was the last time Mrs. Carr saw Don."

"Do you mind staying here alone?" he asked. "No more prowlers?"

"No. If I see one again I shall scream for help. With the FBI beside me and the formidable Mrs. Cox to the rear, I ought to get plenty of protection."

"Have you," he wanted to know, "remembered just when and where you first saw the lady's unfortunate purchase?"

Audrey shook her head. "It was between 1942 and 1944, the years when Don was drinking heavily and drifting from town to town in Connecticut and New York. We were staying in an awful little hotel and I had undressed and gone to bed. When I heard the usual commotion, I got up and put on some sort of thin robe and went to the head of the stairs. Don was almost out and hanging on to a fat man. I should never have remembered the man except for the revolting thing he did. He threw a kiss at me. Even now it makes me sick to think of it."

"Hell-oh-oh!" A rich contralto floated through the door, followed by the bell. "May I come in? It's Beulah Cox."

"Hell," responded Lund, but softly, and went to the door.

"Mr. *Lund?*" she said. "I was rather expecting to see Mr. Peterson or even Mr. Cox. My husband is delayed this evening. Oh, Mrs. Adriance, you are looking better than one could expect."

The glance through her dazzling lenses seemed to have real kindness for Audrey. She sat upon too small a chair and said to Eric Lund, "I was unaware that the federal government interested itself in local accidents. I infer there is nothing but friendliness behind this call, Mr. Lund?"

"Your inference is sound, Mrs. Cox." Lund leaned forward to light his pipe. "There are more than enough officials concerned in these things without me."

"I," she said, and smiled, "have met only one."

"Peterson? He's a good man, Mrs. Cox. Then there's the coroner who is a pretty important factor. By rights the sheriff should be conspicuous but he thought this was the right time to go fishing. And before this is over, you may all hear from the county attorney. I understand he is a recent graduate of the University, able and a good sort."

"I must go before Mrs. Adriance is too utterly tired," said Beulah Cox.

"We'll go together." Lund rose. "I suppose Mr. Dexter has probably returned with his wife. I understand that he was setting her up to a dinner at the best tearoom in town."

"Good night, Mrs. Adriance," said Mrs. Cox. "If ever you are afraid, do send for me."

"I'll do that," said Audrey and received Lund's wink as he escorted Beulah's bulk to the door.

It was a good night, the first that Audrey had ever spent as protector of a child. She slept well and there was something to wake for, a strenuous two hours till the Nursery School taxi came. Waiting in front of her own house, Margaret had a moment of tears.

"My plaid skirt! And the shirtwaist just like the big girls. Mommy said I could wear it today. You didn't let me!" Black curls shook in rage.

"It wasn't in your suitcase, dear. When Mommy comes home—"

"I want it now." A little lady can really howl.

"Here's the taxi. Don't let the children see you cry."

"Can I wear it tomorrow?" She was only sobbing now.

"Yes."

"Do you promise? Audrey, really and truly?"

Audrey remembered the bit of metal shining on the moonlit floor. "I promise."

"O.K." Margaret raised a final wail and let herself be kissed good-by.

The key was still in the pocket of the silver and violet robe of Alfred's choice. Dangling from the small red tag in her fingers it seemed to Audrey a symbol of her muddled relations with the three Grays. A house prowl wasn't going to clarify them nor was it going to be easy to explain to inquisitive neighbors. Better to disarm them in advance.

She dialed the Dexters' number—*6954*. The number that had been strangely important to Don.

"Oh, my dear, what we all do to you!" Rachel Dexter sounded abject but quite healthy once more. She would take Sister, she would run over with some nice fresh radishes from her garden, she would do anything. Yes, of course, she would tell Thornton where Sister was. He'd be sure to call their house when he couldn't get Edna to answer. Thornton always called Edna the minute he got back from anywhere. Edna was most particular about attentions of that sort. And would Audrey bring Sister over for dinner? It would probably be just the old folks. No, Mr. Lund hadn't left but he had said he was expecting a man he'd wanted to meet for a long time.

The morning mail brought no letter from Edna Gray. Audrey had expected a post card might come for the child. Before night there should be word from her father.

The call came at eleven, Thornton's voice over the wire, as filled with emotion as hers.

"Audrey. Dear. Are you alone?"

"Yes," she said breathlessly and then, "No. That is, I'm alone in the house right now, but Margaret is staying with me."

"What Margaret?"

"Margaret Gray. Didn't you know?"

"Know what?"

"She, Mrs. Gray," she couldn't say *Edna* or *your wife*, "had to leave for Iowa early yesterday morning. Her mother is very ill."

He said, "I'll be damned. I'm sorry about Edna's mother. She's been having heart attacks for several years. You get everything handed to you, don't you?"

"Margaret is something pretty nice to get, even for a day or two."

"Well, I agree. I'd rather have her with you than anyone else. She likes you. But that was a hell of a thing for Edna to do."

"You must have worried when you called the house and didn't get an answer."

He said in a deeper voice, "I didn't call the house. I'm at the airport. Just in. It was my one chance to talk to you."

"Thornton, what happened in Washington?"

"Audrey, I think I'm going!"

"Where?"

"It isn't certain yet. Depends on how the war goes in the next few weeks. I'll be in Washington for a while before I go out of the country."

"Oh, Thornton."

"Listen, dear," he said. "I hadn't expected to see you alone. Anyway, not for a long time. Edna certainly does the damnedest things. That foul cake and now this."

"It was a nice cake. The Chief of Police ate half of it at a sitting."

"Audrey, what about the police?"

"I'll tell you when—that is, if you come out."

"I've got a class in half an hour. I'll be at your house about 12:30? All right?"

"You know it is," she said.

CHAPTER XVI

But it wasn't all right to see Thornton again. Beneath her quick, warm response, scruples remained, cold and hard. She must get Margaret's dress at once; no further excuse should take her over Edna's threshold now that Thornton was at home, nor should any little domestic conversations take place.

Audrey sped out into the hot noon light. Beyond the black surface of River Road, trees in tiers, deep and cool, descended the bank to the slow brown current. At the distant corner by the bus stop waited a big woman in white clothes. Voices called from the Dexters' garden: "Alfred, bring my sun hat," and "Cadwallader, come here!"

The walk that led to the Grays' half-timber and diamond panes was shaded by a poplar screen which shut out the houses beyond. On the other side, this Tudor triplet turned its unbroken brick and plaster back of the Great Hall to the Dexters' analogous blank wall, achieving thereby an almost complete exemption from even Alfred's laboratory observation. Only by extended field trips could he have carried out solid research on the social and biological functions of the genus Gray.

Audrey fitted the red-tagged key into a nail-studded door identical with her own. She turned it slowly, delaying an entry that seemed peculiarly indelicate. The door swung out, revealing a small console table bearing a telephone and a Japanese flower arrangement of austere design. It seemed less furtive to leave the door open behind her.

Straight ahead she could see the profiles of chairs and tables in the living-room—curtained against the sun. On the right, tan rep hung stiff at windows and over a cot; books covered all walls and backed the workmanlike desk. The room was in exhibition order and smelled of furniture polish. Alfred Dexter had said: "Thornton Gray uses *his* as a study and a—a study."

This was the kind of thing she didn't want to learn from the Grays' house. She mounted the stairs quickly. The upper hall showed the same perfect order and cleanliness. It seemed impossible that anyone receiving at dawn a message so profoundly disturbing as Edna's seemed to have been, could have achieved rapid packing and departure without leaving a wisp of lint or a rug askew.

The front bedroom bore the same uncanny grooming. All the frippery-flummery of ruffles, rose-painted flacons, and figurines from the Gifte Shoppe displayed the care that Edna lavished on the refinements she had amassed with that income which Thornton rejected. Pink satin lay smooth on the bed and beneath the pillow roll bloomed an enormous red rose, on whose corolla perched a blue butterfly, manufactured to scale.

This single misplaced and somewhat ambiguous object drew Audrey to a closer examination. She walked over thick carpet toward the bed. The farther wall came into view, and then she saw the bags. There were three; a hatbox, wardrobe, overnight case, gray plastic striped with pale blue.

Audrey caught her breath. So Edna Gray had returned. She must be in the house now, in the kitchen or in the small back room. The object on the bed was now quite identifiable. A band of attached blue veiling made butterfly and rose a hat. Adjacent lay more blue, a suede purse and gloves.

It would not be good to explain that she had entered this house with Edna's husband's key, and even though Edna had endowed her with Margaret, she didn't want to be caught rummaging through Edna's bureau drawers. There was only one thing to do. She went into the hall and called down the stairs,

"Mrs. Gray! Mrs. Gray!'

There was no answer. She stood waiting, hearing the blood in her ears and no other noise. Together with the smell of polish and shut-in rugs, there seemed to be a faint human odor.

"Mrs. Gray!" Again she listened. Out on the river a coal barge hooted at the St. Cloud bridge. There was no nearer sound.

Through the door of the oriel room she saw a row of dolls and Teddy bears seated in little chairs and a low painted chest that might contain a shirtwaist like the big girls'. When she met Edna, it would be easier to explain if she were fulfilling Margaret's known desires.

Heavy, slightly tainted air met her at the threshold. Daffodil gauze in precise folds softened the sunlight from the casement straight ahead. Under the side window stood Margaret's bed. Edna Gray lay on the bed. She wore a blue tweed skirt and the over-frilled blouse. Her eyes were closed and one arm dangled, the fingertips nearly touching a rug. No one should have slept through those calls of "Mrs. Gray!" Audrey tiptoed to the bed. Edna's face was wax-white. The lines of her long cheek and chin had an inhuman stiffness but the hard yellow curls were now crushed into the pillow.

Kneeling by the bed Audrey lifted the hanging hand. It was an ugly purple and cool. She couldn't feel a pulse. Her fingers loosened their hold and the arm fell limply and began to swing to and fro.

The slow horror of this pendulum from a body otherwise deathly still crawled through Audrey's nerves. She forced her cringing fingers to push apart the blouse ruffles. The skin where the cloth had covered it was warm in contrast to her own hand which now felt as icy as Edna's. She could feel no heartbeat beneath her palm. Tearing open the blouse, she laid her cheek and ear against the pink crepe over Edna's breast. Nothing to hear, nothing to feel except the mild, unresponsive warmth. She pressed harder with cheek and outspread hand, trying desperately now to find life.

Now she heard a sound. For the moment she had forgotten the world beyond herself and Edna. Dizzily she raised her head and saw that a blur of white filled the door of the room.

"Mrs. Adriance," the voice came from a New England judgment seat, "what are you doing *now?*"

Audrey crept back from the pendant arm. She spoke hoarsely. "I think she's dead."

Mrs. Cox loomed into the room. "Don't you *know?*"

"No." Audrey begged help from the glassy waves that hid Beulah's eyes. "I can't feel any heartbeat, but her skin is warm. Please, will you— feel?"

"Certainly I shall not." The beautiful white coiffure bent accusingly over Audrey. "I know better than to touch a body before I call the police."

"Police? It's a doctor ..."

"Oh, no," Beulah smiled sadly. "Not now. You've changed your mind too late."

Audrey was on her feet. "What do you mean, Mrs. Cox? I came in here a moment ago and found her—like this."

"You came in here," Beulah examined her wrist watch, "exactly fourteen minutes ago. I saw you from the bus stop. Can you guess why I followed you, Mrs. Adriance?"

"No. I don't care. We've got to do something about Mrs. Gray."

"Yes. At once. I came to inquire what you had done with my husband, but that will have to wait now. Go out." She gestured toward the door.

Audrey put out her hand to replace the ruffles across Edna's pallid chest.

"Don't touch her," Beulah's voice rose. "Come downstairs with me while I telephone." She was upon Audrey now, a hand pinching into her shoulder, heaving her forward.

"Take your hand off me!" Audrey wrenched herself from the older woman's mean grasp. "Of course I'll come with you."

"Just a minute, Mrs. Adriance." The red nails that had been piercing Audrey's skin pointed to a blue wastebasket painted with pink bunnies, soap-and-water clean and empty except for a yellow bottle with a druggist's label. "The poison was in that?"

"I hadn't noticed it before."

"No, I'm sure that if you had, it wouldn't be there now." She bent ponderously forward.

"Don't touch it!" Audrey cried out.

"Oh," Beulah straightened, anger-red, "*you* dare to tell *me*..."

"We've got to telephone."

"You're very, very wise to agree."

"Mrs. Cox, both of us can't get through this door at the same time."

Beulah, her face fiery, edged into the hall. Audrey pushed past and rushed down the stairs. The floral art of Japan crashed to the floor as she dialed the red zero.

"Police Department. Emergency." She could feel Beulah puffing up behind her.

"'ello?" sang a Scandinavian voice. "Chief of Police speaking."

"Mr. Peterson ..." The receiver was wrenched cruelly from her hand.

"This is Mrs. Clifford Cox." The heavy breath went over the wire. "I wish to report that Mrs. Adriance has committed another murder. You will find the body at Professor Gray's."

Black pinpoints magnified to marbles by thick lenses, lips slowly moving into a smile, Mrs. Cox lowered the instrument from which Peterson's questions pattered and laid it noiselessly in place. "I'm sorry that your wrist is sore, Mrs. Adriance. It is only a small first installment of retribution, isn't it?"

Fighting faintness and pain, Audrey stood by the newel post, her right hand behind her back supporting the throbbing left wrist, her eyes fixed on the wall above Beulah's triumphant white head, her whole strength concentrated on one purpose: don't speak till the police get here.

Nor did Mrs. Cox say anything further. She brought a chair from Thornton's study, set it in the middle of the hallway, and herself upon it. She no longer resembled a righteous, refined bulldozer; she was a large woman of fifty in an unbecoming white dress, fatigued by emotional strain.

She rallied when the chief tramped up the walk. He too looked old and tired. He came in without removing his cap and leaned against the screen door staring hard from one woman to the other.

"Who's dead now?"

"Mrs. Gray," said Audrey. "Upstairs."

"Which one of you found the body?"

"I did," said Audrey and Mrs. Cox in unison.

Peterson put his head out the door. "Bill." The lanky patrolman who had misjudged the sniffer appeared on the step. "Come in and stay here in the hall. Now, Mrs. Cox, you sit in that room there," he pointed to the dim living-room, "I'll hear your story soon's I get a chance. Mrs. Adriance, you wait in the kitchen. I s'pose it's through this door. All these damn houses are alike."

Audrey sat down on a kitchen stool and laid her hot wrist flat on the cool white worktable. A car came up the drive and parked close to the window. The wiry, red-haired man who jumped out she recognized from her visit to the morgue—the coroner, Dr. Ellison, who was also professor of pathology at the University Medical School. She could hear him give a quick word to the patrolman on guard in the hall and then start up the stairs. A second car drove in, a white police sedan, and two patrolmen, one carrying a camera and a box of flash bulbs, went up to the door.

"Hi," they said to Bill, "business is pickin' up in this burg. Looks like we'll have to put the dog catcher on full time." They too went up the stairs. Audrey said to herself: I'll tell the chief everything. This time I won't hold anything back. Over and over she arranged the details in her mind, placing them in order as facts, things that had happened, without special meaning for herself or for Thornton. The red hands of the electric wall clock loitered halfway around the stupid white face and reached twelve before Peterson came into the kitchen.

Again they faced each other across a kitchen table decorated with a uniform cap. Peterson, nibbling steadily at his mustache, kept his eyes on Audrey's. The notebook did not appear. She told him all she knew, from Edna Gray's telephone call on the preceding morning through Thornton's call of an hour ago; why she had the key and why she had used it; the strange order of the house, her progress through the tidy rooms, the terrified moments at Edna's side and the advent of Beulah Cox.

"Got any idea why she should of followed you in here?" Peterson rubbed a veined cheek.

Audrey shook her head. "She said something about my knowing where Mr. Cox was. I don't remember very well. I was thinking about Mrs. Gray. Mr. Peterson, is she dead?"

"Yes. Doc Ellison guesses it happened three or four hours ago. He'll know more later." He picked up his cap and stood up.

"Mr. Peterson, I do know something about Mr. Cox. I saw him get on the streamliner, yesterday afternoon."

Apparently no remark could have been more bromidic. He yawned and left the room. Indistinguishable words reached Audrey, and then he was back in the kitchen.

"You can go home now, Mrs. Adriance," he said. "Doolittle will stay there for a while and answer the door for you. I'll see you later and go over your story. Now I gotta get Mrs. Cox's side of it."

At the front window of their "study" Alfred and Rachel Dexter nodded sorrowful gray heads as Audrey and the policeman passed. She waved to them and tried to smile. In her hall she watched Bill Doolittle bolt the screen door.

"Has anyone told Mr. Gray?" she asked.

"I donno, ma'am. Sorry, but the chief don't want you to use that phone."

"Oh. Would you like a glass of milk and a sandwich?"

"Don't bother, ma'am. But I kinda would."

She left the door open into the kitchen and he did not follow her. She covered big slices of bread with marmalade and all the butter she had, and poured two glasses of milk. How many times in the last five days had she fed policemen? If Peterson agreed with Mrs. Cox, she would have a chance at a nice life job in some warden's kitchen.

"Oh, golly, thanks." Doolittle sat down on the bottom step of the stairs. "Look, Mrs. Adriance, I ain't guardin' you like a suspect or nothin'; I'm just seein' that nobody gets to talk to you till Pete comes."

"Thank you," said Audrey.

"You're welcome." He took a mouthful of sandwich. "Butter! Say, you *are* a lady!" In gratitude he offered a piece of pleasant news. "City ambulance's just come for the body."

Audrey took her milk to the chair by the fireplace and there in the deep well of the room she tried, between slow, difficult swallows, to think and feel nothing. Twice in a long half-hour she and Doolittle spoke: once he refused to get in touch with Mr. Lund, and again, later, after a short reconnaissance from the street, he returned to tell her that ambulance, coroner, and squad car had just left the Gray driveway and that the chief had also driven away.

At quarter of one nature summoned Officer Doolittle above stairs. It was then that the doorbell rang and Audrey answered it. Thornton, looking as gay as his new blue and gold necktie, was on the step. Before she could speak he had her close. The deep eyes and the black, questioning brows were near her face.

"My girl?" he asked and answered it with his mouth on hers.

"Thornton"—tall and strong as she was, he was hard to push away— "stop. There's a policeman at the head of the stairs. I've got to tell you quick."

"What?"

"It's about your wife. She's dead."

She saw shock dim the vitality of his face and his hands drop heavily to his sides.

Doolittle came sheepishly down the stairs. "You ain't supposed to talk together," he announced weakly.

Thornton said to Audrey, "Tell me about it."

She put her hand on his arm and the three went into the living-room. Between Thornton's chair and Audrey's, the policeman teetered from toes to heels.

"She brought Margaret here at five yesterday morning and told me she had to take a 5:30 bus for Iowa. Just after you telephoned I went over to get some clothes that Margaret wanted. Your house key had fallen out of your pocket here on Friday evening. And in the small back bedroom I found ... she was lying on the bed. I thought at first she was asleep. But the police say she probably died early this morning. Oh, Thornton."

Shadows lay deep between lips and nostrils as he bent his head, looking down at the hands palm to palm between his knees. Doolittle took cigarettes from his shirt pocket and held them out to Gray.

"Thanks," he took one and felt for matches.

"I have a light." Audrey came to him as the bell rang once more.

"Chief probably." The patrolman ran to the door, and in their minute alone, while Thornton drew deeply at the cigarette, she laid her free hand against his cheek.

"Perfessor Gray," Peterson replaced Doolittle between them. "This is a bad business about your wife. The officer told me what Mrs. Adriance just said to you. Well, it seems Mrs. Gray never went to her mother's home in Iowa. We found out her mother wasn't sick and didn't send word of any kind to her." He gave Thornton's bewildered look a hard return. "You had trouble sleeping lately, Perfessor?"

"Yes, a little."

"Did you take anything for it?"

"No. A doctor—Hager at the Medical School—gave me some pills but I never took them."

"But your wife did, didn't she?"

"Not that I know of."

"And you never gave her any?"

Thornton said slowly, "Yes, I did once."

"When, Perfessor?"

"I don't remember."

"Oh. Well, how about last Thursday night? And you had quite a time wakin' her up the next mornin', didn't you?"

Thornton said clearly. "I do remember. It was the night of the thunderstorm. My wife was hysterical and I thought of the pills. The dosage on the label was one to two pills. Because of the state she was in I dissolved two in hot milk. She fell asleep in a few minutes."

"Yayer—well ... Did you suggest to your wife that it would be a good thing if she took those pills right along regular?"

"Good God, no! I didn't tell her there was anything in the milk and she didn't ask the next day. She didn't know I had the pills or where they were kept."

"Where did you keep them?"

"In my study. Behind books on the top shelf near the door. I didn't want my little girl to get hold of them. You're telling me that my wife died of an overdose of sleeping pills?"

"I can't tell you a thing yet." Peterson looked from Gray to Audrey. "It's one of the possibilities. As Mrs. Adriance probably knows."

Thornton found his own cigarettes. "Want one, Audrey?" She shook her head.

"Perfessor Gray, how did you get along with your wife?"

The lines around Thornton's mouth hardened. He controlled evident anger and said, "Things were all right between us. We have never had trouble. We weren't perfectly congenial, which, I've been told, isn't an unusual situation. There had been no domestic crisis."

"Yay-er. Perfessor Gray, how well did you know Mr. Adriance before last Wednesday night?"

"Wednesday? The night we were all at the Dexters'? That was the first time I had seen him. The same"—he anticipated the chief—"is true concerning Mrs. Adriance."

Once again the little diary left Peterson's pocket. "Recognize any of this handwriting?"

Thornton glanced impatiently at the page. "Yes. I wrote my name, the number of my campus office and the hour. Adriance wanted to make an appointment that night at the Dexters'. He had the book but no pen."

"You see this happen, Mrs. Adriance?"

"No. But I was in the garden for quite a while."

"Perfessor, quite a lot's been goin' on here since you left town. It's possible that somebody wrote that in Mr. Adriance's diary after he was dead. To make a kind of alibi."

"Alibi for what?"

Audrey's lips parted. "Thornton, the police think that Don ..."

"Sorry but it's my turn now, Mrs. Adriance. Dr. Gray, where were you from 12:30 P.M. to four, last Thursday?"

"How the devil do I know?" He wasn't going to take much more.

Audrey spoke again. "Thornton, it's important. Please tell him *everything* just as it happened."

"All right," he agreed, toneless and tired. "I picked up my car in front of Abbott Hall where my wife had left it. Right after class. About 12:25 to 12:30. At the foot of the hill in front of the market I saw Mrs. Adriance at the bus stop. I picked her up and we drove around a bit. As a matter of fact out along the county road by the river for five or six miles. We parked and talked for a short time, then turned around and drove back to our respective homes. I unloaded strawberries from the back of my car. The neighborhood women were about to conserve food by wasting sugar. I took a mess of berries over to the Dexters'. About 1:30. Mr. Dexter can probably tell you exactly when I got there. After that," he paused to light another cigarette, "I put my car away and lunched in the kitchen on—if you care—a glass of milk and a banana. Being short of gas, I started to walk back to the University, was picked up at the bridge by Dr. Hager, and got to the campus before two. I then took a walk past the Union and through the Botanical Garden—for which I have no witness—and reached my office at 2:15, early for

Adriance's appointment. You've doubtless checked with my office mate and know how long I stayed there."

"Yay-er, till three. What did you do between three and four?"

"Oh, Lord, let me think! The library stacks, the Campus Club, the anthropology storeroom. I have no idea in what order. And I don't remember seeing anyone I knew. I was back in the office at four."

"O.K. Your partner in Welles Hall, Perfessor, says he never saw you so restless before."

"That was nice of him," said Thornton.

"Well, Perfessor Gray," the chief settled the brass-trimmed cap over his bald head, "you been nice about all this questionin' at a time like this. Believe me, I ain't been doin' it for fun, neither yours nor mine. Doc Ellison wants you should come over to his office in 'bout an hour. I can pick you up here or at your house. You can go home when you like. Everything's been cleared up over there. If I don't find you one place, I'll come to the other. O.K.?"

"Yes. Thanks," said Thornton.

Audrey followed Peterson to the door. "There is one thing I want to ask you. It's for the little girl, Margaret Gray. She won't understand why I haven't the dress I promised to bring her from her own room."

"You're asking if you can go get it?"

"Oh, no," she shivered. "Could Mrs. Dexter do it?"

"I guess so. Here." He tore a sheet from his notebook. "Write out what the kid wants and I'll see that she gets it."

When she came back to Thornton, he was standing, hands in pockets, staring at the rug. "I'd better clear out," he said.

She pushed a cushioned stool toward a wing chair. "Take off your coat," she ordered briskly, "and that very beautiful necktie."

He did not move or speak. "Please, dear. You don't want to go back alone to that house." She felt suddenly shy. "Would you like to go to the Dexters'? You know they think a lot of you."

"No," he still avoided her face, "I'd like to stay here a little while till I pull myself together. But it would look like hell—for you."

"Who would be looking? The Dexters know you are here. And the chief knows more about us than we do ourselves. Give me your coat and your tie."

She moved an end table with ash trays to the side of the chair and went to the hall closet with the coat. "Thornton," she said awkwardly, "you'd like a drink, wouldn't you? I—haven't anything to give you."

He shook the head lying against the chair back. "No," he said, "I don't drink when I'm low. I like to think I can see things through on my own."

Tears came to her eyes. "I'd forgotten there were men like that. Don, you know, was a chronic alcoholic."

"God, no, Audrey. How did you stand it?"

"Most of the time I could realize it was a terrible illness, something he couldn't help. But I couldn't care when he died. I didn't have to go through what you ..."

"Sit down," he said. "I've got to tell you something about"—he added very low—"my married life."

She took a chair distant from his and sat looking at her swollen wrist, waiting for him to go on.

"I don't doubt that you know where I met Edna. Those cherry trees burst into bloom whenever Edna made a new acquaintance. I was homesick for an American girl. She wanted to marry. I knew in a week we were misfits. I don't know when she found it out. I did what I thought was trying to make things work. By the time Margaret was born, Edna realized that I didn't love her like anything she'd read in a book. She compensated by reviving a Victorianism and making herself believe it. Married love, unless a child was the goal, was sin. At the moment she didn't want another baby. Margaret is four years old."

Audrey did not look up while he slowly lighted a cigarette. "A year ago," the words now came with difficulty, "Edna changed her mind or rather her feeling. About married life. She still didn't want another child. There was nothing I could do for her. She'd chilled me thoroughly long before. I was sorry for her and I was through. Then she began to strike at me through Margaret. By calling her 'Sister.' And similar devices. I don't doubt she felt rotten. I didn't feel so well myself. A few years like that were beginning to get the old man down. I'm no saint but I hate a mess. So Dr. Hager gave me the pills to guarantee a good long night's sleep now and then. And it was Edna who took them. God, Audrey, I didn't know she was as unhappy as that!" A dry sob shook his great frame.

"Thornton," Audrey was beside him, steadying his shoulders in her strong hands, forgetting the ache in her wrist. "Thornton, you don't know that she killed herself. She could have died naturally. Don't torture yourself by imagining things. Wait till you talk with Dr. Ellison. He's thorough, you said so yourself, and he's your friend. He'll find out exactly what happened."

She knelt by his side and turned his face to hers, seeking to reach his blank eyes. "Even if she did it, you can't help that now. You've got to think about Margaret. She thinks you're the most wonderful person in the world, much more wonderful than her mother. She talked to me about you the first time I met her out in the garden, and all day yesterday she said dozens of things about Daddy. Mommy's name hardly came up."

"I know. This mood won't last. I won't let Margaret down." Light came back to his eyes. "Audrey, what am I going to do about you?"

Audrey rose from her knees. "You're going to love me. If you want to. Right now, you're going to be fed hot soup."

He was in complete control of himself when Peterson returned. The chief was looking embarrassed. He cleared his throat and glanced from Thornton to Audrey. "Say, Perfessor Gray," he blurted out, "I didn't know till Doc Ellison told me that you had a double loss."

"I don't think I understand you." Thornton buttoned his coat.

"I meant," said Mr. Peterson, "about the baby. Doc Ellison says your wife was goin' to have one in about five months."

CHAPTER XVII

Without a word or a look at Audrey, Thornton had left with the Chief of Police. This was Audrey's darkest hour. In it she faced distrust of Thornton, shame at her relationship to him, pity for the wife their love had killed.

Rachel Dexter, bringing Margaret's dress, cried out, "Oh, my dear! You look so sick. You mustn't feel that way. Not about Edna."

Audrey tried to meet the kind concern in Rachel's face that had grown so old in the past week. "Did you know about—the baby?"

For the first time she heard the stiff note of reserve in Rachel's voice. "I didn't *know*." Silence lay too long in the room before she went on with forced brightness, "Now we must all be just as normal as we can. I'm sure there's nothing else that *can* happen to us. You and Margaret are coming to our house for supper, you know, and Thornton will come, too. It will be quite a family party. Oh, I didn't mean ... Audrey, stop laughing like that! I've got to stop you."

Her big bony hand, stretched long, hovered over the girl's averted head, then descended hard on her cheek. Audrey sprang to her feet, sore wrist pressed against burning face. Terror had brought back the old trick of widening the eyes, but she was no longer shaking with giggles and sobs. She saw Mrs. Dexter take off her spectacles and flap her hands about, while tears ran down her cheeks. "I never thought," she quavered, "that I could slap anybody I liked."

"Here we are." Audrey found face tissues in the pocket of the brown-striped dress. "Look at me, Mrs. Dexter. I'm all right again. Thanks for slapping me back to normal. It didn't hurt. Really! And what if it had? Anything is better than baying like a wolf."

"My dear, you are so sweet. Your cheek is so red. And, my goodness, there's a car stopping out front. Mr. Lund. And who's that man with him?

My glasses are still misty."

Audrey peered between the mullions. The tall detective's companion was a middle-aged man in shirt sleeves, heavy-jowled, and judged by his laggard step, ill at ease. "He's a complete stranger to me."

Wiping lenses on Audrey's tissue, Mrs. Dexter hustled to the door,

"How are you, Mrs. Adriance." Lund nodded, then dropped behind the stranger who slouched to the center of the room and stared hard at Audrey from brown hair to brown ankles. He might have been inspecting war goods. He turned to Lund and shook his head. "Nope, never seen the dame in my life. Not in my place nor anywhere else. Or"—he waved a thumb toward the gaping Rachel—"that lady either." He grinned slightly. "You'd hardly expect I would, but funny things happen."

"O.K. That's that." Lund stood aside and the man walked eagerly to the door. "Thanks for coming. I'll be seeing you."

Rachel whispered loudly, "Who is that man, Mr. Lund?"

"The bartender at the Low Jinks café." Lund's crisp assumption that this occupational classification appeared frequently on her visiting list left her open-mouthed but inarticulate. "Sit down, Mrs. Dexter. Peterson asked me to tell you that you seem to have nothing to worry about. Your Red Cross colleagues are both loyal and explicit. There seems to have been no time or circumstance from the time you parked your car at 12:30 till you drove it away at four when you were without direct observation."

"That was nice of the girls," said Rachel, "and I'm sure they just love the feeling that they have a connection with the case. I suppose they told you all about poor Edna, too."

"It was Peterson they told. Remember, this isn't my case, Mrs. Dexter. I'm the errand boy. About Mrs. Gray. Several women remembered exactly when she left the surgical dressings room and when she came back. It checked exactly with what she had said. From 2:30 to 3:00. During that time which she stated was spent in the Quiet Room there is no witness. Mrs. Dexter, how recently to your knowledge did Mrs. Gray drive your car?"

"Why, I don't think she ever did." Rachel's gray head shook in bewilderment. "Her own car is in better repair than ours and Thornton very seldom used it. She really had a good deal of gas to run around town."

"All right. Now, Mrs. Dexter, is there any doubt in your mind that you took the keys from the car and put them in your purse when you got to the Union on Thursday?"

"Mr. Lund," her tone was troubled, "I've always felt I left them in the car. And yet I agree with Edna Gray that they were in the purse when we started home. Both can't be right. I know it's a little thing, but it makes me feel as if I were losing my mind."

"No, Mrs. Dexter," Lund told her gravely. "I don't think you are. I am going to tell you something that I'd rather you didn't repeat at present, even to your husband. Fingerprints have been taken from Mrs. Gray's body. They match a set found on the wheel of your car. Sorry I can't say more. And now, if you'll excuse me, I'd like to talk alone with Mrs. Adriance."

The screen door closed behind Rachel, and Lund said, "Now that tidbit will travel fast."

"You invented it?"

"No, it's quite true. Mind if I answer that phone for you? Hello ... No, Mrs. Cox, this is not Mr. Cox nor Mr. Gray ... Yes, Lund ... She seems to be quite all right ... Yes, I understand you were upset ... That's asking a good deal of Mrs. Adriance. You made a serious charge without evidence, but at the moment I think she does not intend to sue ... Right ... No, I wouldn't worry about his safety. I think you'll hear from him before the day is over ... Yes, apart from certain theoretical aspects based on the present lag in housing, I should say he was entirely safe ... By the way, Mrs. Cox, I've met a very devoted student of yours ... Yes, extremely interested in everything that concerns you ... No, a coed, a girl named Angel. Good-by, Mrs. Cox."

He came over to the window bench where Audrey was lighting a cigarette—in an attempt to hide curiosity—and sat beside her.

"There is a way, Mrs. Adriance, in which the Federal Bureau of Investigation might possibly enter this case. Don't look so alarmed. Believe me, that would be a great advantage to you. And to Mr. Gray."

She stiffened at the name. "What do you want to know?"

"I'd like to have you tell me everything you remember about your last meeting with Mrs. Gray and about your impressions of what you found in her house."

She seemed to put her whole attention upon the snuffing out of her cigarette.

"You want to help Thornton. Don't you?" She did not answer and Lund said sternly, "Mrs. Adriance, this is the only way you can save yourself."

She looked up at him then in fear. "What do you mean?"

"It's possible that Mrs. Gray committed suicide. She left no note, which is unusual, but it happens. What we need is motive and evidence. Will you tell me what you felt when you were going through her house, as well as what you actually saw?"

"I'll tell you as well as I remember. From the time I went into the hall something seemed wrong. Everything was so orderly. There was a strong smell of furniture polish as if everything had had a thorough cleaning just before the house was shut up. I could see into that room at the right—the study—and nothing was out of place. Upstairs in the hall it seemed more queer. Not as if someone had packed and left suddenly at four or five in the morning. It was as if ..."

"Yes?"

"As if she had planned to go and wasn't expecting to come back."

"Do you think a woman who was about to kill herself would do this?"

"She might, if she cared a lot about what someone would think of her. But, Mr. Lund, she wouldn't pack three bags."

"I agree with you. It looks on the surface that if she committed suicide, the motive arose within the last hour or two of her life. We haven't yet the full autopsy finding, so we're uncertain when she died or how. But let's consider for the moment the possibility that she didn't leave town and return, and that a little while before she came to your house, she decided to die. Did she say anything to you that would indicate such an intention?"

"No." Again Audrey silently reviewed those few odd moments in the kitchen. "She seemed too intense about her mother's illness— particularly when I learned later that her mother had been having heart attacks for some time. There was one other thing. It was when she said good-by to her little girl. She usually called her 'Sister,' Mr. Lund, and the child didn't like it. Just before Mrs. Gray left her, she said, 'Good-by, Margaret.' It made quite an impression on Margaret. Later, she repeated it to me: 'Mommy called me Margaret.'"

"That could mean something, but it wouldn't be much use in court— Mrs. Adriance, the child was with you all of yesterday, wasn't she? And presumably she was the last person except yourself who saw her mother alive. That is, if we assume that Mrs. Gray killed herself. Has the child said anything about her mother that would give you a clue to Mrs. Gray's mood or to the way she occupied herself yesterday morning?"

Audrey put her hand over her eyes, trying to visualize the sequence of Margaret's day. First, she was a bundle in a pink blanket, then unwrapped and having her curls arranged in the middle of the kitchen. Edna led her to the living-room, said good-by. Now Edna was gone and Margaret was peeping through the swing door, hugging an old magazine, like the *Crime Mirror* she had wrenched from Cadwallader's jaws, that evening in the garden. Then they had eaten breakfast ... And on through the day to the trains and Clifford Cox, and the homeward ride on the bus. Wasn't that the only time that Margaret had mentioned her mother? What had she said? Something about pictures and Mommy.

"This is just silly, Mr. Lund," Audrey opened her eyes, "but it's all I can think of now. When we were on a bus in the afternoon, Margaret said, 'I showed the picture to Mommy.' I thought she meant one of the advertising cards in the bus. But I've just had another idea. Probably it isn't any good. Wait a minute and I'll get the magazine she was carrying when her mother brought her here."

She went to the hall closet and took down the raincoat she had worn as a dressing-gown. "Here it is."

Lund took the weary old copy of *Crime Mirror*. "How would the child get this?"

She told him about the sitter and Cadwallader.

He opened the magazine flat on his knees and turned it slowly page by page. Halfway through he stopped and laid his hand across a sheet.

"Mrs. Adriance," he said, "have you looked at this thing?"

She met the probe of his eyes. I'm glad, she thought, that I can tell the truth. I should hate to try to lie to that man.

"No, Mr. Lund." She repeated the circumstances that had led her to put the magazine in the coat pocket.

"The little girl didn't ask for it again?"

"No."

"Mrs. Adriance, what happened in the half-hour or so before she made the remark about showing the picture to Mommy?"

"We had been to the station to look at trains. Margaret is crazy about them, like lots of children who've never been on one. We saw the streamliner go out and then we caught the bus."

"The streamliner," said Lund. "Can you think of any incident in connection with that train that particularly impressed the child?"

"She was thrilled because the engineer waved to her. Oh, and ..."

"What were you going to say?"

"It wasn't something Margaret seemed to notice. I was the one." Perhaps this would interest Mr. Lund no more than it had Mr. Peterson. "I saw Clifford Cox get on the train."

Lund rose from the bench. He dropped the closed magazine on a table, and took out his pipe. "Look here, Mrs. Adriance," he said, "you're very fond of the little girl, aren't you? And she has confidence in you. I think she knows something that will help you and her father and herself in this business of her mother's death. The wrong solution of the case could hang over the child all her life. Do you think that without frightening her, you could get her to tell you what happened? I'd have to be here, too. You see that?"

"I could try, Mr. Lund."

"How soon could you do it? It's 3:30 now."

"She'll be here in a few minutes. In the Nursery School taxi." She picked up the plaid skirt that Rachel Dexter had left on a chair. "If she sees that, she won't think of anything else. They're easily distracted at that age. As you probably know."

"I hope to. The taxi's here."

It was painful to feel such tension while what you waited for was a child. Margaret ran from the taxi, head flung back, curls bobbing. Audrey gathered her up and bore her, kicking and giggling into the living-room.

"I'm dirty." She pointed proudly to her overalls. "I was the en-gine. We played choo-choo train. Right on my tummy in the play yard. Shall I do it now?"

"No, dear. You remember Mr. Lund, Margaret? He lives at Mr. Dexter's house."

"Um-hum," Margaret's mouth started to smile but changed to "There's my book! My ma-ga-zine!"

"Don't pull it away from Mr. Lund, dear." Audrey followed her to the bench where Lund had again taken *Crime Mirror*. "We'll all look at the pictures together."

She let herself be lifted between them on the bench. "You carried the book all the way over from your house," said Audrey, "when Mommy brought you."

"Um-hum." She wriggled. "I wanna go bathroom."

Audrey said to Lund, "We'll be back."

When they returned, Lund boosted the child up on his lap. He was holding the magazine open a few pages before the center. "This is a fine book," he said. "When did you get it?"

Margaret turned a puzzled four-year-old gaze on Audrey who had seated herself on the other end of the bench. "Not *this* day."

"What day, honey?" Audrey stifled anxiety in her voice.

"The day before I went to sleep last night."

"Yesterday?"

"Yes," she said, doubtful but obliging. "Before I came to your house."

"Did you get the book just before Mommy brought you?"

"Yes," she said again. "I wanna get down."

Audrey put her arm around the child. "Margaret, when did you get the book? Was it early?"

She looked perplexed and bored. "It was in the night. I woke up and Mommy had the light on."

Lund said, "Four o'clock war time would be dark in that house."

"What was Mommy doing when you woke up?"

Margaret laughed. "She was sweeping with the sweeper. In the night."

"What did Mommy say to you?"

Margaret was wriggling again. "She said, 'You be good and still,' and she gave me a toy. Out of the big wastebasket that b'longs down in the cellar with the 'cinerator. It was all the way up in my room."

Lund's fingers slowly turned the pages of the magazine. "What was the toy that Mommy gave you?"

"She gived—gaved—me the book. The ma-ga-zine."

As she started to slip to the floor something on the open page caught her eye. She flung herself across Lund's arm and pointed. Her curls and Lund's supporting hand covered most of the page. Audrey could see part of the heading: "... ME-LIGHT." Below were photographs of men.

Margaret smiled up at Eric Lund. "I showed the picture to Mommy. This one right here. I show Mommy the picture of Mr. Cox."

CHAPTER XVIII

"I wish I had had time to fix something interesting. Like a mock duck." Rachel Dexter looked sadly from the plain pink ham on the platter to the almost untouched slices on the plates of her three guests crowded around the gate-leg table. "A mock duck looks so cute."

Only Alfred Dexter chewed steadily, his beard rising and falling in rhythm with the shift of his little eyes from Audrey to Beulah Cox, questing for secondary symptoms of fecundity.

He's the sanest person here, Audrey thought; while the rest of us are concerned with death, he's looking for life.

"Do you mind if I smoke now, Rachel?" Thornton, a cigarette already between his lips, shoved his chair slightly back from the table.

Audrey glanced at his plate beside her own. He had eaten nothing. She was glad that he had been placed where she didn't have to look at him, although it was painful to be moved by the nearness of a man you no longer trusted. It was no greater pleasure to face across the table the woman who had informed the police that she, Audrey, was a multiple murderess. Points of candlelight flickered over the thick lenses, hiding the eyes that had accused.

"This seems like a *little* party, doesn't it? I mean smaller than last week's. Oh, dear!" Rachel had horrified herself. "You must be so worried about your husband, Beulah."

Beulah spoke from the depths: "I am certain, Rachel, that he is dead."

"He's probably taking a pleasure trip," said Alfred.

"I wonder what is behind that remark. I am quite sure he is not. He had no money."

Rachel rushed in. "I wish it had seemed best to have Sister with us. I do think you always feel gayer when there's a child around. Do you suppose she's lying awake crying in that strange room?"

"She's all right," Thornton spoke for the first time. "She slept there last night. And she's got her regular sitter. If she's lying awake, it's because she's wearing out the battery in the horse you pinned on her pajamas. She's crazy about it."

"I'm so glad. Poor motherless baby. The sitter? Oh, the high school girl who reads those funny magazines. I don't mean comics."

Silence came and stayed. When the door bell rang, Audrey gave a startled cry.

"Goodness," Rachel jumped up and followed Alfred to the hall, "we don't want company at a time like this."

Audrey felt Thornton's hand on her shoulder, steadying her, as Beulah Cox said with an ugly smile, "Bad conscience, Mrs. Adriance?"

Three entered the room with the Dexters: Chief Peterson, heavy and solemn in the green suit of detection; Eric Lund, detached and stern; the sleek and panting Cadwallader who sought the far side of the love seat, collapsed, and slept.

"Sorry to interrupt your supper, folks." Peterson was brusque. "We won't be here long. Better put out them candles. You'll be more comfortable sittin' away from the table. I just want to talk to you a little about Adriance and Mrs. Gray. Sort of pull things together once for all."

Thornton, after a questioning look at Audrey, set his armchair near hers. Gaunt, long-bodied Rachel and little round old Alfred on stiff dining chairs were definitely the Dexter Family in contrast to Beulah's mammoth loneliness on the love seat. They had indeed become a small party.

Peterson mopped his hot bald head and cleared his throat. "First, about Mr. Adriance. You know as well as I do that he was found dead in a ditch out where Main Street meets County Road D. It looked like a hit-run case, pure and simple, but we wasn't quite willin' to let it go at that because there was kind of a mystery about how Adriance got out there and why he went.

"He was killed on Thursday. Saturday we got a break. After Mrs. Dexter's accident, I give the car a thorough goin' over. There was a dent in the rear fender and stuck over the right front window where the head hit was hair."

Audrey bit her lips. Rachel's face twitched. Alfred's eyes were polished bright with curiosity. Beulah sat patient and evidently bored.

"It was the old feller's hair all right," Peterson continued. "Matched perfect. But it was different from the hair we found under the left runnin' board. Glued on with blood." He paused a moment. "*That* matched the hair on the head of Adriance."

More than one of the five exclaimed wordlessly. Audrey was sick and still.

"Now, o' course, lots of people's hair can test the same, but it'd be kind of too much of a coincidence, under the circumstances, if identical hair belongin' to another feller had got caught on the car owned by one of the few people Adriance knew in this town. Particularly when you remember that on Friday, the night after Adriance died and before we examined the car, somebody was hangin' around Dexters' garage. And everyone in these four houses had been tipped off by me—and not with any idea of bein' helpful, you can just bet—that there was likely to be evidence on the car that killed Adriance. I told you, Mrs. Cox, and you told the neighborhood."

"I did," came Beulah's tragic tones. "I never dreamed that I ..."

"You all know by now where the car was from 12:30 P.M. to four o'clock. Parked on the campus at the east end of the Union, towards the Botanical Gardens. You've all told me where you was durin' those hours. Most of you fixed up the time a little but it checked pretty good. Mrs. Dexter is completely out as a suspect. If somebody picked up Adriance in the car, drove out to the spot where he was killed, had an argument on the way, and Adriance got out and started to walk home, and the driver ran him down—well, the whole thing could of been done in a half to three-quarters of an hour and wouldn't of used enough gas to show. Mrs. Dexter is in the clear, but there's a time when any of the rest could of done it. That is, there was time when you had no witnesses to your whereabouts. The two Grays and Mrs. Cox admit bein' on the campus. Cox, Perfessor Dexter, and Mrs. Adriance could of been."

"It would have been difficult for any of us without keys to the car," Thornton's eyebrows contracted.

"Yay-er. Sure. But the keys were in the ignition. The person who insisted they weren't was Mrs. Gray. And we know that between 2:30 and 3:00 she drove off, and come back to the Union in that car."

"Edna!" Rachel and Beulah exchanged looks of poorly played surprise. But the shock in Thornton's voice was real. "Prove it."

"O.K. I will. Fingerprints on the wheel and on the key-case where she carried it into the Union and slipped it into Mrs. Dexter's purse."

"Some of that is supposition. She had no motive for killing Adriance."

"Perfessor Gray," said Mr. Peterson, "that's supposition, too. But I'm inclined to agree with you. Motive of any kind's what we've got the least of in this case. The only one that made sense at all was a little personal trouble you may have had with Adriance."

Thornton started from his chair.

"Take it easy, Gray," Lund said quietly from his seat on the step of the dais. "The chief isn't accusing you."

"Sorry," said Thornton.

"Jealousy's a common motive for crime," Peterson went on, "and there was stuff all about wolves, and Japan. But as far as the spy angle goes, I guess the U.S.A. has investigated you pretty fully. But there's your handwriting in the diary and the time you spent strollin' alone in the Botanical Garden. And there's your wife's death."

Words reached Audrey through a fog that stifled thought and nearly all feeling, but she was still dimly aware of the greater suffering this meant for Thornton than for herself. And greater danger.

"Mrs. Gray," the chief was saying, "died from barbituric poisoning. She must have swallowed about 50 sleepin' pills soon after she left the child with Mrs. Adriance. Coroner says many people live two or more days even with a big dose like that. Judgin' by the condition of the body, Mrs. Gray probably went immediately into coma and died in about twenty-four or five hours. She was very susceptible to the stuff, *as you know, Perfessor Gray.*"

Rachel was crying into Alfred's handkerchief, Mrs. Cox's accusing pince-nez were focused on Thornton.

"Mrs. Gray," said the chief, "didn't leave a farewell note. She may of killed herself because of that jealousy we was talkin' about. Maybe she was afraid a divorce was comin' up, and she couldn't take it. With a baby on the way. Or she may have done it out of remorse, if she'd killed Adriance. Like I've already said, she didn't seem to have a reason for that. She drove the murder car between 2:30 P.M. and three, sure, but we think Adriance was killed at or before his appointment with the Perfessor. And besides," he added dramatically, "we know where Mrs. Gray went."

Beulah Cox asked the obvious question the others were too closely involved to ask. "Where did she go, Mr. Peterson?"

The chief ignored her. "It looked like we had maybe a murder and maybe a suicide without known motives. And did they belong together? And there's a third side to this business. A Federal angle."

Lund got up from the dais and walked lightly toward the five white staring faces. He made a gesture toward the hall and the chief swaggered out. Over Lund's quiet ordinary talk as he passed cigarettes and held matches for Audrey and Beulah, they could all hear several masculine voices beyond their view. The "study" door closed and two men came into the room. The sharp younger man in the Palm Beach suit

Lund introduced as the county attorney. The easy-going man with the squint was the sheriff who had come back from his vacation to help solve the case.

Audrey brushed her hair back from her forehead. What would those men have to do with the FBI?

Lund sat on the edge of the refectory table and said, in a clear, quiet tone, "This all begins with a girl named Hilda Hill."

Audrey could hear the others breathe deep in a moment of astonishment and relief. To them it sounded like the beginning of a good story and not too near.

"Hilda Hill was a nice girl with no particular charm or style but she had a little money. In the summer of 1943, in her home town, Providence, Rhode Island—she met and married a man who called himself Stephen Clay."

"Providence!" exclaimed Rachel—delighted at a point of contact. "Why, in 1943 you taught summer school at Brown, didn't you, Thornton?"

"This man Clay took Hilda to Hartford, Connecticut, where Mr. and Mrs. Adriance were both employed in a war plant. Don Adriance was something of an absentee. He met Clay and Hilda in several of the local joints off and on for a week or two. Then Hilda's money was gone and Clay told her he was married, and walked out. Adriance took the girl home to his wife who had never seen the pair. She bucked up Hilda's morale and bought her a ticket back to her family in Rhode Island. The Mann act was involved, and Hilda's father took his daughter's troubles to the FBI. We've found out a good deal about 'Clay' in these past two years. This marriage was one of a dozen or more covering seven years. We knew what he was, but not who he was. He'd never been fingerprinted, and he'd never been arrested. Most of the cases were outdated, but the Hill case is current."

He paused to light his pipe. "The Adriances came here. On Wednesday evening, before he came here to dinner, Don Adriance happened to see his wife's address book open at the page with Hilda's name. Without that chance incident, and one detail he must have observed during the evening, he might never have recognized 'Clay.' I know Mrs. Adriance will forgive my saying that in 1943 Don wasn't always clear about what went on around him."

He smiled at Audrey. "The rest of this story is largely the result of Don Adriance's character and situation. As some of you know, he had suffered for some years from chronic alcoholism. His recent return to the work he cared about and to the good will of his fellow citizens were his intense preoccupations. These strong drives eliminated all others. He was, therefore, at the moment not very close to his wife. On Thursday morning, he took Mrs. Adriance's address book without her knowledge, without explanation checked with her remembrance of Hilda Hill as the girl in question, and left for the University. There he wrote in his pocket diary the telephone number of this house where I am staying. Before four o'clock that afternoon he was dead.

"Things were quiet till Sunday. Then questioning started up. And I stuck around."

Audrey watched the narrow impassive face turn quickly from one to the other of the anxious group. Behind him sheriff and attorney sat expressionless; this was not a new story to them.

"So," said Mr. Lund, "Clifford Cox thought it would be wise to leave town. He had no money and he could get none from his wife. But there was another source. Another woman with a personal income and with whom he had followed what she sometimes referred to as 'scholarly interests.'"

Thornton sat like a rock. So, to Audrey's amazement, did Beulah Cox. She certainly had courage and control.

"Edna Gray agreed to finance Cox's trip, but with the proviso that she go with him. Believe me, Mr. Gray, I'm sorry that I can't do this any other way. The autopsy, as some of you have heard, showed that Mrs. Gray was pregnant."

There was a low moan. Not from Thornton. Alfred Dexter had failed in his special research.

"On Thursday afternoon at 2:30 she telephoned to Cox from the Union. He suggested that they meet at the Low Jinks bar. Outside she happened on the Dexter car with the keys in the ignition. She drove it to the bar, told Cox—not for the first time—about her condition, and was back in half an hour. On Sunday, he was sufficiently afraid of detection and a federal term to come to Mrs. Gray's terms. She was to go by early morning bus, get off somewhere down the line, and join him on the streamliner that afternoon. Leaving Margaret with Mrs. Adriance seems to have been their idea of a joke. Cox left on the streamliner. Mrs. Adriance and little Margaret Gray saw him, and so did the FBI.

"Cox had company on the trip but it wasn't Mrs. Gray. She seems to have stayed up all night cleaning the house, in a sort of perverted respectability. That, I suppose, is how she found the sleeping pills. While she was at work, the child woke up, and to keep her amused, the mother gave her an old magazine from a wastebasket.

"That small act changed all Mrs. Gray's plans. It ended her life. Margaret told Mrs. Adriance in my presence that she showed her mother a picture in the magazine." He pulled the copy of *Crime Mirror* from his pocket and folded back pages. "This," he handed it to Audrey, "is what Mrs. Gray saw. So she killed herself."

The magazine shook in Audrey's hands, as she now saw clearly what she had glimpsed earlier in the day. "In the Crime-light Watch for these fugitives." Under the third of the four photographs was printed: "Stephen Clay. Alias James Clifford. John Stevens. Wilfred DeVere. *Impostor—Bigamist.* Age 44. Height 5 feet 7 inches, weight 200 pounds." She looked at the fat, pop-eyed smirk, the too-long hair, too thin at the temples. She got up and carried the magazine to the Dexters, who sat apart from Thornton.

"But, Mr. Lund," she heard Beulah speak, full, deep, and musical. "This is a most plausible story, Mr. Lund, but I wonder if there is anything behind it. Have you any proof?"

Lund turned away from her to the sheriff. "Bring in Cox."

There was no smirk on Clifford Cox's face when Peterson and the sheriff led him into the room where he had recently been a guest. The face above the soiled shirt collar was baggy rather than fat, and pricked by a dirty beard. Audrey glanced at him and then stared at the floor to avoid Beulah's certain shame. She heard Lund saying tersely, "You told Peterson that you met the Adriances in Tarrytown, in 1941. That was a lie, wasn't it?"

"Y—es," Cox croaked, "sort of. I met them in 1943. In Hartford. Don was always gassing about his mother's swell place in Tarrytown. So I ..."

"Go ahead. Spill the rest."

The sorry, halting version at every point matched Lund's.

"O.K. What did Adriance say to you here when he recognized you?"

"Nothing. He looked at me and laughed but I'm not sure whether he knew me or not. His wife said he didn't. But Edna Gray was sure he did because of some crack he made to her when he saw me being a little nice to her. I wasn't too worried, though. Don was an awful soak. But with a G-Man around I couldn't take a chance. I had to get going."

"You asked your wife for the money. What did you tell her you wanted it for?"

"Well, I told her a little story about borrowing a friend's car and driving it from Iowa to Missouri and finding out afterwards the car was hot. She was wise enough to know that would interest the FBI. But I couldn't get her to take it seriously, so I went to Edna Gray."

"Were you the cause of her pregnancy?"

"She said so. I guess I was. Could be."

Lund rapped out an order. "Sit down, Gray. I'm handling this. It's about over."

"Cox!" A new note in Lund's voice made Audrey raise her eyes. The others—Thornton with lines chiseled from nose to mouth, gripping both arms of his chair, the Dexters holding hands and looking as if they were at a play, Beulah erect with a great dignity—all were staring at Lund and his cringing prisoner. Behind these two, the young county attorney had risen and stood beside the sheriff and the chief.

"Cox," Lund repeated, "when we found you and brought you back here, you begged us to let you tell the truth, knowing it wouldn't shorten your term, but because you were deadly afraid you might be involved in the murder of Donald Adriance."

"That's right," whispered Cox.

"Because you had a motive. Because Adriance knew Hilda Hill. You said only you and Adriance knew about this? Are you sure? Cox, didn't you tell your wife?"

"Christ, no!"

"Then," Lund turned to Beulah Cox, "it was Adriance who told you."

She met him proudly eye to eye. "Mr. Lund, that is not true."

"Mrs. Cox," he pushed the unpalatable Cox toward the sheriff, "do you remember a little talk you had with Peterson about a girl named Amy Angel?"

"Certainly. She was the student who lunched with me on the day of Mr. Adriance's accident." The richness of her voice flowed stickily over the room.

"You remember, Pete, just what was said?"

Peterson stood thick and firm beside Lund. "You said you left Abbott Hall at 1:30. You waved to this Amy Angel who was in Adriance's classroom across the hall. You bought a sandwich in the Union at 1:40 and took it to the Botanical Gardens and ate by yourself till 2:00, and then this Angel girl come along and sat with you till 2:20 and helped finish the grub."

"Quite true." Beulah smiled steadily.

"It is—almost. But this Amy Angel has got a crush on you. She says she hoped to find you when she come out of Adriance's class but you was gone. Students said you let your class out early. 'Bout 1:18. And the Angel girl swears by all that's holy that she didn't catch up with you in the Botanical Gardens till ten minutes past two."

"Well, even if she were right—and I must tell you that she is a sweet but somewhat hysterical child—I can see no significance in these trifling alterations of time. I am not a criminal in need of an alibi."

"Aren't you?" said Eric Lund.

She said quietly, "No."

Lund walked a step or two from Beulah's couch. He spoke in a conversational manner to the others as if he had a good story to tell. "You may not know that the FBI keeps a personal appearance file for all wanted criminals. Sometimes a mannerism will identify a man when the rest of his appearance is almost completely altered. It was like that with the fellow you know as Cox. The women he married were of two kinds—young ones with no boy friends, and old ones with no boy friends. Both kinds, of course, had to have some money. Most of these women were several cuts above him socially, and there was a certain filthy little trick of his that they put up with as a measure of their desperation for a male. When he left them, they all named it. You've seen it. Donald Adriance, drunk or sober, was a gentleman of sorts. He saw it, and then he remembered Hilda Hill." He turned suddenly. "How did you like it, Mrs. Cox, when your alleged husband mopped his forehead on his dinner napkin?"

She still looked at him, the glasses blinking, the face now flushed, the mouth opening. Her feet heaved upward and she screamed.

"That's what he said," she shouted, "when he got out of the car! That's why I ran him down!"

From beneath her wildly thrashing legs Cadwallader wriggled the rest of his length from under the love seat, and rose to shake himself placidly in the middle of the room.

CHAPTER XIX

In the Dexters' oriel bedroom Eric Lund, with the expert hindrance of Alfred and Rachel, was packing his bags. Current prognosis favored his arrival in Washington minus his shaving brush and plus Alfred's beard. "No, she isn't crazy." He maneuvered the catch on his Gladstone from Rachel's puttering fingers. "Her reason for killing Don Adriance wasn't quite so simple as she proclaimed. After we got you people out of the room, she made a perfectly clear and calm confession. Much to the relief, I may say, of Peterson and the county prosecutor."

"You couldn't tell us, could you, Mr. Lund?"

His scarred lips had a smile for the humility of her plea. He glanced at his watch. "I can if I make it short. Cox had told his wife, you remember, about having driven a stolen car over a state line—a euphemism to say the least—and that Adriance, knowing about it, might inform me. I don't know whether she planned to talk to Adriance and urge him to keep still. Anyway she came out of the Union with her sandwich just as he was going in to get his lunch. She held him up, and not wanting to carry on that kind of talk in a congested spot on campus, they got into your car, which she had already noticed."

"The keys?" Rachel wanted to know.

"Were in the ignition." He hurried along before she saw her carelessness as a cause of the tragedy. "While Mrs. Cox talked to him, she drove out past the spot marked X, and stopped to continue the argument. I gather it got pretty hot. Adriance very righteous, Beulah getting madder and madder as a thing she had thought she could swing easily began to seem impossible. In the end, Adriance gave her a good idea of Cox's actual offense and her own status. He got out of the car and slammed the door. Then he did the thing that killed him. He told her why he was certain that Cox and the man who married Hilda Hill were one and the same. No two men in anyone's acquaintance mop their foreheads on dinner napkins."

"And at her age—" Rachel blushed.

"Right. Sudden rage and glandular change happen to quite nice people."

"After all, even though she is a murderess," Alfred wagged sententiously, "Beulah Briggs was a well-bred woman."

"Right. Would you mind relinquishing my vest? Thanks. That foul gesture of Cox's was the symbol of her own shame at her marriage to the only man she could have. She drove up the road a short distance and turned around. Adriance was walking along the left-hand side. He knew she was coming behind him but he didn't look around. There was no logical reason why he should."

"Those men who came in at the end, Mr. Lund. Why did you bring the sheriff?"

"Peterson did." He hunted his Panama. "He wasn't entirely sure where Adriance was killed. If it had happened up the road farther and if the body had been dragged or tossed out of the car, the death would have occurred outside the city limits, in the sheriff's territory. Where the devil did I leave my hat?"

Alfred said pitifully, "In view of your agreement with my wife on the subject of glands, I assume that Beulah Briggs must have sent herself that dress box simply to annoy me. It was a very cruel joke."

"No, no, Alfred. You must be fair." Rachel protested. "Just because she killed somebody, we mustn't believe that she was *mean*. Don't you know that Lane Bryant sells dresses for women with fuller figures? What we used to call 'stylish stouts.' Oh, Mr. Lund, I'm sitting on your hat!"

"I suppose," Alfred looked no brighter, "that Mrs. Adriance isn't going to have a baby either!"

Across the driveway in another oriel room where Margaret Gray and Grane were asleep, a small lamp on the dresser showed two tall people bending over her bed. As Lund looked, the light went out.

"No," he said, "I'm sure she isn't, but I think she might send you an announcement within the next two years."

Audrey snapped off the light and closed the door to Margaret's room. In the dim upper hall Thornton was lighting a cigarette. She dropped down on the top stair at his feet.

"When I go down to Iowa tomorrow for the funeral, Audrey, can I ...?" He stopped.

"Leave Margaret with me? Of course, Thornton."

"You wouldn't be staying here just on her account?"

"I'm in no hurry to leave." She leaned her head against the banister, looking up to find his face in the darkness. "The rent," she added practically, "is paid till the first of August. After that ..."

His words came down to her, harsh with feeling. "What are you going to do after that?"

"I'm going to stay with my father and mother."

She closed her eyes and waited in the dark, smelling the smoke of his cigarette, feeling the silence. After a while she reached up her hand and touched his wrist. "Give me a puff, Thornton?"

His arm went round her, his hand and cigarette reached her lips. He said brokenly, "I have to be in Washington."

She inhaled deeply and held the cigarette to his mouth. "You don't know where my people live."

"In San Francisco?" He put out the cigarette.

"No," she said. "In Washington."

Eric Lund went down the walk to the waiting taxi. Alfred bobbed at his heels; Cadwallader pranced before. Lund gave his bags to the driver and stopped to pat the Labrador's wide head.

"The old strategist turned out to be the best tactician of us all! His rear attack was the final weight that broke Miss Beulah Briggs." He got into the cab and extended his hand to Alfred Dexter.

"It's a pity you have to rush off like this," the round little old man said wistfully. "I suppose you have scented some ultra dangerous criminal."

"Airport," Lund told the driver. In a moment of sympathy for Alfred's frustrated research, he put his head out of the window. "No, Mr. Dexter," he called, "I'm flying home. My wife is going to have a baby."

THE END

www.ingramcontent.com/pod-product-compliance
Lightning Source LLC
Chambersburg PA
CBHW071735190726
48292CB00003B/755